Delia's Place

Also by Lin Stepp

FOR SIX GOOD REASONS
TELL ME ABOUT ORCHARD HOLLOW
THE FOSTER GIRLS

"Well, I've finally come across someone that believes in all the things that I do… love, family, faith, intrigue, mystery, loyalty, romance, and a great love for our beloved Smoky Mountains. Dr. Lin Stepp, I salute you."
- DOLLY PARTON, country music entertainer

"Lin Stepp paints a charming portrait of the Smokies, their people, and a wonderful way of life."
- DEBORAH SMITH, best-selling author.

"A wonderful, new Southern voice."
- JOAN MEDLICOTT, best-selling author.

Delia's Place

Fourth Novel in the
Smoky Mountain Series

LIN STEPP

www.canterburyhousepublishing.com
Vilas, North Carolina

Canterbury House Publishing
www.canterburyhousepublishing.com

First Printing April 2012
Copyright © 2012 Lin Stepp
All rights reserved under International and Pan-American Copyright Conventions.

Book Design by Tracy Arendt

Painting used for front Cover: *April Reflections* by Jim Gray

Author Note: This is a work of fiction. Although there are numerous elements of historical and geographic accuracy in this and other novels in the Smoky Mountain series, specific environs, place names, and incidents are entirely the product of the author's imagination. In addition, all characters are fictitious and any resemblance to actual persons, living or dead, is entirely coincidental.

Library of Congress Cataloging-in-Publication Data

Stepp, Lin.
  Delia's place : [a Smoky Mountain novel] / Lin Stepp. -- 1st ed.
    p. cm. -- (The Smoky Mountain series ; bk. 4)
  ISBN 978-0-9829054-5-6
  I. Title.

PS3619. T47695D45 2012
813'. 6--dc23

2011034376

The scanning, uploading, and distribution of this book via the Internet or via any other means without permission of the publisher is illegal and punishable by law. Please purchase only authorized electronic editions, and do not participate in or encourage electronic piracy of copyrighted materials. Your support of the author's rights is appreciated.

For information about permission to reproduce selections from this book, write to Permissions, Canterbury House Publishing, Ltd. , 225 Ira Harmon Rd, Vilas, NC 28692-9369

Dedication

This book is dedicated to Emma Lee Price, my husband's mother, who welcomed me into her family with love from the first—gave me wise tips and counsel for life, freely shared her creative gifts and talents with me, never wavered in affection for J. L. and me in good times or in bad, and has celebrated joyously with us in the publication of my Smoky Mountain novels.

Acknowledgments

Special acknowledgements to Karen McDonald and Kenton Temple, with the Anna Porter Library in Gatlinburg, for helping me with facts on Gatlinburg's history.

Respectful acknowledgements, also, to any descendants of the Walker family of Gatlinburg—I hope I gave honor to your name through my characters Delia and Hallie Walker with their fictitious links to the Walker family tree.

Thanks and gratitude go to those who helped to make this book a reality:

Wendy Dingwall—President and Publisher of Canterbury House Publishing, Ltd.

Carolyn Sakowski—President and CEO of Distributor, John F. Blair Publishing, Inc.

Angela Harwood—Vice President of Sales and Marketing, John F. Blair Publishing, Inc.

Tracy Arendt—Graphic Artist and Text Designer for Canterbury House

Sandy Horton—Manuscript Editor and helper in making my work "sing"

Final special love and thanks go to:

... J. L. Stepp, my husband, who shares my writing journey, travels with me to signings, and enthusiastically supports my work

... Kate Stepp, my daughter, who encourages me and maintains my author's website

... And to the Lord, who inspires and helps me in all I do.

Cover Art

The beautiful work of art, featured on the front cover of this book, was painted by the well-known regional artist Jim Gray. It is entitled *April Reflections* and shows the magical beauty of a Smoky Mountain stream.

Jim Gray is a nationally proclaimed artist who has been painting Smoky Mountain scenes and southern landscapes for over forty years. In 1966, Gray and his family moved to east Tennessee so that Jim could explore and paint the beauty of the countryside surrounding the Smoky Mountains. Today, Jim Gray has three galleries in east Tennessee and one in Alabama, dividing his time between his homes in the mountains of Tennessee and Perdido, Florida. He has sold over 2000 paintings and 125,000 prints to collectors in the United States and abroad. Jim is listed in *Who's Who in American Art* and has been featured in many publications, including *National Geographic* and *Southern Living*.

Prints of *April Reflections*, or other fine art works, can be purchased in Jim Gray galleries or ordered through Jim Gray's website at: http://www.jimgraygallery.com

Jim Gray's business address is:
GREENBRIAR INCORPORATED
P. O. Box 735, Gatlinburg, TN 37738
Business Phone: (865) 573-0579

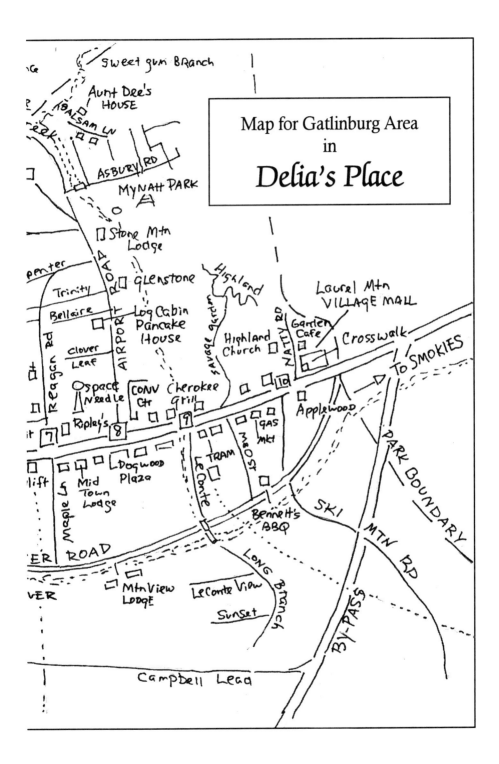

Chapter 1

"Whew, I think I'm finally packed and can head for the beach." Delia stuffed one last duffle into the hatchback of her compact SUV, slammed the trunk, and blew out a long breath. Turning to see the mail truck pull up at the mailbox, she hurried down the sidewalk to catch Mr. Hinton, the postman. He'd delivered the mail to the Walker's Georgian house on Wentworth Avenue in Arlington ever since Delia was a girl.

"Looks like more wedding cards for you," Mr. Hinton announced with a twinkle in his eye, handing Delia a stack of envelopes, several magazines, and a few advertising fliers. "And in the back I've got what looks like another wedding gift addressed to you." He reached behind his seat for a brown-wrapped parcel.

"Thank you, Mr. Hinton." Delia piled the package on the other mail in her arms, flashing her old friend a bright smile.

He smiled back. "When's your big day, Miss Delia?"

"In mid-July." Delia spoke the words in a dreamy tone.

"Well, it'll seem right odd not having you come down to meet me anymore." He winked at her. "But I guess you'll be setting up your own house now. I'll have to find me another little girl who likes my suckers."

Delia grinned at his teasing. "You haven't given me suckers for many years now, Mr. Hinton."

"Well, it doesn't seem so long ago." He scratched his chin. "Why don't I give you one more today for old times' sake?"

"Sure." Delia took the sucker with a grin and, after a few more pleasantries, waved Mr. Hinton off to the next house on his route.

Turning to start back up the driveway, her gaze shifted to her family's spacious, two-storied house situated on an elegant rise of neat, manicured lawn. Delia felt a sudden clutch at her heart. "This won't be my home much longer." She bit her lip. "I'll be making a new home with Prentice, helping him start his practice as a doctor."

Delia's Place

In fact, Prentice had traveled out west to interview with a medical group interested in adding a new doctor to their staff. He would fly back to join her at the family's beach house at Emerald Isle. That's where Delia was headed now. Her parents and all the rest of the family were already there.

"I hope Prentice will take one of the jobs offered back east—like the one with my brother Richard's practice in Baltimore where he interned." Delia sighed. "I'd so love to stay near my family. And it would be nice to live in Baltimore near Richard and Betsy and their little toddler, Helen."

Actually, Delia first met Prentice through her brother Richard. He brought Prentice down to the beach house two years ago for a work break. Like Richard, Prentice was older than Delia—ten years older—but that hadn't kept him from watching her admiringly that first evening. They quickly became a couple as the summer days slipped by, stayed in close touch through the next year, and got together on every holiday.

Delia hugged the mail to herself, remembering last summer at the beach. "We became officially engaged." She looked down at her engagement ring. "But, of course, Prentice had to finish his residency before we could marry. There would be little money until he did. And I needed to finish the last year of my master's program in design at Marymount. It was practical for us to wait." A wistful smile played on her lips.

She stayed on in Arlington, in the townhouse she shared with her roommates, snatching visits with Prentice whenever he could get away. That hadn't been often this last year of his residency. She frowned. "That's all going to change now." Cheering herself with the thought, she skipped back up the sidewalk. "And I'll get to do my first decorating in our new home and maybe even in Prentice's new office."

The phone rang as Delia walked onto the porch of the house. She raced inside to get it. "I hope it's Prentice!" But it was only Frances, her older sister.

Frances was thirteen years older than Delia, her brother Richard ten years older, and Howard Junior, the oldest of the four Walker siblings, sixteen years her senior. Delia had been the late, unplanned addition to the Walker family. In fact, Delia's mother thought she'd started early menopause when she found out she was pregnant with Delia at thirty-six.

"Hi, baby sister," Frances greeted her. "When are you coming down to the beach house? Mother asked me to call and check on you."

"I should be leaving soon." Delia dumped the mail on the entry table. "I only have to make one last sweep, and then I need to find Graham cat and load him up. He's already suspicious about the suitcases and is hiding under the bed."

"Well, I hope you're going to pill that cat to knock him out, Delia. He can yowl and carry on something awful in the car." She made a tut-tutting sound. "I don't know how you put up with it. It personally gives me a major headache."

"Don't worry. The vet gave me something for him." She laughed.

Changing the subject, Frances said, "Listen, Baby, we're doing a barbeque on the beach tonight so head on down this way soon, okay? A lot of neighbors and friends are coming over, anxious to congratulate you about the upcoming wedding. I wish Prentice could be here, too. How long will he be out west on that interview?"

"I don't know. Just a few days, I think, and then he'll be down."

"Well, drive safe, Baby. I'll see you by dinner." Frances made kissing sounds and rang off.

The rambling beach house at Emerald Isle, North Carolina, had been in Delia's mother's family for over fifty years. The Walker clan went, traditionally, to join the Chapmans as soon as school let out every year, staying several weeks and then trooping back for long holiday weekends, whenever they could, throughout the summer months. Delia looked forward to this time with her family, and time with Prentice, too, before the busy season of their upcoming wedding and move.

She sighed. "The next time I go to the island, I'll be married, like everyone else in the Walker family. I won't just be the baby anymore."

Delia sorted the mail she'd dropped on the entry table, taking her personal mail and the gift box into the big formal dining room. She piled the wedding envelopes addressed to Prentice and her on the growing stack of cards on the Queen Anne table. After stripping off the mailing wrap from the parcel, she placed a new silver-wrapped present among the large collection of wedding gifts. She planned to open all the recent gifts and cards with Prentice when he returned.

Delia smiled at that thought, picturing Prentice in her mind with his dark, curly hair and those cute dimples when he smiled. He was very tall, and she always felt so petite and feminine when she stood looking up at him. She could definitely wear heels at their wedding. Yesterday, she'd gone shopping for a wedding dress again but still hadn't found the perfect one. "Maybe I can drive to Wilmington with Frances while at the beach house and look at dresses there."

Sitting down in one of the dining room chairs for a minute, Delia opened the letter she'd received from Maureen Cross. Maureen had been Aunt Dee's best friend and business partner in their crafts store in Gatlinburg, Tennessee, before Aunt Dee died. Maureen wrote that she hoped Delia would come for a visit before they closed on the sale of her aunt's house and property. She also penned several fond remembrances about Dee in her note.

Delia's Place

Delia sighed. "I wish I could see Aunt Dee's place again. I made so many good memories there as a girl, and Aunt Dee felt so proud I was her namesake and godchild."

Dee Walker-Ward and her husband Roland, who passed away when Delia was only a small child, never had children of their own. And when Aunt Dee died this last winter, she left Delia her little cottage in Gatlinburg and a partial ownership in some property. Delia and Prentice discussed the inheritance and decided to sell the property and use the sales proceeds for a down payment on their first home. Otherwise, they'd need to rent for a long time while Prentice paid back his student loans and the money needed to start an established medical practice.

The doorbell rang suddenly, breaking into Delia's thoughts. Looking out the front window, she saw a FedEx truck parked by the curb and a delivery woman coming up the sidewalk. Delia grinned. Probably another wedding gift, she thought, heading back into the entry hall to answer the door with Maureen's letter in hand.

Instead of a gift, the delivery woman handed her an overnight express letter. Delia signed for it and carried it inside, noticing with excitement Prentice's distinctive handwriting.

"Maybe he's learned something about a job or maybe he's coming in earlier." With eager hands, she stripped off the seal to take the letter out, but as she started to read, she sat down abruptly on the hall bench by the door.

Dear Delia ... The letter began.

This is a cowardly way to handle an awkward situation, but I couldn't seem to find the nerve to call you. I got married last night in Las Vegas to MacKenzie Wilkes. You met her this spring when you visited me in Baltimore. We were in residency together finishing our med degrees.

While working together this fall, we became involved. It just happened. I flew out west with MacKenzie to interview with her father about joining his practice. He wants to retire, and he wants MacKenzie and me to begin taking over. It's a great opportunity with a medical practice already well established.

MacKenzie and I have thought about doing this for some time, but neither of us wanted to jeopardize our residency positions with the Baltimore practice your brother Richard partnered by coming forward sooner about our relationship. Richard is your brother, after all, and you and I were engaged and had a big wedding planned. As I said, it was an awkward situation.

I know this is not a very honorable way to break off a formal engagement, but once we finalized everything yesterday with MacKenzie's father, she and I were so excited. And, on a spur, we flew to Las Vegas and got married.

Your family has always been good to me, and I plan to write everyone a note of thanks for that, along with my regrets that our wedding plans didn't work out. You were, in many ways, a little too young and sweet for me, and I'm sure you will meet someone more suitable in time and have much happiness. I wish that for you.

Do anything you want about the gifts that may have already arrived.

... Prentice

Delia read through the letter two more times and sat there, absolutely stunned, trying to take it all in.

Prentice married to MacKenzie Wilkes ... last night. Delia did remember her. She'd been at the doctors' dinner that Delia and Prentice attended in Baltimore only a month ago. Delia remembered her well—a long, leggy, sophisticated type. She even remembered how MacKenzie greeted her when the two of them were introduced.

"This must be Richard's sister, *little* Delia." She offered Delia a smug, patronizing smile and then passed a knowing look to Prentice that Delia found hard to read—like they had some little secret together. Obviously, they did.

The pain and humiliation of the situation hit her fully, and Delia felt waves of humiliation, anger, and hurt begin to wash over her.

"How could this have happened?" she whispered. "And how horrible to learn about it like this. So casually. So nonchalantly. Like an unfortunate turn of events Prentice needed to report. What was the term he used twice in his note?"

She picked up the letter again to read it once more. "There." She stabbed her finger at the words. "That it simply seemed an awkward situation. Was that all our relationship had become to him?" Delia felt sick as she looked back over the letter.

The next cruel reality hit her—she was the only person who even knew about this. Her car stood packed in the driveway, ready for her trip to meet all her family and friends for wedding toasts at a beach barbeque. She pictured that scenario for a few moments and put a fist to her mouth as the tears fell.

"I can't face that right now." She offered the words around broken sobs. "I need time to think first. Time to cry, and wail, and feel sorry for myself if I want to. Time to plan what in the world I'm going to do now." Delia dropped her head into her hands. "Every plan I've made for the last year has been centered around Prentice. Every single plan."

Delia looked across into the dining room at all the presents and cards piled on the table. "Sweet mercy. Someone will have to tell everyone the wedding is off, cancel all the reservations, send back all the gifts and money." She twisted her hands. "And someone will have to hear what Mother has to say about everything that's happened. Not only for today but for days and months to come." A little moan escaped Delia at the thought.

She wiped at her tears, anger and hurt swamping her. "It's simply one more time you've been naïve and trusting, Delia Eleanor Walker. And one more time you've been totally humiliated." Sniffling, she wrapped her arms around herself in agony. "You're just not tough enough for this world. Like Mother often says, you're too nice—too much a dreamer and an idealist. Not a realist."

What had her mother snapped at her after that last break-up? "You look at everything and everyone through rose-colored glasses, Delia."

Delia knew, without a doubt, this whole situation would not be viewed as Prentice's fault in her mother's eyes. It would be hers. "I can already hear Mother talking about all the ways I should have seen this coming. Things I should have done to prevent it—or, at the least, to have headed it off so as not to be stood up and humiliated."

She leaned over on the bench, balling into a fetal position at the thought. "At least Daddy will be kinder. He'll feel sorry for me, pet and hug me." This gave her comfort for only a short moment. "Then he'll be indoctrinated by Mother's point of view. He'll start giving me those pitying looks and slipping in subtle remarks about my maturity. Tell me I need to grow up and become stronger." She swallowed. "He'll start going on and on about all the money he's wasted toward this wedding. Every day mentioning a bill he has to pay, an amount he won't recoup."

Delia hung her head with the thought of going through it all, tears running down her cheeks. "Next, Frances and the boys will start in on me. Gracious heavens, I'd rather be dead than face it. I really would."

The overnight packet slipped off her lap as she reached to wipe away more tears. Leaning over to pick it up, she noticed the other letter still in her hand. The short note from Maureen Cross. Delia glanced down at the words again. "I do wish you could come down for a visit before the close on the house and property. I'd love to see you again. You make me think so much of Dee."

Someone wanted her. Delia bit her lip. She could go see Maureen and stay at Aunt Dee's place. After all, the little house belonged to her. She hadn't sold it yet. She could avoid going to the beach where her family waited for her. She had a plan of escape—an alternate solution to facing her family.

Delia drummed her fingers on the small table beside her. "I suppose I'd be acting as cowardly as Prentice by taking off and avoiding the family at this time—by not really 'facing the music,' as Daddy would say. But I can't bear dealing with everyone right now." She brushed away some more tears. "They won't mean to be unkind, but they'll make everything worse somehow. They always do when something bad happens."

Her eyes fell to Maureen's letter in her lap. Maybe it was a sign from God that Maureen's little note arrived with Prentice's express letter. The more Delia thought about it, the more she wanted to believe it.

"I'm going to Aunt Dee's." She lifted her chin with determination as the idea took clearer shape in her mind. "And that's that."

Decision made, Delia went into full gear with her new plans. She really could accomplish a lot when she wanted to. To be truthful, Delia knew she was stronger than her family believed. And more capable. They'd always simply seen her as the baby because she was the youngest—even called her Baby.

Delia stood up with resolution, folding both letters to put them in her purse. She went upstairs, found two soft-sided suitcases in the back of her closet and started packing the rest of the clothes she'd need for a stay in the mountains. More shorts and tops, more jeans, slacks, and shirts. Some jackets and sweaters for cool evenings. A few business suits, several skirts, blouses, and a couple of nice dresses. Additional shoes, socks, and hose. Hiking boots and thick socks.

Next, Delia sorted through all the boxes she'd brought back from the townhouse and decided on the personal things she'd need. Her laptop. Papers and materials. Decorating books. Jewelry and keepsakes she'd want if she stayed at Dee's for any length of time.

She made quick work of the packing. Finishing her preparations, Delia flipped down the back seats of the Forester and stuffed in her two additional suitcases, another duffle bag, several tote bags packed full, garment bags, and three large boxes. It all fit with the seats down. Thank goodness.

Packing completed, Delia found the cat, forced a travel pill down it, and then sat down at the computer in the downstairs office and started writing out letters—to the caterers, to the church and the minister, to the country club where the reception was planned, to her friends who were participating in the wedding, to family and friends who planned to attend. She printed them out as she finished them, stuffing them into stamped and addressed envelopes.

Actually, once she got a basic form letter created to explain the situation, she simply had to tweak it a little to everyone she wrote. Even the one to her parents. Delia shrugged in resignation. "After all, what can people say? I can hardly marry a man who's already married. It's the best reason to call off a wedding, no matter how humiliating."

Delia took care of everything that needed to be taken care of except returning the wedding gifts piled on the table. She asked her sister Frances to do that in the letter addressed to her, but she knew—even as she asked it—that it would probably be her mother or the housekeeper, Mrs. Beeker, who would actually do it. Delia grimaced. Eventually, she'd hear about that, too. About all the trouble it caused.

She frowned. "At least I can face those complaints later —when I feel stronger and maybe when I can handle them better. Right now, I simply need to get away and have some time alone. Cowardly or not." And for once—just once—she planned to do what she thought was right for herself before everyone took over her life for her.

Delia's Place

Squaring her chin, Delia dug out one of her father's road maps of the southeast U. S. and another of Tennessee and loaded the last of her possessions into the car, including one now very groggy grey Maltese cat, half asleep in his cat-carrier. She filled up her little SUV with gas at the service station down the street and hit the road.

Even amidst the heartache and the hurt, it felt liberating to be out on the highway. To be getting away. To have some kind of plan to move forward, if only a temporary one. The Smokies would be a good place to heal and think. Plus, Delia's memories of Aunt Dee and her place in the mountains were sweet ones. It would be restful to stay at her little place again.

Delia headed down coastal I-95 out of Virginia, mainly because this route south felt more familiar to her. It was the road she always took through Virginia and North Carolina to the beach house. Hours later, as she neared Raleigh and the turns she usually took to the coast, Delia cut west instead on I-85, heading toward I-40 that would lead her into Tennessee.

At the next rest area, Delia finally stopped to call Frances. It was nearly seven. The family would be looking for her by now and starting to worry.

"Hi, Baby, are you nearly here?" Frances asked, answering the phone.

Delia told her quickly what happened, where she was going and why. She started her story matter-of-factly, but before she finished it, she was crying and sniffling into her cell phone.

"Oh, Delia," Frances exclaimed when Delia finally paused on a long sigh. "What are you thinking? You can't go off to Dee's old place in the mountains right now! That's a totally childish and selfish thing to do. You turn your car around right now and come on down here to the beach house, you hear? I know you're upset, Baby, but you need to come and be with your family. This is where you belong at a difficult time like this. You can't simply run off on your own." She blew out an exasperated breath. "Surely you know that's not the right thing to do. You need us right now, Baby. You're upset. We'll take care of you. We'll help you decide what you should do now, see you through this, and handle everything for you. It will be okay. I promise. You'll see."

As usual, Frances missed the point that Delia needed to decide what she needed to do on her own. And that she needed some space and time to do that by herself.

"I'll be fine at Aunt Dee's place, Frances," Delia began. "And I really think this is the best thing for me right now...."

Frances interrupted her. "Baby, why don't I put Mother on," she pressed. "You can talk to her. She'll help you see what you ought to do ...."

"No!" Delia put in quickly. "I'll call her later; I promise. I only wanted you all to know I'm okay. Now I need to get back on the road, Frances."

"Surely you aren't going to drive all night, are you, Baby?" Frances asked with worry in her voice. "You know that's not safe. Especially since you're by yourself."

"I'll stop over when it gets late. Please don't worry, Frances."

There was silence for a minute and a long sigh. Frances put in a typical Walker family comment. "Didn't you see any of this coming with Prentice, Delia? Didn't you sense something amiss or notice something going wrong?"

Delia sighed. Et tu. Even Frances. She bit back a sarcastic comment. "Yeah, Frances, I saw all of this coming. That's why I went out looking at wedding dresses all day yesterday." But of course, Delia didn't say this to Frances. Perhaps she should. Just once.

Instead she said, "I've got to go now, Frances. I'll call you tomorrow and let you know I've gotten to Aunt Dee's safely."

She hung up before Frances could say anything more. Then she turned off her cell phone. If she left it on, every single member of her family would soon be calling her.

Delia shivered as she turned her car back onto the interstate. Her head ached now, and she felt like crying. To make things worse, Graham cat, who'd slept quietly until now, began to yowl.

The strain of the day hit Delia full force as well, and she started to cry along with Graham's yowls. She wept off and on all the way to Asheville. In between the tears, she verbally vented some of her anger and frustration aloud, making her throat sore in the process. But, mercy, it felt good to vent. She needed to be angry, needed to cry and feel sorry for herself.

On the outskirts of Asheville, Delia finally stopped for the night, sneaking Graham cat into her room on the backside of the motel complex. As usual, Graham quit yowling and meowing as soon as he got out of the car. After cautiously exploring the motel room and using his cat box, he curled up on the bed beside Delia and fell asleep.

Surprisingly, Delia slept, too, despite her grief. Probably just emotionally exhausted, she decided. The next morning, after picking up some continental breakfast items and coffee, she rolled back onto the road once more.

The highway beyond Asheville rose in scenic majesty along the eastern boundary of the Great Smoky Mountains, the green ridges of the Smokies on one side and the Pisgah National Forest on the other. Delia hadn't visited here for a number of years, and she'd forgotten the beauty of the mountains in this part of the country. Graham obviously disagreed, and he yowled groggily in his cat carrier as Delia's blue SUV wound in and out around the mountains' curves.

"It's not much longer, Graham," she told him comfortingly, reaching inside the carrier to stroke his soft, gray fur. "Then we'll be at Aunt Dee's place."

Delia wished longingly that her Aunt Dee could still be at the little house behind Gatlinburg, waiting to greet her. Not having any children of her own, Dee always claimed Delia as "her girl." It made Delia feel special for many, many years. As a young girl, Delia spent long weeks of her school vacation time with her Aunt Dee every summer, so she felt familiar with the simple stone house near Mynatt Park that her aunt owned. It nestled in a neighborhood of small scenic cottages that many homeowners used only as summer homes while others lived in year round. Aunt Dee and Uncle Roland knew all the families in the little neighborhood at the foot of the mountains. Delia had come to know many of them, too, on her visits.

She tried to keep her thoughts focused on happier girlhood pleasures of trips to the mountains, but memories of Prentice kept inching across her consciousness instead. Scenes of their happy times together scrolled through her mind like clips of past movies, and Delia indulged herself in them, letting herself remember and cry.

"Prentice always acted so sweet to me." She chewed her lip. "How could he have been seeing someone else without me sensing it? When we talked, even on the phone, he always spoke so romantically. And when we shared times together, he never acted cold or distant, like someone else occupied his mind."

Delia couldn't understand it. "I thought we were so good together." She said the last out loud on the edge of another sweep of weeping.

By the time she turned off the freeway to catch Highway 321, leading from Cosby into the back of Gatlinburg, she thought she'd finally cried herself out. At least for now. Stopping at the W. T. Market, a small gas station, to refuel the car, she went in the restroom to wash her face, brush her hair, and fix her makeup.

A soft, round face with warm brown eyes stared back at her in the bathroom mirror. Petite in size, only about five foot three, Delia had dark, thick, almost black hair hanging to her shoulders and what everyone said was a nice smile. She tried smiling at herself encouragingly, remembering that. Her eyes still looked puffy, and she felt travel worn, but she decided she didn't look too bad overall.

She wanted to look nice now. She'd be coming into Gatlinburg soon and needed to stop by the Crosswalk store downtown to get keys for Aunt Dee's place from Maureen Cross. She certainly didn't want Maureen to know she'd been crying, and she hoped she could keep her sorrows to herself while here and not make too much of her broken engagement to everyone.

"After all." She sniffed again. "People break up all the time. At least, if Prentice didn't really love me, I found out before I married him. That has to be a positive. As Aunt Dee always said, look on the bright side. Surely there's one somewhere."

Driving into Gatlinburg twenty minutes later, Delia could see the summer tourist season already well underway. Traffic crawled back-to-back along the main highway through Gatlinburg, even on a weekday.

Gatlinburg, which started as a rough mountain settlement, grew gradually into a small, picturesque vacation town, and then blossomed into a major tourist destination at the base of the Great Smoky Mountains National Park in the 1950s and 1960s. Many of the quaint shops and early hotels along the old Parkway and the Pigeon River remained, keeping the town charming in character, but it had definitely grown and spread over the years since Delia began coming here. The Great Smoky Mountains National Park had become the most-visited national park in America. Throngs of tourists strolled up and down the sidewalks of the Gatlinburg Parkway this May afternoon, enjoying the unique arts and craft shops and colorful dining and entertainment venues amidst the spectacular views of the mountains above the town.

Delia watched the crowds, gawking and pointing, laughing and talking—all having a wonderful time. She smiled in spite of herself. She'd always enjoyed Gatlinburg—such a happy place, full of interesting shops and galleries and friendly, open-hearted people.

After driving up and down several streets near Maureen's Crosswalk store, Delia finally found a parking space. She cracked the window for Graham, walked up a side street, and then down the main road to reach the Mountain Laurel Village Mall, where the Crosswalk Crafters Store stood on the corner. Delia smiled to see Maureen Cross helping one of the store clerks at the front counter as she walked in the door.

She looked the same as Delia remembered—her reddish brown hair pinned up in the familiar bun she'd always favored, her makeup minimal, her form still tall and overly lean, her wire-rimmed, oval glasses resting low over the bridge of her nose. Maureen had a stern, no-nonsense look about her, but Delia knew a very warm heart lay underneath. For as long as Delia could remember Maureen had been her Aunt Dee's best friend and, for the last eighteen years, her business partner in the store.

When Maureen glanced up to see Delia inside the doorway, she broke into a bright smile of pleasure. It was a treat to get a smile from the serious-natured Maureen, but even nicer to get the warm hug Delia received next. Generally, Maureen wasn't a demonstrative person, but Delia cherished her impulsive welcome today. It made what had been a terrible day seem, suddenly, a little bit better.

"Delia Eleanor! What a truly wonderful pleasure!" Maureen held Delia away to take a long look at her.

To Delia's surprise, Maureen teared up and put a hand to her mouth. Delia tried to remember if she'd ever seen Maureen cry.

"Forgive the tears, Delia." Maureen's voice had a little catch in it. "But you look so much like your Aunt Dee, and I'm still not over losing her, you know. Simply seeing you brings back so many wonderful memories. You do know how much she loved you, don't you?"

"I know." Delia bit her lip. "And I know how much she loved you. Seeing you makes me feel sad, too, Maureen. It makes me miss Aunt Dee even more. I'm so sorry I couldn't get down for her funeral."

Maureen waved a hand dismissively. "It was the middle of winter with you in the midst of exams, darling. Everyone knew that. Besides, the remembrance we held was a small one, like Dee wanted, with only a few good friends present."

Leaving that subject behind, Maureen looked at Delia. "Now what brings you down to see us? Not that it isn't a joy, of course. I hoped you might come, but I thought you'd probably be too busy for a last visit with us before your big wedding."

Delia had carefully prepared her answers to questions like this as she drove down from Virginia, but now, as she heard Maureen's words, she found herself fighting back a fresh spate of tears. In addition, she felt a lump rising in her throat and couldn't seem to find ready words in reply.

Maureen watched her for a moment and smiled gently. "There. There." She leaned closer to pat Delia's cheek with fondness. "Something has happened and we'll not talk of it now. It's a painful thing when the heart is hurt, and this is just the place for you to heal when that happens. Dee would have wanted that, you know. And I'll be right here for you, too—as Dee would have been—if you want to talk about anything later on."

Delia managed a small smile, reassured with the comforting words. She felt glad not to hear any suggestions from Maureen that pointed a finger of blame her way.

The doorbell jingled behind them, and Maureen waved a greeting to someone coming in the front door. "Look who's here!" she called out.

Delia turned to see a young man strolling into the store. He wore a starched blue button-down shirt, a subdued red silk tie, and held a dark suit coat hitched casually over one shoulder. Definitely preppy, Delia thought, with his neat short haircut, tailored slacks, and shiny cordovan loafers. Although not tall, like Prentice, he was well built, and something looked vaguely familiar about his tanned face.

"Well, well, if it isn't the little princess," he observed, offering her a broad grin and a teasing bow.

A fresh sweep of humiliation spread over Delia as she recognized Maureen's son, Tanner Cross, her old playmate from childhood summers. The last time she'd seen him she made an absolute fool of herself over him with some silly girlhood fantasies. Seeing him again today—of all days—was exactly what she didn't need. It seemed just another reminder of how naïve and foolish she could be in matters of the heart.

Taking a deep breath to try to settle herself, Delia plastered a bright smile on her face, and reached out a hand in greeting. "Tanner, how nice to see you again," she lied politely.

Chapter 2

Tanner Cross worked his way down the busy sidewalks of the Gatlinburg Parkway. He'd just finished a meeting with Hiram Sheffrum that went better than expected. As Hiram Sheffrum's CPA, Tanner had leveled with his client over a late lunch meeting. Sheffrum was overspending in his business. If he didn't rein in on his expenses, he could face bankruptcy. Fortunately for Sheffrum, it wasn't in the essentials that he played too loose a financial hand, but in the perks and extras. Hiram Sheffrum liked to live and dine well. He liked the best, even in office furniture, art, and equipment. And he loved new technology.

The business meeting hadn't been one Tanner looked forward to. Hiram Sheffrum, an egotistic man, had a tendency to excess in his spending and his temper. Tanner had, luckily, caught him on one of his better days—helping Sheffrum to see, with only minimal grousing, where his continued overspending could lead. Sheffrum agreed, for today at least, to Tanner's well laid out plans for some new and greatly needed economies. Things had gone well overall, Tanner thought.

The afternoon felt warm as Tanner walked back from Howard's Restaurant. He took off his suit jacket and hitched it over one shoulder as he strolled along. It was easier to walk in the Burg whenever you could instead of driving. Finding a parking place always posed a challenge, even as a local when you knew all the back streets.

Tanner whistled cheerfully, watching the mill of tourists with pleasure as he made his way up the sidewalk of the Parkway. He stopped to give directions when asked, chatted with a few friends he ran into. Gatlinburg had always been home to Tanner and he loved it here.

The T. Cross Accounting Firm lay upstairs in an office suite over the Crosswalk Crafters Store that Tanner's mother owned in part. On the side of the building, outside stairs led to the accounting offices, but Tanner decided to head in through the store first to tell his mother how the lunch meeting had gone. She knew Sheffrum and the trouble he could cause.

As he pushed into the front door, he glanced up to catch the end of his mother's "look who's here" words. She stood smiling with pleasure by the front register, her arm looped around the shoulders of a young woman. Probably one of the high school clerks his mother hired for summer help who'd dropped back by to say hello. It happened a lot.

The girl was definitely cute, Tanner noted. Not too tall, maybe all of five two or three. Tanner always noticed height, being only about five foot eight himself. He remembered when he was younger trying to stretch himself taller with some exercise book and equipment he'd ordered from a magazine. Of course, it hadn't worked. And, in time, he'd come to terms with his height.

The girl wore fitted jeans, a scoop-necked white t-shirt, and had a sweet little figure. Really, really sweet, Tanner thought to himself, studying her again. And nicely filled out, too. Her hair fell down on her shoulders, dark brown and wavy, almost black, and when she looked up at him, he saw pretty eyes of a rich, warm brown flecked with white. Her face was round and soft, her lips full and touched with a light red lipstick. Something seemed oddly familiar about her, too. Suddenly it hit him.

My word, he thought, it's little Delia Walker. Seeing the start of recognition on her face, as well, Tanner fell immediately back into his old teasing mode from their younger years.

"Well, well, if it isn't the little princess," he observed, using the pet name he'd called her when she tagged around after him in dress-up clothes and an old tiara. He always wanted to play cowboys or pirates, but she loved to play prince and princess—with particular notions about how Tanner should bow and act like a real prince.

He bent over now, doffing a pretend cap and grinning. However, she didn't smile back at him. Instead her face blanched white and she looked stiff and pained as if she might cry—given half a chance. She collected herself quickly, though, and put on a forced, bright smile, holding out a hand to him.

"Tanner," she said liltingly, in the same sweet voice he remembered so well. "How nice to see you again."

Tanner took her hand in greeting, nodding and offering back a few similar polite words in return. He could tell Delia would prefer telling him to go eat nails if she could do so politely. He wondered what he'd done to make her so upset with him. And so soon. She'd always been an emotional little thing. Guess that hadn't changed much over the years.

Glancing down, Tanner realized he still held Delia's hand in his and that she struggled tactfully to pull it away. He clamped down harder on it for a moment and looked more closely into her eyes, seeing a redness about them with puffy skin underneath. She flushed under his scrutiny, and Tanner let her hand go.

Delia's Place

"Thought you wouldn't have time to come see us Appalachian folk again with your big wedding coming up," he teased, trying to lighten the moment.

Her eyes reddened more, and she turned her head away.

Maureen gave him a warning look and a shake of her head. "There's been a change in those plans, Tanner. And I, for one, am simply delighted, because that means Delia will hopefully stay with us for a long time this summer. To be frank, I could really use her help in the store with the tourist season coming in, and Aunt Dee's old place could benefit from some company and cleaning up."

Tanner's mother, always a master of conveying "telling looks," passed him a second significant glance, and Tanner picked up on her message this time.

"Yeah, I think that house has been a little lonely." Tanner took his cue. "Needs somebody to stay in it for a while. Wants some TLC and such. You know."

His mother smiled. "Tanner, why don't you go get the keys and take Delia on over and let her in to the cottage? I really need to stay here until five when John comes in for his shift. We're busy today, Delia. Bess took off early to go to the doctor, and I'm covering for her until John arrives."

"Oh, please, don't go to any trouble." Delia waved a hand in protest. "No one needs to go with me. I know the way and I can let myself in just fine." She sent another plastic smile Tanner's way. "I'm sure Tanner needs to get back to work, too."

"No, I'm actually through for the day," Tanner put in, just to provoke her. He knew she wanted to avoid being with him for some reason.

His mother rummaged behind the counter for the key to Aunt Dee's house. "Oh, by the way, Tanner, how did your meeting go with Sheffrum? I almost forgot to ask."

"Better than I expected." He leaned against the counter. "Sheffrum actually agreed to cooperate with almost every part of the spending reductions I laid out for him, and he didn't grouse too much about it, either. In fact, when Bogan came in as we left the restaurant, Sheffrum told him in that booming voice of his that I was the best gall-darned CPA in all of Gatlinburg."

"Well, that did go well." Maureen smirked.

They both laughed.

Remembering Delia still waiting, Maureen turned to her. "Now, Delia, you drive on over and let yourself into Dee's house. Here are the keys; this one opens the front door, this one the back, and this one the shed. Dee labeled them all. While you settle in, I'm sending Tanner to the food store on 321 to get you some groceries. I'll make out a list of basics. There's absolutely nothing in that house, you know, and you don't need to get out and go shopping in this traffic after driving all day like you did."

Delia tried to argue, but Maureen quelled all arguments, and soon sent Delia on her way to Dee's place on Balsam Lane. After Delia left, Maureen found a scratch pad at the sales counter and started scribbling off a grocery list.

"Tanner, something hurtful has happened to that child about her upcoming marriage," she said, as she wrote. "I don't think it's just a spat, either. Delia wouldn't have come all this way to Gatlinburg over a little upset with her fiancé. Plus she didn't deny it when I mentioned her plans had changed."

She looked at Tanner over her glasses. "You tread carefully with her, you hear me? Don't tease her too much. You know how you are about that, especially with Delia. Sometimes you don't know when to back off."

Tanner shrugged. "I'll be careful, Mom. I've been tiptoeing around little Delia Walker's emotions for years now. It won't be like it's anything new to do it once more."

"Hush that talk, Tanner Harmon Cross," Maureen admonished with a firm glint in her eye. "Delia was only a little girl, five whole years younger than you back in those childhood days. Five years made a big difference when you two were young. So did her being a girl among you and your rowdy male friends."

Tanner rolled his eyes.

She crossed her arms. "You can see Delia's a grown woman now, Tanner. She'll be twenty-three years old on her birthday in July."

Maureen paused, thinking. "You know, it seems to me the last time you even saw Delia was the summer you graduated high school before she turned thirteen. That was a long time ago, Son. The two of you are both grown and more like equals now. You need to remember that. Plus, Delia doesn't need to be teased and treated like a little child if she's going through a painful time. I know."

"Yeah, yeah. I'll put my best foot forward, Mom. Don't worry. I can be a real sensitive guy."

"Hmmmm. Well, we'll see." She gave him a sharp look. "You keep in mind, too, that Dee Ward was my very best friend in all the world, and she loved that girl with all of her heart. You and I are going to do everything we can to help Delia if she's going through a difficult time. Do you hear me, Tanner?"

"I hear, I hear." He draped his coat over his arm. "But I wonder why Delia came here instead of going to her family if she's experiencing a tough time, Mom?"

Maureen snorted. "You don't know her family well, or you wouldn't ask that. Especially that hard, unyielding mother of hers, Charlotte Chapman Walker. I never did like that woman. Her husband—Dee's brother Howard—always let Charlotte lead him around by the nose, if you ask me."

Tanner knew better than to reply to his mother's observations.

"I'll go get the groceries," he said instead, making his escape.

Tanner enjoyed the wind in his face as he drove his classic silver Mustang convertible down the Parkway and then up Highway 321 to the Food City, the only large grocery store in the Burg. The sporty convertible had been one of his Atlanta yuppie purchases when he worked with a top CPA firm there and started making the big bucks.

Seeing Delia today reminded him of his college days and the choices he made after graduation. "Worked my butt off day and night in The Big Peach and was miserable in the bargain," he added out loud.

It still amazed Tanner that he'd lived and worked in Atlanta for so long. But he wanted to live out his big city success dream after college and stayed in Atlanta for nearly four years. He'd known success there, too. Been promoted quickly in one of the nation's top three accounting firms and jumped on what might be termed 'the upwardly mobile track for rising young CPAs.'

Tanner shook his head remembering. "Maybe it was Dad's death that made me determined not to come home sooner. I felt angry fate took my dad so young. Left Mom a widow. Robbed me of one more good fishing trip or long talk with my father."

Thomas Cross was a true friend to Tanner as well as a fine father. Raw pain still lanced Tanner's heart when he thought about his dad's death too much.

His thoughts slipped back. "It took an unexpected realization to make me want to come home. Dee Ward called it an epiphany." Tanner grinned at the memory. "It happened in a flash one fine spring day when I went walking in the park on my lunch hour. I stopped to look around, the scene froze, and I realized I wasn't where I belonged." He drummed his fingers on the steering wheel. "The Cherokee Indians believe everybody has a place they belong to that calls to them. That spring day, I got my call clearly and knew I needed to come home."

He phoned Barry Claibourne, his father's old employee in the T. Cross Accounting Firm the same day. "Hey, Barry. You think there might be enough business for me to come back to Gatlinburg to work?"

"Well, it's about time I got this call," Barry grumbled into the phone. "I thought you'd never wake up and realize where you belonged, boy. We've been overworked here since your father died, struggling to keep up the work load these last years." The older man paused. "Something wrong there, boy? You in trouble?"

"Nah, I just had a wakeup call, Barry. Figured out where I belong," Tanner answered candidly.

"Hummmph." Barry snorted. "Well, it would have been nice if you'd had this wake-up call before tax season finished. We just passed through the worst time of the year short-handed and overloaded, you hear? When do you think you can get your sorry ass up here and get to work?"

Tanner laughed, remembering the call and knowing the reprimand was Barry's way of welcoming him back to the firm. Tanner got his ass back to the Burg within the month—the best decision he ever made. He was exactly where he belonged now. It had just taken him a little time to know it.

He'd moved back in with his mother for a short time when he returned, then tore down the old shed on the side property and built a small complementary house on the old foundations. Even saved the trees. He liked the Mynatt Park neighborhood and didn't mind living beside his mother. They'd always been close. But as a grown man now, he wanted his own space. His mother understood that. Probably wanted hers, too.

Tanner's new place and his mother's house both lay on the same side road, named Balsam Lane, where Dee Walker-Ward's house stood. Eight houses lined Wesley Drive that led up to Balsam, but only three homes nestled on the short cul-de-sac angling off the end of it. The Crosses owned the property on the left side of the street, and the Wards owned the property on the right.

"Now little Miss Delia Walker's going to be living right across the street for a time in her Aunt Dee's old stone cottage. Well, well." Tanner turned that idea over in his mind, and grinned. "It might be sort of fun to see what comes of that."

Tanner still remembered Delia's first stay at her Aunt Dee's at only five years old. "Her father brought her down and left her for two weeks while he went to North Carolina to furniture shows. Little Delia had two stumpy, little ponytails then and acted shy at first." He shook his head. "I admit, at ten, I was fascinated by her, not having younger siblings. She possessed a keen imagination for only five, and we played pretend games together every day. Of course, the fact that she idolized me didn't hurt, either. That felt good to my ten-year-old ego."

Tanner let his mind drift over the years. "Delia came every summer after that, often for a whole month." He curled his lips in a smile. "I developed a boyish crush on her as soon as I figured out such things. I knew she was crazy about me, too, as I got older. We have some history—me and Delia Walker. Some childish history, but some history."

He pulled into the grocery parking lot and started looking for a space. Tanner angled into a spot near the door, frowning at his next thought. "I admit I felt secretly upset last summer when I learned Delia got engaged. Even though I hadn't seen her for years. And, now, here she is again—not a cute little girl anymore, but a real knockout." Cheered by his own words, he headed into the store.

By the time Tanner arrived back at Balsam Lane with groceries for Delia, he'd started feeling downright wolfish. He pulled his Mustang in beside her

Delia's Place

blue SUV in the open carport and started to unload. He banged on the back door before he let himself in, but still he startled her. And watched that cute little flush crawl up her face again.

"Sorry if I surprised you," he apologized, setting the grocery bags down on the kitchen counter. "Why don't you start putting these groceries away, where you want them, while I unload the rest?"

"You mean there are more?" She stared at the pile of bags he'd already hauled in.

"A lot more." He laughed. "Mother sent me to the store with a two page list."

"Oh, she really shouldn't have done that," Delia protested. "And I want to know exactly how much I owe her for all this, too."

Tanner shook his head. "On the house. Welcome gift from Maureen. You'll hurt her feelings, Delia, if you don't accept. She's so pleased you're here."

"Well, if you're really sure." Delia mumbled the words reluctantly, starting to unpack the bags. "But it doesn't seem right."

Tanner headed out to his car for more of the groceries. Ten minutes later he'd hauled everything in and was helping Delia find places for it. Working together had started to ease a little of the initial tension.

"There's enough food here for an army." Delia stacked canned goods into the pantry shelves.

"Well, Mom tried to think of everything you'd need to get started." Tanner put a carton of eggs in the refrigerator. "When you decide on more things you want, the big grocery is a few miles up 321 on the left. Around the corner—closer—on Cherokee Orchard is a pick-up market where you can buy milk, bread, or cokes. You may remember it. We used to bike down there."

"With the incredible Jack Gang." Delia turned to give him the first genuine smile he'd seen. "What happened to those boys, Tanner?"

"Believe it or not, they're all living and working right here in the Burg." He smiled back. "Perry and I left for a number of years but then both wandered back home. Keppler and Bogan never left the area except to go to college."

"J-A-C-K—for James, Ammons, Cross, and Kirkpatrick ..." Delia remembered. "You took the first initials of all your last names to create a name for that silly boys' club you started in the old tree house."

"Yeah, and you were the first girl that got to come up into that tree house," Tanner reminded her.

"Was I really?" Delia turned to him wide-eyed.

"Yeah, but don't get too smug about it. It was only because you cried for an hour at the base of the tree that we let you up at all. We couldn't stand to listen to you yowl anymore."

"Ohhh, you mean thing." She punched him on the arm. "You didn't have to tell me that and burst my bubble. I thought for a minute I was special."

"You were always special, Delia." Tanner spoke the words in a soft voice.

She looked at him. Surprised. Then turned away to wipe at tears that started to trickle down her face. "Don't be nice to me today, Tanner. Okay? It's not a good day for me."

"Okay," he replied, noticing her tears. "I'll try to think of all my best insults instead." He paused, propping against the counter to grin at her. "Remember that time we all took turns thinking of insulting names to call each other, Delia? Everybody wrote down all the worst stuff they could think of and then we read them off. You were here that summer."

She laughed. "I remember. All of you came up with such awful names, especially Bogan."

"Like Fart Face and Booger Breath?" Tanner made a face. "Bogan actually used those insults for years, you know."

She giggled.

"I remember the worst one you thought of was Fairy Poof." He sent her a smirk. "We didn't even know what it was but still died laughing over it."

"I told you what it was." She lifted her chin, a little piqued.

"Yeah. One of your imaginative concepts for fairy bowel movements. Your explanation cracked us up more than the term."

She frowned and crossed her arms. "Keppler and Bogan teased me over that and called me Fairy Poof for weeks afterwards. I was awfully glad when they finally quit."

Tanner grinned. "Mother heard them, gave us a lecture, and made us quit," he explained. "She made us feel guilty and creepy for picking on you, with you only seven and all of us twelve."

"I never knew that." Her eyes grew wide with surprise. "But I'm grateful. It was hard for me always being so much younger than the four of you."

"You did all right." He shrugged.

She smiled again. "Those were good times."

"Want to have some more good times?" He stashed cleaning supplies under the sink while he spoke. "We're all getting together for my birthday this Friday night. Having a cookout right here at the park. Everyone would love to see you, Delia."

"I'll think about it." Her face fell and she turned away, busying herself with the groceries.

"Listen, Delia," Tanner put in, catching her eyes with his when she glanced back his way. "No one down here cares a rip about whether you changed your mind about getting married. Or whether he changed his mind. It's not a big deal to us. The guys will just say, 'Hey, way to go, Delia. You escaped the noose just in time.' You know how they are. Real laid back. Real easy."

"Real teases." A tentative smile touched her lips again.

"Maybe, but only in fun," he added. "But they'll think more of it than it is if they know you're here, and you don't come. It is my birthday, after all. It would seem odd if you opted out. They'll think you don't like me anymore or something."

"And should I like you?" she challenged saucily. "You never wrote me all those years once you became a big college boy."

He leaned against the counter again. "We never wrote much anyway, Delia. Just the occasional kiddy postcard or Christmas card."

"Maybe," she conceded.

"Besides, I was engaged in Atlanta part of that time. Melanie probably wouldn't have appreciated me writing to other girls, even old childhood friends. In fact, I'm absolutely certain she wouldn't have."

Delia bit her lip. "What happened with that, Tanner?"

"I'll tell if you'll tell." He flashed her an arch smile.

Delia hung her head.

"Aw, come on, Chicken Butt. How bad can it be?" he teased.

Her eyes flashed at him. "All right. But you first." She lifted her head with a little challenge.

"Okay. Here's the story. I broke up with Melanie; that's the gist of it." Tanner shrugged. "She was running my life. Telling me what to do, who to be friends with, what to think, and what to eat. The final straw came when she decided that I shouldn't lead a scout troop I'd already committed to help. Told me in a snooty tone it wasn't an upwardly mobile move for me, that it would be better if I learned to play golf. She said negotiations on the golf course would take me further than messing around with a bunch of little kids doing good deeds."

"I see." Delia considered this. "Was she pretty?" She blushed self-consciously as she asked.

"Stunning." Tanner popped a cold cola and took a drink. "Sleek, blond, sexy, and a snake from the pit of hell. Just took me a space to figure that last part out."

"What about you?" He leaned his forearm against the doorframe.

Delia hesitated and started to tear up again.

"None of that crying crap, Delia. Just spit it out. We had a deal."

"All right! He married someone else," Delia snapped at him. "So there!"

"Is that all?" Tanner asked casually, baiting her.

"No. He sent me an overnight letter to tell me about it the day after." She almost shouted the words at him now, her face blotching. "Like it wasn't even a big deal." She clenched her fists in anger. "And he left me to face everybody and to take care of everything all by myself!"

He took another swig of cola. "So? It sounds to me like you're better off. Guy sounds like a jerk."

"He is a jerk! He'd been seeing this other woman for almost a year." Tears trickled down her cheeks. "He didn't even have the decency to tell me there was someone else. Just let me go on thinking we were getting married. Let me make plans and send out announcements and everything."

Tanner sat his cold drink on the counter, considering that. "Why in the world would he do that?" He scratched his head.

She shrugged, stopping to think about it herself. "I don't know. He was completing his residency with my brother's medical group in Baltimore. Both he and the woman he married were residents with Richard's medical practice. Prentice said in his letter they thought it might hurt them professionally if Richard found out they were seriously involved."

Tanner picked up his drink again. "Well, Richard might have punched his lights out for being unfaithful to you, but I doubt he'd have kicked the guy out of his residency."

"Well, who can say now?" snipped Delia. "It wasn't as though anybody bothered to ask me—or talk to me with decency and candor about anything."

"Another major point to his disfavor." Tanner made a face. "The guy sounds like a coward, too, Delia. And certainly not good enough for you."

She turned wide eyes to his. Surprised again. "Thanks for that, Tanner," she said, sniffing.

He crunched up his cola can and tossed it in the trash. "Listen, Delia. I know you're mad and hurting and going through a hard time with this. But surely you can see this wasn't the kind of guy you wanted to spend your life with. He was obviously way below your level."

"And what's my level?" Her voice softened.

"Well, honey, everybody knows you're a princess." He winked at her.

"Tanner, this isn't a time to make jokes." Delia crossed her arms angrily, her eyes starting to pool again.

"Okay, no jokes." He chose his words carefully. "Did you love him that much, Delia?"

She shot him a dark glance. "I'd hardly have planned to marry him if I hadn't. Didn't you love Melanie?"

"I thought I did." He paused to consider this. "Maybe I did for a time. But sometimes people change."

He heard Delia let out a soft sigh. "So how does anybody know what feelings they can trust?" she asked him. "How can anybody know what is real?"

"Well, that's a big question to think on." Tanner stuffed the now empty shopping bags in a box under the sink. "Maybe that'll be our "Question for the Night" this Friday for the Jack Gang."

Delia giggled despite herself. "Do the four of you still play that old game?"

"Absolutely." He grinned at her. "It's how we arrive at the answers to many of life's great problems and mysteries."

"Oh, you." She waved a playful hand at him. "You guys all sat around and wrote out three answers to the Question of the Night on the backs of napkins and read them out loud."

"Well, sure," he answered. "But out of that accumulated wisdom, we always seemed to figure out the right answer."

She smiled. "You're so funny, Tanner. I've missed that."

"Well, that's something then, isn't it? Does that mean you'll come to my birthday party?"

"I guess," she conceded. "Do I have to bring a present?"

Glad to see her tears drying, he answered in fun. "Yeah, and I want a new silver sheriff's badge like the cool one I had that you lost. And a bag of jacks, cause I bet I could still beat you."

"I did not lose that sheriff's badge." Her face flushed. "You always blamed that on me and it wasn't my fault."

"Well, you were the last one who had it," he stated, grinning.

"Whatever." She put the last of the canned goods on the shelf in a huff. "I doubt you'll get a new sheriff's badge or any jacks for a birthday present, but I'll think of something."

"You're just afraid I'll beat you at jacks again."

She crossed her arms and cocked her head at him, in the way he remembered so well. She always did that when she got provoked at him.

He chuckled, glad to see her tears dried up at last.

"Don't you have something else to do except hang around here all day?" Delia scowled at him. "I need to unpack and rest after my trip. And I need to call home."

"To boo-hoo and cry to your big sister Frances?" he goaded.

"No, smarty." She pushed at him in irritation. "But I do need to let them know I got here all right. I haven't called them yet, and they're all down at the beach. Probably worried about me."

"Want me to stay while you call?" he asked, picking up on her change in mood.

"No." She went to open the kitchen door for him. "And tell your mother thanks for the groceries. It was wonderful of her to do that for me."

Delia was dismissing him now. Tanner didn't argue, but he lingered in the doorway. "Delia, do you remember where the old boat shed used to be— back in that stand of trees across the street?"

"Yes," she answered. "Why?"

"Well, where it used to be is where my house is now." He glanced in that direction. "And Mother's place is still the next lot down—right where it always was. So if you need anything, just come find us. Or call. Here's my number."

Tanner pulled out a business card from his pocket. "My cell phone's on here and my business phone. I'll write my home phone number on the back for you, too." He scribbled it down.

"Okay." She took the card. "I'll be all right, Tanner. I don't need a babysitter anymore like when I was little."

He grinned rakishly at her. "I could stay and baby-sit again if you'd like, Delia. You could sit on my lap and I could read you a story."

"Honestly, Tanner," she protested, flushing and dropping her eyes.

"Listen, Delia," he said, watching her. "In case you haven't noticed, you've become a very beautiful woman. I don't know what that doctor jerk was thinking to choose someone else over you, but he used sludge for brains when he did. You keep that in mind and don't wallow in this too much, you hear? And when you call your family, you stand up for yourself and don't let them give you a hard time." He lifted her chin to look into her eyes. "Okay?"

"Okay." She gave him a small smile.

Tanner turned to leave. "By the way. What was this guy's name?"

She hesitated. "Prentice Ginsberg." She said the name with reluctance.

"Yuk." Tanner stuck his tongue out. "Ginsberg. Sounds like the name of a Nazi spy or a hot air balloon like the Hindenburg. You'd have been Delia Ginsberg if you'd gone through with it. That's a yuk name. And your initials would have been D. E. G. – almost like dig or degradation. See? You got out just in time."

He had her smirking before he left.

"You're a goof, Tanner," she informed him. She smiled when she said it, and her eyes looked better now.

Tanner left, whistling by the time he'd driven halfway down Balsam Lane heading out of the park. He'd made progress. And it was turning out to be kind of fun. He even got Delia to tell him why she wasn't getting married now. Poor kid. That guy really treated her like crap. The bum. No wonder she felt so hurt and had run off.

He'd help her get over it. Not just because his mom told him to, either. Tanner was beginning to suspect he might have his own little agenda in mind for cheering up Miss Delia Walker.

Chapter 3

*E*arlier that day, after leaving Maureen and Tanner at the Crosswalk store, Delia experienced a rush of memories when she drove up the narrow, shaded street and pulled into the driveway at her Aunt Dee's place for the first time in years. The weathered grey stone house still looked welcoming with its peaked gables, steep rooflines, and bright red front door. Ivy twisted up over the stone chimney and spread itself merrily across the front windows, just as she remembered. And here in late May, Dee's spring flowers created a sunny show of yellow, red, and white in the front flower beds.

As Delia looked closer, she saw weeds in those flower beds, too, plus leaves and debris on the front porch and stairs that needed to be swept off. Even the old sign that read 'Delia's Place' fell over to one side on its stake by the front steps. She reached down to straighten it, experiencing a touch of nostalgia as she remembered the day she and Aunt Dee bought the sign at one of those woodcraft shops on the Gatlinburg Parkway. Every summer when Delia visited, Aunt Dee always created unique, one-of-a-kind times and memories for them to hold fast to during the year.

Inside, the little house looked as charming and colorful as Delia remembered. Aunt Dee's decorating style belonged in a Mary Engelbreit magazine with its warm, colorful patterns and cozy crafts for decoration. Dee's favorite colors, rich reds and sunny yellows, spilled over in every room, mixed with the bright chintzes, busy prints, colorful quilts, and richly patterned rugs Aunt Dee loved so much. It had always seemed a gay and happy house to Delia.

The cottage was a small one in its floor plan. A roomy living and dining area centered around a big stone fireplace on the main floor, with an eat-in kitchen, small side porch and pantry in the back. The door off the little side porch by the garage led out to a broad, shaded screened room that spanned the back of the house. Two bedrooms and two baths were also located on the downstairs floor. Upstairs a third bedroom, a small bath, and a little office hid under the gable peaks.

She smiled as she looked around. "I remember my special play haven was that long bedroom upstairs under the slanted rooflines of the cottage, but I always slept downstairs in the bedroom across the hall from Aunt Dee." She carried her luggage into that room now, stopping to peek out the window across a woodsy back yard full of hardwoods and evergreens. "Every morning when I woke here as a child, I could hear the birds and squirrels chattering in the backyard—and in the evening, the sounds of tree frogs and cicadas lulled me to sleep."

Woodland filled most of Dee's property, with the exception of a small cleared, grassy yard near the porch that led to a back shed smothered in climbing roses. Beyond the back yard in the open woods, the forestland spread deeper leading into the Great Smoky Mountains National Park. A narrow, side trail wound its way from Dee's yard into the woods and eventually to a trickly mountain creek named Sweet Gum Branch. If you hopped the rocks across it and followed the trail to the right, it met up with other trails that led back into the parkland in different directions. Delia looked forward to exploring some of these familiar paths again while here.

She smiled to see the cat creeping out of his carrier, beginning to explore the house now. "Make yourself at home, Graham." She'd chosen the gray Maltese from a friend's litter when she moved into the townhouse with her friends. At home, her mother never wanted pets—especially one that spent much time inside. So a cat was one of the first things Delia sought when she moved out on her own.

"It's surprisingly clean in the house," Delia told the cat. "I thought it might be dusty or dank from being shut up so long. Maybe Maureen's had someone in to clean."

Deciding the bed sheets might be musty, Delia peeked in the bathroom closet and discovered clean sheets and towels. She put fresh sheets on the high bed in the back bedroom and remade it. Then she made sure clean towels hung in the bathroom for later on. She'd started to explore the kitchen when Tanner startled her, letting himself in the back door with an armload of groceries.

Admittedly, Tanner cheered her by coming. Delia hadn't planned to restart their relationship, but she realized now she could hardly avoid it. They'd been friends since childhood, after all. And it wouldn't hurt to have a friend or two right now.

Delia walked through the house to the front window and watched Tanner's car disappear down the road. Across the street through the trees, she could see a neat, tan house trimmed in white with black shutters, reminiscent of Maureen's cottage a half block down the road. It was thoughtful that Tanner built his own house to look like a guest cottage of his mother's place. The look fit for the Mynatt Park neighborhood. And for Balsam Lane.

Delia's Place

As Delia started down the hall, she smiled at herself in the antique mirror hanging on the wall. "It didn't hurt that he flirted with you today either, Delia Walker. You have to admit that it made you feel better about yourself. Probably why he did it, too. Tanner was always able to pull you out of your moods with his flirting and teasing."

Bracing herself for the inevitable now, Delia turned on her cell phone and called the main phone at the family's beach house. Her mother answered on the second ring as though she'd been sitting by the telephone.

"Delia, are you all right?" she challenged as soon as she heard Delia's voice. "We've all been worried sick here. And we've been trying to call you ever since yesterday evening. We couldn't get through on your cell phone. Where are you?"

"I'm at Aunt Dee's and I'm fine, Mother." Delia sat down on a chintz chair.

"I couldn't believe it when Frances told me what happened," her mother exclaimed. "And to learn you'd run off to Dee's old place to brood rather than dealing with this like you should. Truly, Delia, I'm very disappointed in you."

Delia sighed. What else was new?

"Mother, I dealt with everything that needed to be done before I left Arlington. I thought Frances would have told you that. I sent letters to the caterers, the church, the minister, the people in the wedding, and the guests who planned to attend. I didn't avoid dealing with things before I left."

Her mother interrupted her. "So what possessed you to run off down to that junky tourist town rather than to come here and be with your own family? Honestly, Delia, your father and I are deeply hurt over this. As is the rest of the family. Surely, you owed it to us to come in person and talk about this."

"What was there to say, Mother? Prentice ran off and married someone else."

Her mother snorted in annoyance. "And did you know that was going to happen, Delia? Had Prentice been telling you things were not all right? Did you avoid dealing with the growing problems in your relationship like you usually do—just continuing to plan a wedding, hoping everything would magically work out?"

Delia gritted her teeth. This was why she'd come to Dee's place instead of going to her family. But she couldn't say so.

Instead she said, "Mother, I am not at fault here. I did not have any idea Prentice was even seeing another woman until I got his overnight letter. That's how he informed me about this, Mother. He sent me an overnight letter to tell me he'd impulsively gotten married the night before in Las Vegas."

"Well, that doesn't sound like Prentice at all," her mother interrupted, her voice petulant. "He was always so practical and sensible. So honorable. And very up-front."

"Well, he wasn't up-front this time, Mother," Delia informed her, annoyed now. "Nor was he honorable. He'd been having an affair with MacKenzie Wilkes since last fall, Mother, and they knowingly concealed it from all of us."

"Why ever would Prentice do that, Delia?" Her mother sounded genuinely shocked.

Delia sighed. "I don't know, Mother. He said it was because he and MacKenzie both interned with Richard's group. Said he thought it might reflect badly on them professionally or jeopardize their careers, if they came forward about their relationship sooner."

Delia heard her mother sputter. "Now, whatever makes you think a thing like that, Delia? Is that your overly active imagination making up a plausible story to explain all of this?"

A flash of anger rose up in Delia. "No, Mother, it's not," she replied tightly. "That's what Prentice told me in the letter he sent. I was looking at wedding dresses the day before I received his letter instead of plotting stories to tell you."

"Don't be sarcastic, Delia. It's not becoming," her mother criticized. "And please tell me you didn't buy a wedding dress yesterday? It would be just one more bill to pay in all this mess."

Delia hung her head. A few tears started a silent course down her cheek. Not one word of love and kindness, she thought. Not one "I'm so sorry" or "My heart is just grieved for you over this." Not a single word of hostility toward Prentice either, who'd let her down and broken her heart. Only accusations and criticisms.

"I didn't buy a wedding dress, Mother." She spoke the words quietly.

"Well, thank heavens for that." Her mother sighed in relief. "Now, when are you coming back up here to the beach with us, Delia? You'll need to make some other plans for your life now, you know." She paused to think. "I suppose you could live at home and work in the family business for a time until you find yourself."

It didn't sound like a warm invitation to Delia.

"I think I'll stay here at Dee's while I think about other plans," she replied. "I do own a house here, you know, and have money in savings. I'll be all right for a time."

"I thought you planned to sell that place." Her mother's tone sounded cross. "Your father said you already scheduled a date to turn Dee's house and business property over to a new owner. If you stay on, you might lose that good sale, Delia. And it might not be easy to get rid of that old house at a later time. It was only a little summer cottage, if I remember, hardly modernized, and filled with all Delia Ward's bargains and crafts. It might have been fun for you to visit as a little girl, but surely you don't want to stay there for any length of time. I personally always disliked the place."

Delia looked around the living room where she sat. Aunt Dee's cozy furniture, print pillows, shelves of books, and mountain handcrafts winked back at her. A wonderful homemade quilt in rich tones lay sprawled over a side chair invitingly. Beautiful patterned rugs covered the hardwood floors and Aunt Dee's photographs were crowded in a cluster on a side table. It was a wonderful house, and Delia should know. She was an interior decorator, after all. She pulled herself upright at that thought. She had a master's degree in interior design. She could find her way in the world if she needed to, and she didn't need anyone telling her what sort of place was suitable for her to live in, either.

"I like it here, Mother," she said with what firmness she could muster. "I'm going to stay here until I decide where I'd like to work. I have my resume, license number, and all my work materials; I can network and job hunt from here as well as anywhere else. Plus I can enjoy a nice vacation at the same time. The mountains sit right at my back door. I can walk and hike. And Maureen's house is across the street. I'll be safe and well here, Mother."

"You've never been sensible like my other children," her mother snapped back in annoyance. "And it hurts us very much that you shut us out at a time like this when we've all experienced such a shock."

Delia stiffened. "You need to remember I had the worst shock, Mother. And I need some time on my own to get over it."

Her mother gave an exasperated sigh. "Well, your father is going to be terribly disappointed in you over this."

Charlotte Walker always used Delia's father as a final weapon when nothing else would yield a win. It was her way to make Delia feel more guilt on yet another count.

"I'll call and talk to Daddy later this week," Delia promised.

"Well, I simply don't know what else to say to you, Delia. We had such high hopes for you with this marriage to Prentice. You would have been so well set with him. Richard says he's going to be a fine doctor."

Delia counted to ten under her breath. "But he's not a fine man, Mother."

"Well, there must be some sort of explanation for all of this," her mother said. "Prentice spent so much time here with the family. This is simply not like him."

"I'll send you a copy of Prentice's explanation by fax." Delia gritted her teeth. "Maybe that will help you understand. It's all I can offer you." She knocked on the wall beside her. "There's someone at the door," she lied. "I've got to go. I'll call you later this week. Tell everyone I'll be fine."

She hung up before her mother could say more. Then she disconnected her cell phone.

"Sweet mercy, I made the right decision coming down here." She walked over to sit down on the couch with Graham cat, who'd curled himself against an old embroidered cushion on the sofa.

Delia looked slowly around the cozy living room again. She couldn't understand why her mother disliked this place so much. Come to think of it, her mother hadn't visited Dee's place for over twenty years. Even as a little girl, Delia sensed some awkwardness between her mother and Aunt Dee. She didn't understand what lay behind that, but she knew instinctively, even as a child, that her mother didn't approve of or like her father's sister. Or her place in Gatlinburg. She'd never learned exactly why, but she knew it was true. She found herself wondering about that now.

"From what I remember, Graham," she told the cat, "my paternal grandfather, Howard Walker, came from Gatlinburg originally. Some of our family still live off Highway 321 here in Tennessee, and I think they own a furniture store there."

She picked up a sofa cushion to hug it. "As a young man, Grandad Howard met Dorothy Wells, and her widowed father Buckner Wells, when they visited in Gatlinburg trying to locate handmade items for their Virginia corporate sales and lease business, Arlington Corporate Furnishings. Grandad Howard told me he fell in love with Dorothy at first sight and that Dottie's father approved of a match between them. He liked Howard's moxie, his furniture know-how, and ambition. Howard followed Dottie and Buckner back to Virginia. He married Dottie after a short engagement and joined the corporate firm Buckner Wells had established in Arlington."

Delia searched her memory for more. "Howard, and later my father, expanded the business to become one of the top corporate and rental leasing companies in the Arlington area. Grandad Howard only rarely returned to Gatlinburg to see his family. He worked long hours, and the corporation became his world."

She propped her feet on a small stool. "According to Aunt Dee, no one in her family showed much interest in their Appalachian heritage except her. Aunt Dee was the only one attracted to the Walker past. At nineteen, a college scholarship to Arrowmont School brought her here to learn more about mountain arts and crafts. She met Roland Ward, a forest ranger, married, and never returned to Virginia. Aunt Dee said she never regretted her decision, even though her family thought she'd married beneath her."

Delia's own father had married Charlotte by then, and Delia knew her mother violently opposed Dee's match from a few hushed conversations she had overheard. In fact, her mother refused to even come to the wedding. Delia never learned why. She asked her father about it once, and he refused to discuss the matter.

"It's a mystery, Graham, one I still don't know the answer to."

She felt a sudden empathy with Aunt Dee, remembering the old story. Neither of them held much favor with Charlotte Chapman Walker. That fact made Delia even more comfortable in Aunt Dee's little stone house. She felt somewhat like a family outcast herself now.

Delia's stomach growled, and she realized how little she'd eaten today. She padded out to the kitchen to see what she could find for supper. "Mercy knows, I have enough food here." She grinned as she opened the loaded refrigerator.

Tanner had brought a big container of homemade chicken salad that he bought at a little diner next to the grocery store. Delia pulled the container out of the refrigerator and fixed herself a plate of chicken salad and chopped up fruit. She made a pitcher of tea, poured out a glass, and took her tea and dinner to the back porch to eat.

The shady, screened porch had always been one of Delia and Aunt Dee's favorite places in the house. Roland added it behind the cottage after he and Dee married. The floor was painted in black and white checks, the furniture a hodgepodge of rustic twig armchairs, colorfully painted sidepieces, and comfortable hand-me-downs. On the side tables stood old lamps with Dee's whimsical collection of metal sculptures marching along the porch rails. Typical of Dee, everything on the porch laughed with color.

Delia turned on a whimsical lamp, settled into the corner of a worn cushioned sofa, and started to eat.

"Is Tanner finally gone?" a girlish voice called out of the darkness, startling Delia and almost making her dump her plate.

A young girl appeared out of the gathering darkness in the yard. "Don't be scared," she called out. "I'm just your cousin."

The girl walked closer, letting herself in the side door, and offered a tentative smile.

"How do you know who I am?" Delia watched her nervously.

The girl shrugged. "It isn't hard. Your pictures are all over the house. Dee always showed them to me and talked about you. You really do resemble the Walker women, you know. Short in stature, dark hair, round face with brown eyes, a full figure, and ..." She stopped to pat her chest. "Stacked at the top."

She studied Delia. "Actually, you look like Dee when she was young. And your cousin Ina Ruth Walker and you look a world alike. Do you know Ina

Ruth? Never could figure out why she never married. My Grammie Rayfield called it typical of the Walker women. A lot of them are real independent and never marry."

"Who are you?" Delia finally got in.

"Oh, sorry. I'm Hallie Walker." She extended a hand to Delia. They shook hands and Hallie plopped down on a chair opposite Delia.

"Where do you live, Hallie?" Delia asked, wondering how this girl came to be wandering in her back yard at night.

Hallie shrugged. "I sort of live here right now. I hid out in the back shed all day until I figured out who showed up at the house. When I realized it was you—and finally decided it might be safe to come introduce myself—Tanner Cross showed up. Then I had to wait until he left before I came out."

"You mean Tanner doesn't know you're here?" Delia frowned trying to follow the girl's story.

Hallie saw Delia's confusion and laughed. "It's a long story, Cousin Delia. I'll tell it to you if you want. I don't have much choice really. From all the groceries I saw Tanner hauling in, I guess you're going to be staying here for a while. I can hardly hide in the shed for weeks. Besides it gets cold out there at night. There's no heat."

While Delia started to pose another question, Hallie leaned forward to study Delia's plate of food. "Hey." Her eyes brightened. "Do you have any more of that chicken salad left? It looks great, and I haven't had much to eat today. There wasn't much food in the house when I got here."

Delia thought for a minute before answering. "There's more chicken salad in the refrigerator in the white container on the top shelf," she said at last. "There's more fruit there, too, and some iced tea. Crackers are in the tin by Dee's breadbox. Do you want me to fix you a plate?"

"Nah, I know my way around Dee's house. I've been coming here with my Grammie Rayfield ever since I was only a little thing. We both loved Dee Ward. Grammie cleaned for Dee for years and years. I know you must have met my Grammie when you came here to visit your aunt."

"Etta Mae Rayfield was your grandmother?" Delia's eyes widened in pleasure.

Hallie nodded.

Delia smiled in remembrance. "Etta Mae was one of my favorite people. She always told me the most wonderful stories when she came to clean. And she made the best peanut butter cookies I ever ate."

Hallie's face fell and her voice grew quiet. "She was the best."

"Is she not living any longer?" Delia asked, remembering Etta Mae Rayfield with her head of pure white hair from years ago.

"No, she died last year. I still miss her, like I do your Aunt Dee," Hallie stood up. "I'll be back in a sec after I get something to eat."

Delia's Place

She came back soon, and Delia had a set of questions ready to ask her.

Before Delia could begin, Hallie said, "Listen, I know I don't look like a Walker, but I really am." She held out a card to Delia. "Here, this is my ID from school. We all got fingerprinted and got IDs last year. The picture's not good, but you can see it's me."

Delia looked at the card. It read Hallan Garrett Walker, the photo definitely one of Hallie.

"My red hair comes from the Rayfield side of the family." She laughed. "A lot of the Rayfields are red-headed—many totally bright carrot-tops like me and usually pale complected and freckled. My mother's fair-skinned and red-headed, too, but she didn't get the freckles."

"Your hair is a gorgeous color." Delia studied the rich waves of red hair tied behind Hallie's neck with a band. "And I really like your freckles. Honest."

"Well, I like your boobs," Hallie quipped back. "That's a Walker trait I'd like to have inherited. The Rayfields aren't very endowed in that area." She flattened down the knit shirt she wore to demonstrate the fact.

"How old are you?" Delia asked her.

"Seventeen," Hallie answered. "But I graduated high school, and I'll turn eighteen in the fall. How old are you?"

"Twenty-two," Delia replied. "I'll be twenty-three in July."

"Wow." Hallie studied her. "You don't look that old."

Not too sure if that was a compliment or not, Delia said, "I think you'd better tell me what you're doing here at Dee's place now, Hallie."

Hallie wolfed down the rest of her chicken salad before she answered. "Okay, but let me go back a little. My daddy was Lawson Hallan Walker. His daddy, Raymond Walker, was the son of Gordon Walker, one of your granddaddy Howard's brothers. There were three Walker brothers from John and Margaret Jane Walker, our great-grandparents—Eldridge, the oldest, then your grandfather Howard Walker, and then my great-grandfather Gordon. We're, like, second cousins through those granddaddies."

She took a drink of tea before continuing. "Your granddaddy Howard went north to Virginia to marry Dottie Wells. Gordon and Eldridge both still live here. Eldridge is a minister in Happy Valley, over on the western end of the Smokies below the Chilhowee Mountains. Gordon and his son Ray run the Walker Furniture Store on Highway 321. Ray's son Vesser works with the business, too, but he's more the artisan of the group. He builds handcrafted furniture. Vesser made this furniture here." She gestured to the twig armchairs.

She paused to drink more tea and finish off the last of her fruit. "My mother was a Rayfield. My grandfather Ben Rayfield and Grammie Etta Rayfield owned a big farm over in Greenbrier, raised three boys and two girls.

I don't guess you want to hear all they're doing now, since they're not your direct kin. But Sissy, the youngest Rayfield girl, was my mother. She married my father, Lawson Walker, the year she graduated high school. My father worked in the furniture business with his father Ray Walker like most all the Walkers did. He was the middle child of three—first Willine, who married and is Willine Dalton now, then Lawson, my father, and then Vesser."

Delia remembered her Aunt Dee told her that mountain people almost always started any family story with a long lineage account. She tried to remain patient, hoping Hallie would eventually get to the point.

Hallie scratched at a mosquito bite, frowning. "When I was a little thing, about three years old, my father got killed in a car wreck. Just one of those tragic things. They say it clearly devastated my mother. She moved back home with me to my Grammie Rayfield's farm, but didn't recover well. Grammie told me she fell into a depression. Couldn't seem to handle my daddy's death. She got real wild and rebellious in her ways. Nobody seemed to know how to help her. When I turned four she took off. Met somebody traveling through, an older man named Lou Clower. Ran off with him to Alaska, of all places. Married him. And left me with Grammie to raise."

"I'm sorry." Delia didn't know what else to say.

"It can feel hurtful sometimes," Hallie admitted. "But I was lucky I had my Grandpa Ben and my Grammie Rayfield. Also my uncle Hobart Rayfield lived across the street on the other half of the old Rayfield farm. I had lots of cousins and lots of relatives that loved me on both the Rayfield and Walker side. I wasn't neglected or anything. Plus, I couldn't have had anyone better to love and raise me than Grammie Rayfield." She gave Delia a stony look. "I'd fight anyone that says different."

"So why aren't you there with the Rayfields?" Delia asked.

"I'm getting' to that," Hallie insisted casually, not willing to be hurried along in her story.

Delia reined in her patience while Hallie finished her dinner and casually propped her feet up on a stool, stretching like a cat. Delia admired her long legs while she waited, guessing Hallie to be about five foot seven, maybe four inches taller than she.

Hallie finally sat her plate on a side table and continued her story. "My mother hardly kept up with me through all the years I was growing up. I tried writing and sending her little school drawings and such when smaller, but I never got a reply. She seemed to want an all-new life away from her past memories—with me another old memory of Lawson she wanted to forget. I kind of came to terms with it over time, although I never understood it."

She shifted in her seat. "Then when I started into high school, my mother came home. Her husband got killed in some logging accident up in Alaska. She sold out her place there and moved back to Tennessee. She didn't move back in with Grammie, though. She bought herself a little house over in Cosby. Went to work managing a motel in Newport. Seems that's what she'd done all that time she lived in Alaska—managed a hotel there. I didn't know any more about what brought her back than I knew why she'd left. But she insisted I move in with her."

"She did?" Delia found herself being drawn into Hallie's lengthy saga despite herself.

Hallie looked at Delia pointedly. "Yes, and I didn't want that. I loved my Grammie Rayfield, and she was a widow by then. She needed me. I helped her with the house and with the farm. With everything. I didn't want to change high schools and leave my friends. Sissy got the law involved and made me move to Cosby with her whether I wanted to or not because I was a minor. Grammie never actually got legal custody of me through all those years."

Delia leaned forward. "When did this happen?"

"The summer before my junior year, and I can tell you moving in with my mother didn't work out well at all. You can't just pick up with someone after all those years like nothing happened. Nor can you expect them to gain a fondness for you when you disrupt their life against their will."

She scowled and looked out into the night. "We fought a lot. Rayfields have a bit of temper when riled. She wanted me to forgive her and for us to have a relationship. But by keeping me from Grammie and my friends, I wasn't willing for that to happen. We went on that way, disagreeing for a year. Over the summer, Sissy let me go stay with Grammie. She took up with Jonas Cole that summer while I stayed at Grammie's farm. He was a real estate agent that lived in Newport, a sharp looker and a real charmer. But no good at all. He schmoozed Sissy at a time when she needed it, I guess, and she was stupid enough to marry him."

"What happened then? Did she let you stay at your Grammie's after she married again?" Delia asked, into the story now.

Her voice grew brittle. "I'd hoped for that. But, no. She insisted I come back, move in with her and Jonas. Thought we'd be a happy little family together. But Jonas was a slime. Word soon got around that he preyed on young girls for kicks. It wasn't long until he started making moves on me when Sissy wasn't around. Oh, he acted subtle for a long time. And I kept my distance. He drank sometimes and always drank too much. He had a bad temper when he drank. I began to hear stories about him beating up on people. I started worrying about myself and about Sissy, but she wouldn't hear a word against him when I tried to talk to her. Didn't believe anything I told her. Thought I was only trying to make more trouble for her."

"All of this happened this year?" Delia asked. "When you were a senior?" It horrified Delia to think this had happened to a girl only seventeen.

"Yeah." Hallie grimaced. "Things came to a head about time for me to graduate. Jonas came into my room one night when Sissy was gone and tried to rape me. Said he thought I'd been out catting around and that he wanted him some."

Delia winced. These weren't the kinds of stories she heard in Wentworth Heights, the prestigious section of Arlington where she'd lived.

"I got lucky that night." Hallie paused. "My mother came home early. And Jonas clambered out of my room real quick when he heard her coming in. Warned me not to tell her. Said she wouldn't believe me anyway. Then he leered at me and said he'd be back one night soon to finish the job he started."

"Why didn't you go to your Grammie's?" Delia stared at her, dumbfounded.

"I couldn't. She'd died that winter. Probably another reason Jonas knew I was vulnerable."

"What did you do?" Delia asked, enthralled with Hallie's story. "Did you go to the police?"

"No. With my background of not wanting to live with my mother, running off sometimes, and having to be brought back by the law, I didn't think the police would have put much credence in any story I brought to them. I planned an escape instead. Senior classes were done, grades in, and only senior events and graduation to finish out the year. So I decided to leave. Go somewhere and stay until I turned eighteen. Then they couldn't make me go back. No matter what."

Delia's mouth dropped open. "But aren't people out looking for you if you just took off?"

"Not really." She wiggled her eyebrows at Delia. "They think I went to New York City. I planned it so they'd think that. It was partly because of Dee Ward I could get away at all. She left me some money when she died. That got the idea started of staying here at her place for a time. I knew nobody lived here. That the house sat empty."

"How did you get here without anyone knowing?"

"I hiked in from the back," she said nonchalantly.

Delia stopped to think, confused now at this twist in the story. "But didn't you say you lived over in Cosby? That's a long way from here."

Hallie stretched her legs out again, pointing her toes in a gesture Delia now recognized as characteristic of her.

"It is, but I got here." She looked at Delia. "I hid out from Jonas as best as I could until I got my plans laid to leave. Made sure I was never alone with him. I would have waited longer somehow if my senior classes hadn't been officially over and all my exams taken. It was important to me to graduate—even though I missed the graduation ceremony with my class. I want to go to college later."

Delia's Place

She paused, picking up the thread of her story. "Once all my plans were made, I bought a bus ticket to New York. And I made sure someone got on that bus with my ticket that looked a whole lot like me."

"How did you do that?" Delia asked, intrigued.

"I knew a girl that worked in Greenbrier that really wanted to get away from home and go to New York. I offered to pay her way if she'd go as me. That way, her family wouldn't know where she took off to, either. And mine would think I rode the bus to New York City."

"Wouldn't her family have worried about her?" Delia ventured.

Hallie gave her a flat look. "You've obviously led a real sheltered life, Cousin Delia. This girl's folks were drug addicts. I did her a favor by helping her get a new life away from them. They'd made her work since she was only a kid, and then they took all her money for drugs. It wasn't a good situation. She knew someone in New York she could go live with, but she'd never have gotten the money to go if I hadn't helped her. So I bought the ticket, bold as brass, being sure to talk to all kinds of people at the bus station about where I was going and giving my name out a lot. At the last minute before the bus left, I went in the restroom and me and Rita Jean swapped clothes and everything. I'd even bought Rita a red wig to wear and me a black one that looked like Rita Jean's hair. It worked perfect. She got to New York safe, and we've stayed in touch since. She's okay. Got herself a nice job. I figure I did her a good turn while helping myself."

Delia gaped at her. "What did you do next?"

Hallie laughed. "I did a lot of walking—after I left my car in Greenbrier by the stable where my uncle Hobart Rayfield works. I left a note on my car, too, telling Uncle Hobart I was going to New York. I asked him to keep my car safe for me. I told him when I turned eighteen I'd come back and get it."

"Are you going to go live with him then?" Delia interrupted, hoping this long discourse might finally be drawing to a close.

"I could." Hallie shrugged. "But I'll probably go live with my aunt Tabby and her husband Cas who live in Grammie's old farmhouse now. I know Tabby and Cas would be glad to have me, and it wouldn't be far from their house to drive to Walters State Community College outside Sevierville. I'm going to get my college degree there."

She smiled at the thought. "I have good grades from high school and I can go free on the Tennessee lottery scholarship. This last winter, I went over and applied, got accepted and everything. I called the college before I took off, and they said I can start in January instead of September. I'll be late getting my college started, but still get to go. I just need to stay clear of folks who might recognize me until November when I turn eighteen. Otherwise, they might send me back to Sissy and Jonas."

Hallie looked at Delia pointedly. "I've taken a big chance confiding in you, but I didn't know what else to do. If you won't let me stay here, just tell me. I'll figure something else out. I'll go somewhere. Rita Jean said I could come to New York and stay with her if I needed to."

She sat up and leaned toward Delia. "Tell me straight out, Delia, if you don't want me to stay here," she repeated earnestly. "Don't rat me out or turn me in, thinking you're doing me some kind of big favor. Jonas Cole will rape me and beat me up, too, if you send me back. He's done it to other young girls. I know. I've heard stories. He meant what he said when he told me he'd get back to me."

Delia shivered. "I won't tell anyone, Hallie. And I guess you can stay here. It might get tricky when people start to drop by and visit though."

"You mean like Tanner or Maureen?" Hallie sipped at her tea. "Or other neighbors from around here?"

Delia nodded.

"Well, I'll go upstairs or out to the shed to hide if you know anyone is coming. I only need to stay here until November. It's only six months. Are you even going to be here that long?"

"Probably not," Delia answered truthfully. "I just came for a few weeks. Maybe a month or two at most. While I look for a job."

"You mean while you get over some jerk dumping you," put in Hallie candidly. "Sorry, I was listening at the window while you and Tanner talked earlier. Checking to see if he'd left. The windows stood wide open. I didn't mean to eavesdrop."

Delia hung her head.

"Look," Hallie pressed. "It looks like you and I have both been through our own kind of bad time lately. Maybe we can be company to each other. You know, like, talk about our futures together. Have some good times. Get acquainted. It's been really lonely for me here by myself. And I was starting to worry about going to the grocery, even in my black wig, without someone recognizing me. For a while, at least, you can do the grocery shopping. I'll clean the house and cook. I'm really good at both."

"Have you already been cleaning here?" Delia looked around.

Hallie nodded.

"I wondered why things looked so nice and clean." Delia smiled.

Hallie leaned forward, watching Delia. Tense. Guarded. Delia could sense her wariness. She'd risked a lot to tell Delia all that happened to her.

"You know, I didn't know I had cousins here," Delia confessed. "I guess I knew I had relatives, but I didn't think about some of them being girls not far from my own age."

Hallie still watched her.

"It's okay, Hallie." Delia reached over to pat her leg. "I'm not going to throw you out. And I'm not going to call the authorities or your family and tell them you're here. We'll take a few days and think on all this. See how we get along. We'll both have a chance to think about how this will work out, sharing a house together. If I change my mind about this situation, I'll tell you first. Give you a chance to make your own next plan, so you can stay safe."

"Thanks." Hallie sighed in relief. "I risked a lot to share with you. And I only really got scared about it toward the end. Thinking maybe you wouldn't believe me."

"I believe you, Hallie." Delia reached for her own tea. "It's too incredible a story for someone to make up."

"Yeah, I can't believe you were engaged to a creep who would get married to someone else and then send you a telegram about it later. Saying, 'Hey, by the way, babe. I just got married out here in Vegas.'" Hallie scowled.

"He sent an overnight letter, not a telegram," Delia corrected.

"Well, whatever." Hallie shrugged. "Anyway, I agree with Tanner that Delia Ginsberg would have been a yuk name."

They both giggled at that.

"Want some ice cream?" Delia asked her then. "Maureen sent over three whole cartons. Can you believe it?"

"Cool." Hallie's eyes lit up. "What flavors?"

They went into the kitchen to check out the ice cream.

"By the way, I'm sleeping upstairs," Hallie told her. "There are no front windows there, and I made a blackout sheet for the one side window so no one would see light from it at night."

"You make me feel like I'm hiding a criminal." Delia wrinkled her nose.

"No, you're keeping me away from a criminal." Hallie dished out ice cream into two bowls. "I'm telling you that man Jonas Cole is dangerous. It worries me to death to think my mother is married to him. I mean she's really blind to him, you know. I worry it all might blow up in her face someday."

They sat down at Aunt Dee's little kitchen table to eat their ice cream. Hallie picked butter pecan, and Delia chose French vanilla.

"You know, you're lucky you didn't marry that Prentice person," Hallie claimed, waving her spoon. "He doesn't sound like he's a very good kind of man. I mean he's not as bad as Jonas Cole or anything, but who would carry on for a year with another woman and not break it off honorably with the person he was engaged to? What did he say to you when he wrote you, anyway?"

Delia went over, got her purse, and fished out the letter from Prentice. She laid it before Hallie to read.

Hallie read it slowly while eating her ice cream.

"What a rat," Hallie exclaimed as she finished. "I can't believe he was such a cad that he'd just call everything that happened an awkward situation. Unbelievable!"

She stabbed a red-painted nail at the letter again. "Here's the real answer to all this right here," she announced. "He thought he had some future opportunity set up with you through your brother Richard and your well-to-do family to get into a practice. Then along came rich Miss MacKenzie Wilkes with her daddy in the medical field, too, and, obviously, a better opportunity to pursue. I think your Mr. Ginsberg is just a pure opportunist. An old fashioned gold-digger. You know the type. May the richest girl with the best offer win. Thinking of his own fine self before anyone else."

Delia's face fell. "I never thought of that. Do you really think Prentice only used me and never cared for me at all?"

"Hey, I don't know." Hallie's face fell, obviously worried about the effect of her words on Delia. "I'm just supposing. Maybe Ginsberg's family is really rich, too, and he wouldn't need to be an opportunist."

"No, actually they're not." Delia sighed. "He grew up somewhat poor in Chicago. Just with his mom. And he talked about money a lot. Admired people who had it. He liked to spend time with people with money. Cultivated those kinds of friends. He was very impressed with what people had financially. Sometimes, he made jokes about people who didn't have much." Delia looked at Hallie thoughtfully. "I never liked that about Prentice."

"A lot of people suck up to money." Hallie shrugged.

Delia bit her lip. "Yes, but I didn't even see that in Prentice's letter until you mentioned it. Hallie, you could be right. Prentice may not have wanted to burn his bridges with me until he knew he had a sure thing with MacKenzie in her father's practice."

"Bummer for MacKenzie if that's true." Hallie ate a bite of her ice cream. "What if an even better opportunity comes along later on? She may get dumped herself."

They both thought on that for a minute.

Graham entered the kitchen meowing and jumped up on Hallie's lap.

"Nice cat." She stroked Graham until he started to purr. "What kind of cat is this? He has really soft fur for a cat."

"Graham is a Maltese. They're noted for their thick, soft fur." Delia felt pleased to see Graham warm to Hallie so quickly. "You know, Graham doesn't usually like strangers, but he obviously likes you."

"Well, animals always like me." Hallie scratched Graham under the neck. "And Graham here is more interested in my ice cream dish than in me anyway. Can I let him lick the bowl?"

Delia nodded, and Hallie put her dish down on the floor for Graham. They watched him lap up the last of the ice cream with pleasure.

Delia's Place

Delia looked around thoughtfully. "Hallie, you know Aunt Dee left me this house, don't you?"

"I'd heard that. But I also heard you planned to sell it, too, so I didn't expect you to come back."

"Prentice talked me into the idea of selling the house and the other property Aunt Dee left me. He told me we'd need the money for a house of our own and to help him get set up in a medical practice. He said we didn't need a pokey little place down here in the Tennessee mountains."

"Ouch." Hallie grimaced. "And what did you think about that?"

"That's just it." Delia wrinkled her nose. "I didn't think. I went along with most everything he wanted to do." She stopped and looked at Hallie. "I've been really stupid, haven't I?"

Hallie grinned. "If I said yes, would you throw me out?"

"No, but thanks that you didn't." Delia frowned and looked around fondly at the cozy little kitchen where they sat. "Look at this place, Hallie," she observed. "This is mine. This wonderful little house is mine. And I almost lost it."

"Well, someone up there must have been looking out for you." Hallie reached down to stroke the cat again.

"That sounds like something Aunt Dee would say." Delia licked the last bite of ice cream off her spoon.

Hallie's eyes followed her actions. "You're not one of those atheists or agnostics or anything, are you?" She asked the question tentatively.

"No. But I'd like to have beliefs more like Aunt Dee's. She had a stronger faith than mine and more of an intimate relationship with God."

"Yeah, I remember that," said Hallie. "She talked to God—and things like that. It was kind of neat, I guess. You know, there are some old books of hers here about faith stuff she used to read a lot and booklets she wrote in. Maybe you and I can learn some of what she knew in those."

"Maybe," agreed Delia. "I'd like that."

Delia looked out at the darkening sky. There were no lights here in the mountains at night. It had grown almost pitch black now.

"It's getting late." Hallie followed her eyes to the window. "Are you tired?"

"I am," admitted Delia. "And I'm kind of glad I won't be here alone tonight."

"Me, too," shivered Hallie. She reached across the table to put her hand on Delia's. "I think we're going to bond, Cousin."

Delia smiled. "Maybe we will, Hallie," she said. "Maybe we will."

Chapter 4

Tanner woke up the next day thinking about Delia Walker. In fact, he'd gone to bed thinking about Delia Walker. She sure had changed from that awkward, young girl he remembered at thirteen, but she acted a lot the same, too.

He wanted to spend time with her. Get to know her again. See how much she'd changed. He wanted to know what she thought about and liked to do now. What she wanted out of life. He knew she'd finished her schooling this year. Gotten a master's degree in design or something. He admitted he didn't know much about that. He'd have to ask her.

Tanner sat at the kitchen table, drinking a second cup of coffee after breakfast. He'd looked over at Aunt Dee's house when he went to get the newspaper. The house looked dark and quiet. He figured Delia would sleep in for a while, but maybe later on he could get her to come down and have lunch with him in the Burg. Business was quiet at the office right now. He could take the afternoon off. Walk around and play tourist with her. Besides, he needed to talk about business with her, anyway. He was handling Dee's estate, and there were things he needed to discuss with Delia.

He looked at the kitchen clock. It read almost eight-thirty. He could call her. He doubted Delia knew he'd kept Dee's old phone line connected and put a message on her answering machine. He and Maureen thought it safer if people thought someone lived in the house. They didn't want people breaking in, thinking the place empty.

Tanner knew the bedroom Delia slept in. A phone extension sat right by the bed. She'd probably kill him for calling this early. He tapped his fingers on the table considering it, then he grinned and dialed Dee's number. It rang a few minutes and a tentative, sleepy voice answered.

"Hello?" It was Delia.

"Hey, it's Tanner. Are you up yet?"

"What do you think?" Her voice grew annoyed. "And why didn't you tell me last night you still had the phone connected. You scared me to death, Tanner. I was sound asleep."

"Sorry," he confessed. "But I wanted to check and make sure everything was all right before I went off to work."

"Everything's fine," she said, her voice snippy.

"Look, why don't you come down to the Burg and have lunch with me today." He drummed his fingers on the table. "I'll show you around the offices and the store. Let you see some of the changes Maureen and Dee made. Then we can poke around Gatlinburg. See the sights. Like old times."

"Well ... I don't know," she began hesitantly. Tanner could almost sense her coming up with an excuse.

"Also, we need to talk business, Delia." He offered these words in a more professional voice. If he couldn't win one way, he'd try another. "You know I'm handling your aunt Dee's estate. Several decisions are pending. I think we should talk about these as soon as possible. And I have time in my schedule this afternoon."

He heard her sigh. "All right," she conceded. "I'll come down at lunch. But I want to get some things done here first."

"I have work to do this morning, too. One o'clock would be good for me." Tanner suggested.

"Fine." Delia agreed, resigned.

Tanner smiled. "Walk up above the store and find me at the office when you get there," he said. He rang off quickly before Delia could find a way to change their plans.

"Gonna' be a good day," he told himself, heading out to his car to drive to work. "A really good day."

The morning flew by, Tanner busy working on late tax returns for one of his clients. He also shuffled in a meeting with a new client, Zola Devon, who'd bought one of the corner shops in the Mountain Laurel Mall. Crosswalk Crafters Store and the T. Cross Accounting offices formed a corner anchor of that mall. The new client wanted his advice in developing a better financial plan for her business and help with her yearly tax preparation.

As they concluded their meeting, she asked, "Can you come by the store later? I want you to look at the ledgers I set up. Tell me if they're adequate."

"Uh. Well, I have a lunch meeting and then business with a client." Tanner hedged.

Zola looked across at him. "You can bring her along," she suggested, her dark eyes studying Tanner with a hint of mischief. "I'd like to meet her. I've sensed her all day. She's going to be an important presence in your life."

Tanner had been warned that Zola Devon was the tiniest bit odd, but now he had it confirmed. He studied her in return. She even looked like a gypsy—with that head of thick black curls and those dark European eyes.

"Oh, never mind." She stood and smiled at him. "I didn't mean to make you nervous. I just see things sometimes. You shouldn't worry over it." She paused. "She's a very good person. Your friend. But I think you already know that."

"Well, I'm glad we could meet today." Tanner stood, reaching out his hand to shake hers and avoiding a personal response. "If there's time today, I'll try to stop by. If not, I'll certainly walk over to look at those books tomorrow."

Zola gave him a small catbird smile as she left, letting him know she wasn't fooled by his evasions. As she started to walk out the door, she turned back. "Take her to that bear store." She smiled. "There's something there that will delight her."

She left before Tanner could reply.

"Weird," he said to himself, shaking his head as he turned back to his desk to look over the last of the morning's phone messages he needed to answer.

Delia stuck her head into his door a little before one. "Lavonne isn't out front. I saw an Out to Lunch sign on her desk, and the other office doors were closed. So I guessed you had to be in here."

"Come on in." He gestured. "Let me write down a few notes to remember from this last call, and we'll be ready to go. Lavonne should be back any minute to cover the office."

Delia sat down on the couch across the room. She picked up a magazine, thumbing through it. Tanner watched her out of the corner of his eye.

She had on an emerald green, short-sleeved blouse tucked neatly into sleek black slacks today. Pearls winked at her ears and a pearl teardrop hung on a thin, silver chain around her neck. Her eyes were clear and rested today, and she looked fantastic.

"I thought you were doing paperwork," she commented, looking up to find him watching her.

"I was," he conceded, grinning at her. "I finished. And you look good today."

"Thanks." She stood up with a little blush. "I parked out back in Dee's old parking space today. I hope that was all right."

"It's fine. No one uses it now. It can be yours whenever you want to come down. The sign in front of it does say Delia."

She smiled at that. "So it does."

Lavonne Magee stuck her head in the door. "Lordy, Lordy … is that little Miss Delia I hear in here? Let me look at you, child. It's been an age."

Lavonne Magee, a fixture at T. Cross Accounting, was well into her sixties now, but still working and active. Her bleached, short blond hair poufed around her face and she sported a million-dollar smile.

Delia's Aunt Dee always claimed, "Whatever you want to know about anybody in Gatlinburg, Lavonne probably knows it."

Lavonne's husband, Bill, a long-time policeman in Gatlinburg, had settled into an administrative position with the force now. He and Lavonne stayed heavily involved in all the main civic groups and activities around the town.

Lavonne came in Tanner's office, turning Delia around with pleasure to look at her. "Good gracious me, girl. You've grown up from a gawky little thing into a real beauty. Hasn't she, Tanner?"

Tanner grinned obligingly.

"I can tell you for a fact, I'm tickled pink Dee Ward left you her little place. I hope that means we'll keep seeing a lot of you down here in Gatlinburg." She stopped to shake her head, her face wistful. "You know, as long as you're living, child, Dee Walker-Ward will never really be gone. The likeness of you to her when she was only a girl is real strong."

Tanner raised an eyebrow at that.

"Now, Tanner, I know Dee Ward put on considerable weight as the years went by. But I remember her well, about this same age, when she first moved to Mynatt Park with her husband Roland. There's a little picture of Dee in her early twenties—over on her old desk across the hall. You go look at it and you'll see what I mean. She's wearing a brown, straw hat and standing in front of some flowers in a field. Roland took it of her, and she always cherished the picture for that reason."

Tanner closed the file on his desk and stood up. "Well, I'm going to take Delia to lunch if you're back to cover the office," he told Lavonne. "We might do a little sightseeing in the Burg afterwards, since Delia hasn't been down here for a while. Let her see how things have changed."

"Well, you take Delia somewhere nice to eat, Tanner, like the Peddler, Calhoun's, or the Cherokee Grill. The Grill has real nice steaks and seafood, Delia."

"And good shrimp?" Delia asked with interest.

"Very good shrimp," answered Tanner. "We'll make it the Grill."

Soon they strolled down the Gatlinburg Parkway heading toward the Cherokee Grill that stood on the main road a few blocks away.

"You know, I want to explore Crosswalk when we get back." Delia bounced along beside him, looking around with pleasure. "And I want to walk through the Mountain Laurel Village and look in all the shops I remember so well."

She noticed his small scowl. "You don't have to come with me if you don't want to, Tanner. You can go back to work."

"We'll see how our time goes," Tanner remarked.

Delia pleaded to stop at two shops along the way to the restaurant. In the first, she bought a stack of postcards and in the second two Gatlinburg T-shirts and two bill caps with the word Gatlinburg across the front.

"Doing the tourist thing?" Tanner asked her, amused.

"Absolutely," Delia replied with zeal. Tanner enjoyed the way her eyes sparkled as she skipped out of the store.

As they walked on down the Parkway, she pointed out familiar landmarks with joy and almost babbled remembering stories from past visits. Tanner watched her with increasing pleasure. She might be nearly twenty-three, but she still had the same bright, delightful enthusiasm for life Tanner remembered so well. When she stopped to ogle the characters in a wax attraction show, Tanner laughed out loud.

"What?" She turned to him. "There's no crime in looking. And they're funny."

"I know," he answered. "I'm just enjoying seeing everything through your eyes."

"Well, I haven't been here for a while," she explained, justifying her excitement.

"You've been here a million times, Delia, but you always see things with fresh eyes. It's charming and I like it."

"Are you making fun of me?" She eyed him suspiciously.

"No, I'm complimenting you," he assured her. "One of the things I've always remembered about you is that you enthusiastically enjoyed everyday life. You noticed things. You got excited about things. I'm glad you haven't changed."

"Well, thanks, I guess. But are you really trying to say I'm still just a little kid and acting like one?"

"Do you know there have been self-help books written that encourage people to recapture their inner youth so that they can live happier lives? You don't need to read them, because you never lost yours. That's the charm."

"Hmmmm. I think you've grown up and gotten smarter on me, Tanner."

"Only a little wiser," he said. "And here's our restaurant."

At Delia's insistence, they settled into a window table so she could watch the people walk by while they ate. "Is this where you met your client for lunch yesterday?" she asked.

"No. He's a steak man. We met over at Howard's."

The waiter came back with drinks, and they placed their orders.

"You know," Delia commented after a little idle chit-chat, "I remember you always said you'd be an accountant like your father. Do you like it?"

"I do," he replied.

Delia's Place

"You also used to say you wanted to go to a big city to practice. To get away from the Burg. I remember you went to Atlanta after you graduated. Aunt Dee told me you worked with a big accounting firm there. Why did you come back?"

He drank some of his tea before answering. "I realized one day it wasn't where I belonged. But I'm glad I had that time there. It taught me more about myself, I suppose. Let me know what I wanted. Made my choice to be here feel more secure."

Their food arrived and Delia stirred dressing into her salad. "Do you think you were drawn back here because it felt familiar? Because it was home?"

Tanner thought about that for a second. "Maybe a little. I don't know. The Cherokees say everyone has a place where they really belong. A place they belong to in spirit." He buttered a roll from the breadbasket. "They say a person can't be truly happy until they find that place. It isn't always the place where they were raised either. It may be somewhere else entirely, but the Cherokees believe it calls to you and draws you to it. Then it holds you, so that you don't want to leave."

"I like that," she confided. "Do you feel that way about Gatlinburg now?"

He thought about that as he cut into his fish. "I feel that way about the mountains here. This is where I can most be myself. Where I feel a sense of rightness. That's important." He grinned at her. "Do you have a place that calls to you, Delia?"

"You know, I've never really thought about it." She tilted her head in that cute way of hers, biting on one lip.

Tanner felt a little rush of male virility watching her. Especially when she started chewing on that lip. She did things to him. Attracted him physically. She always had in a childish way, but this was certainly different.

"I guess I've just always been wherever my family was." She sighed.

"You went off to college," he added between bites.

"Not really," she explained, after sampling one of her shrimp. "At first, I stayed at home and commuted to Marymount University right in Arlington. I decided to do my master's work there, too. I did move away from home and into a townhouse with three friends. They needed a fourth. Rent is really high in Arlington."

Their waitress came to refill their drinks, and Delia talked about her friends and the jobs they'd become involved in since graduation. "They've all doing exactly what they wanted to do," Delia enthused. "I'm so proud of them."

"What about you?" he asked her, between bites. "What were your goals?"

She looked panicked for a moment. Then her eyes teared up. "I suppose I had some," she whispered. "But when I met Prentice I guess I started to forget about them."

"What did Prentice want you to do?" Tanner asked carefully, watching her face.

She bit her lip. "I guess be supportive of him. Go wherever he went. Decorate our house and, maybe, start a family. We never really talked much about it."

"Let me guess." Tanner's tone grew sarcastic. "Prentice was too busy talking about himself and all he planned to do and be. You know, Delia, I'm liking this guy less and less by the minute."

The hint of tears turned into a rush of genuine weeping now.

"Oh, dang it, Delia. Don't start dripping all over the place again. I wish I hadn't brought the guy's name up, okay?" He clanked down his fork and looked out the window. He hated to watch her cry.

Delia pulled herself together and blew her nose. "Prentice broke the engagement only three days ago, Tanner. It's not sensible to think I'm going to blithely forget about everything overnight. That I won't have some bad moments."

He didn't reply.

She leaned forward toward him. "Did you forget about Melanie overnight when you broke up with her?" she challenged. "Did you just break up with her and go right on with your life? Was it all simpler for you?"

He looked at her. "No, but I'd gone through my worst times with her before I ever broke up with her. Trying to be what she wanted me to be. Whatever I already was never seemed to be quite enough for Melanie Lane."

"And afterwards?"

"Okay. I had some bad moments." His jaw tightened. "But I didn't go around sniffling over it."

She gave him a considering look after those words, making him think of his mother. He read the message in her look loud and clear without any words spoken.

"Yeah, yeah, I get your message. Crying's a girl thing. I should cut you some slack."

A smile tugged at the corner of her lips. "I'll bet you got all irritated and cross when you had your bad moments," Delia said. "Snapped at people. Sulked. Maybe got physical and kicked something. I have brothers, you remember. That's how they handled their breakups with girls."

"Eat your lunch," he demanded, wanting to change the subject.

She complied, much to his surprise. And they ate in silence for a while.

"You know," Delia said thoughtfully after a time. "What I wanted to do passionately before I got so involved with Prentice was corporate interiors. I grew up around corporate furniture at Arlington's, our family business. Studied the catalogs and furniture. Read the office magazines. And whenever I went down to the store, I played around with the room designs when no one was watching. Changed a few things. Moved some pillows or pictures. Imagined how much better everything could look with changes I envisioned. So many corporate offices are so unimaginative."

Tanner looked up, intrigued. "Very interesting, Delia. Did you take any coursework in that area when you did your college work?"

"Yes. What things I could. I took courses in corporate and modern office design." She paused again, obviously thinking back. "Somewhat like your father became your inspiration, Tanner, I had someone who inspired me, too, when I was younger."

"Your mother?" He raised an eyebrow.

She frowned at him, and he knew he'd gotten that one wrong.

"Who then?"

"Her name was Maria Antonelli. A great Italian name, huh?" She smiled at him brightly. "She worked for my father's business part-time when I was a little girl, doing free-lance jobs for Arlington Corporate Furnishings. Sometimes she came in-house and did room set-ups for the store. I loved to watch her and talk to her. She often let me help her. She was the first person that suggested I might think about design as a career."

"And?" Tanner asked, wanting her to tell him more.

Delia smiled again. "Maria was very dramatic and flamboyant. In her dress, her speech, and in her decorating style. I remember she waltzed in to see my parents one day and announced with a swish of her hand, 'I think this child of yours has a natural flair. She could be a very creative decorator. You should nurture that in her. And you should remember, later on, that Maria Antonelli foresaw it.'"

Tanner tried not to laugh.

"It's all right to laugh," she said, grinning. "Maria was always overblown in the way she did things. It's one of the reasons she didn't continue working long for my family. She occasionally got a little too outspoken with our clients. Also, she could be somewhat unbending in her creative ideas. However, I fell completely under her charm. I'd never been around anyone quite like her before in my life."

"And she was the first to recognize your gift," Tanner added.

"I guess that's one way to think of it." She paused.

"So, Delia. You gonna fly with that idea now? Get into corporate decorating?"

"I don't know." She heaved a sigh. "I'm having to revisit all my goals now, Tanner. Reexamine where I want to go with my life. I thought I could do that while staying here. I have a master's in interior design and am a licensed designer in Virginia. I have the title—that's the next step above having a degree in design." She stopped to think. "Sort of like sitting for the CPA and passing that is a step above being just an accountant. You have your accounting degree and your master's in accounting, but you've also attained your CPA."

He considered this. "So what would you put on your shingle hanging outside your door? Licensed interior decorator?"

She shook her head. "Absolutely not, Tanner. Anyone can call themselves an interior decorator and, as you say, hang out a shingle. I'm a Certified Interior Designer. Just to take the qualifying certification exam, you need six years of education and either an internship or full-time interior design experience. There's a very big difference between a decorator and an interior designer."

Tanner wiggled his eyebrows at her. "And to think I could learn something from little Delia Walker. I didn't know there was any difference between the two terms at all."

"Well, now you do," she said primly.

He laughed. "So, while I'm Tanner Cross CPA, you're Delia Walker CID."

She giggled. "Can't you ever be serious, Tanner?"

"I am serious," he said. "You decide to hang out your shingle here in the Burg, and I'll jump right in there helping you to rustle up some business."

"Well, usually corporate designers have to work in relatively large cities." She straightened her back. "But thank you, Tanner."

"Look around you, Delia," he challenged. "The Burg is one business right after another, and there are even more businesses down in Pigeon Forge and Sevierville. I think you could find yourself a lot of work here if you wanted to. You already own a house and an office, too. Think of the overhead you'd save."

She looked at him with a slightly stunned expression. "I could hardly take off on my own in the corporate design business, Tanner. Young graduates have to start out working for larger firms. Learn the ropes. Work their way up. I don't have the experience to simply jump into an independent design business without any more background than I possess now."

He raised an eyebrow at her. "Well, if you think so, Delia. But I'll bet there's no law saying you couldn't do it if you wanted to." He leaned toward her. "If you had the confidence and the moxie to try it."

She glared at him, spots of color coming into her cheeks. "That wasn't a very nice thing to say, Tanner. And just when I'd almost started to like you, too."

He held up both hands in a mock surrender. "I guess I stepped out of line on that one. Do I need to apologize?"

"No," she snapped, still annoyed. "But I'm ready to go now."

Tanner paid the bill and worked on jollying her up as they started down the sidewalk. He wasn't sorry for the idea he seeded in Delia's mind. As a business consultant, he knew it a sound one. Delia could easily start her own business here. Her credentials were impressive, and with the limited living expenses she'd have, she could afford the risk to see if she could make a go of it here in Gatlinburg. A large number of interior designers were self-employed in America. Even Tanner knew that. Besides, selfishly, Tanner would like to see Delia stay around the area. He wanted more time with her. If she found herself a job in Washington or Chicago or New York right away, she'd take off, move there, and that would be that.

A block from the restaurant Tanner spotted the bear shop. He remembered Zola's odd words suggesting he take Delia into the store. "Let's go in this shop," he said impulsively, turning her off the sidewalk and into the door.

Inside the store resided a world of colorful bear items. Not only were there stuffed bears to buy, and clothes and accessories to choose for them, the store boasted bear toys and bear bric-a-brac of all kinds, bearskin rugs, bear mugs, bear purses, pins, and key chains. It was a typical tourist mecca capitalizing on a single Smoky Mountain item. Looking around, Tanner felt immediately bored.

Delia, however, appeared enchanted. She oohed and aahed over everything, picking up teddy bears to hug and examining items up and down every aisle.

"Oh, look!" she exclaimed. "I am so buying this!"

Tanner looked at what she held in her hands. "What is it?" He studied the flattened bear shape in her hands.

She eyed him in exasperation. "It's a bear backpack. Isn't it cute? See, it looks like a little black bear and it goes on your back with these little straps."

"And you'd wear that?" he asked, incredulous.

"Absolutely." She lifted her chin. After she paid for it, she demonstrated just that by stuffing her other purchases into the bear and putting it on her back.

Tanner shook his head. "I can't believe I'm going to walk down the main street of Gatlinburg with a grown woman wearing a bear on her back."

"You can walk down the street without me, you know." She headed out the door with a saucy smile. "I don't need an escort to poke around the Burg with me. You can go back to work."

"No. I guess I'll deal with it." He rolled his eyes. "Maybe I'll get myself an Indian headdress or a bow and arrow to hang over my shoulder, so we'll make a better tourist match."

"Whatever you want." She practically skipped. "This is a day to be impulsive."

Leaving the bear shop, Tanner and Delia stopped to order a cola before heading back to the office, settling at an outdoor table to enjoy it. Delia quibbled over the table choice, wanting to sit in the sunshine to watch the tourists stream by. Tanner enjoyed the friendly tug of war between the two of them. It brought back memories of their childhood escapades.

"Do you see the Jack Gang often?" Delia asked.

"Yep. We always meet at the big round table in the front right corner of George Deacon's restaurant every Wednesday morning." He stirred his cola with his straw. "The restaurant is behind the Mountain Laurel Village Mall on Natty Road and close to my office."

"Do I know George Deacon?" Her eyes searched his face.

"I doubt it, but he married Keppler's sister, Ruthann. Keppler sends business George's way, and George returns the compliment, recommending Keppler's motel—you remember, the one near the end of Airport Road that's been in his family for years. It's less than a block from the back end of Mynatt Park."

She smiled. "I do remember. We used to go swimming at the motel's pool." Delia leaned forward, propping her elbows on the outdoor table where they sat.

"Is Keppler married, Tanner? You need to catch me up on everyone since I'll be seeing them all Friday night."

"Keppler is definitely married and has two sons. Lives in a white frame house off Cherokee Orchard Road." He sent her a grin. "Keppler married Sherilynn South, his younger sister Ruthann's best friend. She grew up in the Burg with all of us—family owns a car and jeep rental business out on the east parkway. Her brother is the best mechanic in town if you ever need one."

She blinked in astonishment. "Wasn't Sherilynn that little pigtailed girl that hung around with Ruthann?"

"The same, but she's changed a lot since then." Tanner took a swig of his cola. "Keppler's changed since you last saw him, too. He's five foot nine now, solidly built, not skinny any more, and has a few streaks of white in that dark hair of his."

"Time slips by, doesn't it?" She sighed. "Tell me about Bogan."

"Bogan started a print shop and gradually added a production line to it handling promotional books, tourist pamphlets, mountain music CDs. He calls it Mountain Productions. It sits across the parkway in that small strip mall as you start up Ski Mountain Road."

Her expression sharpened with interest. "I remember Aunt Dee told me he'd gotten involved in printing and media production." She smiled. "Bogan Kirkpatrick. He was always the tallest and biggest in the Jack Gang, talked the most, and laughed the loudest."

Tanner shook his head with a smile. "That hasn't changed. Bogan's still burly, over six feet tall, looks like the football player he was in high school—if

Delia's Place

a little heavier now. Married a girl he met in college who grew up in Knoxville. They have twin girls and live in a chalet home on the mountainside a few miles above Bogan's business."

"What about Perry? I think Aunt Dee wrote me that Perry became a minister. That really surprised me." She looked thoughtful. "He always seemed somewhat bookish compared with the rest of you, but..." Her voice dropped off.

"But is right." Tanner interrupted. "Perry's decision to go into the ministry surprised all of us. He didn't even go to church as a kid." Tanner loosened his tie and shifted his chair to catch the shade of a nearby building. "Maybe you don't remember, but Perry's father divorced his mother and left the area when Perry was only a kid. Perry took it hard, often said he felt mad at God because his folks split up."

Tanner lifted a shoulder. "We were shocked when Perry told us he'd 'found the Lord' at an area evangelistic meeting and felt called to preach. We thought he'd get over all this newfound zealousness after a space, but we were wrong. He went off to Bethel College on scholarship when he graduated from high school and became an ordained minister in the Cumberland Presbyterian Church. He worked as a minister in Kentucky somewhere—I forget the town now—and got married."

"So what brought him back to Gatlinburg?" Delia leaned forward with wide eyes.

"Bogan and Keppler." Tanner grinned at the memory. "A friend of Bogan's father wanted to sell his wedding chapel on Highway 321 above Gatlinburg, and Bogan and Keppler persuaded Perry to come back and run it. The rest is history."

She sent him a bright smile. "What's the name of the chapel? And does Perry preach there as well as do weddings?"

"He preaches some to fill in for Rev. Madison at Highland Cumberland Presbyterian Church, where he's also the part-time youth minister—that's where your Aunt Dee went—but he only does weddings at the chapel. It's called Creekside Chapel." Tanner finished off his cola. "Perry's wife Tracie works in the business part-time, too—bakes wedding cakes and runs a side catering business. She's a cracker jack of a girl, a nice foil to Perry, who's always been more serious."

Tanner crossed an ankle over his knee, trying to get more comfortable on the metal seat. "Perry and Tracie bought a rustic house in the woods above the Creekside Chapel. They have two mutt dogs, a pet raccoon, a big parrot that quotes scripture, and a new baby—born this winter—named Caleb Joshua."

Delia giggled and looked down at her hands. "Then you're the only one not married in the gang."

"That's right, and they never let me forget it." Tanner snorted. "They're always trying to do some sort of matchmaking with me." He leaned back in his chair, enjoying his time with Delia, but wishing he wasn't in a dress shirt and tie.

Two hours later, he and Delia climbed back up the stairs to the T. Cross Accounting offices, Tanner tired and hot, Delia wired and enthusiastic. She still wore her bear backpack and had donned one of her Gatlinburg bill caps as well, tucking her thick dark hair through the back, in a ponytail, to get it off her neck. Tanner had rolled up his shirt-sleeves. The day had warmed up considerably while they explored.

"Well now, don't you two look like a couple of regular tourists!" Lavonne exclaimed as they walked in the door. While Tanner went back in his office to check his messages, Delia showed Lavonne all the things she'd bought while out exploring.

Tanner returned looking for Delia, and Lavonne told him that she had gone across the hall to Dee's old office. Tanner found her there sitting at Dee's desk looking at photographs.

"Here's the one Lavonne was talking about," Delia said, holding out a silver-framed picture of a young Delia Ward for him to see. "I do look a lot like Dee."

He studied it, noting the resemblance. "Well, see that you don't progress to look like Dee did later on."

"I won't." Delia set the picture back on the desk. "I know weight helped to bring on Dee's diabetes and put pressure on her heart, so she had an early stroke. She simply wouldn't take good care of herself."

"But she was a wonderful person," Tanner added. "Always cheerful, upbeat, positive, and full of fun. Beloved by everyone who knew her. You know, people used to come in to the store just to see her, Delia. She had a real gift with people."

"I remember." Delia sighed.

He studied her, sitting in Dee's old chair. "You look good behind that desk, Delia." Tanner framed the scene between his two hands. "We could make you a little CID plaque for the door, and you'd be set to go."

She frowned at him in annoyance.

"Only kidding." He held up his hands in surrender again. "But we do need to talk business now, Delia. Do you think we could do that?"

"All right." She gave him a wary look. "But I bet it won't be fun."

"Well, I'll tell you what." He sat down in the chair across from her. "I'll skip to the fun part. And we'll wait to go over all the more boring, detailed parts later. How's that?"

"Okay." She offered him another of her sunny smiles.

Delia's Place

He crossed his ankle over his knee, leaning back in his chair. "Well, first off, your aunt left you her house. You know that. It's worth more in value than you might think because of the increased property values in Gatlinburg now. However, like Dee's other property, it has business clauses on it. Mainly, Mother has first right to buy both the house and business. Which, as you may know, is exactly what we planned to do."

Her mouth dropped open in surprise. "You mean you were the buyers for Dee's house and the property?"

"We were," he told her. "Dee and Mother started the business together about eighteen years ago, not long after Roland died."

"I was only a little thing then." Delia bit her lip.

"Dad had been renting the upstairs of this building since he started his business, and after Roland died, Dee began working for the craft store on the lower level. She came and told Mom and Dad one day that the owners wanted to sell out. Said she had a wonderful vision for a business to put there instead of just another craft store—a crafters mall, where different artisans, collectors, and dealers could rent booths to sell their items."

Tanner shifted and put his feet on the chair across from him. "Dee had seen a similar store in another city, so Dad researched the idea, and he and my mother figured out a financing plan. Mom used to work with Dad in the accounting firm before she and Delia started their business. She still occasionally works in T. Cross during tax season. Anyway, Dad bought the building, and Delia and Mom put in equal financial investments to start the crafts business downstairs together. The property you inherited is really Dee's part of the crafters mall."

"I remember Dee and your mother named it Crosswalk Crafters Store by combining Cross and Walker."

"Yeah, the Walker part of Dee's name worked better than the Ward part in the titles they were considering back then. And Dee liked the idea of giving credit to the Walker side of her family since she'd come to know many of them here in Gatlinburg."

"So." Tanner steepled his fingers. "The fun part is that you own a house and part of a thriving business." He paused at her surprised look. "Aunt Dee loved you, Delia, and she always told Maureen she worried about you."

"Why?" Delia looked at him in surprise.

"She thought you were a throwback to the Walkers, more like her. And she didn't think you were fully appreciated—or understood—by your family. She wanted you to have something of your own in case you needed it." He shrugged. "Plus I think she hoped her place held some special meaning for you. That you'd enjoy keeping it and using it, if only for a summer vacation place."

The room fell silent. "And I was ready to just sell out everything." Delia's voice barely whispered the words.

"Well, Dee was always idealistic and sentimental." Tanner shrugged.

"She was wonderful," Delia said, tearing up again. "And I was so infatuated with Prentice this last year that I didn't even see what she'd done for me. Prentice wanted me to sell out as soon as he heard of the inheritance, so we could use the money to buy a house and help start his practice."

"The more you tell me about this guy, the less I like him." Tanner scowled, dropping his feet to the floor.

"I'm beginning to agree with you," Delia mused with another frown. "I almost sold Aunt Dee's house without even thinking it through, Tanner."

"Does that mean you may not want to sell now?" He deliberately kept his voice casual.

"It means I really want to think about it carefully." She dropped her eyes. "But I do think I should sell Dee's part of the business to Maureen. That seems only right. I don't know anything about running a craft business, and Aunt Dee was always a working partner, not a silent one."

"Have you ever looked over any of the paperwork about the business, Delia?"

"Not really. Daddy and Prentice looked it over. And Mother, I think. They thought it would be more profitable to sell. I remember they all said there was a sure buyer because someone had a first option and wanted to exercise it."

"That was Mother, and she still does want to exercise that option," assured Tanner. "However, maybe your family should have mentioned to you that you'd have a rather nice little income from the business if you kept it. Dee had a nest egg put away for her future, and that's yours now, too. She left some of her money to friends and family members she'd grown close to and wanted to help, but most everything else went to you. There were no children, and she said her only brother – that would be your father – really didn't need it. Nor did she think he and your mother would appreciate getting the house. She assumed they'd sell it right away."

Delia nodded, remembering her mother's earlier words.

"My point here is that you received a rather nice inheritance from your Aunt Dee. It's not a fortune, Delia, but neither is it something to sneeze at. Right now, the other 'fun thing' for you to know is that you can draw on the income from the business while you're staying here—without needing to worry about having basic funds. There is plenty of income to maintain the house, pay the bills, and keep you in groceries and bear packs until you decide what you want to do about everything."

Delia studied Tanner thoughtfully. "Daddy didn't tell me all of this," she told him candidly. "Neither did Mother. Or Prentice. They just made it sound like I'd inherited an old house, and I wouldn't be able to afford the upkeep or taxes in order to keep it. Plus they said I'd inherited some property I wouldn't have any need for or want."

Delia's Place

Tanner shrugged. "Maybe they didn't really look it over very carefully."

She leaned forward. "Or maybe they did and didn't want me to know what I had," she snapped, two spots of color coming into her cheeks now.

"They might have been scared you'd move here and leave them," Tanner put in quietly. "Families sometimes do things from mixed emotions, Delia, viewing a situation as not right for someone they love when the truth is it's not right for them."

"That could be." She placed her palms on the desk. "But it was still my life they made decisions about. And without letting me have much part in it."

"I'd watch being too mad," Tanner advised. "They are your family. And they undoubtedly love you. Quite candidly, you need to be fair and admit that you could have demanded at any time to see all the paperwork, or you could have contacted the executor, which was me, for more information you wanted to attain. You were of age, you know, and it was your inheritance."

"Meaning I was stupid." Delia fixed her gaze on him. "You might as well say it, Tanner. It's true enough. It's not as though I was a minor. You're right. I just let everyone think for me and handle everything for me." She paused. "Like I always seem to do."

Tanner stayed quiet over that one. Sometimes a man needed to know when to be still and wait.

"Listen, Tanner," she acknowledged at last. "You've been kind about all this, and obviously, there's a lot more I need to look at, learn, and think about. You have told me the fun part—that I'm okay to stay here for a while if I want to, that I have a house I can live in and a little income I can draw on. That's comforting right now. Do you think I could come down another day to let you go through everything in detail with me? Let me look over all the papers. Understand all the options. Be clear about everything."

"That would be fine, Delia. You've had rather a lot to deal with the last few days. Take a rest. Enjoy the remainder of the week and the weekend. We'll talk some more next week sometime. How's that?"

"That's fine." She closed her eyes for a moment.

"In the meantime, if you need money ...."

"I don't," Delia interrupted. "At least not today." She smiled. "I have money in savings and money in my bank account. I'll be all right."

"Fine." He stood. "But I'll keep paying the bills for Dee's house from the office until we talk more. They all come to me now – lights, phone, power, garbage pickup, that sort of thing. As stipulated in the will, they're being paid from Dee's ongoing income from the business. So don't think it's charity or anything. Nor will it be charity when you decide you want to start drawing on that money. It's been funneled directly into savings while we waited to get everything resolved."

Delia stood, also, putting her hands on the desk. "Tanner, I'm truly humbled Dee would have done this for me. Ashamed, too, that I haven't been more appreciative of it. You and Maureen must think very badly of me."

"No." He shook his head. "And don't put me in a noble role, Delia. Actually I tried to convince Dee that you probably wouldn't want to keep any of the property here. Especially when I heard you were engaged. I actually advised her to reconsider how she'd written up some aspects of her will. I knew it would make things more complicated."

"You didn't want her to leave me the house?" she asked, surprised.

"No. And I wanted her to change aspects of the will about the Crosswalk business. I thought she ought to leave it to Mother. They've always been like sisters, and the two of them grew and developed the business together, you know."

Delia studied him. "If your mother had died first, would her half of the business have gone to Aunt Dee?"

He had the grace to actually flush. "No. It would have gone to me."

She grinned. "Well, I feel a little bit less like a heel now, Tanner," she confided. "And thanks for being honest."

She started for the door and then turned. "You know, I may not have acted very much like Aunt Dee's girl these last years, Tanner, but that's going to change now. I'm going to honor Dee's beliefs in me, and I'm going to decide how to wisely use what she's left me. And be more appreciative of it."

Tanner watched her, a small smile starting as he listened to her talk.

She strapped on her bear backpack, and his smile turned into a broad grin.

"Would you quit laughing at me about my bear pack?" she quipped. "I like my bear. Besides, if I remember right, it was you that dragged me into that bear store anyway. So you have no one to blame but yourself."

She walked over to where Tanner stood and leaned over to kiss him on the cheek.

"Thanks for all you've done for me. I really owe you."

Tanner got a whiff of some soft, sweet scent as she leaned near him, felt her breasts press against his shoulder. She slipped out the door, waving and tossing him a final smile over her shoulder.

"Oh, yeah, little Miss Delia," he ground out as the door closed. "You owe me big time for giving me some breezy little kiss and thinking that's enough for me. I may be biding my time for now, Princess, but I'll certainly be back for more."

Chapter 5

"You stayed gone long enough," grumbled Hallie when Delia let herself back into the house at nearly six.

"I had a lot to do," Delia explained. "And why are you acting so grumpy about it, anyway?"

"I guess I felt bored," Hallie admitted sullenly. "And jealous you get to go out and run around while I'm stuck here."

Delia shifted the bags she carried, so she could turn around to shut and lock the front door.

Hallie giggled. "You didn't really buy that lame bear backpack while you were out, did you?"

"You're worse than Tanner." Delia glared at her. "I like my bear. And if you don't shut up about it, I won't give you any of the presents I bought you."

Hallie's eyes lit up. "What presents?"

"I bought a few things when I went out with Tanner." She headed into the living room to dump her bags on the sofa. "After I left Tanner's office, I explored the booths in Crosswalk and shopped in Mountain Laurel Village Mall and some of the nearby stores." She turned to smile at Hallie. "I forgot how much fun it is to poke around in Gatlinburg. There are so many cute stores!"

Delia began unloading the bear pack and her other bags. "Here, Hallie. I got you this soft grey T-shirt with a mountain scene on it. And this ball cap to match."

"I assume the other ball cap and shirt with Smoky Mountain black bears on it is yours," said Hallie, giggling again. "What's it with you and black bears, Delia?"

"I like bears," Delia replied absently. "Oh and look, I got a box of mountain taffy for us and postcards to send to my nieces and nephews over at the beach. I bought these gorgeous note cards of mountain photo prints at the Jackson Gallery, too."

She paused to grin at Hallie. "And," she added with a flourish, dumping out her other shopping bag onto the sofa. "I got you all this stuff on sale at this darling little clothing shop – a raspberry T-shirt, a cute yellow top, and these two pairs of shorts to match." She held up a pair of shorts for Hallie to see. "I know they're the right size because you left a pair of jeans draped over the sofa last night; I saw the size this morning when I folded them up."

Delia rummaged in the bottom of one bag. "I got you these awesome leather flip flops, too. And this sweet sundress—that is so you—in a wonderful shade of green to match your eyes."

Delia turned to see Hallie scowling at her and not smiling anymore. "Am I your new charity case or something, Delia?" She put a hand on her hip, eyes flashing. "Because I don't need charity. I can take care of myself just fine."

Delia sat down abruptly on the corner of the sofa, totally surprised at the change in Hallie's mood. "I was only being nice, Hallie Walker," she said quietly. "I thought you'd be pleased I thought about you. I certainly didn't imagine you'd get mad at me."

"Why'd you do all this?" Hallie crossed her arms and moved to sit stiffly on a high back chair.

"Like I said—just thinking about you." Delia shook her head. "I knew you weren't able to bring much with you from home. I thought it would be fun to surprise you with a few things. I didn't think it would upset you, Hallie. Honest, I didn't. I'll take everything back if you really don't want it."

When Hallie didn't respond, Delia found her eyes welling up with tears. "I can't seem to do anything right these days," she complained. "And I'm really trying."

Hallie watched her sullenly. "Why are you trying so hard to do things right with me?"

Delia looked across at her in annoyance. "Well, actually, Hallie Walker, I don't have an answer for that," she snapped. "I was simply being thoughtful. I'm a thoughtful person—but maybe that's a word you don't understand. I like to do things for people. It's the way I am. It doesn't mean I believe you need charity or anything. Personally, I think you're being really rude and overly sensitive when I only tried to do something nice."

"Maybe," Hallie said, shrugging uncomfortably. "I only wanted to be sure you didn't think you had to do stuff like this for me because I ran away from home. Or because you felt sorry for me."

Delia glared at her. "Actually, I only feel sorry for you because you're so unappreciative, Hallie. You shouldn't be."

Surprisingly, Hallie giggled at that, her mood shifting like quicksilver. "All right, Delia. I'll be appreciative." Grinning now, she jumped up from her chair, peeled off her jeans and top, and proceeded to put on a pair of her new shorts and a knit top. Then she pulled off her tennis shoes and slipped into the leather flip-flops.

"Okay. What do you think?" She struck a pose.

"Everything looks great," Delia announced with pleasure, deciding to overlook the quick turnaround in Hallie's mood. "You're tall and slim; I bet almost anything looks wonderful on you. You're lucky in that, Hallie."

Hallie walked over to the long mirror in the hallway to check herself out. "Thanks, Delia," she said, coming back into the living room. "And you're right that I couldn't bring many clothes with me. These extra shorts sets will really help."

She held up the little dress against herself and went over to the mirror again to see the effect. "This dress is pretty, too. You have great taste." She swirled around. "I'll wear it when John Dale comes back."

"Who's John Dale?" asked Delia, glad Hallie's emotional scene was past.

"The man I'm going to marry," Hallie pronounced with a smug smile. "Come into the kitchen, Delia, and I'll tell you about him. I made dinner for us—a casserole my Grammie taught me how to cook and a sweetbread I want you to try. The bread is a new recipe I've been playing with, and you can tell me whether you like it or not."

Delia trailed Hallie into the kitchen. There, Hallie pulled out a hot casserole from the oven, sitting it on a trivet on the counter beside a plate of fresh sliced tomatoes and cottage cheese. A sweet, gingery smell filled the air from the loaf of warm bread she'd baked, which Delia saw sitting on a cutting board by the stove.

"You did all this?" Delia eyed the array of food in surprise.

"I told you I'd cook and clean if you let me stay here," Hallie replied matter-of-factly, starting to spoon casserole onto a couple of plates. "Sit down. I'll make you a plate and pour us both some tea."

Finding Hallie a little unpredictable, and not wanting to get into an argument again, Delia complied agreeably.

"Ummmm," Delia said a short time later after trying the casserole. "This tastes like homemade chicken pot pie."

"That's the idea." Hallie sent her a bright smile. "But it's really simple to make and will be a great dish to use later on at the bed and breakfast."

"What bed and breakfast?" Delia looked up in surprise again.

"The one John Dale and I are going to run in Greenbrier at his grandmother Mary Ogle's place. She owns this big Victorian farmhouse with wraparound porches and gingerbread trim. It even looks like a bed and breakfast." Excitement threaded through her voice. "And since John Dale is off in Charleston studying hotel management right now, I'm trying to do my part here to figure out foods and desserts we can serve the guests. That's why I'm working on sweetbreads, you see. We can use them on the breakfast buffet and then wrap and sell them to make more money. John Dale and I want to do this right, you know. That's why I'm going to get my degree in business at Walters State Community College, so I'll know better how to help run the place."

Delia felt more confused now than before. "Hallie, I'm missing way too many pieces to follow this whole story. Why don't you back up and fill me in more."

Hallie shrugged in typical teenage nonchalance. "I forget you're not from around here, Delia, and don't know everybody. When you've always lived here like me, it's easy to forget that."

Delia got up to pour more iced tea and get another small helping of casserole.

"Okay, it's like this," Hallie continued, when Delia sat back down at the table. "John Dale and I started making these plans for a bed and breakfast way back in high school when he and I realized we were a love match and wanted to get married. We used to hike this little mountain behind his grandmother's place, look down over the house and grounds, and make our plans."

"I hate to interrupt again, Hallie, but who exactly is John Dale?"

"Oh." She looked astonished. "John Dale Madison. You know. He's the son of the preacher at your aunt Dee's church. I figured you knew that. The Madisons live right here in Mynatt Park. You've met them, even if you don't remember right off." She paused. "See, that's another reason I'm being real careful about staying in hiding over here. The Madisons may not live on this street or anything, but they do live at the back of the park off Chewase Road on Dogwood Lane. You know where that is. Their place is the little white house on the corner with all the crepe myrtles in the yard. You've probably walked by it a hundred times."

Delia nodded. She did remember it. "Is John Dale's father the minister of the church on Natty Road behind Aunt Dee's store?"

"That's the one—Highland Cumberland Presbyterian. Dee used to take you when you visited. I saw you there when I came to church with my Walker kinfolks. But most Sundays, I went to Beech Grove Baptist Church in Greenbrier with my Grammie Rayfield."

Delia raised a hand to get Hallie to pause. "Whoa, Hallie. You need to remember I only came down here in the summers for a few weeks every year or so. My memories are limited, and some of this story doesn't make any sense to me. For example, why wouldn't John Dale's parents be supportive of this problem you're having with your stepfather, Jonas Cole, if you're planning to marry their son? I'd think they would take you in and help you if they knew what Jonas tried to do to you."

Hallie rolled her eyes. "You obviously don't know John Dale's parents," she observed. "Rev. Vernon and June Madison don't think I'm good enough for John Dale. And they certainly don't want us to get married. That's one reason they sent John Dale away to college in Charleston. They think if we're separated for long enough we'll grow apart."

"You are very young," Delia put in, reaching for a roll from the plate in the middle of the table.

"Well, thanks for being on my side." Hallie's eyes flashed. "Being young doesn't mean you can't be sure. Plus John Dale's almost three years older than me. He's a junior in college this year. We've only got one more year to go. And we neither one have changed our minds one little bit. So there."

"Sorry." Delia winced.

Hallie stuck her chin up. "Most of the problem with John Dale's parents is with his mother. June Madison is a big priss. You'll pick up on that when you get around her. When she comes to see you, she'll be sure to tell you she's an Ogle on her daddy's side and a Boone on her mother's side, which means she's kin to some original Revolutionary family that still owns a historic plantation near Charleston. John Dale's shown me pictures of it. It looks like *Gone with the Wind* or something. She'll also tell you her husband Vernon's people go back to the fourth President of the United States James Madison. Which is kind of cool, I guess, if June didn't think it makes her family a little better than everyone else's."

Delia scratched her head. "Your family all sound like fine people to me, Hallie. And I remember your grandmother, Etta Mae, as a wonderful person. I can't see what the Madisons have to criticize."

Hallie rolled her eyes again. "June Madison thinks my people are trashy because my mother ran around wild after my daddy died, and because she ran off and left me to be raised by my Grammie. Also, my mother coming back here and taking up with the likes of Jonas Cole hasn't helped things much. Or that my mother's been married three times. I heard June Madison tell John Dale once that "blood tells" and that she didn't want that wild Rayfield blood running in her little grandchildren's veins one day."

"She actually said that, and she's a minister's wife?" Delia's mouth dropped open in amazement.

"Yeah, she said it." Hallie reached to get a roll for herself. "Actually, to be fair, she's a pretty nice lady in most ways. But she has a really big blind spot about family genealogy and stuff."

Hallie paused in thought. "Funny thing though. Her mother, John Dale's grandmother, isn't a bit like that. Mary Boone-Ogle is as good as gold and doesn't have a snobby bone in her whole body. And Mary is the one who's a fancy Boone, came up here to visit in the mountains one summer, and married John Dale's grandfather John Ogle. Not that some of the Ogles don't have money or anything, but you'd think it would be Mary with her nose stuck in the air about her Boone ancestry and not her snooty daughter June a generation later."

Delia tried to take all this in. "What does Mary Ogle think of your and John Dale's idea to make her place into a bed and breakfast?"

"Oh, she thinks it's a great idea. She wants John Dale to have her home place when she's gone. Her only son lives in Charleston and is a doctor or something down there. He doesn't want the house, and Mary doesn't want the old place in Greenbrier sold. It's got some kind of historical significance. She's thrilled John Dale and I are going to turn it into a B & B. In fact, she's going to work with us and help us run it." She turned a sunny smile on Delia. "Mary even has a guest house on the back of her property she's going to let us fix up and live in after we're married."

"What if John Dale's parents are still opposed to your marriage when John Dale finishes college?" Delia drank a sip of iced tea.

"Well, too bad if they are." Hallie shook a fist in the air. "They've made us wait all this time when we didn't want to. If June Madison hadn't been so prissy, and if the good Reverend hadn't gone along with her and threatened not to send John Dale to college if we married too young, I'd have caught a bus to Charleston when this mess with Jonas Cole happened. I'm graduated from high school now. I could have stayed down there—safe from creepy ole Jonas Cole."

"You're still underage to marry," Delia reminded her. "You'd need your mother to sign for you in order to get married, Hallie."

Hallie frowned. "I didn't think of that." She popped the last bite of her roll into her mouth.

"So you have another year to wait before you and John Dale can get married—after you turn eighteen this fall and he graduates this spring." Delia clarified. "Do you see him often?"

"Whenever he comes home for holidays." Hallie leaned back in her chair. "Sometimes he gets a long weekend and comes then, too. The last time was at his spring break in April. I saw him every day." She smiled. "He either came to Cosby or we met halfway at Mary's or Grammie Rayfield's old place, where Aunt Tabby and Uncle Cas live. Sometimes we met at the Ramsey Stable where Uncle Hobart works and went riding together. We camped out once, too. It was great."

She propped her elbows on the table. "You know, Grandmother Mary's place adjoins my Grammie Rayfield's farm. That's how John Dale and I first met. We started playing together as children when John Dale's daddy moved here to take the church in Gatlinburg. John Dale came over to stay with Mary a lot. We met when I found him in my old playhouse in the woods. We almost had a fight about that, but became friends instead."

"You go back a long way." Delia got up to take their dishes to the sink.

"That we do," Hallie said, smiling at the thought.

"Does John Dale know what happened with Jonas and that you're staying here at Aunt Dee's place?" Delia asked as she washed up the plates.

"Yeah, I had to tell him. If he'd heard the story that I ran off to New York, he'd have freaked out. He's worried enough as it is, but he'll be home soon and you'll get to meet him. His mother is going to Charleston to stay with his sister Mary Alice when the Reverend picks John Dale up. She's having another baby, and June's going to help out. That will make things easier for us this summer. Vernon is always at the church, so John Dale can slip over through the woods to see me. You won't mind, will you?"

Delia considered this. "I don't see why that wouldn't be all right."

"Wow, I'm glad you came," Hallie jumped up to give her a quick hug. "Now, leave those dishes. I want you to taste my sweetbread and see what you think about it. This one's almost like a gingerbread." She walked over to the counter to cut Delia a slice. "You could put whipped cream on it or ice cream. Or serve it with apple butter or applesauce. See what you think."

Delia took a bite of the warm bread. "Ummmm. I think I'm going to gain weight if you keep cooking like this all the time I'm here," she teased. "This bread is really delicious. What do you call it?"

"I think I'm going to call it Ginger Loaf. I need to write down the recipe for it before I forget it, too." Hallie went to retrieve a pen and paper from a kitchen side drawer. "I thought up this bread recipe while reading an old gingerbread recipe I found in your aunt Dee's recipe box."

"Hallie," Delia asked quietly, leaning against the counter. "How did you know John Dale was the one? I mean, you said you both knew early, and you tell me you're both still sure."

"You're thinking about the fact that your relationship with Prentice busted up again, aren't you?" Hallie sent her a knowing look.

Delia hung her head. "I guess I am, Hallie. Here you are, only seventeen and so sure. I'm almost twenty-three, and I've had three or four relationships I thought were serious but crashed on the rocks—the one with Prentice the worst. It's the only one where I got engaged and dumped less than two months before the wedding."

Hallie shook her head. "My Grammie always used to say there's a right time for most everyone. She told me even the Bible says one of the greatest mysteries of life is of a man with a maid. So maybe your question's not an easy one. I was lucky to find my other half early. Some people don't find theirs till late in life. You read enough books to know that. Grammie used to say 'It'll happen if it's supposed to happen and when it ought to happen.'"

Delia sighed. "That's not a very encouraging answer."

Hallie finished writing the rest of her recipe. "Well, what do you think the answer is then?"

"I don't know."

"Hmmmm. Well, I guess you'll have to study on it." She tapped her pen on the table, thinking. "I used to watch couples in love after I turned twelve and started to get interested in stuff like that. It seemed to me something different happened when they even came in a room together—a change in the energy in the room or a way they seemed aware of each other more than anybody else." She grinned. "You know. Like sparks shimmering in the air."

She giggled. "With older couples I watched, I saw the relationship more comfortable—like they were a mix of each other and not as complete on their own as when together. Grammie and Grandpa Rayfield were that way. They seemed so easy and comfortable together. Sometimes, in a room with them, I used to think I could feel the love rays passing between them."

Hallie waved her pen in the air. "There are some real scientific studies, you know, that discovered that atoms pass back and forth between people who are in love, so each soon carry atoms from the other inside them. The energies, or shared atoms between them, recognize each other when they get together and draw the couple toward each other every time they meet."

Noticing Delia's amazement, she stuck her chin up. "Just because I haven't been to college yet doesn't mean I can't read!"

"I can see that." Delia smiled. "You're very wise for your years, Hallie."

Hallie shrugged. "It's just mountain raising," she replied matter-of-factly. "Plus I didn't have much opportunity to be sheltered or spoiled or anything. I had to grow up pretty early."

Delia bristled. "You think I've been sheltered and spoiled?"

"What do you think?" Hallie smarted back.

"I don't know." Delia bit her lip. "But it seems like I ought to be smarter than I am by now. Certainly tougher. Maybe able to read people better."

"We've all got different gifts." Hallie turned to start washing up the dishes. "You simply haven't figured out exactly what yours are yet. Or you'd have more confidence in yourself."

Delia picked up a dishcloth to help dry the dishes. "You don't think I have confidence in myself?"

"Nope, not as much as you should have," Hallie replied candidly. "You seem to be always worried about what somebody else is thinking. Touchy and crying about little things. Reluctant to say your own mind sometimes. Not always even knowing your own mind. Seems like you ought to be more sure of yourself at nearly twenty-three."

"Well, great." Delia put a hand on her hip in annoyance. "So now a seventeen year old is telling me I'm immature and lacking in confidence."

"Not exactly immature." Hallie rinsed off a glass and handed it to her. "But you could definitely use some work in the confidence area. You know, kind of like shining up silver when it gets dull. So you can see more who you

Delia's Place

are. Feel stronger in yourself. And act stronger. I'm figuring you kind of got submerged in that big family of yours and never really came into your own self well. My friend Ruby was like that for a while, being the youngest in her family. Plus your mother sounds like a real control freak from what you've told me. It's hard to find your true self with someone like that around, always trying to make you into something you're not."

Delia felt a little silly getting philosophical advice from a seventeen-year-old. But it was, admittedly, pretty good advice.

"You're kind of like a patchwork quilt," Hallie continued, handing her another glass to dry. "A little of what this person pieced in and a little of what that person sewed on. More other people's patchings and stitchings than a creation all your own design."

She smiled at Delia. "Grammie Rayfield shared that advice with me when I started high school, and she worried I was letting other people shape my ideas and thoughts too much."

Delia wanted to defend herself in some way against Hallie's analysis, but she struggled to find words to do so.

"Hey. Let's finish cleaning up the kitchen and play Parcheesi." Hallie was off on a new subject again. "I found Aunt Dee's old game while cleaning yesterday. I love Parcheesi. We can sit out on the back porch, play, drink tea, and listen to the night frogs. And tomorrow, I want to take you hiking to the Walker sisters' cabin. You need to see where some of your kin came from and hear some of their stories."

She carried the last of their dishes to the sink, still talking. "It's a weekday and not many people take that trail then. I can hide my hair under a hat, and it's unlikely we'll see anybody who might know me. It'll be fun."

It did sound fun—a board game on the porch listening to the night sounds and a hike in the mountains tomorrow. Delia thought she'd spend her days at Aunt Dee's all by herself, but now she had this saucy cousin for company instead. Hallie acted moody sometimes, but then, admittedly, so did Delia. Perhaps they'd end up being good for each other.

"I'd love to play Parcheesi and go hiking tomorrow." Delia laughed. "But you need to know I play games very competitively. I will not be nice and let you win."

The rest of the evening flew by, and it wasn't until later, when Delia lay in bed alone with Graham cat curled up next to her, that she found time to think about her day with Tanner. An odd, flirty sort of attraction flickered between Tanner Cross and her. Or at least it seemed that way. Delia's radar about men hadn't been that great lately. Prentice sure fooled her royally, romancing and kissing her even last month in Baltimore over spring break.

She wondered if MacKenzie knew about that. Looking back, it seemed MacKenzie assumed Delia and Prentice had a platonic relationship, but that wasn't so. Not that they engaged in an affair, as Prentice did with MacKenzie. But they did more than hold hands and moon over each other across the table. What sort of man could play two women like that? Delia cried into her pillow thinking about it.

Now Tanner Cross was flirting with her. Ten years ago Delia would have given anything for Tanner to pay attention to her. She'd been twelve that long ago summer, just turning thirteen—beginning to get a bust, but still with a little girl's rounded body. Not much of a figure. Her sister Frances tried some sort of a perm in her hair that summer, too, and it frizzed too short around Delia's full face.

Tanner had turned eighteen in May. Changed from the gangly highschooler of two summers before into a young man. Went to the university that year, and suddenly everything felt awkward and different between them. Tanner didn't climb trees anymore or ride his bike with his hands off the handlebars. He worked part-time in his father's business weekdays instead and partied with his friends on weekends. He still babysat her a time or two and took her to Douglas Lake one day when he and the gang went fishing and swimming. They tried to teach her to water ski behind Bogan's daddy's boat, but she made a fool of herself trying; however, not as much a fool as she made of herself the night Tanner came by and found her playing dress up in Aunt Dee's old dancing dress.

Aunt Dee had gone to a dinner theatre show with friends that night, and Delia insisted she could stay by herself alone. It shouldn't have surprised Delia that Aunt Dee sent Tanner over to check on her anyway.

Delia, lost in her fantasy world in the upstairs bedroom, hadn't even heard him knock. In fact, she didn't even know Tanner had come upstairs until she heard him say, "Well, well, isn't the little princess dressed up tonight."

She whirled around to see him lounging in the doorway, grinning, as he so often did. He looked so handsome, still in a dress shirt and dark slacks he'd worn to work. She knew, too, that she looked sort of pretty in her Aunt Dee's dancing dress—ice blue, low cut, and covered with silvery beads. Delia had pinned her hair up on her head underneath Aunt Dee's jeweled tiara. And she'd been dancing around the room with a pretend partner while listening to big band music on Dee's old record player. When she heard Tanner at the door, she couldn't help but wonder how long he'd stood there watching her.

He arched a brow teasingly. "Want me to play prince again so you don't have to dance by yourself?" he said. Before Delia could answer, he walked over, took her in his arms, and started slow-dancing her around the room.

Delia grew giddy and light-headed dancing with him, smelling the male smells of him and feeling his heart beating under his shirt when she dared to lean her head against his chest. He was patient and sweet with her, dancing her gently across the floor, careful not to step on her bare feet.

But when the music stopped, she leaned back and looked up at him with naked longing in her face. Wishing he would somehow magically kiss her. She wanted him to so much.

He looked at her and smiled, then touched her cheek sort of sweetly. Somehow, Delia knew he saw exactly what she was thinking. But she didn't care and she didn't look away.

Then he said softly, "Just for the moment and the memory, Princess." And he leaned over and kissed her. Really kissed her. It had been wonderful and different from all those giggly spin-the-bottle kisses with the gang in summers past. This kiss made Delia's heart pound and her knees feel weak. And she felt funny down near her stomach.

Tanner broke away suddenly. Looked mad and upset. Backed away and turned to leave.

"Don't stay up too late," he told her curtly on the way out. "And tell Dee I remembered to stop by to check on you, okay? I'll see you tomorrow."

He didn't see her tomorrow. Or the day after. He didn't even come to say goodbye two days later when she left.

The next summer, Delia didn't come to Gatlinburg. She went to stay with her sister Frances all summer, after Frances' fourth child Kenneth was born. The following summer, when Delia turned sixteen, she traveled to Europe with Aunt Dee on a long, wonderful trip. She didn't actually return to Gatlinburg again until the summer she turned seventeen.

"I secretly looked forward to seeing Tanner again on that visit," she whispered to Graham, scratching the cat's neck. "I knew he'd be more grown-up and I wondered what he'd think of me—older now, too." Delia sighed. "But I arrived to find that he had moved to Atlanta and was engaged to be married. Even if it was silly, I climbed up in the gang's old tree house and cried over it for hours."

Delia punched her pillow to fluff it. "That's why I felt so humiliated to see Tanner again the other day. I hadn't seen him since that night when I practically begged him to kiss me—a silly little thirteen-year-old in love with an eighteen-year-old man."

Love. What did she know of love? "Tanner was my first real love, and that came to nothing. Next I thought I loved football star Jack Helton in high school, who broke up with me to date the head cheerleader. After that, I fell in love with Hal Graham, visiting with family at the beach. We wrote for a time, and then he married some girl in New Jersey. Let's see, what humiliation came next?"

She thought back. "Oh, yeah. Vince Rawlings, the son of a business associate of my parents. We dated two whole years, talked about our future. Mother and Daddy loved Vince, but I showed up at Vince's apartment unexpectedly one afternoon and found him in bed with another woman. I thought

I'd die—cried and screamed at him when he tried to follow me out to my car to explain. For three months, he tried to make up with me. Apologized to my parents. Even proposed. Mother stayed provoked with me for a year afterwards because I wouldn't be more forgiving. She never really forgave me until Prentice came along."

Tears trickled down Delia's cheeks now. "Prentice simply oozed masculine charm and charisma. It was so easy to fall in love with Prentice. And my family adored him. Now, I wonder if any of us ever knew Prentice at all." She reached over to get a tissue to blow her nose. "How can anyone know if love is real? And I must really be an idiot to be flirting with Tanner Cross after everything I've been through."

Delia sighed again, and crawled out of the bed to go look at an old picture Aunt Dee had framed and put on the chest of drawers. She'd seen it in the moonlight filtering in the window—a photo of Tanner and her at nine and fourteen, sitting on a big rock in a mountain stream, their feet hanging down in the cold water. Grinning and enjoying a wonderful time.

"Wonder why Tanner is flirting with me after all these years? I don't know what to think about it. And I don't know what to do about it, either. Probably nothing. His timing is horrible, and nothing good ever comes of my relationships anyway." She crept back to bed. "Maybe Hallie's right. Maybe I'm just a patchwork quilt of bits and scraps other people have sewed on to me. Maybe that's why everyone loses interest in me when they get to know me better." Delia let the tears flow again.

Images of all her failed relationships filtered through her mind, giving her no comfort. The cat curled back up beside her as she settled under the covers again. "You know, Graham, I think I'm going to figure out who I am and get focused," she told him. "And I'm going to quit falling in love so easily. Men are just not reliable and bring nothing but grief."

She poked her pillow. "And that includes Tanner Cross, too. He can flirt away all he wants. But I'm locking my heart up safe from him. And from anyone else, too."

Graham purred in agreement, an easy man to please.

And Delia soon fell asleep.

Chapter 6

On Wednesday mornings, Tanner had a standing breakfast meeting at the Garden Cafe with his three best friends since first grade, Keppler James, Perry Ammons, and Bogan Kirkpatrick—the Jack Gang. Tanner pushed his way into the Garden Restaurant and headed toward the corner table where his friends sat already working on breakfast. He was the last to arrive.

"Yo, T. Cross," Keppler called out. "You'd better hurry before we finish up all the pancakes."

Tanner grinned as he joined them. "Deacon will make more—and usually has to at the rate you eat them."

"Hey." Bogan changed the subject. "I saw Tanner leaving Howard's this week with Hiram Shreffrum."

Keppler laughed. "Was Tanner holding him up and helping him walk out the door, or was Sheffrum sober this time?"

Bogan waved a fork full of pancakes. "He was sober this time, at least partly, and he boomed out to me, and about half the restaurant, that Tanner was the best gall-darned CPA in all of Gatlinburg."

"We all know that," Perry added loyally.

"Whoo-ee, Tanner." Bogan shook his head. "It must try your patience to work with that man. I dread every time I see him coming in my door to get a print order done. Half the time he isn't pleased with anything we do for him."

"Mostly he's just trying to get out of paying full price," Perry observed. "I'll bet half the time he tries to talk you into giving him the job for free, too."

Keppler raised an eyebrow. "Now, what kind of way is that for a preacher to talk?"

"You forget, I'm a businessman, too." Perry poured maple syrup over another pancake. "And Hiram has tried to rip Tracie and me off for work we've done for him several times now. In fact, he complained again last week about one of Tracie's cakes he ordered for an office birthday party."

Bogan laughed one of his deep, rumbly laughs. "Lordy mercy, I wish I'd been there to see how little Miss Tracie-spitfire handled that one. She's not as easy-going as you, Perry. What did she do?"

Perry chuckled. "Hiram complained Tracie put one too many layers on his party cake, hoping, undoubtedly, to get the price knocked down. Tracie raised an eyebrow at him, commented he might possibly be right, and then proceeded to whack off the top layer of the cake with her spatula. Folks probably heard Hiram gasp and holler for half a mile about how she'd ruined his cake."

They all laughed, imagining it.

"Did she make him another one?" Tanner asked.

"Nope." Perry grinned widely. "She told Hiram he could buy himself a nice two-layer cake down the street at the grocery store if he wanted one. Then she walked out, carrying what was left of her cake along with her."

Bogan hooted. "Good for Tracie! Hiram needs to get a little of his own now and then. It's not like the man is hurting for money. He certainly spends enough when he wants to."

Tanner felt like saying Amen to that. But he always kept the financial affairs of his clients totally confidential.

"What happened to the cake?" Keppler asked.

"Oh. Tracie put another top on it, repaired the icing, added little wedding bells to it, and sold it to a couple from Ohio that I married later that night. They shared it with their wedding guests and acted thrilled to have it."

Their talk went on like this, sharing stories and updating each other on their lives while they ate breakfast. After pancakes, they ate eggs, sausage, grits, and biscuits with white cream gravy. Plus several pots of coffee. Tanner always felt stuffed for hours after their Wednesday morning breakfasts.

He looked around the table with affection at his old friends.

"Earth to Tanner. Earth to Tanner," Keppler intoned, interrupting Tanner's wandering thoughts. "We're ready to see who has the best news flash of the week."

This was another of the Jack Gang's many games. Whoever brought the best news flash got their breakfast tab picked up by the others that day.

"All right, here's mine," challenged Bogan. "I got lucky enough to get Dolly Parton's signature last week on one of her photographs."

"Awww," complained Keppler. "That was only because all you publication owners went to that big Sevier County meeting she attended for publicity. Plus I hear nearly everybody there got her signature."

"Well, maybe so." Bogan drained his coffee. "But I did get it. I've framed that picture and put it right up behind my cash register, too. You got something better?"

Delia's Place

"Maybe." Keppler offered a smug smile. "My flash is that Sherilynn and I are going to have another baby. Found out this week."

"Well, dang, congratulations to you!" exclaimed Bogan.

Perry and Tanner both joined in to offer their best wishes.

"Maybe it will be a little girl this time." Perry poured out another cup of coffee. "So Randy and Dennis will have a little sister."

"Well, I'd sure like to have a boy." Bogan jumped into the conversation. "Rona and I are trying, you know, now that Rylie and Kaylin are older. It took me awhile to talk Rona into another baby after she had to raise two at one time all these years with the twins."

They laughed again as they passed more biscuits across the table.

"That reminds me of my news flash." Perry steepled his fingers. "I married two identical male twins this week to two women who were sisters. Pretty unusual, huh? The similarity in the couples was uncanny. Tracie said she hoped they clearly labeled their wedding pictures so they didn't get them mixed up."

"That's a pretty good one." Bogan slapped a hand on the table. "All right. What's yours, Tanner?"

Tanner smiled a little slyly. "Mine is the news that little Miss Delia Walker has come back to town. And she's coming to my birthday party over at the park this Friday, so you'll all get to see her again."

"Well, I'll be jiggered," declared Bogan. "Little Miss Delia. Glory-be, we haven't seen that girl since she was about twelve or thirteen."

"Actually, the last summer we saw her she'd just turned thirteen," Perry pointed out. "I remember we had a little party for her down at the park in the gazebo."

"Boy-oh-boy, that old gazebo sure holds some memories for me," Bogan said. "We used to play spin the bottle down there. I remember Miss Delia played that game right along with us one summer. She about died of embarrassment the first time one of us kissed her. Seems like she was only nine or ten back then."

Keppler jumped into the conversation. "You know, the first time I ever kissed Sherilynn was when we played spin the bottle at the gazebo. I wasn't happy that night either when the bottle pointed to her. She was Ruthann's best friend, you know, three years younger than me, and I knew she had a crush on me."

"Well, it must have been a pretty good kiss." Perry punched him on the arm in fun. "You married the girl."

"Yeah, but it wasn't that kiss that talked me into the idea of marrying her. She had her lips all scrunched up that first time, but some later kisses we tried out sure did have an impact." Keppler grinned.

This brought on another round of good-natured laughter.

"You know, seems like it was always Tanner that Miss Delia Walker had a crush on." Bogan wiggled his eyebrows. "Followed him around everywhere—if I remember it right. Got right mushy-mooney over him that last summer or two. Plus, we had to put up with her every time she came down here over the years because Tanner's mother made us be nice and play with her."

"I remember Delia as a really good kid," countered Perry. "Bright and imaginative. Always game to try about anything we got up to and always had the best ideas. We had fun with her, even if she was much younger than all of us. She looked up to us with such adulation that it felt kind of good to our egos. She thought us so grownup and cool."

"We were cool." Bogan pumped a fist. "Still are. The girl was simply admiring quality."

More laughter erupted.

"You know," Perry said. "I thought Maureen told us last year that Delia got engaged to be married. That still happening, Tanner?"

Bogan leaned toward him. "Yeah, Tanner. Has she brought herself a Yankee boy down with her for us to tease a little?"

"No." Tanner shook his head. "The wedding and engagement were called off. Came as a kind of a shock. Seems the jerk was running around with someone behind Delia's back. Then up and married the other woman in Vegas. Sent Delia an overnight letter to let her know about it. It's been kind of hard on her. I think that's probably why she came down here just now. Wanted some time to get away and get over it."

"Bummer," declared Bogan. "I hate that happened to her."

Keppler fluttered his eyes. "And have you let her cry on your big shoulder?"

Tanner scowled.

"Man alive, that girl could cry buckets," interrupted Bogan. "That's one thing I sure do remember about Delia Walker was how often that girl cried."

Keppler took the floor again. "Hey, what does Delia look like now, Tanner?"

Tanner smiled and shook his head a little thoughtfully.

"Dang, I know that look." Bogan leaned foreward with interest. "When Tanner smiles like that and can't find any quick words to say about a woman, that means she's really hot."

Keppler scratched his head. "It's hard to think about little Delia Walker being hot. Is she hot, Tanner?"

"Let's just say you better be sure your wives don't see you ogling her too much on Friday night," warned Tanner with a grin. "Little Delia has changed quite a bit since we saw her last." He paused, frowning. "Listen, you all be

Delia's Place

nice to her on Friday if I bring her, you hear? I don't want you razzing her or giving her a hard time."

"Owww-eee, aren't we being protective now?" Bogan wagged a finger at Tanner.

"Hey." Keppler smirked. "Since Tanner's the only one of us not married yet, maybe we can help get him and Miss Delia Walker together while she's visiting."

"Yeah, he can soothe her broken heart." Bogan rubbed a hand over his chest.

Tanner's eyes flashed with annoyance. "Look, I thought you guys might like to see Delia again," he groused. "That doesn't mean you need to start trying to match me up with her. And I don't want you saying stuff like that around her when she comes down to the park Friday, you hear? Making her feel uncomfortable. She's getting over a bad relationship. Cut her some slack, okay?"

"He doth protest too much, me thinketh," remarked Keppler with another smirk.

Tanner scowled at him, but everyone only laughed.

"All right. All right," Perry intervened. "Let's give Tanner a break here." He grinned at him. "You're the only unmarried one we can tease any longer, Tanner. So don't take it too seriously."

"Yeah, lighten up." Keppler punched a fist against his arm. "And, listen, you just bring Miss Delia Walker right on down to see us on Friday night. It'll be a treat. We'll talk about old times and catch up. And, don't you worry, Tanner, we'll all be nice. We always were nice to Delia, if you remember."

"Shoot. If we weren't nice, she was likely to cry," put in Bogan. "And, boy howdy, we all hated it when she tuned up to do that. It took forever to get her quieted down once she started."

"Yeah. We even let her climb up into our tree house once to shut her up," Keppler remembered. "And that was our Boys Only place."

"Listen, you all, as Mom reminded me the other day, Delia was five whole years younger than us back then. That made a big difference," Tanner explained. "She's grown now. More an equal to us—just received her master's degree in design. She's a woman now... let's remember that."

The guys all passed a knowing look around the table, further annoying Tanner.

"Hey, let's vote on the best news flash," demanded Bogan, changing the subject. "What'll it be?"

"I vote for Keppler's news about his new baby coming," said Perry. "You can't get much better news than knowing they'll be another addition to the Jack family line."

Everybody laughed and decided to agree. And it was Keppler that day who got the free breakfast prize.

Later, as Tanner walked back over to Crosswalk, he popped in downstairs to say hello to his mother. He found her putting homemade candles into a display case by the front counter.

"These are almost the last of Dee Ward's candles," she told Tanner. "Only one box more in inventory. Dee loved the art of candlemaking. What a shame there won't be any more. I remember when Dee came down to Arrowcraft to a series of summer craft workshops and first met Roland Ward."

Tanner remembered Roland well—a tall, gentle man and a forest ranger for the park service. Animals and people always seemed magnetically drawn to Roland. And Tanner remembered he told wonderful stories about nature and outdoor life.

Roland frequently went fishing with Tanner and his father, and he always seemed to know the best places to go fishing, no matter what season. Roland and Dee and Tanner's mother and father, Maureen and Tom Cross, had been the best of friends. Tanner spent many evenings with them enjoying dinners, games, and music. It shocked Tanner when Roland died. Only nine, Tanner had never known anyone that died before. His mother told him Roland had a defect in a valve in his heart. No one knew about it, but that caused his death.

Delia's father came down to visit Dee that summer after Roland's death and brought Delia, almost five. Tanner's mother said the visit helped to cheer Dee and gave her something new to live for.

Tanner studied the candles Dee had made, remembering all this.

His mother's words interrupted his thoughts. "You know, Dee learned many crafts over the years, but when she started making candles, she discovered a craft she especially enjoyed. She liked working with wax and adding the dyes and scents. After she ran out of people to give candles to, she started bringing them down here to the store to sell. People loved them. Dee always put so much scent in her candles. They didn't just smell good when you opened the jars to sniff, they smelled good when you burned them. The scents Dee used were rich, natural aromas, too. She never made any of those overly sweet or cloying scents."

Tanner nodded in understanding. He'd grown up with the smells of Dee's candles in his home and office, and they sold well in the store. "Maybe we can find someone else to make candles we can sell here."

"It wouldn't be the same," his mother acknowledged sadly. "Everyone would come looking for Mountain Way Candles and they'd be disappointed to get anything else. Dee's recipes were so special."

As Maureen finished putting the candles into the display area, Tanner saw an old friend coming into the store—Hobart Rayfield, who worked for one of Tanner's clients, Harrison Ramsey, at the Ramsey Stable in Greenbrier. He wore his standard uniform of old jeans, flannel shirt, ranch boots, and a brown leather cowboy hat. Tanner always thought Hobart looked somewhat out of place whenever he came into the city. He'd much rather be at the stable or at his old farm place off Laurel Creek Road.

"Hey, cowboy, what brings you to town?" Tanner reached out to shake Hobart's hand. "Did Harrison send you over with some papers for me?"

In deference to Maureen, Hobart took off his hat and held it awkwardly in his hand. "Howdy, Maureen," he said. "Good to see you. You, too, Tanner."

Maureen stood up from her task on the floor, brushed off her dress and the Crosswalk apron she wore. She held out her hand to Hobart. "I haven't seen you in an age, Mr. Rayfield. What brings you into my place today? Looking for a gift for someone?"

"No, ma'am, although there's right fine stuff here, and that's a fact. I'm here today because my niece has gone missing. Hallie Walker."

"Hallie?" Maureen asked with surprise. "When did this happen? Is this Etta Mae's girl you're talking about?"

Hallie, well known to both Maureen and Tanner, had frequently come with Grammie Rayfield to clean both Maureen and Dee Ward's houses. She'd worked for Maureen last summer in the store when she turned sixteen and had been a good employee.

"Yep. It's Etta's and my Hallie," Hobart confirmed. "She just graduated from the high school this year, you know. Had high grades and got her a scholarship to go over to Walters State this fall. Planned to stay over to Tabby and Cas's nearer to the college if we could have talked her ma into it." He hung his head.

"I know things were never very good between Hallie and her mother, Hobart," Maureen said gently. "And it was a shame Etta died last year when she did. It hit Hallie hard losing her."

"Well, Etta and my brother Ben, were like her ma and pa all her life," he explained. "I was real close to her, too. I know that girl. It ain't like her to just run off." He looked up with angry eyes. "I think there's something we're not knowing of."

Tanner narrowed his eyes. "What do you know about where she might have gone?"

"Well, supposedly she's gone off to New York City." He twisted his hat in his hands. "She finished her classes, started those last senior days at the high school, and then jest up and took off one night. Bought herself a bus ticket to New York City, and there's plenty of witnesses say they saw her get on the bus and leave. She left her mother a note explaining she knew a friend with a job for her in New York. She brought her little Volkswagen over to my place and left it for me with a note. Told me the same thing. She also told me not to sell the car—that she'd be back for it when she could start school later. Maybe in January. She asked me not to tell her mother she might be coming back."

He stopped to scratch his head. "None of this is like Hallie at all. She ran off and didn't go through her graduation ceremony. And she'd rented the gown and all two months back. Paid for it herself. She told me about it, and she looked forward to that day. Planned to go to the senior breakfast, too. Even told me she might get some recognitions and awards fer her grades and such. So it don't seem right she'd go off afore all that."

"Did something happen?" asked Maureen.

"Well, you know, that's what I'm a thinkin'," said Hobart. "There's something real oddish about this whole thing. Hallie didn't never have any desire to leave this valley. Her heart belonged right here. Her plans and dreams were here. She'd confided in me a lot, you see."

He didn't add more to that. Nor did they ask.

Hobart shook his head. "She still had her little horse Foxey over at her Grammie's stable. Went over to ride that mare every weekend, more if she could. She told me to see to the horse while she was gone, or to get Cas or Aunt Tabby to. That wasn't like Hallie, either."

"What can we do to help, Hobart?" Maureen reached out to put a hand on his arm.

He shuffled his feet. "I don't know for sure where she is, you see? I thought she might try to make contact with some folks she knew after a time. She worked here for you last summer, and she liked you, Maureen. Knew you, too, from helping Etta Mae clean your house over the years. I was hoping if you heard from her, you'd let me know. That you'd ask her to call me, too. Let me know she's okay."

"Oh, Hobart, of course I will," Maureen assured him. "Tanner will, too, if she calls here when I'm gone or calls his place. It must be frightening for all of you to think of her up in New York, or wherever she is, so far away from her family."

"Yes, ma'am, that it is," he confessed.

He looked at Tanner. "This is about to tear Vesser apart, too, Tanner. I know you two fish together a lot. Maybe you can be a bit of comfort to him."

"I'll bet Vesser misses Hallie helping him with his children, too." Maureen smiled. "Since his wife died, Hallie has been wonderful to spend time with Isabel and little Lawson. She brought them in here one day to see me, and it seemed obvious that both those little children were foolish about her."

Tanner looked thoughtful. "Do you think she's really in New York, Hobart?"

"Well, the police think so." His brows drew together in a frown. "Her ma and that Jonas Cole are convinced that's where she's run off to. All the evidence points to that."

"But you're not sure?" Tanner watched the old man.

"Aww. Just one of them old superstitious feelings." He twisted his hat again. "That something ain't right about all of this somehow."

"And Hallie didn't talk to anyone before she left? Give any explanation for this?" Maureen straightened a row of candles absently.

Hobart nodded no.

"Well, I think you're right." Maureen looked up. "That isn't like her. Hallie is much too conscientious about her family and much too level-headed to be this impulsive."

Hobart stiffened. "There's those who say she's jest a chip off the old block. That she's acting wild like her ma did, and at about the same age, too."

"Well, I am certainly not one to agree with that for even a minute." A touch of angry color came into Maureen's cheeks. "And you can be sure, Hobart, that if Hallie calls me, I'll have a talk with her. Try to find out what's going on."

"Do you think this might have anything to do with Jonas Cole?" Tanner asked thoughtfully. "I hate to say it, but I've heard some pretty bad rumors about that man. I hear he's roughed up a few people. Some of them girls."

"I've heard worse than that," Hobart said flatly. "That worries me a lot. If I learn Jonas has hurt Hallie, I may find me a way to see he pays. Sissy ought never to have married a man like that. That girl hasn't been straight in her thinking about men ever since Lawson died all them years back. It did something to her good sense."

Hobart put his hat back on, indicating that he'd be leaving now.

"If we hear anything at all, Hobart, we'll call you," Tanner assured him. "Thanks for coming to tell us. I'll try to talk to Vesser, too, when I can."

"Thank you." Hobart turned to leave. "And if you think of it, I'd appreciate it if you'd put a word in for Hallie to the Man Upstairs. You know?"

"We'll certainly pray," Maureen promised. "And we'll be in touch."

After he left, his mother looked toward the door throughtfully for a few minutes. Then she turned to Tanner. "Hobart's right that it's not the least bit like Hallie Walker to run off like this. I'd stake my life on it something's happened to upset her. You know, I told Hallie she could work here again this summer, and she never even called to tell me she wasn't planning to come in. That isn't like her either."

"Well, try not to worry too much, Mom. Maybe Hallie will call you soon. Or write to you once she gets settled to explain things."

Despite his comforting words to his mother, Tanner found his thoughts drifting off in Hallie's direction several times that afternoon at work. Like Hobart, he worried about the girl's safety alone in the big city of New York. Heck, Hallie Walker hadn't been further than Knoxville in her whole life. What in the world possessed her to get on a bus and go to New York City?

Chapter 7

A fine sunny day greeted Delia and Hallie as they set out for their hike. Before they left Aunt Dee's house, Hallie pointed out their route on a local map, and then she hunkered down on the floorboard in the back seat, out of sight, until they drove out of the Gatlinburg area. Once on the Little River Road, heading into the mountains, Delia pulled into an overlook to let Hallie climb into the front seat.

To conceal her identity, Hallie had braided her bright red hair into pigtails and put on a brown floppy hat of Aunt Dee's. Since the day dawned warm, both Hallie and Delia wore shorts, t-shirts, high socks, and well-worn hiking boots. The girls had stuffed a light lunch and bottles of water into two backpacks—the lightweight pack Hallie had brought with her and Delia's new bear pack, despite Hallie's jibes and protests.

"That's our turn ahead on the right at Metcalf Bottoms Picnic Area," Hallie said, after they'd driven in and out along the twining mountain road for about eight miles. "I'll watch for a good parking spot as we go in and point it out to you. We need to walk across the bridge over the creek to get to the beginning of our trail, so we don't want to park too far from that."

Hallie directed Delia into a parking place beside the creek and bridge, and after a quick stop at the picnic area restroom, the two set out on their walk.

"I can't tell you how glad I am to get out of that house for a while," Hallie enthused, stopping on the bridge to look out over the mountain stream that tumbled in a riot below them. "And I love this part of the mountains."

The May day had heated up quickly; children already played on the rocks in the creek below the bridge and waded in the cold mountain water. Further up stream, Delia could see tubers floating in the swift rapids, angling themselves artfully between the rocks and boulders, shrieking in pleasure.

The hiking trail started to the right just across the bridge and then ran alongside the stream. The rustic sign at the beginning of the trail read "Metcalf Bottoms Trail."

Hallie set off down the trail in a lilting walk. "This trail follows the Little River for a short distance and then swings left over the ridge top and back down to the Little Greenbrier Schoolhouse," she explained. "The whole trail to the schoolhouse is only a little over a half mile. A lot of people like to walk to the school from the picnic grounds."

Delia soon spotted clumps of silvery glade ferns along the trailside, spires of white foamflower, and daisy-like chickweed. "Look, there's a late trillium under that tree." Delia pointed toward it. "I've always loved the trillium."

"You need to come sometime in April if you really want to see pretty trillium." Hallie smiled at her. "A good place to see a show of them is on the Little River Trail out of Elkmont. We passed the entrance to that coming in."

"I always visited in summer every year," Delia put in. "Most of the wildflowers are gone by then."

"Well, this trail isn't a very good one for wildflowers, but we may see some along the way anyway, like yellow ragwort, wild violets, or maybe some fire pink by the stream later."

Delia stepped over a rock in the path. "You know, Aunt Dee always tried to teach me the names of the flowers, trees, and ferns. I still remember many, but I wish I remembered more."

They walked quietly along through the woods, enjoying the day. Noisy squirrels chattered at them from high in a creekside tree and Hallie pointed out a lizard scuttling under a sunny rock. The trail climbed uphill after angling left, passing over the ridge top and then starting downhill through a rhododendron tunnel.

"See all the buds here on these rhododendrons?" Hallie gestured. "It will be pretty here in July when they all bloom out."

"At least I did see the rhododendron when I visited in the summers." Delia slowed to study a pink bud. "My favorite place for the rhodos is higher up the mountain at Alum Cave Bluff trail."

"Oh, yeah, that's a great place." Hallie shook her head in agreement. "The stream sides and hillsides along that trail are simply a glory of blooms if you catch that trail at the right time—some years are better than others in the mountains for rhododendrons and other blooming things, just like for vegetables. One year we had so much squash in the garden at Grammie's, we ran out of people to give them away to."

Delia laughed. "Always living in the city, we never grew a garden."

"Oh, a garden's wonderful. But they're a lot of work, too. Planting, tending, picking, canning, and freezing. There's work to do from spring till the end of summer. If you grow turnip greens and have apple trees, the work keeps going right up into the fall. Something is always coming in that needs to be picked, used, or put up. From the time I could walk down a garden row and carry a bucket, Grammie had me working and doing chores in the garden."

"Will you put in a garden when you have the bed and breakfast later on?" Delia asked.

"Oh, for sure." Hallie nodded. "And an orchard, too. There's nothing better than serving people fresh vegetables, fruits, and the great dishes you can make from both."

The trail wound down into an open valley in the woods as they talked. A little stream ran alongside the path, bubbling merrily over the rocks. Delia found it easy to imagine the old homesteads that probably stood in the cleared areas long ago.

"Be careful crossing this bridge," Hallie warned as they came to a log bridge over the stream. "Sometimes yellow jacks build underneath it. If you see any, just run like heck." She laughed.

They tripped over the bridge and on to the historic, one-room schoolhouse on the other side. Stepping inside to explore, they found the worn desks and blackboards still in place, as though school just let out earlier in the day. Delia sat in one of the desks to check it out, while Hallie walked up front.

"All right, class," Hallie intoned, mimicking a stern schoolteacher's pose as she turned around to grin at Delia. "We're going to recite the poems we each learned today, starting with Delia Walker. Delia, please stand and recite your poem aloud."

Playing along, Delia stood to her feet while searching her mind quickly for a poem she could remember. "Life is a wonderful thing and sweet," she recited after a moment. "If we let it swirl around our feet / And know that we are a living part / Of all the world's pulsating heart."

"Well, I'm impressed." Hallie lounged against the aged teacher's desk. "That was nice, Delia. I thought you'd do 'Roses are Red' or something. Where did you learn that?"

"From a little book of poems and thoughts. I can't remember the author." She shrugged. "What would you have recited?"

"Probably a childhood poem I heard so often that I finally memorized it, like 'The Owl and the Pussycat' or something."

"I love that poem," Delia put in with excitement. "Aunt Dee used to read it to me. Let's see how much of it we can remember as we hike. Okay?"

This got them both giggling and remembering childhood poems, rhymes, and songs as they made their way from the schoolhouse to the next part of the trail.

The trail name changed as they walked on, becoming Little Brier Gap Trail. Broadening from a narrow path into an old mountain roadbed, Delia and Hallie could walk side by side now, rather than in single file as before.

Delia's Place

After a mile, they turned to the right down a side trail leading to the old Walker home place.

"I can't believe you've never been here before." Hallie gestured ahead as they entered the homestead area after a quarter mile. "Your direct relatives once lived here. Your great-great-grandparents, John and Margaret Walker, settled this homestead and raised eleven children here in the mid-eighteen and early nineteen hundreds. The mountains were pretty primitive then, nothing like you see now."

"What's that building there?" Delia pointed. "And why is it over the water?"

"That's the springhouse." Hallie headed toward the small structure. "It's built over a spring or creek so the family can keep milk or cheese or other perishables inside it. There weren't any refrigerators, you know, or inside plumbing or electricity. Early mountain families had to be very self-sufficient. I read that a lot of outbuildings once existed at this farm when the family lived here, like a smokehouse for meat and an apple house. I'm sure a bigger barn stood at one time, too, but now all that's left is this springhouse, the corn crib that looks like a barn, and the log house the family lived in."

Delia explored the house and grounds with Hallie before the two sat down on a bench on the front porch of the old cabin to eat their lunch and rest.

"Most of the Walker kids married and moved off eventually." Hallie unpacked a ham sandwich and chips from her back pack as she talked. "And like I told you before, one of the brothers that we're descended from moved away and started a furniture business outside of Gatlinburg. His name was John Lawson Walker. My daddy Lawson got named for him and your granddaddy Howard was one of John Lawson Walker's sons. Have you ever gone to any of our big Walker reunions?"

Delia shook her head, unpacking and starting on her own lunch.

"Well, they're great." Hallie grinned. "And a wonderful place to hear a lot of family stories."

She passed Delia an extra snack bag of granola and dried fruits before she went on. "Your granddaddy Howard and my great-granddaddy Gordon—who's your uncle—both worked in the furniture business in Gatlinburg with their father John after Eldridge went off to become a preacher. And, of course, you know the story about how your granddaddy went north to get married and work there. So now, it's only my great-granddaddy Gordon, his son Ray, who's my grandfather, and Ray's son, Vesser, my uncle, who work in the family business. Ray manages things and works in the store with Granddaddy Gordon, and Vesser builds handmade furniture and is a craftsman. He also repairs and refinishes old furniture, and he can hand cane chairs real nicely, too. I'm especially close to Uncle Vesser. He kind of took on fathering me after my daddy got killed."

"I've never really gotten to know many of my Walker relatives except Aunt Dee," Delia admitted. "She did take me to meet my grandfather's brother Gordon and his wife Inez one time. I think I met Ray, his wife Louise, and some of their family at church once, too, but I don't remember any of the rest."

"My father's sister, Willine, married an upholsterer – handy with the furniture business in the family. In fact, that's how Willine met Cale Dalton. And, by the way, he's the best upholsterer in the area if you ever need something done."

Delia smiled. Hallie was always so loyal and supportive of her family members.

"Don't you think your Walker relatives are worried about you now?"

"I'm sure they are." Hallie's eyes dropped. "And the Rayfields, too. But it can't be helped. They couldn't keep me from going to my mother and Jonas Cole before. It's not likely they could do anything to change things now, Delia, even if they knew Jonas tried to hurt me. There's no proof except my word."

She paused. "Besides, I'd be worried, too, that Vesser or Hobart might go after Jonas if they knew what happened. Hobart's old, and even though he's tough, he might get hurt or get in trouble with the law. Vesser's a widower with two little kids. I wouldn't want him to get locked up or anything when he has Isabel and little Lawson to look after. They're only five and three."

Hallie finished the last bite of her sandwich. "I've done what I thought was the right thing, Delia. The time will pass fast until I'm eighteen. Then I can live wherever I want."

"Maybe, but it all worries me, anyway." Delia frowned.

"You shouldn't worry." Hallie sent her a sunny smile. "We Walkers come from an independent stock of women. Maybe you don't know it, but five of the Walker daughters born and raised in this cabin never did marry. They just continued living right here in this little house on their own land until they died. It was part of their deal with the park service. The Walker sisters got to be sort of famous as time moved on for living here and taking care of themselves on this primitive farmstead.

"Which reminds me, here's a poem I meant to read to you back in the schoolhouse. I brought it in my pocket knowing we planned to come here. Louisa Walker, one of the Walker sisters, wrote it about this old cabin. This poem and some other poems of hers are printed in a little book I found at Aunt Dee's place."

Hallie dug out a folded piece of paper, opened it, and read:
There is an old weather beaten house that stands near a wood
With an orchard near by it, for most one hundred years it has stood
It was my home in infancy; it sheltered me in youth

Delia's Place

When I tell you I love it, I tell you the truth

Delia looked around at the rustic log homestead and wrinkled her nose. "It's hard to believe a woman loved a primitive home like this enough to write a poem about it. It only has two rooms, plus that loft above that you need a ladder to reach. Those sisters probably slept in one room together and used the other for living and cooking. The house doesn't have electricity or running water. It's dark with few windows, and it looks drafty."

"Yeah, but it's peaceful and quiet. And it's beautiful here." Hallie leaned back against a porch post. "You know, I'd come here to hide out if Jonas ever came after me, and I didn't know where else to go. He'd never think of looking for me here."

"Well, you'd better hope that doesn't happen in the winter." Delia barely disguised her shock. "It would be bitterly cold here. And if you started a fire in the old chimney inside the house, park rangers would see the smoke and that would be the end of your little stay."

"Maybe." Hallie shrugged, obviously hating to give up on the idea. Changing the subject, she posed a question. "What are you going to do now, Delia? I mean, now that you're not going to marry Prentice charming. You've told me about your school and degree and what you can maybe do. But where do you think you'll want to work as an interior designer?"

Delia giggled. "Well, Tanner says I should put out my shingle in Gatlinburg and be a designer here. Isn't that crazy?"

"I don't know. What else did Tanner say?" Hallie lifted a brow curiously.

She waved a hand. "Oh, he said that since I already owned a house and could use Dee's old office space in the Crosswalk offices, that I'd have no overhead. He thought it would be a good set-up for me—that I could start up my own design business here without much financial risk." She rolled her eyes. "Tanner may know a lot about finances, but he doesn't know much about the design field. I mean, a lot of people do set up their own businesses eventually, after they gain experience in the field or become well-known, but they don't just start out at first on their own."

Delia stood up and brushed the lunch crumbs off her shorts. "I guess I'll search the internet for job opportunities and start sending out my resume soon," she added. "I have networks through school I can explore. Something will open up that will be right for me. It's not like I can't move anywhere I want to, since I'm on my own, you know."

Hallie got up, too, and strapped her backpack on.

They started off down the trail, heading back towards their car.

"You know," Hallie volunteered after a while. "It's not really such a dumb idea Tanner had about you starting your own business in Gatlinburg, Delia. I don't see why you couldn't do it."

Annoyance prickled Delia at her words. "Look, I've tried to explain. I've only had part-time work with my father's business over the summers and my internship in D. C. before I graduated. I don't have enough experience to start out on my own."

"Or maybe just not enough guts and confidence." Hallie tossed her head. "If you wouldn't have any overhead and didn't have to worry about income, I don't see what you'd lose by trying. The worst that could happen is that you'd bomb."

"Yes, and I'd really like another humiliation right now," Delia snapped.

"You see? It really is because you're afraid." Hallie gave her a smug smile.

"I'm not afraid." Delia's jaw clenched. "I'm only trying to be smart and sensible."

"All right, Miss Smarty," Hallie pressed. "What would it hurt to try your hand here while you look around? I bet our family in the furniture business could send some business your way if you asked them. And you said Tanner was supportive. He and Maureen know a lot of people. You could make up some business cards or fliers and give it a try."

"It's simply not a practical idea." Delia felt an angry flush rise up her neck. "You don't understand about the design business. Besides, you and Tanner both assume I might actually want to stay in Gatlinburg and live here."

"Well, excuse me." Hallie waved a hand. "I guess I forgot you might not want to live down here with your hillbilly cousins. I suppose a pokey, little town like Gatlinburg isn't fine enough for you coming from fancy Arlington, Virginia."

"I didn't say that!" Delia exclaimed.

"Well, it sounded like that to me," Hallie said, miffed.

They walked along the trail in silence, Hallie kicking pine cones whenever she could find them.

The woodsy trail wandered in and out of dappled sunlight, while to the left a small stream gurgled over mossy rocks. Delia heard the caw of a crow in the distance and, closer by, she thought she caught the *check, check* call of a warbler. She craned her head to look for it in the trees. Aunt Dee had taught Delia to know the sounds of many birds and to recognize them if she could see them.

"Let's not be mad," Delia offered at last, giving up on spotting the warbler. "Deciding on a first career job is a big decision. I need time to think about it, to know what I most want to do. Where the best opportunity will be. It is my life, you know, Hallie. You're always saying I should make my own decisions."

"Fine, so do it," returned Hallie sullenly.

Delia slowed her pace. "Why are you so interested in seeing me stay around here, anyway?"

Hallie turned to look at her. "Gee, that's a hard one. I thought we were becoming friends or something, Delia."

A little wave of surprise washed over Delia. "You'd like me to stay because we're friends?" she asked quietly.

"Well, sure." Hallie shrugged. "I guess that's the same reason Tanner wants you to stay, too. Unless there's something more with him."

Delia felt a slight flush creep up her face.

"Hmmmm," Hallie muttered. "That little blush is interesting. Has Tanner been putting some moves on you, Delia?"

"No, just flirting like always." Delia looked away. "You know how he is."

"Actually, I've never had Tanner Cross flirt with me ever." Hallie grinned, still watching Delia. "Maybe now and then I hoped he might, but he never did."

"Well, I've always noticed he flirts with just about everyone," Delia replied snippily, a little flustered now at this turn in the conversation.

Hallie giggled. "Do you like him?"

Delia sighed in resignation. "I used to have a big crush on him as a girl," she admitted. "But that was a long time ago."

"How long?" Hallie slowed her pace with interest.

"Well, the last time I saw Tanner I'd just turned thirteen. So you can see it was a really, really long time ago."

"Tanner is a good man," Hallie observed.

"I'm sure he is." Delia squared her shoulders. "But I'm not interested in getting into a relationship with anyone right now, Hallie Walker. So don't start trying to stir up a romance where there isn't one, you hear me? I already told you the other night about all my disasters with men. I've made a firm decision that I'm signing off on all men for a while. They're too much trouble. I want to get my life together instead. It seems like I'm always planning things around men, and when things don't work out with them, I'm back to square one. This time I want to get something going on my own that's all my own with no men involved."

"Well, you told me off right smartly there." Hallie lifted her eyebrows in admiration. "I think you might have some spunk and gumption after all, Delia Walker. I may have misjudged you earlier."

Delia blushed. "I didn't mean to be rude," she started.

"Now, don't go backing down," Hallie interrupted. "You go find your own life and make your own plan like you said. But don't be so stubborn that you can't consider ideas other folks may throw out now and then. Sometimes the best ideas sort of come to you at random, you know. My Grammie used to tell me that. She said sometimes we toss and worry and think and try to figure a way to a problem. And then one day the answer simply plops right in. You might dream it—or wake up one day and suddenly know what you've been trying to figure out all along."

"I've actually had that happen to me," Delia admitted, laughing a little. "I wish I'd known your Grammie Rayfield better. She seems to have been a very wise woman."

"Grammie had good common sense even though she didn't get much schooling." Hallie picked up her pace again. "I sure miss her sometimes."

The girls passed by the schoolhouse again and headed back over the ridge toward the stream and picnic grounds where they parked.

Hallie slanted Delia a glance. "Will you keep in touch with me when you move away?"

"Sure," Delia smiled. "I'll come see you at your bed and breakfast later on—if only to eat more of your good cooking and buy some of your breads."

"You think I'll really be good at that?" Hallie asked, a small touch of timidity slipping out from underneath her usual bravado.

"I think you'll be great at it," Delia assured her.

As they walked on back to the car, Delia found herself oddly touched by Hallie's desire to keep her close and by the fact that both Hallie and Tanner thought she had the ability to start her own design business. Delia was more used to people telling her what she couldn't do or shouldn't do. It felt novel to have anyone suggest she could do more than she'd even considered. And kind of flattering, too.

Chapter 8

Tanner sat in Aunt Dee's house tapping his foot impatiently. Seeing Delia head out earlier, he'd decided to check out a niggling theory about Hallie. He headed over to Dee's place and let himself in the house with his spare key. Sure enough, he saw plenty of evidence to prove Hallie Walker was staying here with Delia. He found her clothes and belongings in the upstairs bedroom, as well as personal identification in the billfold in her purse. From the Gatlinburg area map laid out on the kitchen table, it looked like the two girls had gone somewhere on a trip. Tanner had no idea where, but he hoped Hallie wouldn't get Delia into some kind of trouble.

Knowing the girls would probably be out for a while, Tanner went on to work. He found it hard to concentrate through the day, and at four o'clock, he took off early to come back to the house, finding the girls still not back. He'd sat here now for thirty minutes, watching the clock and wondering whether he ought to call the police. Something might have happened to those girls.

Delia's gray cat lay curled up beside him on the couch napping, obviously not worrying one little bit about his absent mistress and her stowaway friend. The cat had hissed at Tanner when he first came in, then ran and hid. Eventually, though, he came out cautiously to where Tanner sat in the living room, probably because Tanner had gotten cheese and crackers to snack on from the kitchen. Evidently the cat liked cheese, and Tanner soon lured the cat into a semblance of friendship by feeding him cheese bites.

As the cat lifted his ears now suddenly, Tanner offered him a nod of respect. He'd heard Delia's car pulling in even before Tanner did.

Hearing the girls let themselves into the back kitchen, laughing and giggling over something, Tanner rounded the corner to confront them. "It's about time you both got back." He scowled at them. "I was just about to call the police."

"Oh, my gosh," Hallie gasped, startled and scared at finding Tanner in the house. She began to quickly look around for a route of escape.

"Settle down, Hallie," Tanner assured her. "I figured out you were staying here, and I know about how you've supposedly run off to New York. You must have some good reasons for being here, and I'm open to hear them. I give you my word I won't do anything to blow your cover until I do. So calm down and quit looking around for the next quick jet out the door."

Delia, recovered now from her own shock, found her voice. "What are you doing in my house, Tanner Cross?" She glared at him. "You don't have any right to come over here and let yourself in whenever you want. And I think you need to give my spare key back to me right now."

"Look, Delia." He stiffened. "Just because you got yourself busted for hiding Hallie Walker over here doesn't mean you need to get up on your high horse about it."

He watched both the girls hesitate for a minute, eyeing each other, obviously trying to decide what they should do about this situation. "Let's go sit down and talk." He tried to sound nonchalant. "That's the sensible thing to do."

Tanner started into the living room and heard Delia and Hallie following him, Delia still muttering snippy complaints about how he had his nerve letting himself in her house and nearly scaring them both to death. He ignored her.

Hallie and Delia perched nervously on the couch together across from Tanner, while he settled into one of Dee's easy chairs. He noted the girls' dusty boots, and remembered they'd carried backpacks when they came in.

"Been hiking?" he asked casually, trying to lighten the mood.

"I took Delia to the Walker sisters' house." Hallie lifted her chin.

"You must have hidden in the floorboard of the car when you left." He picked at a nail. "I saw Delia leave, but I didn't see anyone else in the car with her."

"How did you know I was here?" Hallie blurted out. "I've been real careful since I got here last week."

"I agree." Tanner kept his voice casual. "I live right across the street, and I never saw a light or a sign anyone was here before Delia came. After Delia arrived, I never saw signs you were here, either."

Hallie leaned forward, curious. "Then how did you know?"

"Hobart came down to the store yesterday, worried about you. He told Mother and me about you running away to New York. He thought maybe you might contact one of us in time. Hoped if you did, we might tell you how much he wanted to hear from you, to know you were all right."

Hallie waited, watching him.

"Hobart and Mother kept saying how it wasn't like you to run off as you did. They both think something happened to upset you. Hobart's guess was Jonas Cole."

Delia's Place

Tanner saw Hallie wince and Delia look her way in sympathy.

He picked at his nail again. "Hobart said something, too, that got me to thinking later. That he had an intuition that maybe you hadn't really gone to New York, no matter how it looked. I've always trusted Hobart Rayfield's intuitions. There's Cherokee Indian in the Rayfield bloodlines—or so your grandmother told me—even with so many of you being redheaded amongst the black-haired ones."

His glance moved to Hallie's hair. "Anyway, it got me to thinking. I knew how close you were to Dee Walker and that she left you money. I also knew you'd be one of the few to know her house sat empty. So after I saw Delia leave, I thought I'd come and snoop around. I thought you might be staying in the shed or camping out in the area nearby. Maybe slipping into the house when Delia left. Just a hunch I wanted to follow up on. Instead, I find you neatly settled in, and obviously, Delia harboring your stay."

Hallie jumped in defensively at that comment. "Listen, Delia didn't even know I was here at first. So don't be mad at her. I confronted her on the back porch that first night after you left. Pretty much begged her to let me stay. I can leave if you don't want me here, Tanner. But I hope you won't tell anybody you saw me."

Delia leaned forward. "Hallie has a really good reason to need to be hiding out here, Tanner."

Tanner watched her slip her hand into Hallie's and he found the gesture touching somehow, even though he still felt provoked with them. "So tell me the reasons why you need to be here hiding out, Hallie." Tanner propped his feet up on the ottoman and crossed his ankles. "I've got time to listen."

Hallie related her whole story. About the problems she'd experienced with her mother and Jonas Cole, how Jonas tried to rape her, threatened her, and how she planned her escape and made her way to Delia's place.

"Well," Tanner pronounced when she finished. "I'm right glad—in a way—to know you helped Rita Jean get away from those druggie parents of hers. She certainly deserved a break." He paused thoughtfully. "And you say she's all right in New York, that she has someone to stay with and a good job?"

Hallie nodded.

"I need to think on all this for a while." He ran a hand through his hair. "In the meantime, Hallie, you've gotta tell me how you hiked all the way to Dee's house from way over in Cosby." He grinned at her. "Honey, that's a long way. You couldn't have hiked it in one day, even if you really pushed it."

"It did take me a while." Hallie relaxed a little, settling back against the couch. "Originally, I picked up Rita Jean in my little Volkswagen, but we had to hide it out somewhere and walk into the bus station when she left. Later, when dark fell, I sneaked back to the car, drove it to Greenbrier, and left it by the stable with a note for Uncle Hobart. Then I hiked up to that old Ramsey cabin on the ridge above the stable and spent the night there. I had my camping backpack, some food, and a bedroll, so it wasn't too bad. I felt safer sleeping by myself in that old cabin than outdoors."

"I know where that old place is," Tanner commented. "Harrison Ramsey keeps it nice. You were safer to sleep there than outside by yourself. That was smart, Hallie."

Hallie smiled a little at his praise, before picking up her story again. "The next morning early I hiked from the cabin up the horse trail to Grapeyard Ridge Trail. I followed it over the ridge and down to the old Cole cabin off the Motor Nature Road. I stopped there to rest and eat, and then walked the road a ways before catching another trail that brought me out near the upper end of Twin Creeks Trail where the Ogle cabin is. I rested there again. I'd come about eight miles by then and felt pretty worn out."

Tanner couldn't help smiling. "How'd you avoid the tourists who always drop in to see the Ogle place?"

"Oh, dusk had fallen by that time and no one was around." She shrugged. "It wasn't a problem. Before pitch dark fell, I walked in the last two miles down Twin Creeks Trail and cut through the woods path into Dee's back yard. Her place looked a welcome sight by then, and I felt real glad to find an old house key still hidden on top of the shed window. Dee always kept it there in case she locked herself out or in case Grammie did when she was cleaning."

Delia sat open-mouthed by now. "You came all that way by yourself?" she asked incredulously. "And spent the night in some old cabin alone?"

"I grew up in these mountains." Hallie sent her a smile. "I wasn't really afraid, only worried someone might see me before I could get here."

"I'm forced to admit you devised a good plan, Hallie." Tanner shifted his feet off the ottoman. "Also, you made effort, even when upset, to leave notes for people, trying to reassure your family you'd be all right, that you had someone to stay with in New York. You could have left with no word."

"Like my mother did when I was little." Hallie scowled and crossed her arms. "She just up and left one day. Weeks and weeks went by before she sent word about where she'd gone or even that she was all right."

"Did you ever try to talk to Sissy about Cole?" Tanner asked her.

"I told you I did." Her anger flashed. "More than once, too. The second time she lost her temper and slapped me. Told me I'd better not come to her with any more made-up stories about Cole simply because I didn't like him."

Delia shook her head. "I can't believe she wouldn't believe you about something like that."

Irritated, Hallie snapped at her. "Well, your fancy mother wasn't so quick to think the best of you about Prentice charming, either. I heard you trying to convince her on the phone you hadn't caused him to dump you."

Delia's Place

Delia flushed and dropped her eyes.

"Don't take it out on Delia because you're upset," Tanner cautioned with a warning edge to his voice.

Hallie frowned. "My point was, Tanner, that mothers aren't always the loving saints picture books paint them out to be. Delia's mother included."

"You're right," Delia admitted with a sigh. "My mother might not have slapped me, but she's certainly thrown her share of verbal abuse my way."

Hallie stood up suddenly, breaking everyone's thought pattern. "I'm hungry," she announced. "I'm going into the kitchen to heat up the rest of the chicken casserole from last night and make some things for supper. Do you wanna eat with us, Tanner?"

"Sure," he said. "If you've got enough."

"I have plenty, and I'm going to make some salad and bread, too. You two can sit here and argue over my fate while I do."

With a defiant toss of her head, she turned to start toward the kitchen, but then paused to look back at Tanner. "I'll ask you the same thing I did of Delia when I came, Tanner. If you feel you can't keep my secrets, or if you don't want me to stay here, you just tell me. I have other places I can go. But don't call the police or my family thinking you're doing me a favor. They'd send me right back home to Jonas. You know they would. He'd really make me pay for running off. You've got to know that. Jonas Cole likes to get what he wants. When he doesn't get his way, he can turn nasty."

She turned and walked around the corner into the kitchen.

"The sound of that man really scares me," Delia whispered, with a shiver. "Do you know him, Tanner? Is he as bad as Hallie says?"

"Yeah. I'm afraid he is." Tanner's jaw clenched. "And maybe worse. I've heard some pretty bad tales about him—especially when he got drunk or vengeful. I always thought Jonas had a loose spark up there somewhere. Sometimes he can seem totally normal and charming, but other times ...." He left the thought unfinished.

Delia winced. "Will you let Hallie stay here, Tanner? It's all right with me. She is my cousin, after all. Actually, I've been glad for her company." She looked away, a shadow crossing over her face. "It's helped to keep my mind off things."

Tanner studied her face. "Well, I need to think about all of this," he replied candidly. "And if Hallie plans to stay here for any length of time, we need to tell my mother she's here. Mother's house is half a block away. Inevitably, one day she's going to figure things out. See Hallie coming or going. Come to the house and catch her here. I may decide Hallie can be harbored for a time, but I don't want to lie to my mother. Besides, Hallie may need Mother's support and friendship when you leave later on, Delia. Especially if she really intends to stay here until November."

"Hallie might be upset if we tell your mother," Delia worried, biting on her lip.

Tanner watched Delia absently chewing on her lip and suddenly found his thoughts drifting off into an entirely different direction. He let his eyes slide over Delia admiringly. She wore little red shorts. Short shorts, with her cute rounded legs curled up on the couch underneath her. And that snug little stripy t-shirt hugging her well-rounded breasts. Just looking at them now caused Tanner's heartbeat to escalate.

"What?' she asked, sensing a change in his focus.

He gave her a wolfish grin. "You do things to me sometimes, Delia Walker," he told her softly. "I don't know quite yet what I'm going to do about it."

Her eyebrows lifted in surprise. "Honestly," she huffed. "Well, I certainly know what I'm going to do—go to the kitchen to get something to eat." She flounced out of the room as she spoke, but Tanner watched a flush rise up her neck and over her face as she headed towards the kitchen. He got up to follow behind her, enjoying the view from the back as she walked ahead of him.

Hallie had set the table on the back screen porch for their supper. As typical of Hallie, she'd thrown together a tasty dinner in quick time, and had even lit one of Dee's jar candles on their dinner table. A subtle scent of vanilla fragrance filled the air.

As they ate dinner, Tanner asked Hallie questions about John Dale and learned that he knew where Hallie hid, also. From her chattering about the bed and breakfast and their future plans to marry, Tanner figured the two of them still a serious item.

"I remember when John Dale moved here," Tanner told Delia. "He was about eight years old, seven years younger than me, and his sister Mary Alice a year older than me. The Madisons only live a few streets away, Delia. Rev. Madison is the minister at Mother's and my church—and the one your Aunt Dee went to."

He chuckled as he buttered another of Hallie's rolls. "I recall Mary Alice hated it here in Tennessee, missed South Carolina, and went back to Charleston to college as soon as she graduated. Married a local boy there. Has one child and another on the way now." He bit into the roll. "John Dale was just the opposite. Took to the mountains like a duck to water. Loved it here. Spent a lot of time out of doors at his grandmother Ogle's place and constantly hiked and explored the mountains around Mynatt Park and Gatlinburg."

Tanner could remember taking John Dale fishing with him and his father several times. John Dale had been a Scout like Tanner, and Tanner remembered helping with John Dale's Cub group, too. He always liked the boy and could still recall the summer when John Dale and Hallie started lighting up sparks whenever they sat in a room together. They'd always been friends, but then suddenly something else kicked in.

Tanner found himself studying the candle on the table while thinking back. The inviting aroma of vanilla drifted up from it.

"Penny for your thoughts, Tanner," Hallie asked.

Not wanting to tell her exactly where his thoughts wandered, he said instead, "Actually, I was looking at this candle and wondering if you ever helped Dee make her candles when you hung out here."

"Sure." Hallie licked a last bite of casserole off her spoon. "Especially when Dee's health started to suffer the last year or two. I came and helped her mix and stir the wax, and pour out the candles every week. It's hard physical work when you're making a big batch, you know."

He lifted an eyebrow in interest. "Think you could do it on your own?"

"What?" She looked briefly bewildered. "You mean make candles?"

"Yeah," he replied, the idea beginning to take shape now as he thought about it. "We've only got one more box of Dee's Mountain Way candles in the storeroom at Crosswalk. Mother was regretting the other day there wouldn't be any more. They sell well, Hallie. You could start making them for something to do while you're here and we could sell them. It could make you a little money."

"Well, maybe." She squinted at him. "I'd have to go out to the shed and see if Dee's old candle recipes and notes are still there. Then I'd have to experiment. See if I could do it alone." She frowned. "I don't have much money for supplies, though, Tanner. I might be limited in what I could do."

"I'll front you." Tanner grinned. "Just to keep the candles coming into the store. Whatever profit we make from them you can keep. Also we'll let the public believe we're still selling off Dee's old surplus for now."

"It might work," said Hallie, obviously considering it.

"Is it hard to make candles?" Delia asked.

"Yes and no." Hallie turned to her. "It's kind of like cooking. Most anybody can follow a recipe and do it, but with some artistry and experience, you get a better product. I know Dee worked for a long time to get her recipe exactly the way she liked it for her jar candles. She used beeswax in her mix and was real fussy about her scents. She played around with the colors, mixing and experimenting, until she created some really unique color blends that were sort of her signature."

Tanner smiled. "You see. I knew I was getting a great idea the minute I thought of this. With summer moving in, you could really make some money, Hallie."

Her eyes brightened. "I'll go out to the shed and look things over tomorrow."

"Maybe I could help you," Delia offered.

"Maybe." Hallie gave her an appraising look. "But I'd much rather see you do a little decorating for some offices around Gatlinburg." She sent Tanner a sly look. "I'll bet Tanner's office and the Crosswalk offices could use somebody to give them a nice face lift. Maureen sent me upstairs on an errand once, while I worked at Crosswalk, and I remember everything looked pretty old and dated. . ."

Tanner interrupted. "Hallie, that's a great idea. The offices could use some sprucing up." He turned to Delia. "It would give you a little something to put on your resume, Delia. You could take before and after photos and use them to help you in your job searching. Call it a summer experience after graduation."

Delia crossed her arms and gave them both a glare. "You two are simply not going to give up on this, are you?"

They shook their heads conspiratorially.

"Well, I'll think about it. And that's all," she warned. "But I don't see why I can't try to help you make candles, too, Hallie. Sometimes I used to watch Aunt Dee make candles when I visited over the summers."

Before Hallie could answer, a voice floated in from outside the screened porch. "Here you are, Tanner." Maureen laughed. "You were supposed to come over to supper tonight, and when you didn't drop by, I started looking for you. I saw your car parked in your driveway and the lights on at Dee's, so I guessed I might find you here."

As Maureen opened the screened door, her words dropped off. "Hallie Walker? Is that you? Good gracious, child, everyone's been so worried about you!"

Hallie, Delia, and Tanner gave a collective groan.

"I guess that idea of mine, of bringing Mother into the picture about Hallie, is going to be sooner rather than later," Tanner muttered.

Hallie got up to hug Maureen and, to Delia and Tanner's surprise, burst into tears as she tried to tell Maureen why she was here.

After Maureen sat down, Hallie told the whole story all the way through again, and Maureen agreed the best place for Hallie right now was anywhere away from Jonas Cole. "If this situation becomes a problem or if anyone learns Hallie is here," Maureen stated matter-of-factly, "I'll take Hallie down to my sister's place in Mississippi. Harriet would be glad to have her. And she'd be safe there."

Hallie grinned at Maureen in relief. "Well, I wondered how I was going to make candles to take into the store for Tanner without you figuring out something was going on. I guess that won't be a problem now."

"What's this?" Maureen asked excitedly, leaning forward. "Do you really think you can make Dee's candles?"

Naturally, this led Maureen and Hallie into an animated discussion about Dee Ward's candles. Tanner looked over toward Delia and gestured toward the dishes still sitting on the table. "While you two talk about candles, Delia and I are going to clean up the dishes from dinner. Did you eat, Mother, or do you want me to bring you a plate out?"

"No, I ate at home." She waved him away before turning back to Hallie again.

In the kitchen, Delia found some plastic wrap and food containers and put the leftovers away. She and Tanner made quick work of the supper dishes.

"Wanna walk me home?" Tanner suggested afterwards. "I'm tired, and I have an early meeting in the morning."

"It's only across the street," Delia grumbled. "You hardly need me to walk over there with you."

"I thought we could go to the old swing on the way and look at the stars."

Delia smiled in spite of herself. "Is that old swing still there?" Her voice sounded wistful. "I thought it would have fallen apart by now."

"No, it's still there."

An old metal two-seater swing had hung off the limb of a big oak at the end of Balsam Lane ever since Delia first started coming to see Aunt Dee. It sat back behind a hedge of forsythia bushes, not readily visible from the road. Aunt Dee had called it the star-gazing swing, and she took Delia out at night to sit in the swing, lean back, and look up at the stars in the night sky. Sometimes Tanner joined them, since Aunt Dee often took him out to the green metal swing to teach him the stars and constellations, too.

As they grew older, Delia and Tanner started going out to the swing at night to star gaze by themselves. They'd sit in the old swing, lean back, look up into the night sky, and see who could name the most stars and constellations.

Tanner could see Delia's mind remembering, as a soft smile drifted over her face. "Oh, come on," he pressed. "Mom and Hallie are on a roll out there talking about candle-making. They won't even miss us."

"All right." Delia smiled. "But let me go tell them you're leaving, and that I'm seeing you out. Okay?"

She did so, and the two of them walked into the darkness and headed toward the end of Balsam Lane. The forsythia, in full bloom now, created a golden hedge at the end of the little street. From the woods beyond, Tanner could smell the honeysuckle on the air and, against the shadows, see the lightning bugs blinking off and on.

"Look!" Delia said, pointing to them. "Remember when we used to run around and try to catch them?"

He nodded. "Yeah, and you'd pout if I didn't let every one of them out of the jar before we went home."

They found the old swing and settled down on it, both leaning back so they could look up at the night sky. Delia was soon pointing out the dippers and looking for all the familiar night sky constellations. Tanner played along with pleasure, enjoying the feel of her in the swing next to him, liking the occasional wafts of some soft, floral scent that still lingered on her skin at the end of the day.

Sitting here with Delia and looking up at the stars seemed familiar, but many of Tanner's feelings felt new and surprising to him. He found himself drawn to Delia in a strong, fresh way he wasn't sure he understood yet. He knew he felt physically attracted to her; that was easy to discern. Every time he came close to her now, it seemed like every electrolyte in his body got aroused.

Antsy with that physical attraction stirring him now, Tanner stood up and turned to put his hands on the back of the swing to look down at her. "Are you going to be all right having Hallie with you?" he asked. "She's still a teenager, underage, and might be a handful for you sometimes."

"I think it will be all right," Delia answered on a soft note with a catch in her breath.

Tanner realized then she felt aware of him, too. "It's a lot the same and yet a lot different between us now, isn't it, Delia?" he asked huskily, moving a little closer until his legs were on either side of hers.

She didn't answer, but he heard her suck in her breath rapidly and felt her knees tremble against the side of his legs as he stood looking down at her.

The next thing he knew, he'd leaned over to brush his lips over her mouth. Just softly back and forth while he cupped her face in his hands—a sweet and instinctive moment, and not the wolfish assault he'd thought about so often.

Delia sighed, a soft little sigh. Relishing the moment, Tanner held himself back from taking the kiss deeper. Instead, he pulled Delia to her feet to hold her against him for a moment. He buried his fingers in her hair and savored the feel of her against the length of his body. Enjoyed the pleasure of feeling her heart beating against his.

Tanner fully expected Delia to bolt any minute, but she seemed surprisingly compliant. When he drew her back to look down into her eyes, she smiled wistfully, watching him with wide-eyed innocence.

For once, Tanner couldn't quite decide what to do. He felt like anything he said to her now would seem silly. And he was afraid if he kissed her again that he'd lose this moment of sweet control.

Just when he'd started to decide it really didn't matter—that he'd risk losing control—Hallie called to them from the house. "Delia, your sister's on the phone!" Her voice rang out. And the moment was broken.

Delia's Place

To Tanner's surprise, Delia chuckled softly in the dark. Then she gave Tanner a quick kiss on the mouth and took off for the house, calling to Hallie, "I'm coming."

Tanner stood shaking his head for a moment, wondering what would have happened if the phone call hadn't come when it did. Then he shrugged and headed off toward his house. Delia Walker had only just arrived here at Balsam Lane. There would be a lot more opportunities to test the waters between them. He distinctly looked forward to that idea.

Chapter 9

Delia lay in the bed the next morning, berating herself for yielding to the moment and kissing Tanner Cross. "Whatever is the matter with you, Delia? First you gave him that kiss in his office and now you kissed him out by the swing. There's no telling what Tanner must be thinking about you for acting like this—shamelessly flirting and kissing some other man with your engagement to Prentice barely ended." Delia moaned and tucked her head into her pillow.

Last night, she had struggled for hours with a tormenting mix of emotions while trying to fall asleep. First remembering how sweet Tanner acted at the swing, how he made her feel, all light-headed and fuzzy. Then remembering—that only last month—she'd been kissing Prentice, feeling all light-headed and fuzzy with him.

She groaned. "What's wrong with you? Are these feelings with Tanner the same or different than the ones you had with Prentice?"

Prentice made her feel excited, but she never felt the tenderness for him she felt with Tanner. Or felt as comfortable with Prentice as she did with Tanner. She bit her lip. "To be honest, Prentice often made me feel silly – laughed at my thoughts and fancies, chided me when I got excited about a full moon or stopped to watch a sandpiper darting in and out of the waves down at the beach." Tanner took as much joy as Delia did in small things – catching lightning bugs, naming constellations, or just remembering old times.

"Well, no matter what, I'm still glad I made the decision to come to Gatlinburg." Delia sighed. "But I sometimes wish Tanner hadn't been here to confuse things so. I'm really not ready to start new feelings about someone else right now." She punched her pillow. "In fact, I hate myself for still having feelings for Tanner Cross and for being attracted to him after all these years. It's pathetic that I'm so excited he's interested in me now that I've grown older. And simply pitiful how easily I've followed along with his little flirtation with me."

Delia frowned, turning restlessly under the covers. "I really shouldn't lead Tanner on. I have no intention of getting involved with anyone else right now. And I don't want Tanner to get the wrong idea."

Sounds from the kitchen let Delia know Hallie was up. She needed to get up, too. Pulling herself out of the bed, she padded into the bathroom.

"Delia Walker," she told herself in the mirror. "You've got to stop this flirting with Tanner Cross. And get your life together." With new resolve, she pulled on some clothes and headed out to the kitchen.

"Good morning." Hallie glanced up from the stove as Delia came in the kitchen door. "I'm trying out an omelet recipe I found in a magazine. Sit down; it's nearly ready."

Delia thought about telling her that she usually only ate cereal, but the smells wafting around the kitchen quickly changed her mind. "What's in that?" she asked instead, sniffing the air.

Hallie grinned. "Onions, peppers, and mushrooms that I stir-fried ahead of time, then eggs, two kinds of cheese, some chopped tomatoes, and some secret spices."

On the table, Hallie had already set out two plates, with sliced oranges in a side dish and two slices of wheat toast hot and waiting in the toaster.

"How do you stay so thin if you eat like this all the time?" Delia groused.

"I have a high energy level." Hallie cut the omelette into two pieces and slid them neatly onto the plates. "And eating healthy foods doesn't make people become overweight. It's junk food that does that."

"Eating too much of any kind of food can cause people to become overweight." Delia dropped into a kitchen chair and picked up an orange slice. "And my genetics are predisposed to excess weight on the Walker side."

Hallie glanced her way. "So tell me what you usually eat for breakfast."

"Cereal, milk, juice, maybe fruit. Sometimes a bagel or a muffin."

"Well, if you added up the calories in all that, this breakfast would have far less calories overall—and also way less carbohydrates."

"So when did you become a food expert?" Delia asked, a little annoyed.

"I've been studying up." Hallie gave her a smug smile. "You have to know all these things to run a bed and breakfast inn." They bantered about food and nutrition while they settled down to split the omelet Hallie made.

"Ummm. I have to admit, your omelet is wonderful." Delia finished the last bite with reluctance. "I wish I'd learned more about cooking as I grew up."

"Didn't your mother teach you?" Hallie spread jam on her toast.

"Not hardly." Delia snorted. "By the time I was born, Mrs. Beeker, the housekeeper, did most of the cooking. She lived in with us, above the garage in her own apartment. Mother stayed home with her first three children. By the time I came along ten years after the others, she'd gone back to work in the store and didn't want to come home to do another baby. Mrs. Beeker took care of me and kept the house, too. She got more money, but I think she wished things had stayed the way they were before, with the other three children out to school all day. Richard—the youngest—was already ten, Frances thirteen, and Howie sixteen when I was born. All neatly three years apart."

Hallie nibbled on her toast. "So your mother wasn't excited when she found out she was pregnant again?"

"No. Absolutely not." Delia got up to pour herself another cup of coffee. "At thirty-six, she thought she'd started early menopause when she skipped her first periods with me. Mrs. Beeker always called me 'the mistake.'"

Hallie's mouth dropped open. "How mean of her to say that."

"Mrs. Beeker was never noted for tact and never very fond of me."

"Why not?"

Delia looked back. "I was a dreamy, moody, imaginative little thing—Mrs. Beeker, precise, factual, and scheduled, with not an imaginative bone in her body. We were as different as night and day. I always felt I intruded into her well-ordered life and schedule. In fact, she often told me I did."

"You're kidding?" Hallie propped her elbows on the table. "She sounds really awful."

"She had this big daily calendar on the refrigerator with the day's schedule on it," Delia remembered. "With a posted time for everything listed on it. Mrs. Beeker liked everything done on schedule at the right time." She sighed. "Babies and small children don't fit rigid schedules very easily, so I was always inconveniencing Mrs. Beeker."

"Sheesh." Hallie rolled her eyes. "Was she that way with the other children when they were little, too?"

"Mrs. Beeker didn't join the family until Howie, Richard, and Frances were well into school. So they only had to deal with her in the afternoon when they got home." Delia grinned. "Mrs. Beeker never quite got the other kids in line with all her rigid routines either. They'd known a lot of freedom before—and not as much restriction with Mother not working. Frances often told me Mother was more fun and relaxed in those early years."

She ate a last bite of orange thoughtfully. "Howie and Richard called Mrs. Beeker 'The Beek.' Even to her face they often called her Mrs. Beek instead of Mrs. Beeker." She giggled. "Frances and the boys never seemed to take Mrs. Beeker as seriously as I did. And they didn't get in trouble for not obeying her to the letter like I did, either."

"Poor little Delia." Hallie's lips twitched. "Sounds like you had it rough. But, hey, get over it. You're a grown woman now. That's the past."

Her flippant tone rankled Delia. "That's easy to say, Hallie, but don't you still hear your Grammie's corrections in your mind? Don't you hear your mother's criticism? I hear Mrs. Beeker and Mother in my mind all the time—and it's never uplifting."

Hallie leaned forward. "See. That's where you and I are different, Delia. If I did hear that, I wouldn't let it dictate to me. I didn't listen much to what people told me growing up unless it seemed sensible. Unless it felt right. Or unless I knew they were telling me something I could learn from. When people's words are just mean-spirited and don't mean you well, you need to let them slide off you. Don't let them sink in."

"That's easier said than done." Again, Delia marveled at the insight of this seventeen-year-old.

"Look." Hallie put her palms on the table. "Obviously you had some things about your childhood that weren't so great. So did I. But some things were good. Admit it. You had your needs met probably 90% better than most kids. You had a lot of privileges and opportunities most kids never get. Trips and traveling. Lessons in stuff like piano and swimming. Camps and clubs. Pretty clothes. Probably more toys. You got your education paid for, and two degrees, too." She grinned. "Look on the bright side, Delia. It could have been a lot worse. Nobody beat you. Nobody was an alcoholic or hooked on drugs in your family. You never had to worry if you were going to eat. You never had people laugh at you in school because your clothes weren't nice. A lot of my friends had bad stuff happen in their lives. And they've moved on. Gotten past it."

She got up to put some dishes into the sink. "Hold on to what's good now and get over the rest, Delia. It's only going to hurt you to keep dwelling on all the bad and to keep thinking about all the negatives."

Hallie poured out some more coffee and came back to sit down at the kitchen table. "Tell me a good memory about your mother," she demanded.

Delia stopped to think a minute, and smiled. "Mother always loved to watch Frances and me twirl. We took baton and were both majorettes in school. Mother always came to watch our recitals and took pictures. She always came—no matter how busy she was—and she made Daddy and the boys come when we marched in the parades or performed at football games. She created a special shelf for our twirling trophies, too."

"You won trophies for twirling?" Hallie grinned. "You must have been good."

Delia shrugged. "Frances started teaching me early. I loved it because it was something I could do with her. Mother hired a seamstress to make me a little costume exactly like Frances's high school majorette costume, and I got to march out with all the majorettes for the games. I loved that."

"See?" Hallie waved a finger in the air. "Your mother was proud and supportive of you sometimes. And she made your whole family get in there and support you. It also sounds like you had a good sister if she played with you and included you like that."

Delia sighed. "I lived for Frances, Howie, and Richard to come home from school. The whole house came alive and became a fun place. They were all good to include me in little things in their lives, even though I was so much younger."

Hallie smiled in satisfaction. "All right, now remember something good about Mrs. Beeker."

Delia made a face. "That's hard."

"Come on," Hallie pushed. "There's got to be something."

Delia struggled to recall a good memory to humor Hallie. "Okay. She saved magazines for me. She knew I loved house and decorating magazines, and she saved me old magazines from her apartment and let me have them to cut up. She also bought me paper dolls. Of course, she knew I'd sit for hours and play with these and stay out of her way, but, still, she did buy them for me. I think she even bought some of them with her own money, but I can't be sure."

"See how you're starting to feel better now that you're remembering the good stuff?" Hallie insisted. "My Grammie used to make me do that. She was a big one to look on the bright side. She even had a favorite hymn about always keeping on the sunny side of life. One of her favorite scriptures that she quoted by memory was how you should always focus on whatsoever things are good, true, lovely, of good report, and all that. That you should think on those things instead of negative stuff."

"Well, I do have happy family memories," Delia admitted. "More happy ones than bad. It's just seems lately the bad ones came swamping in on me when all this stuff with Prentice happened."

"Everybody gets in a funk when they get dumped." Hallie shrugged. "It's natural. If you'd figured out what a creep Prentice was before all this happened and before he dumped you, you'd have dumped him first. Then you'd be feeling good now. In the cat bird seat."

Delia thought about that. "Maybe that's why Tanner doesn't feel so bad about his broken engagement with Melanie. Because he broke it off and not her."

With the mention of Tanner's name, Hallie lifted her eyebrows. "Seems to me like some subtle little fireworks were going off between the two of you last night."

"No. There weren't. Don't think that." Delia stiffened. "It's too soon for me to be having feelings for someone else after Prentice! And Tanner is only flirting. I told you he does that."

"If you say so," Hallie replied nonchalantly.

"Hey." Hallie changed the subject. "I'm going out to the shed and get into Dee's candle making stuff now. See what's there. Find out what materials are on hand and see if I can find some recipes, so I can start making up some candles. I know I saw lots of boxes filled with jars out there earlier. Dee got to where she only made jar candles."

"I'll come help you," Delia offered.

For the next hour or two the girls explored the shed and then got out cleaning supplies and cleaned the place from top to bottom. While Delia made an effort to sort through and organize supplies on the shelves, Hallie began reading over Dee's old handwritten candle recipes and looking for the items needed in Dee's notes. She got increasingly testy with this task, and finally Delia got provoked.

"You're getting cranky and bossy over all this now," she complained. "Every time I try to ask you anything, you snap at me."

"Huh?" Hallie asked, surprised. Then she grinned at Delia. "I'm a real crank when I'm trying to get something figured out, Delia. Give me a little while to read and study and get this place all set up the way I want it, and then I'll be nice again." She looked back down at an old recipe she was studying. "Why don't you go down to Gatlinburg and get Tanner something for his birthday. You're still going to that party thing tonight with him, aren't you?"

"Oh, mercy, I'd almost forgotten!" Delia exclaimed. "Thanks for reminding me. But are you sure it will be all right if I go off and leave you?"

"Sure. Go. Maybe when you get back I'll have all this sorted through and be in a better mood. Maybe then we can try making some candles if I can make sense of Aunt Dee's notes here."

"Okay," Delia agreed, glad to be off to a happier task. "Do you want me to bring you anything from town?"

"Certainly not a bear pack," Hallie teased.

"Smarty. Maybe you won't get anything at all!" Delia sauced back at her.

Hallie looked up from her task. "Get me something to give Tanner for his birthday." She stopped to think. "Maybe a trout fishing book. The guy loves to fish. Or a jar of stick candy from that candy shop in Laurel Village. Aunt Dee sometimes used to get him a jar when I went to town with her—said it was a favorite of his."

"I'll see what I can do," Delia promised.

As she drove down to Gatlinburg, Delia found herself thinking back on her breakfast conversation with Hallie. Considering that Hallie had known a rough upbringing, she held a surprisingly good outlook on life—practical and positive in her thinking, more like Frances. She didn't seem to wear her feelings on her sleeve either. That's what Delia's mother said Delia did, while Frances shrugged things off more easily.

Well, maybe she could change. Maybe she could get tougher and more confident. Work on not being so sensitive. Perhaps Hallie was right about how focusing on the negative always made things worse. She needed to look more on the bright side. As Hallie said, try to "move on and get past it."

Delia thought about Prentice, too, as she drove along. "If I had known that Prentice was involved with MacKenzie when I visited Baltimore this spring, I would have broken up with him. Right then, too. Just like I did with Vince when I learned he was cheating on me. I probably wouldn't be grieving so much now, either. Hallie was right about that. It only hurt so much because he made a fool of me—dumped and humiliated me in front of all my friends and family."

She imagined being with Prentice now that she knew all she did about him, and found herself turning up her nose. "He cheated on me, lied to me, and probably used me and my family." She gripped the steering wheel tighter with the thought. "Hallie's right. I need to get over him."

But Delia found it hard to get over old dreams. Quite frankly, her heart still hurt, and she felt bruised and wounded. Granted, she felt a little better each day, but there was still pain, and she knew bad moments. "Oh, well," she told herself. "With time, maybe everything truly will be better."

Later, after poking around in Gatlinburg for an hour and buying a jar of stick candy for Hallie to give Tanner, Delia found exactly what she wanted for Tanner's birthday. Glancing at her watch and noticing it was nearly noon, Delia decided to see if Maureen had time to get a salad or a sandwich with her for lunch. She had a few things she wanted to talk to her about.

After checking in the store, she found Maureen upstairs in the Crosswalk office, working on a pile of paperwork and making phone calls. A woman named Bess directed her up the back steps leading to the offices above the store. As Delia walked through the downstairs craft mall, she noticed it was beautifully arranged—interesting and colorful with its aisles of craft items and sales booths. Upstairs, however, the charm stopped.

Delia looked around the entry area as she got to the top of the steps, wrinkling her nose in distaste at the bland and sterile off-white walls, droopy, fake ficus plants, and a handful of chairs covered with orange vinyl. Ugh. A decorator's nightmare.

Tanner's office hadn't been as bad. The wood furniture was of good quality, and the brown leather sofas in the entry area looked somewhat new; however, admittedly, the rest of the T. Cross décor appeared bland—the walls decorated only with an assortment of accounting plaques and sun-faded mountain prints.

Letting herself into the Crosswalk offices, Hallie waited in the entry area for Maureen to get off the phone in her adjoining office. A comfortable sofa and a few chairs filled the space here, but the floral upholstery on the sofa and chairs had seen better days. In addition, the symmetry of the framed prints and photographs on the walls was uninspiring. Delia fought to keep her mind from clicking with ideas for improvement—always a problem as a designer.

"Sorry I made you wait," Maureen offered now, coming out of her office. "I'm trying to catch up on books and ordering today. I was on the phone talking to one of our suppliers in Ohio. I order shop bags and boxes from them."

"It's all right." Delia smiled. "I just dropped by to see if you'd had lunch yet. I thought maybe we could go out together."

Delia saw the pleasure light Maureen's face. "No, I haven't eaten yet—been too busy. What were you thinking about for lunch?"

"Hallie's feeding me so well, I thought I'd order a big salad today. Any suggestions? Perhaps a place near by—something you'd enjoy, too?"

"Absolutely. The Garden Café, right behind the store, has some wonderful salads." Maureen hunted for her purse. "There's a delicious Cobb salad on the menu, a nice Caesar, and an excellent salad entree topped with grilled chicken, mandarin oranges, and sugared pecans. George always serves a homemade soup every day, too. I think on Friday it's tomato dill."

They walked to the nearby Garden Cafe and settled into a table on the patio porch. Like in most areas of Gatlinburg, hanging baskets spilling with colorful flowers hung outside the porch windows. Bees hovered over the blossoms, and as Delia watched, a hummingbird darted in to slip its long bill into a pink trumpet-like bloom.

Delia pointed to the bird in delight.

Maureen nodded. "George planted a row of butterfly bushes behind the patio wall a few years ago. Butterfly bushes draw in the hummingbirds, you know, and sometimes a few sneak over here to sample the flowers in the hanging baskets."

Maureen had introduced Delia to George Deacon, the owner of the restaurant, when they arrived. It seemed obvious he and Maureen were well-acquainted.

When the waitress came, Delia ordered a house salad and tomato dill soup, and Maureen ordered a vegetable plate.

"Where's Hallie today?" Maureen asked.

"Working out in the shed trying to figure out how to make candles." Delia grinned at Maureen. "I helped for a while this morning, but then I left Hallie poring over Dee's old recipes and came downtown to do a little shopping."

Maureen squeezed lemon into her iced tea. "I can't tell you how delighted I am that Hallie remembers as much as she does about making candles with Dee. I guess I'd forgotten how much she worked with Dee in the shed those last two years. She told me Dee paid her to help after school. The work evidently got too intensive for Dee when she started having problems with her health."

"Hallie said if she could figure out some of the recipes that we might try a batch of candles when I get back this afternoon."

Maureen unwrapped her silver and spread a napkin over her lap. "Well, it might take some experimenting, and some trial and error, before Hallie and you are able to make candles on your own. It isn't as easy as you'd think."

"Maureen, are you really all right about Hallie staying with me at Dee's for a while?" Delia asked. "I've been worried that you and Tanner might think badly of me for taking her in and letting her stay with me... and, especially, for not telling either of you."

"No." Maureen waved a hand. "I know Hallie, and I doubt you had much choice." She smiled. "Also, Hallie would have bolted if she thought you planned to tell anyone at first. Even though Hallie acts plucky and strong, she's scared now. In my opinion, she has a right to be."

Delia bit her lip. "Do you think people will look for Hallie around here?"

"No. I think most people really believe she's gone to New York. If Hallie gets her friend Rita Jean to write a letter, supposedly from Hallie, postmarked from New York that will help to keep the story going." Maureen paused. "Hallie does not need to go back around Jonas Cole, and, frankly, it worries me that Hallie's mother, Sissy, is married to a man like that. He's a time bomb that could go off someday. I think he has some serious mental issues."

The waitress brought their food, interrupting their conversation. When she left, Delia said, "You know, Maureen, despite the fact that Hallie's mother left her as a child, Hallie seems a wonderful and well-adjusted person."

"Adversity often builds character." Maureen looked up from her plate. "And don't forget Hallie had her Rayfield grandparents in her life—very fine people. I was especially fond of Hallie's grandmother, Etta Mae. You probably remember she cleaned for me and for your Aunt Dee for years." Maureen smiled. "Etta Mae often felt real sorry for Dee and me because we both had so few domestic talents in comparison to hers. She gardened, put up food, and was one of the best cooks I've ever known. I'm afraid my culinary and gardening efforts pale in comparison to hers."

"She seems to have passed her cooking genes and talents along to Hallie," Delia remarked. "Hallie will hardly let me in the kitchen, and she insists on doing all the housework, as well."

"She's proud," said Maureen, finishing off a portion of macaroni and cheese. "She wants to do her share and earn her keep. That's a good trait, really. When she worked for me at the store, she was one of the best young clerks I ever had. You know, a lot of young girls haven't learned how to work hard and don't exhibit very good work ethics on the job either. That wasn't true of Hallie Walker, and she made a surprisingly good sales person, too."

"It's hard to believe she's only seventeen sometimes," Delia remarked.

Delia's Place

They talked on about other things, including reminiscing about past times with Aunt Dee as they ate. After a while, Delia told Maureen all about Prentice and what happened to their engagement.

"And how are you doing with all that now, Delia?" Maureen asked kindly.

"Well, actually I'm beginning to question my feelings for Prentice at this point." She willed herself not to get teary. "Prentice was much older than me – ten years older, very charming and very smooth. I think I felt fascinated with Prentice and flattered that he took interest in me. I'm not sure now that I ever knew or loved him. That's hard for me to admit, but ours was mostly a long distance romance those two years. We only spent time together on holidays and occasional long weekends, and I didn't know Prentice as a person very well. I'm beginning to believe, too, that much of what I thought of as romantic love on Prentice's part was mostly an act with him."

"There's healing already occurring if you can talk about things as honestly as you are now." Maureen patted her hand. "That's a good sign."

As they started back to the office, Maureen launched into a new topic. "Tanner tells me you might redecorate the offices for us upstairs while you're here." She turned to smile at Delia. "I hope that's true, because I know they really need it. We haven't done much with the space for years, partly because none of us knew what to do. And partly because we've been too busy doing other things. I hope you'll consider giving us some time. We'd insist on paying you, of course. I know you're a certified designer, and I'm sure you'll make those old upstairs rooms look beautiful."

Delia smiled. "You're all so nice to want me to gain some decorating experience while I'm here, but it's really not necessary."

"Maybe not for you." Maureen put a hand on her hip. "But it is for us. Seriously, Delia, you know the offices look very dated. Since we both have clients coming there to meet with us, we really need to have those rooms redone. I've been considering it for a long time, but I simply didn't know anyone to trust with the job. Some of the decorators around here are either terrible or a bit shady. A lot of people have encountered some bad experiences, especially on the corporate side."

Delia considered the idea. "Well, if I do decide to do some redecorating, I'll draw you up a plan and get your approval first," she explained. "I'll also write up estimates on the work that needs to be done, and I absolutely will not allow you to pay me for my time. It's bad enough Dee left me an interest in your business, and that I'm not doing any work toward earning the money I'm receiving from Crosswalk."

They argued for a time over this, but Delia finally won. Or at least she thought she'd won. As she drove home, she realized she'd solidly committed herself to redecorate the T. Cross and Crosswalk offices.

Chapter 10

Tanner dropped by to pick up Delia at about six o'clock. He'd come to Dee Ward's door to get a younger Delia hundreds of times during her summer visits in the past, but things felt different this time. This felt like a date, even though he wore blue jeans and a faded blue chambray shirt.

He found Hallie sitting out on the back screen porch, her feet propped on a small table with a book across her lap.

"Hey, birthday boy," she chorused. "Have a seat. Delia will be out in a minute. You can open that little package while you wait."

"Ummm, I hope this is what I think it is." Tanner picked up a cylindrical package, wrapped simply in white tissue paper and tied with a string.

"I had Delia buy it," she told him. "Since I couldn't get out to shop."

Tanner tore off the tissue to find the hoped-for jar of homemade stick candies he'd always liked so well. He screwed open the jar to look for a favorite flavor. "Thanks, Hallie." He sent her a wide grin. "Want one, too?"

"Yeah. Find me a clove stick. They're always the yellow and brown striped ones."

Tanner handed her one. "What are you reading, Hallie?"

"One of Dee's books on candle-making," she answered. "Delia and I got the shed cleaned up, and we did a little experimental candle-making this afternoon. But I don't know if the candles we made turned out that great. I'll check them tomorrow."

"You'll get it right," Tanner encouraged her.

Delia interrupted from the doorway. "Hi, Tanner. I didn't hear you come in."

Tanner turned toward her voice and caught his breath as she walked out onto the screen porch. She wore a lacey, black skirt that swirled when she walked, and, above it, a creamy, see-through blouse with little tucks and ruffles down the front. Underneath the blouse flirted a matching camisole with spaghetti straps that fitted Delia like snug underwear. Lord help him.

She'd done something fussy with her hair, too. Pulled some of it back and tied it up with a scarf. Made herself up more than usual, too. Also, instead of her usual socks and canvas shoes, she had on black, strappy sandals that showed her pretty little feet with coral-painted toenails.

Hallie laughed. "Delia, you must look even better than I thought. I think Tanner just swallowed his tongue."

"You dressed up." Tanner managed to say, at a loss for better words.

"It's only a skirt." Delia looked down at herself anxiously. "Do you think it's the wrong thing to wear?"

"No, you look absolutely fabulous," Hallie assured her. "We girls need to dress up every now and then. Come on, Tanner. Tell her she looks great before she goes back upstairs and puts on an old pair of jeans or something."

"You really do look beautiful, Delia." He swallowed hard. "I can't wait to see what the Gang will say to see how you've grown up."

"Well, watch where your eyes travel when you say that, Tanner." Hallie wiggled her eyebrows at him. "It isn't polite to stare at girls' boobs that obviously."

"Aw, shut up, Hallie." Tanner colored. "I was only noticing she had on a pretty blouse."

Hallie stuck out her tongue at him.

"I got the blouse in DC shopping." Delia smoothed the fabric. "The skirt, too."

"Well you look gorgeous," Hallie said again. "Want a stick of Tanner's candy?" She held out Tanner's jar of stick candy toward Delia.

"Oh, you've already opened it." Delia's mouth formed a pout. "And before I got here." She swooped up a second wrapped gift from off the side table. "Well, you'll have to wait to open mine until later, Tanner. I'm going to take it down to the party."

"Sure. If you want to," Tanner agreed, beginning to regain his composure now. "There will undoubtedly be some other stuff there. A few nice gifts. And some gag gifts probably lacking in taste. Don't be shocked, Delia."

"There's little Bogan Kirkpatrick and Keppler James can do to shock me anymore," she said saucily. "Ready to go?"

Tanner and Delia said their goodbyes to Hallie, walked around the house to the street, and started down Balsam Lane toward the park.

"Are you going to be all right in those fancy shoes walking around in the park tonight?" Tanner asked.

Delia laughed. "They're just fussy on the top but canvas soled underneath. See?" She lifted a foot so he could see the bottom of her shoe. But mostly Tanner focused on the nice expanse of leg and thigh she showed him.

She skipped ahead of him, and he had to walk fast to catch up with her. Always cheerful and youthful, he thought.

"I enjoyed a nice lunch with your mother today." She flashed him a smile. "And she invited Hallie and me over to eat dinner with her Saturday evening."

"I heard about that lunch," Tanner said. "I also heard, with gratitude, that you're going to redecorate the offices."

She sighed. "Your mother made it hard to say no."

"So, have you got any ideas of what you're going to do?"

"A few ideas," she answered evasively. "But I always like to get thoughts from my clients. What ideas do you have, Tanner, for the T. Cross offices?"

"Just don't do them in pink and blue or sissy colors." He scowled. "Or with a lot of flowery prints. Bogan had some decorator do his office and it's all pink and green floral upholstery with big rhododendron blooms on the walls."

"For a publishing and printing office?" Delia asked, surprised.

"Yeah." He laughed. "Bogan's wife owned some pretty rhododendron prints she thought would be nice, and the decorator sort of went nuts with the idea."

Delia giggled.

He turned to her, serious now. "Don't do anything like that in T. Cross, okay? It's mostly a guy's place except for Lavonne."

"I'll keep that in mind." Delia smirked. "I usually like to run my plan by my clients before I begin. To get their input and to see if they like where I'm going."

"That sounds sensible." Tanner felt relieved at that idea.

Delia pushed a loose tendril of hair from off her neck. "What things would you really not want to see changed in your offices?"

"Well, I think we have good office furniture. You know, good desks and conference tables. Nice desk chairs and stuff like that. Some of the pieces are old, but they're quality." He looked at her to gauge her response.

"I agree," she conferred, smiling. "You and your father invested well there."

He sighed. "And I really like the brown leather. I bought the sofas two years ago when a client sold out one of his business locations." He looked her way again.

"The leather's okay," she told him.

"So what else is there?" He shrugged. "Office furniture and some sofas for clients to sit on until you can see them. What more do you need?"

Tanner saw her smile slowly. "Oh, maybe we can think of a few accessories to make everything look a little more polished," she replied casually. "Some rugs would be nice. Maybe some new art for the walls. But not rhododendron blossoms."

Tanner laughed. "One of my clients in Sevierville owns a rug and carpet business. He owes me. I bet he'll give you a big discount if you tell him that what you're buying is for me."

"I'll get his name,' Delia promised.

They chatted on a little more about decorating. As they started down Wesley Street, Tanner pointed at a sign beside one of the driveways. It said, "Two Oaks."

"Remember the summer when you decided all the houses and cottages should have names?" he asked her. "I think you were ten or eleven. You spent days thinking up names for all the houses and then made signs for them on poster board tacked to sticks. You made me go around and help you put them in all the front yards."

Delia giggled. "I remember that. It was so much fun."

"Well, the Bartlett's actually liked the little name you thought up for their place. Later, they had this larger sign made and their place has been Two Oaks ever since."

"Honest?" Delia stopped to look more closely at the wood-burned sign beside the driveway. She studied the Bartlett's house. "I thought Two Oaks a good name because of the two white oaks on either side of their house. The trees are still there, too."

They walked on down Wesley Street, past the small homes and rustic cottages characteristic of this quiet mountain neighborhood. Many had screened porches across front or back, rustic rock walls or chimneys, decorative shutters, and gingerbread trim. Some were of native stone or weathered wood, others painted in colorful tones—one was even painted pink with charming white trimmings.

"The houses are so unique," Delia enthused. "It's always been one of the reasons I loved it here so much. Every house has such character. Look! There's the Dancing Bear house. I always thought it had the cutest name."

"Many of these houses were built as part of a Methodist assembly grounds in the early 1900s." Tanner told her. "People came for camp meetings and extended revivals. Later when the Methodists moved their assembly headquarters over to Junaluska, on the other side of the Smokies in North Carolina, this became a summer camp for children."

"Really?" Delia smiled. "I never knew that. Do you know what it was called?"

"Chewassee Camp. A good Indian name."

"That's where the street named Chewassee got its name." Delia's eyes brightened.

"That's right and, fortunately, as Gatlinburg developed, the city bought part of the old Chewassee camp and made it into a park."

"I'm glad they did. So few cities hold on to green spaces today." Delia said these words regretfully. "There is so much greed in the world. And more and more parks, and remaining woods and fields, are being taken."

"Some areas around here show poor planning, too," admitted Tanner.

"Yes, but there is still so much beauty."

The park came into view now, and Tanner and Delia walked across Asbury Lane and down toward the picnic tables along LaConte Creek. They could already see Tanner's friends beginning to gather.

"Great day in the morning! Is that little Miss Delia?" called out Bogan. He came over and swooped her up in a big, sweeping hug.

"Whoo-ee," he exclaimed. "You sure have grown up fine!"

"It's good to see you, Bogan."

"This is my wife, Rona." He put his arm around a tall, blond woman with a warm smile as he introduced Delia to her. "I met her at college and persuaded her to come back home to the Burg with me." He pointed. "Down there wading their feet in the creek are our two twin girls, Kaylin and Rylie."

"Pleased to meet you, Delia," Rona offered. "Here. Give me that present you brought and I'll put it on the table with the others."

"Hey. I'm getting a hug, too." A smiling, dark-haired man, walked over from the charcoal grill. Delia had to look closely for a minute to recognize Keppler.

"Oh, Keppler," she said with pleasure as he swept her into another bear hug.

"Keppler, you be careful or you'll pull her back out!" admonished a short, tanned woman in bermuda shorts. "Do you remember me, Delia?"

"Sherilynn?" Delia's mouth dropped open.

"I've changed a lot from that little girl with buster brown bangs, braids and braces, haven't I?" She laughed. "But so have you!" She gave Delia a hug, too.

Sherilynn Carpenter and Keppler's sister, Ruthann, had been the only two girls that ever played much with the Jack Gang—mostly because Keppler's parents often made him bring his kid sister and her friend along to their play outings. Although Sherilynn and Ruthann were older than Delia, Tanner knew Delia had always felt pleased when they came to the Jack Gang's outings. It evened up the numbers some.

"I guess Tanner told you I married Keppler," Sherilynn said.

"You always did have a crush on him," Delia remembered.

"Yeah, but it took a long time before I could get him to notice me as anything other than his bratty sister's best friend." She pointed toward the basketball goals. "Those are our boys over there, Randy and Dennis. They're trying to see if they can throw a basketball high enough to get it into the goal. They're a little small yet, but that doesn't seem to keep them from trying."

Bogan's voice boomed out. "Here come Perry and Tracie."

Perry soon collected his own hug from Delia, and then introduced his auburn-haired wife, who held a smiling baby on her hip who looked about seven months old.

"Bogan, can you set up that play bed over by the table where Caleb can see everybody?" Perry's wife Tracie asked. "He'll play happily there if he doesn't think he's missing out on anything."

"You've grown up on us, Delia." Perry surveyed her with a smile. "And I'm pleased you've come down to see us all again. We missed you."

"Thanks, Perry." She looked up at him. "You've certainly grown taller."

"Yeah, even taller than Bogan now, and that really irks him."

"It irks me, too," put in Tanner. "Even Keppler got taller than me."

"Tanner said you've become a minister," Delia said to Perry.

"Yeah. Rev. Perry Ammons now." He raised an eyebrow at her. "You need prayer or absolution or anything?"

Delia laughed. "No. But I'll keep it in mind, Perry."

"You do that," he countered seriously now, taking her hand to squeeze it. "I'm good at what I do when I'm on duty for the Lord."

"He really is," Tanner said loyally. "I'll take you to hear him preach one Sunday when he fills in for Rev. Madison."

Everyone started milling around the grill and picnic tables, getting hungry from smelling the hamburgers and hotdogs cooking over the coals. For the monthly gatherings of the Jack Gang, everybody always brought food to share, with Tanner exempt tonight because of his birthday.

An assortment of side dishes spread across the picnic table to accompany the grilled hamburgers and hotdogs—baked beans, buns, and chips from Bogan and Rona; potato salad and relishes from Keppler and Sherilynn. Tracie had baked one of her homemade birthday cakes, which sat invitingly in the middle of the food table. They'd also brought a freezer full of homemade vanilla ice cream.

Tanner, leaning against a picnic table, enjoyed watching the faces of the Jack Gang as they first saw Delia tonight. Once Bogan sent Tanner a thumbs up signal when Delia wasn't looking, his sign that Tanner had been right about Delia becoming a real stunner.

He watched Delia himself now, interacting with his old friends, still comfortable with the guys after all this time. She'd made friends quickly with Rona and Tracie and taught Bogan's seven-year old twin girls a clapping rhyme, quickly overcoming their shyness with her. Earlier when the baby cried, Delia swooped him up to comfort him as if she'd taken care of babies all her life. Tanner supposed she'd become used to kids, hanging around all her nieces and nephews. Still, not everybody handled small children comfortably like Delia did. Just another new thing Tanner discovered about her tonight. She seemed a continual surprise to him these days.

Opening his gifts later, Tanner found some embarrassing, as expected. Bogan and Keppler saw to that. Other gifts were nice—new fishing flies, a shirt, a gift certificate, and two guest passes from Keppler for the Ripley Aquarium.

"I thought you might like to take Delia," Keppler explained. "The Aquarium is pretty new to Gatlinburg, and she might not have seen it yet."

"I haven't." Delia sent him a smile. "And I'm going to remind Tanner one of those passes is meant for me."

Tanner opened his gift from Delia last. On the top sat two bags of jacks, which got a laugh from Bogan right away. Underneath the jacks lay a leather belt. Tanner took it out to examine it. On the front of it was a star buckle—the star shaped like a Texas sheriff's badge.

"I did my best to get what you asked for." Delia gave him a saucy smile.

Tanner looked at the card under the gift, a funny one, and found inside it a kid's silver sheriff badge, a lot like the old one Tanner had as a boy.

"That's cool," said Keppler's little boy, Dennis.

"So it is." Tanner laughed and pinned it on his shirt. Then he traded out his old belt for the new one with the sheriff star on the front.

"Well, hey." Bogan studied the kid's badge on Tanner's shirt. "That looks like the old sheriff's badge you used to wear all the time as a little kid, Tanner. Didn't you lose that thing somewhere and get all whiney over not being able to find it?"

"Yes, he did, and he always claimed I lost it." Delia lifted her chin. "So I got him another one."

Everyone laughed at that.

"You're a real 'all star' guy now," quipped Keppler. "But, heck, I'd probably paste a star right on the front of my forehead if a pretty little thing like Delia gave it to me."

"Maybe I'll drop by your motel and give you one," Delia chipped back.

Tanner smiled to see that she gave as good as she got now. Not that she hadn't made an effort to do so when she'd been younger, but her comebacks always showed her age back then—always five years younger than the rest of them.

He let his eyes rove over her, sitting on the edge of the picnic table, her shapely legs swinging below her little skirt. She chattered to Bogan, smiling, relaxed, and absolutely beautiful. When had Delia become so beautiful?

Tanner remembered again the day when she turned thirteen. He thought that night at Dee's he'd seen a hint of what she might become. It scared him—what happened then. He meant to give her a little birthday kiss that evening, because she gazed up at him with those big eyes of hers, wondering if he would. Obviously wishing he would. He expected the kiss to be like any other of their childish kisses of the past. Like the times when they played spin the bottle out in the gazebo. But it hadn't been. The kiss turned passionate. He'd felt it, and she felt it. That's why he pulled away and left

Delia's Place

when he did. She'd only been a little girl, turning thirteen, and he eighteen, finishing his first year of college. Toying with her would have been wrong. And he knew better.

He watched Delia bite on her lip now while she laughed at one of Bogan's stories. Delia certainly wasn't a little girl anymore. Perhaps tonight he'd see what really kissing her would feel like—with both of them older.

After they waved good-bye to everyone later that night, Tanner had the perfect opportunity. Delia wanted to see the old gazebo before they went home, so he walked her down the dark path beside LeConte Creek until they came to the white gazebo hidden among the trees.

She walked around inside it, noticing landmarks—like all their initials carved on an old post—and fondly remembering past times. The moon hung nearly full in the sky tonight, and Tanner could see Delia's face in the moonlight.

"Did you have a good time tonight?" he asked her.

"Actually, I had a wonderful time." She sent him a soft smile. "I hope you enjoyed your birthday."

"I did," he replied huskily, moving closer to her. "But it might get better." He pulled her firmly into his arms and kissed her. Really kissed her. Not like that teasing little peck she'd given him at the office or those soft butterfly kisses he'd offered her last night. No, sir. This was the real thing.

Delia gave a startled sound at first, stiffening in surprise and trying to pull away from him, but then she stopped resisting and moaned softly as Tanner deepened the kiss and slipped his hands under her hair. He felt a surge of triumph when Delia grew soft in his arms, when she leaned into him and slipped her arms around his back. She fit so nicely against him, like she'd been made to fit there. He pulled her closer, savoring the feel of her. He kissed her face and eyelids—tasting her, hearing her breathing escalate with arousal, reveling in the soft scent of her floral cologne, filling his senses with her.

If Tanner wished for fireworks on his birthday, he savored them now. The feelings Delia aroused in him flared with intensity, more so than the time long ago. Tanner soon lost himself in her mouth, in the feel and smell of her. He buried his face in her hair, his mouth tracing itself down her neck and into the soft skin above her breasts. Delia, fallen back limply in his arms, suddenly jerked away from him, stepped back—almost fearfully—gasping and holding her hand to her chest. Scrambling to get away from him.

Tanner pulled himself gradually back to reality. "What's the matter, Princess?" he whispered huskily, still holding her hand and trying to draw her gently back towards him again. "It's all right if it's exciting and good between us."

She shook her head back and forth. "Oh, no, Tanner, I'm so sorry. We shouldn't be doing this. I shouldn't be doing this. I didn't mean for this to happen."

"Sometimes things just happen," Tanner told her silkily, smiling at her in the moonlight. "And it's all right. There's no reason we shouldn't be attracted to each other. Mercy, Delia, surely you can see it's really good between us."

"I know, but I don't want it to be good between us." She stepped back further. "I should never have spent so much time alone with you tonight. Never let you think there was something going on that wasn't. I shouldn't have flirted back with you. Or made you think I had feelings I don't have."

Tanner felt a chill now. He grabbed her wrist. "Are you trying to tell me you've been playing tease, Delia? That this has only been a little game for you?"

"Well, I thought it was for you," she offered apologetically.

He grew quiet. "You thought I'd been playing a game? Is that what you still think?"

"I don't know, Tanner." Her voice sounded anguished, and she twisted her hands. "I just don't know. I'm confused."

She started to cry, but Tanner found himself growing angry.

"You're not thirteen anymore, Delia," he snapped. "You're a grown woman and you responded like a grown woman here tonight. I don't see what's confusing to you about this."

"Well, it is," she wailed. "I don't want to be involved with anyone right now, Tanner. Not you or anybody. I just went through one bad breakup and I'm not ready to start into a relationship again. Any relationship."

"I see. So, tell me, Delia," hissed Tanner. "If you were so interested in not being involved with anyone, why did you flirt with me? It hasn't all been me, you know. You flirted with me as much as I with you. You kissed me. Let me kiss you. To me, that isn't signaling you'd like me to keep away. What did you expect me to think, Delia?"

"I don't know," she murmured, hanging her head and continuing to sniffle.

Tanner felt disgusted. "Come on. Let's go home." He turned his back on her. "I don't feel much like partying any more."

He stalked to the picnic table, picked up his bag of gifts, and started retracing his steps towards home. He soon heard Delia trailing along behind him, still sniffling.

After a time, she moved to walk beside him. "Are you mad at me, Tanner?" He noticed she'd quit crying now, although her eyes looked red and puffy.

Delia's Place

He moved a few steps away from her. "Yes, Delia. I'm still mad. But I expect I'll live."

"I'm sorry," she said quietly.

"For what?" He shoved at his hair.

She hesitated. "For messing up your birthday?" she questioned.

"Try again," he snapped, knowing anger crackled in his voice.

"Look, Tanner. Can't we just be friends?" She tried to walk closer to him again. "We've always been friends. I don't want to mess that up."

He looked at her tear-streaked face. "I'm not sure I want to be just friends with you, Delia. But I'll give it a try."

"Oh, good." She tried offering him a tentative smile, moving nearer.

He pulled away from her, frowning. "Don't push it, Delia. Tonight I don't even feel like being friends. Tonight I feel like being pissed."

"Oh," she whispered quietly.

They walked along in silence until they got to the end of Balsam Lane. Tanner turned toward his own place, figuring Delia could make her own way to Dee's house at this point. He had no plans to walk her to her door.

"Good night, Tanner." Her voice floated softly into the night as he started down his driveway. When he didn't answer, he heard her running up behind him.

"You've got to say goodnight and say it's okay, Tanner," she pleaded, running around to step in front of him and reaching to put her hands on his shoulders.

"Is that right? Well, here's my goodnight." He caught her up, before she realized what he intended, and kissed her again. Then he pulled back from her, studying her flushed face. "You can say what you like, Delia Eleanor Walker, but there is something special starting to happen between us." He glared at her. "Trying to deny it or trying to hide from it isn't going to change things. You give it some thought, you hear? It doesn't matter who you broke up with before or when. It doesn't matter who we had in our lives before now. This is different, Delia. I can feel it, and you can feel it if you'll be honest with yourself. It's a real shame you couldn't take a little pleasure in the discovery of that fact tonight."

With that, he turned and stalked off toward his house at a brisk pace. Any more time close to Delia Walker in the dark, and he probably wouldn't be so reasonable.

Tanner hardened his heart at the sound of her sniffling as he heard her walking back to Dee's. Let her sniffle. He wouldn't mind a good cry himself this particular night. He'd had enough of Miss Delia Walker for one day.

Chapter 11

Delia found with relief that Tanner still spoke to her and didn't try to avoid her, even after Friday night. In fact, he showed up for dinner at his mother's the very next night, acting cordial and entertaining to everyone. He gave no indication over dinner that he felt upset with Delia in any way, acting towards her as he used to when she was a child. This mostly meant he paid no particular attention to her whatsoever. Delia tried to act natural and normal during the evening, but she came across as overly bright and gay in her effort not to reveal her strained feelings.

"What the heck's going on with you and Tanner?" Hallie asked before they'd walked halfway down Maureen's driveway on their way back home.

"Nothing." Delia tried to respond casually. "Why do you ask?"

"Good try, Delia, but I'm not buying your act," Hallie returned sarcastically. "Last night, I went to bed early with a good book in case you and Tanner wanted some time alone when you came back. However, I'm pretty sure I heard you come in alone. And you've been acting weird all day today."

"I have not been acting weird." Delia bristled.

"Pooh. You have, too. You were so distracted I had to run you out of the candle shed earlier today. We had the waxes melted and the color and fragrance in. I had you stirring while I finished getting the containers out of the oven, so we could get ready to pour. I looked around and you stood there daydreaming—and not stirring."

Hallie snorted in annoyance before continuing. "Delia, you know you have to stir the wax well at that point so the oil and color bond together. And you were supposed to be watching the temperature, too, to be sure it stayed at around 170 degrees. You weren't. You let it get too hot. That's dangerous, Delia, not just because it can ruin the candles, but because wax can burn, too."

"I was thinking about other things." Delia looked away. "I have a lot on my mind these days, you know."

"Hmmph. You simply don't want to tell me what happened." Hallie's eyes narrowed.

"You don't need to know every little detail about my personal life." Delia tossed her head. "I do have a right to my privacy."

"Well, la de da." Hallie waved a hand foppishly. "Aren't we prissy? So, I guess I'll have to ask Tanner what happened."

"You'd better not!" exclaimed Delia.

"Oh, yeah?" pushed Hallie. "Maybe I'll ask him what happened to cause you to act so weird and moody all day. I'll bet he'll tell me something."

"Hallie, please don't do that," begged Delia.

"So, you tell me then," Hallie demanded.

Delia dropped her eyes. "We kind of had a little disagreement. That's all."

"What kind of disagreement?"

"Just a difference of opinion," Delia replied, two bright spots of color coming into her cheeks now.

Hallie studied her. "He put some moves on you," she guessed.

"Okay. Yes. And I didn't want him to." Delia crossed her arms against herself. "So we had a small disagreement about that. I told you, it wasn't much."

"If it wasn't much, you wouldn't be upset," Hallie argued. "Did he feel-you-up and want to have sex?"

"Hallie!" exclaimed Delia, shocked. "Of course not!"

"Oh, pooh. What if he had? All boys want to have sex. It's not like it's some secret that nobody knows."

Delia lifted her chin. "Well, I assure you, that issue never came up, Hallie Walker."

"So, is all this only about kissing?" She wrinkled her nose. "Surely you didn't get in a snit over him simply kissing you or something."

Delia didn't answer.

Hallie studied her again. "So Tanner kissed you and put some moves on you and you got mad. Is that it?"

"It's more complicated than that," Delia insisted.

"Only with you." She rolled her eyes. "Everything's more complicated with you, Delia."

"You don't have to be mean, Hallie."

"So explain it to me so I'll quit guessing around."

"All right." She hesitated. "We enjoyed a great evening with all his friends, and I had a wonderful time. We walked back to see the old gazebo before we started home, and suddenly, Tanner started kissing me. You know, really kissing me. When I wanted him to stop and told him I didn't want to get into a relationship with anyone right now, he got mad. That's what happened."

"Hmmm." Hallie thought about that for a minute and then raised her eyebrows at Delia. "Is Tanner a good kisser?" She giggled. "It's a sweet thing when a man knows how to kiss good. I've heard that when a man really knows how to kiss slow and sweet and good, that it's an indication he'll know how to do other things slow and sweet and good, too."

"Hallie Walker!" Delia sputtered. "You're only seventeen years old. Where in the world do you get all these ideas?"

"I can read," she grinned. "So, did he? Did he kiss good?'

"Maybe," Delia replied evasively.

"That means yes. If it had been no, you would have said so." She smiled in triumph.

Arriving at the house, the girls let themselves in the back door to the kitchen. Graham met them, meowing a welcome, and Delia gave him a few pets and kitty greetings.

Hallie turned to look at Delia in the light. "So, you got upset because Tanner Cross kissed you, and it was really good. And because you don't want to risk falling in love again and getting hurt."

Delia's lips tightened. "Yes. I told you; I don't want to get involved with anyone right now."

"Tanner isn't like Prentice." Hallie spoke the words softly.

Delia sighed. "I know that, Hallie."

She cocked her head. "Did Tanner tell you he loved you?"

"No! And I hope he doesn't. I really meant what I said, Hallie, I don't want to get involved in a relationship right now. Period."

"So what is Tanner supposed to do if he's getting feelings for you?" Hallie leaned against the kitchen counter.

"I don't want to talk about this anymore, Hallie." Delia felt herself growing testy.

Hallie shook her head. "So, fine," she complained. "But things don't go away, Delia, just because you avoid them. Or don't want to talk about them."

Eventually, Delia managed to get Hallie off the subject of Tanner that night. But she found it harder to get her own thoughts away from what happened with Tanner in the gazebo as she tried to settle into sleep later.

When Hallie politely ran her out of the candle shed again the next day, after further inattention, Delia went for a walk to think. She decided to drive to Aunt Dee's old office to work and think some more. She knew Tanner wouldn't be there on Sunday with the Crosswalk and T. Cross offices closed. Maureen had gone to church and then visiting—and Tanner was fishing with a friend. She'd have the upstairs offices all to herself.

Delia carried her decorating materials, books and files, and her laptop into Dee's office, and spent an hour or two cleaning and setting up her office space to make it more her own. Next, she made some calls and did several internet searches to locate potential design jobs she thought she might like to apply for. After what happened with Tanner on Friday, she felt a little panicked to think of staying here in Gatlinburg for too long. She wrote cover letters, printed out resumes, and sent off packets to three corporate design firms—one in Richmond where her friend Holly Davis lived, one in Wilmington near the beach house and Frances' family, and one in DC.

Finally, because she'd promised Maureen, Delia walked around the upstairs offices to think about how she might like to redecorate them. She carried a spiral sketch pad with her, making rough drawings and notes as she explored the spaces. The upstairs offices of T. Cross Accounting and Crosswalk were laid out on either side of a wide upstairs hallway. Toward the back of the entry hall, behind the stairs, sat a large storage room that both offices shared.

The entry area flooring, covered in old flecked linoleum, showed tears in several places. "This floor will need to be replaced with wood or tile," Delia said. "Maybe tile, since the area carries so much traffic." She wrinkled her nose. "And these dusty, droopy ficus plants and faded orange vinyl coverings on the chairs need to be dumped. Ugh." Delia squatted down to determine the quality of the chairs, turning them over to examine the construction, deciding they might be salvageable. "Recovering might work here." Standing again, her eyes scanned the walls. "New paint is a definite for the walls—a unique color and texture to catch the eye."

Delia let herself into the T. Cross offices. "As Tanner said, there is good furniture here—cherry desks, shelves, tables and chairs in all three of the offices and in the entry area—but no decorative touches, no warmth. No theme. And simply no color." She sighed. "All the walls are the same off-white as the entry hallway, the hardwood floors and sofas both brown. The only color is in those faded, cheaply framed mountain prints on the walls." She scowled at them. "They're not even arranged well and there's no unity between them."

Delia found the office bathroom no better—painted a sickly green with plain white fixtures and not even a picture on the wall. Dismal.

"At least Tanner's office seems a little better." She stood inside it, looking around. It sported another small brown leather sofa with a matching chair, Tanner's desk, and two bookshelves loaded with books. The only piece of art on the walls, except for plaques, framed certificates and diplomas, was a large, old world map. "Hmmm. That map isn't framed well, but it's actually quite nice." Delia moved around to study it from several directions. "I think I can use that."

Across the hall, the Crosswalk office spaces were, at the least, more colorful—the entry area stuffed with a faded floral upholstered sofa and some coordinating side chairs grouped over a patterned area rug. Delia examined the furniture pieces, finding them to be sound. "I could keep these if I recovered them. And I could redecorate the bath off the entry area to match the colors I decide to use."

She walked back to the conference-kitchen area, where staff often held meetings and shared a meal. "Yuk. No color scheme here at all." She looked around, shaking her head. "But it's a sunny room and it could look welcoming with a little effort and creativity."

Moving through Aunt Dee's and Maureen's offices, she frowned at the stained and frayed rugs and scuffed hardwood floors, but smiled at the contrast between Maureen and Dee's offices—Maureen's neat and stark, Aunt Dee's cluttered and full of bric-a-brac and notions. "Both these offices need work, and I want to make an effort to respect Maureen's personality when I redecorate her space."

Noticing yet more frayed chair fabric, Delia suddenly remembered Hallie telling her one of the family members ran an upholstery business. "I'll go talk to them about the work I want to do first. Get estimates. Maybe look through the family furniture store and their catalogs for furniture and decorative items I need. For art prints, I'll probably need to go elsewhere, but I'll have little trouble finding art in the Gatlinburg area."

Delia was on her knees taking measurements in the hallway, when Tanner walked up the stairs.

"Making measurements for decorating?" He stopped in the doorway.

"Yes." She pushed a wayward strand of hair back from her face and stood up. "I thought you went fishing."

"I did this morning. Caught some nice trout. Then came back to the house, mowed the yard, and cleaned up." He glanced at his watch. "It's nearly five, you know. Hallie saw me in the yard and came over to say she was worried about you. Said you'd been gone nearly all day. Plus she's cooking up something for dinner she wants you to be sure to get home to sample."

Her eyes met his. "So you came looking for me?"

"No," He leaned casually against the wall. "Actually I needed to come to the office to drop off some papers I'd been looking over." He held up the folder he carried.

"Oh," Delia replied, a little rattled with his nonchalance.

He straightened a picture on the wall. "Let's have a cola before we head back home," he offered. "I'll get two out of the refrigerator in the kitchen. Diet for you, regular for me. We'll drink them out on Little Italy."

"Little what?" Delia looked up, distracted by his last remark.

A small smile touched the corner of his mouth. "It's what we call the covered patio over the front entry. Everybody in Gatlinburg sits on their rooftop porches to watch the world go by, Delia. It's tradition." He grinned. "Let yourself out the door there." He pointed. "It's nice outside today. I'll join you in a minute with the drinks."

Delia actually preferred to avoid Tanner's company for any length of time, but she thought it might seem churlish to refuse a cola when he'd been acting

Delia's Place

so nice. Perhaps he wasn't upset anymore about what happened? Maybe he just wanted to be friends now, like she suggested?

Letting herself out through the double doors onto the porch, Delia looked around in pleasure. An array of painted metal furniture and a few weathered rocking chairs stood scattered up and down a long, narrow balcony enclosed with decorative, black wrought iron. "I'd forgotten how nice this porch is." She leaned over the rail to look down at the crowds milling on the sidewalk and then sat down in an old rocker to enjoy the view.

Tanner soon joined her carrying two canned drinks. After handing her one, he dropped into the rocker beside her.

"It's been a beautiful day," he commented, settling back and plopping his feet on a low table across from them.

"Why do you call this Little Italy?" she asked, remembering his comment from before.

"Oh, it's an old family joke." He grinned. "Mom and Dad always hoped to travel abroad, and one of the places they most wanted to visit was Italy. Mother bought a pile of coffee table books showing scenic pictures of Italy, and she and Dad often planned what they'd do and see when they finally got to go. But, of course, always working and busy, they never found time to get away. Dad used to laugh and say the closest we'd probably ever get to sitting on a balustraded villa porch, like the ones in those Italian brochures, was right here on our own Little Italy in the Burg. Of course, he meant this old roof top balcony. Somehow, the joke stuck, and we started calling our porch here Little Italy."

"And they never got to go?" Delia sipped her cola.

"No. But it was a good dream. Maybe it's something Mother and I can still do some day. I remember Dee went to Europe and Italy one summer and took you along. She tried to get Mother to go, too. But Mother found her excuses."

"It's beautiful in Italy." She told Tanner some of the things she remembered most from her trip.

"You really make me want to visit," he confessed, sitting back in his rocker and downing the last of his cola.

Delia studied him as he leaned back with his eyes closed.

Sensing her watching him, he opened his eyes and smiled lazily at her. Delia suddenly felt light-headed and a little dizzy.

"You know, Hallie's making homemade chicken soup for supper and some sort of yeast rolls," he told her. "She invited me to come eat. Is that all right with you?"

"Of course." Her heart sank. It would seem petty to say no after Hallie invited him. And especially since Hallie cooked the dinner.

He chuckled. "Actually, I think Hallie's real motive in inviting me is because she wants to play Clue after supper. It takes three people to make a good game with that. Hallie really likes games, you know."

"I know. So do I." Delia brightened. "I haven't played Clue in ages."

"Who do you like to be when you play?" he asked teasingly, referring to the characters each player used in Clue's board game.

"Miss Scarlett." She didn't hesitate. "What about you?"

"Always Colonel Mustard," he replied with a grin.

Tanner stood up to leave, winking at her. "I'm going on back. I want to pick up a bottle of wine or two on my way home. My contribution to dinner."

Without thinking, Delia said, "You're not mad at me anymore, are you, Tanner?"

"No," he answered, leaning over her in the rocker and looking down at her. "But whenever I get even this close to you I feel like I need to take a cold shower." He gave her a slow smile. "It remains to be seen whether that will pass off or not."

Before Delia could think of a reply, Tanner sauntered off.

"Don't forget to lock up," he called as he left.

Delia sat in the rocker breathing rapidly and trying to calm down. "This is no little teenage boy you're dealing with now, Delia Walker. That man is dangerous." He'd made her heartbeat escalate when he sat down beside her in the rocker, made her nervous and uncomfortable, too. And when he leaned over to look down at her, she'd felt like she might drown in his eyes. "Heaven help me, I even found myself wishing he'd touch and kiss me again."

She jumped up. "This is crazy," she told herself. "It's just some kind of after reaction from what happened before." As Delia went back inside, locking the porch doors behind her, she hoped against hope this was true. "I do not want to get involved with someone else right now," she told herself sharply. "I've only been un-engaged from Prentice for eight days. No one can trust feelings they have for anyone when they've only been un-engaged for eight days."

Delia could only imagine what her mother or Frances would say if they knew that she'd been kissing another man so soon after her engagement ended. Gracious mercy, she hoped they'd never, ever find out!

She went inside to turn off all the lights in the office and finish locking up. But as she walked through the entry area, she suddenly stopped and looked around with a smug, slow smile. She had the perfect inspiration for her design theme! She'd use the concept of Little Italy from Tanner.

Excited now, Delia reopened the doors to both offices and walked back through all the rooms, her mind whirling. She talked out loud to herself as she walked. "Here in the T. Cross offices, I'll put patterned European rugs on the hardwood floors and hang prints of Italian vineyards and landscapes on the walls. Maybe apply some of the rich tones from the prints in decorative items."

She turned around slowly, inspiration rising. "I'll put some tasteful brass pieces on the walls, maybe an ornate mirror with scroll and medallion accents. A Bordeaux coat tree by the door. Maybe a brass umbrella stand, too, and a few rich pillows on the sofas."

She walked into Tanner's office. "An old world theme with an Italian touch will work nicely here," she observed. "I'll have that map of Tanner's rematted and nicely framed." She waved a hand. "Add a subtle Italian landscape to the wall and maybe a few small sienna photo prints. Put a standing globe in the corner. Add a few pillows and decorative items on the sofa and chairs." Delia smoothed her hand over the sofa back as she talked. "I can use some of those same ideas in the other offices. It will look wonderful." She smiled with pleasure as her thoughts whirled.

Delia decided to paint all the rooms in a soft, golden tone that would warm the office areas and complement the theme. She'd carry that color into the bathrooms, too. Find some wallpaper border with an Italian theme or use some grapevine stenciling. Hang rich colored towels on a brass rod for additional color and locate a nice mirror and a few prints for the walls.

Flashing across the hallway, she stood and looked around the Crosswalk offices. Here she'd use deep reds in the entry area. Wouldn't that be striking and cheerful? Maybe re-upholster the sofas and chairs in crimson twill. Use rich throws and gold color accents. Find some elegant, patterned, old world rugs.

"It would be perfect to hang a big painting of a field of poppies on the primary wall in the Crosswalk entry room. To set the tone for the reds. I've seen a print like that in one of my catalogs. I can find it." She formed a frame with her hands, imagining it.

She skipped toward the back rooms. "Perhaps some paintings of Italian street scenes here in the conference and kitchen area would be nice." She looked around. "I can pull out colors and ideas from the scenes to use in the décor."

Feeling a new idea rise in her mind, she headed for Maureen's office. "I'll get Tanner to tell me the names of some of the places in Italy that Maureen most wanted to visit. Then I can find photo prints of those places and frame them in a well-planned grouping. Maybe locate a nice Italian tapestry for the wall. Bring the colors from it into the upholstery for the side chairs."

She felt like hugging herself with excitement. "I can do something similar in Dee's office but with different colors. Perhaps indigo blue and gold."

Slipping out of the Crosswalk offices into the bland entry hall space again, Delia turned around slowly seeking more inspiration. "I'll put down soft-red tiled floors here to replace the worn linoleum and texture the walls to look like old European stucco. Hang a decorative clock or scrolled mirror."

She smiled as the vision fleshed out. "Then I'll have someone paint window murals on the walls like the windows of an old Italian villa. Rounded on the top with deep sills." She traced the shape on the wall, imagining it. "It will make a person feel like they're looking onto a rural Italian scene—seeing a rolling landscape or acres of lush vineyards. It'll be charming, but tasteful, too. I'll be careful about that." She'd be careful, also, to reupholster the chairs in the entry area in subtle tones and to add only a few tasteful brass accessories on the side tables or walls.

Delia danced back into her Aunt Dee's office to sketch and write notes rapidly to get all her ideas down. Finally, she leaned back with satisfaction, knowing she had a solid plan firmly in place for her decorating project. "I think Maureen and Tanner will really like this idea, too." Locking up the offices now with a happy heart, Delia headed out to her car.

To Delia, these wonderful moments of inspiration provided the greatest joy in being an interior designer. She loved the deeply creative times when the visions for designing personal and corporate spaces came flowing into her mind, dominating her senses and almost seeming to suspend time. It was so satisfying.

Of course, she'd need to run her ideas by her clients now, get their initial approval, then shop and begin to plan a budget. Next, she'd want to present a second proposal with more detail and cost estimates. See if the clients were still in approval before she could begin the work.

She drove home to Dee's feeling heady and excited. She was running a little late getting back, but she knew when she explained everything that Hallie would understand. Hallie was a creative person, too, after all.

The last thing she expected when she let herself into Dee's front door was to find Hallie weeping inconsolably on the sofa with Tanner sitting beside her trying to comfort her.

"Good heavens," she exclaimed. "Whatever has happened?"

Chapter 12

"I don't know what's happened," Tanner answered, relieved to see Delia. "I walked in and found Hallie crying like this. She won't tell me what's wrong. She just keeps saying her life's ruined."

Delia dropped her purse on a chair and went over to sit down beside Hallie on the sofa. "Hallie, what is it?" she asked gently, reaching over to push Hallie's hair back from her face. "Has Jonas Cole been here? Has he called or has someone else called to upset you?"

"No," she wailed, clutching a pillow to herself. "It's worse."

Delia searched her mind for something worse. "Has someone died? Your Uncle Hobart? Your mother? One of your relatives?'

Hallie shook her head, still sobbing.

"Has something happened to John Dale?"

This brought on a fresh burst of tears, but still no answer but a series of wails.

"Oh, bugger it, Hallie." Tanner snapped. "We're tired of playing twenty questions here. Tell us what the heck has happened, so we can try to help you."

Delia glared at him in annoyance.

Hallie, however, turned her tear-streaked face Tanner's way and said angrily, "I'm pregnant, Tanner. So how do you think you can help with that? Nobody can help."

She started to sob again, and Tanner wished instantly he hadn't accepted the invitation to dinner now. This was definitely women's stuff. And too much friggin' information for him.

"How do you know you're pregnant, Hallie?" Delia took Hallie's hand. "Maybe you're jumping to conclusions. Maybe you're only late or something. It's not as though you've been to the doctor or anything. Maybe you're wrong."

"I'm not wrong," she pronounced on another sob. "I took two pregnancy tests and they both showed positive. Both of them!" She began to cry again.

Tanner scratched his head. "How did you even get any pregnancy tests to take?"

"I went to the store and got them." She sent him a dark look. "I hid my hair under a hat and put on an old coat, so no one would recognize me. But I had to know. I had to!"

"Look, you seemed fine this afternoon." Tanner sat back. "What suddenly gave you the notion you needed to get yourself a pregnancy test all of a sudden?"

Hallie glared at him. "I was working in the kitchen making bread for tonight and I noticed a grocery list Delia had started on the refrigerator. She'd written a note: Get feminine products and ask Hallie what kind she wants."

While Hallie talked to Tanner, Delia slipped out of the room for a minute to get a box of tissues from the bathroom, and Hallie pulled one out of the box now and blew her nose. "I got to thinking suddenly that I hadn't had a period since the first of April. I always come right at the first of the month. Always. I realized I hadn't come this month at all, and I freaked. I had to know. So I sneaked out to the drugstore and came back here and did the tests. I even got two, so I could be totally sure."

"This is too much information for me." Tanner shook his head and stood to leave.

"Don't you dare leave, Tanner." Delia reached out to grab his arm. "We need you here right now. For balance. For another view. Besides, how could you even think of leaving right now when Hallie is so upset?"

He sat back down in defeat. "Fine. Fine. I'll stay." He rolled his eyes. "I guess the next question to ask is whose baby this is."

"It's John Dale's, you creep," Hallie practically snarled. "What do you think I am, Tanner? Some kind of little slut who sleeps around? You know John Dale and I have been promised for years."

Tanner shrugged, moving himself back a little from Hallie's fingernails that curled in attack mode when she snapped at him.

"You might have handled that a little more diplomatically," Delia said on the side.

Tanner rolled his eyes again.

"Listen, Hallie," Delia offered. "Those pregnancy tests are wrong sometimes. Especially if you haven't actually ... well, if you and John Dale haven't really ..."

Hallie turned an irritated gaze Delia's way. "It's no wonder you have issues about getting well-kissed when you can't even bring yourself to say the word sex, Delia. Honestly! I know some people get pregnant from fooling around the edges, but I can guarantee you that isn't the case here. Nor is this any immaculate conception."

Tanner sniggered at that.

"I wouldn't laugh right now, Tanner Cross," Hallie threatened him. "I'm not feeling overly fond of the male race at this moment."

"Ever hear of protection?" Tanner bit back, annoyed.

"Yeah, I have, smart ass. And obviously the statistics about protection sometimes failing are far more accurate than I'd care to think about right now!"

Tanner sent Hallie a grin. "Well, personally, Hallie, I'm glad you're mad now instead of just crying." He crossed his leg. "I can relate better to mad."

Delia glared at him over that comment.

"Heavenly days, what am I going to do?" Hallie dropped her face into her hands. "As if I don't have enough trouble on my plate already. And now this."

"Maybe the first thing you should do is to tell us when this happened, Hallie. Or when you think this happened." Delia slipped off her shoes and curled her feet under her on the sofa.

"Well, that's a long story," replied Hallie, trying to wipe away the last of the tears on her face with another of the tissues.

Tanner wasn't sure he really wanted to hear too many details. "Maybe we should eat first," he suggested. "Afterwards we can all sit down and you can tell us everything."

"Tanner Cross!" Delia exclaimed. "How can you even think of food at a time like this?" She shot him a chiding glance.

"Oh, he's just being a typical male, Delia," Hallie put in, almost chuckling. "Very little gets in the way of appetite for them. In fact, problems only make a lot of men hungrier."

Tanner shifted uncomfortably, knowing he'd been labeled as insensitive. But, dang it, his stomach was growling. And this thing was bound to go on all night. It wasn't as thought there could be some kind of quick fix for this.

"You know, Tanner's right," Hallie agreed, sighing. "I think we should go eat. The soup's ready and simmering. Probably needs to be stirred and the heat cut off. And the bread's done and sitting in the warmer. We might as well eat while we talk." She wiped at her face. "I've thought of suicide already and decided I'm not the type for it. So I guess I'm going to have to find some way to live with this situation. And figure out what I'm going to do about it."

Tanner waited this time, certainly not going to be the first one to get up and head for the kitchen.

"Are you sure you want to eat at all, Hallie?" Delia asked. "You don't have to."

"Listen, I worked on that soup for hours," Hallie put in practically. "It's a new recipe I'm trying. And I want to know how it came out. So, yes, I want to eat. I want you and Tanner to eat, too. We'll go get some food and take it out on the screen porch. I set up the table earlier today before all this mess happened."

Delia patted her on the knee. "I'm so sorry I wrote that note on the refrigerator, Hallie," she apologized.

"Well, not seeing that note today wouldn't have changed anything in the long run, Delia. I was bound to have figured this out eventually. I guess today's no worse a day to learn about it than tomorrow." Hallie stood up, sighing. "I'm gonna go wash my face. And then I'll meet you both in the kitchen. Go on out there and get some bowls down from off the shelf. I'll be there in a minute."

"Do you want me to go with you?" Delia twisted her hands anxiously.

Hallie actually grinned. "No, Delia. I can still go to the bathroom by myself in this condition, and I'd just as soon do so. And I'm not gonna' slit my wrists or do anything dumb, so don't worry."

Delia blushed at that. Hallie went into the bathroom, and Delia and Tanner started out towards the kitchen.

"I'm so glad you're here, Tanner," Delia told him nervously. "I honestly don't know what in the world to say to Hallie about this. Or what to tell her to do. Plus I don't really know very much about … well, you know … very much about …"

"Sex." Tanner grinned at Delia. No wonder this girl acted so spooky about passionate encounters. He was beginning to think she'd never experienced any before.

"Delia, have you never been in the sort of situation where this could have happened to you?" he asked casually.

"Absolutely not!" Delia replied, offended.

Tanner smiled.

"Why are you smiling?" Delia asked defensively.

"Oh, I just had a happy thought, I guess," he replied lightly.

"Well, this is hardly a time for happy thoughts," she spluttered, turning to hunt for bowls in the kitchen cabinet.

"I'll stir the soup," Tanner replied, still grinning and savoring his own little discovery in the midst of this nest of trouble.

They ate Hallie's chicken soup and homemade yeast rolls out on Aunt Dee's screened porch. Dark had fallen, a full moon hung in the sky, and fireflies and tree frogs filled the night with lights and sounds. Despite the crisis here, the world moved on.

"Great soup," Tanner told Hallie, trying to cheer her up. "I especially like all the chicken in it. Plus the fact that it's thick, full of vegetables and noodles, and not all brothy. A lot of soups are mostly liquid. Not hearty like this." A crisis seldom affected Tanner's appetite, but he noticed that Delia and Hallie both merely picked at their dinner.

"You must both think I'm an awful person, getting pregnant and all like this," Hallie ventured at last.

Delia's Place

Delia looked to Tanner hopefully for a comment.

He shrugged. "Stuff happens, Hallie." He knew it wasn't a great philosophical reply, but it was all he could think of at the moment.

"Well, that's very astute, Tanner." She frowned at him in irritation.

Tanner spread his hands. "Look, how have I gotten in the attack seat here? I was a guest invited over for dinner, if I remember right. I'm doing my best here in an awkward situation. Especially for a guy."

Hallie leaned forward. "So as a guy, what do you think I should do, Tanner? Get an abortion? Go off somewhere and give the baby up for adoption? I could probably get in one of those homes. Harrison Ramsey's wife Alice, over in Greenbrier, could probably help me. She's in social work, works with foster kids, and helps place babies in good families. Everybody already thinks I'm in New York City. I guess no one would ever have to know."

"Do you want to do that?" Delia asked, wide-eyed.

"I don't know; I'm thinking here, Delia." Hallie's voice snapped back. "What do you think you would do? Run home to your mama? That's not really an option for me."

Delia hung her head. "You don't have to be mean, Hallie."

"I'm naturally irritable right now," Hallie returned. "But I really would like to know what you think you'd do, Delia."

Delia hesitated. "I guess I'd talk to the father if possible. That would seem to be the first right thing to do. Especially if it was someone I loved, and someone who loved me. Someone I had a history with, like you do with John Dale."

"So, then what?" Hallie shook a fork in the air. "John Dale drops out of school to take care of me and this baby. His parents have a hissy fit. He doesn't finish his degree, and his parents cut him off financially. His grandmother Mary probably gets mad at us, too, and reneges on her promise about the bed and breakfast. I don't ever get a chance to go to college. John Dale starts cooking in a fast food restaurant. We live in some little dump apartment and try to get by somehow. And both our lives go down the toilet."

"It might not be that bad." Delia suppressed a sigh.

"No, it might be even worse." Hallie left the table and went over to slump into one of the porch chairs.

Tanner gestured to Delia, and they both got up and went to sit on the old sofa across from Hallie. "You got any idea when this pregnancy took place?" Tanner studied a nail as he asked the question.

"Yes. Early April when John Dale came home for his Easter spring break. He stayed ten days from the fifth through the fourteenth. My guess for a date is the ninth or tenth of April—the weekend we went camping in the mountains." She frowned in remembrance. "We might have been a little careless."

Delia did a little mental arithmetic. "So you'll be due about January ninth. You'll be eighteen before then. You and John Dale can get married."

Hallie snorted. "Actually, we're already married. At least sort of."

Tanner sat up in awareness. "How can you be sort of married, Hallie?" he asked skeptically.

"Well, we got tired of waiting." Hallie crossed her arms and scowled. "It got hard. You know. Especially after John Dale went off to college. When he got home last summer, we both decided to make some changes. We falsified a copy of my birth certificate, to make me appear a few years older, and then we drove over to this wedding chapel in Townsend and asked them to marry us. John Dale had a South Carolina address and his school ID, and they thought we were a sweet little couple who'd come to get married and honeymoon in the Smokies. We didn't have any problem."

"Oh, isn't that wonderful!" exclaimed Delia with relief. "You're both already married, and the baby will be legitimate and have John Dale's name. Surely, when you explain all this to John Dale's parents, they'll understand and be supportive of you. After all, you tried to do the right thing."

Hallie gave Delia a withering look. "So, now I look real virtuous because I did the right thing and got married first. I knew that bothered you, Delia."

Delia lifted her chin. "Well, I was raised to believe that's what couples are supposed to do before ... well, you know ... before...."

Tanner laughed. "Mercy, let's not stumble over that again. I think all of us were raised that way, Delia. And, Hallie, even I'm glad you and John Dale thought more with your heads than your emotions when you made a decision to start sleeping together. At least, as Delia suggested, you tried to do the right thing."

"I wouldn't have wanted Grammie Rayfield to look down from heaven and be ashamed of me," Hallie claimed, hanging her head. "I guess she will now, anyway. I guess this is another time when John Dale's mother will say my wild Rayfield blood was showing itself."

"Nonsense." Delia's brow creased in annoyance. "This was as much John Dale's decision as yours. I don't believe it's all on the girl."

"I agree with that." Tanner got up to snag another brownie from the table. "But I'm not totally sure about all the legalities of a marriage when one partner is underage and when the couple knowingly uses a falsified birth certificate."

"Do you think we could get arrested for what we did?" Hallie's mouth dropped open, a new horror dawning on her.

Tanner shook his head. "No. It's unlikely, but you might be required to get remarried to fully legalize the marriage. Your families could hardly annul the marriage when it happened last year, and when there's a baby on the way now."

Hallie got up to pace. "We intended to get married again officially when John Dale graduates next summer. Tarnation, I wish this hadn't happened."

"You'll need to tell John Dale when he comes home," Tanner said. "When will that be, Hallie?"

"This weekend. Saturday or Sunday." She slumped in her chair at the thought.

Delia's eyes brightened. "Maybe John Dale will have an idea about what to do."

Hallie shook her head. "It was all I could do to keep him in school, and to keep him from taking off and coming up here when all this happened with Jonas Cole," she complained. "This is really going to mess things up. I don't want him to drop out of school. He's only got one more year, you know."

"There are other ways to finish a degree," Tanner put in. "I went to the University of Tennessee in Knoxville. I lived in an apartment there with Bogan and Keppler, but we could have commuted to Gatlinburg. UT has business degrees and hotel administration degrees. John Dale could finish there, Hallie. It wouldn't necessarily mean he'd need to quit school if he lived here now."

"But his parents wouldn't pay for his school." Hallie frowned. "And neither of us has the money to send him back to school and manage to get by, too."

"There are student loans for college," Delia assured her. "A lot of students go through all four years of school on student loans. I'm sure John Dale could get money to go for one year."

"It's not what I want though." Hallie ran a hand through her hair in irritation. "I want him to finish college where he started. He's going to cooking classes on the side at this chef school nearby in downtown Charleston, and he's really learning so much. I'd rather wait until he finished there. Then we can get married like we always planned and, afterwards, do the bed and breakfast."

"Sometimes plans get changed, Hallie," Tanner offered sensibly. "It doesn't mean things won't be good again. Like with Delia. Her plans got changed. It's been painful for her, but she's going to be all right. She's going to have a good life, make some adaptations, and find her way. She'll be fine. I believe she'll get another chance to make plans to marry and satisfy that part of her life, too."

Tanner enjoyed the surprised, and then tender, look he saw on Delia's face as he said this. He'd never really given much thought to how all this crisis with Prentice had torn her up inside.

Hallie crossed her arms. "Well, no matter what John Dale thinks, I want him to go back to school in Charleston." She lifted her chin stubbornly. "I'll stay here until I'm eighteen, and then I'll move over to Aunt Tabby's and Uncle Cas's at Grammie Rayfield's old place. They'll help me with the baby until John Dale graduates next May. Then John Dale will have his degree, he can get a good job, and we'll manage."

Tanner finished off his brownie before responding. "And how do you think Rev. Madison and June are going to feel about their son marrying a girl with a baby already in tow next year?" he asked.

"Who cares?" Hallie snapped back. "It's their fault we're in this mess, anyway. We wanted to get married three years ago when Tanner graduated from high school."

"Ah, come on, Hallie. You're not being logical about this at all," Tanner argued. "Three years ago when Tanner graduated from high school you were fifteen years old! Neither your mother nor your Grammie Rayfield—who was still alive then—would have wanted to see you married at fifteen. They would have never given their permission. So I don't know how you can be faulting John Dale's parents solely for this."

"That's true, Hallie," Delia put in.

"Oh, both of you are a great support." Hallie's temper flared.

Tanner shook his head. "No. You just aren't being realistic. You and John Dale fell in love very young, Hallie. I know it's hard to wait when you want to marry. But quite truthfully, it would have been better if you had. Surely you can see that now. It's not really that anyone set out to keep you two from happiness. They only wanted to see you both grow up more."

"Oh, fine. Have it your way," Hallie complained. "And I guess you've never been so in love that you didn't want to act sensibly?"

"Well, I know needs are kind of tough to deny sometimes." Tanner gave Delia a pointed glance and enjoyed seeing her blush.

"Okay. Okay." Hallie lifted both hands in surrender. "We've talked about all the ways John Dale and I acted stupid. The way some of my thinking has been twisted, according to you two. How about some ideas now for how this can work out some way? How am I going to manage here alone this fall being pregnant if I can talk John Dale into going back to school? You could be right, and we may have to tell his parents we got married and all, but I'd like to wait to do that until I'm eighteen. I've still got the Jonas Cole problem going on. The law might make me go back with Jonas and my mother with my marriage license being sort of shaky. I can't risk that."

"No. That's a point." Delia tapped her chin thoughtfully. "It would be awful if Hallie got legally sent back to Jonas Cole. She has a baby to think of now, too."

"So what's your idea, Delia?" Tanner asked her.

"I'm beginning to agree with Hallie," Delia confided. "I think she needs to stay right here, quietly hidden if she can, until she turns eighteen. Then I think she and John Dale need to legalize their marriage ... marry again or whatever ... and then tell his and her parents. At that point Hallie can either go to Charleston to stay with John Dale until he finishes school, if she gets some support from the Madisons, or as she already suggested, she can go stay with her Aunt Tabby and Uncle Cas. Or she can stay here with me until next summer when John Dale graduates."

"With you?" Hallie leaned forward, catching that last part of Delia's words. "Would you stay here with me, Delia?'

"Of course." Delia reached across to take her hand. "You're my cousin. My own blood. And my friend. I wouldn't leave you here to have a baby all by yourself, or send you away somewhere alone. I'll stay here with you until everything works out. As Tanner told me, I have a nice income you and I can live on. I helped my brothers and their wives when they had their children. I stayed with Frances when she birthed her last baby and I took care of her, the new baby, and her three little girls while she recovered from being ill." She smiled. "I know a lot about babies. I may not be as smart as you about many things, like cooking and baking or candle making, but I do know a great deal about babies. And I'm very good with them."

Hallie burst into tears, jumping up to throw her arms around Delia. "Oh, Delia, I won't ever forget this. Not ever. I swear."

Tanner, captivated, watched the scene. "Would you really change all your plans to stay here for Hallie?" he asked Delia.

She looked at him in surprise. "I'd change any plans I might have for someone I truly loved, for someone who needed me. Believe me, I wouldn't even consider letting Hallie go away with strangers at a time like this, or stay here on her own. No one wants to be alone and without family when they're having a baby."

Tanner smiled. "You're a good person, Delia."

"Not especially." She shrugged. "Anyone would do the same. Plus, we'll need your help in this, too, Tanner."

"How's that?" he asked warily.

"Hallie will need to see a doctor. I don't know any in this area, and I don't have any contacts here. You'll need to find us a doctor for Hallie. One that can be discreet, and we can trust. And someone who's a very good doctor, too."

"I'll give some thought to that," Tanner replied.

"Maybe I can wait and go to the doctor when I turn eighteen," Hallie suggested, curling back up in her own chair now.

Delia shook her head. "Oh, no, that's out of the question. And dangerous to both you and the baby. You need to be checked regularly and put on some good prenatal vitamins. You also need to be sure you eat in a healthy way."

Tanner grinned. "Well, considering how Hallie cooks, I don't think the latter will be any problem." He reached over to snag another of her brownies from the table.

Delia, ignoring him, continued thinking out loud. "We're going to need maternity clothes later on, and baby things if Hallie stays here with me after the baby is born. You know, if you do stay here, Hallie, we can make that little office beside the upstairs bedroom into a nice baby's room. We could paint and decorate it, and it would be really sweet."

"Oh, gracious, Delia." Hallie's eyes grew wide. "This is actually real, isn't it? I'm really going to have a baby."

"Actually, it's rather wonderful." Delia sat back with a sweet smile. "It may not be the best time to have a baby for you. But any baby is such a beautiful gift. You'll see that one day. It seems like it's not something you want right now, but when the baby comes, you'll feel differently."

Hallie bit her lip. "Do you really think so?"

"I know so. You'll need lots of support through this. I'll be a support, and Tanner will be a support. John Dale will be a support, too."

"I hope John Dale will be a support," Hallie whispered. "He may be mad at me."

"Why would he be mad?" Tanner's temper flared. "You didn't do this by yourself."

Hallie looked away, embarrassed.

"If John Dale doesn't step up to the plate about this honorably, I'll be very surprised," said Tanner. "I've known him ever since he was a little kid. He's a straight guy. He may be a little shocked about this at first, like we were, but he'll come around."

"Goodness, I dread telling him," Hallie confided.

"You want us to be there with you?" Delia reached a hand across to her.

"Thanks for offering," Hallie squeezed Delia's hand. "But I think it would be cowardly if I said yes to that. It seems like I ought to talk to him private about this on my own first."

Tanner held up a fist. "And if he isn't a champ about all this, I'll go bust his lip." Tanner felt pleased to see Hallie giggle.

Hallie yawned then and looked at her watch. "Listen, I know it's early, you guys, but I'm exhausted from all this emotion and crying and stuff. Would you two mind if I go on up to bed early? I feel kind of nauseous, too."

Tanner and Delia exchanged a pointed look. "You go right on, Hallie." Delia stood up. "I'll clean up everything in the kitchen and see Tanner out."

Hallie smoothed her hair back. "I don't really feel much like playing Clue right now, either," she offered apologetically. "Maybe some other time, okay?"

"We'll have lots of other times," Tanner assured her. "Don't worry about the kitchen. I'll help Delia tidy up before I go home. You get some rest, Hallie."

After Hallie left, Tanner helped Delia clean up from supper. Both were quiet while they worked. "Let's sit out on the porch for a minute before I have to leave," Tanner said at last. "It's nice out."

He saw a guarded look cross over Delia's face. "Oh, get a grip, Delia." He frowned at her in annoyance. "I'm not trying to get you into a compromising situation. I simply thought we could relax for a minute on the porch. Get some of the kinks out. It's been kind of a stressful night."

"All right," Delia agreed, dropping her eyes.

"I'm opening one of those bottles of wine I brought to go with dinner, too," Tanner told her. "I forgot I even brought them with all that was going on. Personally, I think a little after-dinner wine would be perfect right now. I'll pour you a glass, too. I bought both a red and a white. Which would you like?"

"The white," she answered, hanging up her dishtowel and starting toward the porch.

He brought two glasses out for them a few minutes later. "Boy, this has been some night, hasn't it?" Tanner fell into a chair and propped his feet up.

Delia sipped her wine. "Yes, and I'm feeling a little ashamed for worrying so much over my problems when Hallie has such bigger ones. Bless her heart."

"Things will work out somehow," Tanner said. "Hallie's a strong girl. She'll be all right."

Delia turned worried eyes to his. "But she's only seventeen, and she's having a baby, Tanner."

"Girls have had babies at younger ages than that."

"Maybe." Delia bit her lip. "But she's still so young."

"It was good of you to tell her you'd stay here with her. See her through this time. Even help her with the baby, if it comes to that."

Delia sighed. "I think she'd have done it for me, too. I kept thinking about how afraid I'd be in the same situation. Wondering what I would do. What options I'd even have. I don't think my family would support me. I think they'd send me away."

Tanner played with his wine glass. "How soon does Hallie need to go to a doctor?" he asked.

"Within the month if she can," Delia told him. "It might be wise to take her to someone in a nearby city. People talk, you know. Even if the doctor is discreet, his staff might not be. Hallie might run into someone she knows in the waiting room."

"That's a good point." Tanner tapped his finger on his wine glass, thinking. "We might find her a gynecologist in Knoxville and drive her down there. It's only an hour away. She can go to that doctor until she turns eighteen, and then maybe that doctor will refer her to a colleague he knows here."

"That sounds like a good idea, Tanner."

They sipped their wine and sat quietly in the darkness, listening to the wind rustling in the pine trees and enjoying the night sounds.

"The cicadas are out," Tanner commented.

"I hear them," Delia replied, smiling.

"Are you going to be okay if I go on home now?" Tanner asked, finishing his glass of wine.

"Sure. And, Tanner, I'm really glad you were here tonight."

"Well, I wasn't glad at first," he answered honestly, grinning at her. "But I am now. A few good things came out of this evening."

"Like what?" She seemed surprised.

"I learned you'll be staying around for a little longer." Tanner watched her drop her eyes and fidget. He chose his next words carefully. "Delia, I know you've been through a rough time, and that I've rushed you. I didn't see that at first, but I do now."

"I didn't mean to make you mad at me, Tanner," she whispered.

"I know. And I think I understand better now why you said you felt confused. It hasn't been long since you ended an engagement. When I came back here, after I broke it off with Melanie, I wouldn't have been eager to get hooked up with anybody else."

"You got hurt in that relationship?" She lifted her eyes.

"Sure," he acknowledged. "It was a raw and painful time for a while."

She nodded.

Tanner reached a hand across the sofa to lay it on Delia's. He felt her flinch, but after a minute, he could feel her heartbeat escalating where his thumb touched her wrist. "If this nice static between us could be seen, I think it would look something like those lightning bugs out there," he told her, laughing softly.

She avoided looking at him, obviously embarrassed.

"Listen, Delia. If you're confused, I want you to know I've been a little confused and surprised by all this, too. We've been friends a long time, and I hadn't expected such strong feelings between us. Just touching hands here is getting us both excited. You know it's true." He turned her face to look at him. "I'm not sure what this means for us, Delia. But I'm glad we'll have some time to figure it out."

She looked at him with big soft eyes, nervously biting on her lip.

Mercy. He could have done without that temptation right now.

"I won't push you." He got up before he reached over to kiss her. "But I want you to know I'm glad that you're staying."

"Thanks for being so understanding," she said softly, twisting her hands nervously in her lap.

"I'm doing my best," he answered.

Then he left, while he still could.

Chapter 13

Two months later, on a warm July day, Delia sat in one of the new chairs on the balcony outside the T. Cross and Crosswalk offices. The summer weeks had zoomed by since the night of Hallie's news. Where Delia once counted the days and hours from her breakup with Prentice, now she seldom had time to dwell on it. Her life had become busy and full, her pain and hurt more and more a distant memory.

Maureen and Tanner readily approved Delia's plans and cost projections for the office decorating and renovation, and the work was almost complete now. It proved challenging and satisfying, handling her first real decorating job on her own. With no one to advise and guide her, Delia learned by doing—networking locally for contract work, locating and visiting merchants and vendors for supplies and furnishings, researching and tapping old contacts for items she needed to order. To her surprise and pleasure, Delia found herself very competent in dealing with people and in negotiating prices. Locating the resources she needed excited her, like engaging in a treasure hunt, and seeing her ideas come to life felt truly satisfying. Delia loved it.

She called and talked to her friend, Holly, in Arlington, about it. "I started the decorating project with Maureen and Aunt Dee's Crosswalk office area first. When the work finished there, I moved the accounting staff across the hall temporarily to paint and decorate their area. Last week, I saw the work on the balcony finalized, and this week the final touches to the entry hall are being completed."

Delia found it hard to contain her excitement. "Holly, I found this fabulous local artist to do the Italian murals on the entry room walls—you know, to establish the Little Italy theme I told you about. They turned out even more stunning than I envisioned."

She giggled. "Tanner's friend, Bogan, printed business cards for me as a surprise and gave them to me at one of the Gang's regular get-togethers. He printed Delia Walker Interiors as my business name, added my credentials and affiliations, even noted that I specialized in commercial interiors."

"I like that name, Delia," Holly said. "It's simple and straightforward. Do you think you'll get any other business from this job?"

"Well, Bogan and Rona want me to redo their publishing offices next—take away the overkill of magnolias and floral prints their former decorator left them stuck with."

"That's the way business builds, Delia, little by little. Maybe you've found your niche there." Holly worked for a large interior design firm near DC and often yearned to start her own business.

"I don't know," Delia answered. "But the jobs will look good on my resume."

She listened to Holly tell about her latest project and then saw Maureen coming through the door. "Gotta go now, Holly. Maureen's brought us lunch. I'll call again, soon, okay?" She rang off and waved to Maureen.

"Sorry I'm late." Maureen dropped her purse on a chair. "There was a major traffic tie-up—typical for summertime in Gatlinburg. Gracious, I've never seen so many people in town! Seems like more tourists come every year." She grinned. "But I can't complain when it's so good for business. You better tell Hallie she needs to send some more candles down to the store. They're selling wonderfully. I'm getting call-ins for repeat orders every day, too. Especially on the vanilla and that new fig candle she created. I burned one of those in the front of the store yesterday, and the smell is simply heavenly. Musky and subtle. Everybody wants to know what it is, so they can buy it."

Maureen spread out their lunch on the table while she talked. Like many introverts, she might appear quiet in a group, but she could be very talkative one-on-one with people she knew well.

As the summer weeks slipped by, Delia had established a strong bond with Maureen Cross, working with her at the Crosswalk offices nearly every day. She'd come to admire Maureen's quiet strength, her business acumen, her calm under pressure, and her loyalty. She could understand now why Aunt Dee loved her so much.

"I splurged and got club sandwiches at The Brass Lantern for us. No salads today—I ordered their nice mozzarella sticks as a side instead of fries. Tanner does taxes for the manager so I worked a trade. Plus I got two slices of cheesecake."

Delia groaned.

"Oh, stop groaning. You've been eating salads for weeks now. And we needed a little celebration today for the offices being almost done. Delia, I can't believe how marvelous everything looks. I think Melinda Harvey is doing a wonderful job on those Italian scenes in the entry. In that first window mural she finished, I feel like I'm looking right out onto a view of the Italian countryside."

Delia's Place

"I'm pleased with it, too," Delia reached for a sandwich. "I love the second one she's starting that will look out across an Italian vineyard."

Maureen smiled wistfully. "Those scenes make me remember all the plans Tom and I made to go to Italy long ago."

"It doesn't bring you pain to remember, does it?" asked Delia with concern.

"Oh, no, darling," Maureen said reassuringly, patting Delia's hand. "Just good memories. The look you've created in all the offices is so polished and beautiful. I can't wait for everyone to see it all at the open house."

Delia's brows drew together in a frown. "I wish Tanner hadn't insisted on that."

"Well, you can blame me as much as Tanner for that." Maureen handed Delia a cold drink. "We all want everyone to see it and meet you."

"It's only a little decorating job for an office," she mumbled.

Maureen peered over her glasses at Delia in disapproval. "That sounds like something your mother would have said to you, Delia. You know everything starts with one first beginning. You should be proud to let people see the fine work you've done."

"Well, I don't want people to think I'm pushing myself."

"Pooh. As if they would. Everyone knows it's Tanner, Lavonne, Barry, and I wanting to show off our new offices. It's simply the icing on the cake having you at our open house, too—introducing you as the decorator." She looked at Delia thoughtfully. "Many people have missed your Aunt Dee, too, Delia, and want to meet you because you're Dee's niece."

Delia frowned again, picking at the sandwich in front of her.

"What's really bothering you in this, Delia?" asked Maureen.

"I told you," she murmured.

Maureen waited in her usual patient way, watching Delia thoughtfully.

"Oh, all right," Delia said, breaking down. "I don't want people to get the idea that I'm setting up business to stay here."

"Would that be so bad?"

Delia shrugged. "After Hallie gets things straightened out, I'll probably check with some of the firms that have been contacting me. Get into a big corporate decorating company, so I can learn and grow. Become a more accomplished designer in the field."

"Having this little open house won't get in the way of that, Delia. You know you're free to go whenever you think you should. Even with Hallie, I can watch over her and take care of her. I raised a child before, you know. I think I could do all right again." She smiled at Delia.

Delia poked at her sandwich, shifting it around on her plate.

"You're worried about Tanner, aren't you?" Maureen asked candidly. "Worried he'll get his hopes up that you will stay."

Delia looked up at Maureen in surprise.

"I'm not blind or dumb, Delia. I can tell my son has feelings for you."

Troubled, Delia blurted out, "Maureen, you know I wouldn't deliberately do anything to hurt Tanner, don't you?"

"Oh course, Delia."

"Well, it's just complicated." She swallowed hard. "Tanner and all the gang, and even Hallie, are all putting pressure on me to stay. Wanting me to set up business permanently and to stay on here in Gatlinburg."

Maureen smiled. "It's nice in this world to have people that care about you, Delia."

"Oh, I know." She fidgeted in her seat. "That's what makes it so hard. But I don't want to simply take what is the easy way. The way I just sort of fell into."

Maureen raised an eyebrow. "You'd prefer pain and suffering, is that it? Working your way up from the bottom in a large corporate firm. Probably receiving little recognition for years. Often not having any of your own ideas implemented even when they're good. Having a senior designer get credit for your ideas that do get implemented. Spending most of your time carrying out someone else's plans. Living in a little apartment in the city and riding the metro into work. Coming home to a nice cat and making a TV dinner. Yes, there's a lot to be said for that, Delia. You might miss all that by staying here."

Delia stuck her tongue out at Maureen. "You don't know it would be like that."

"Maybe. Maybe not. But think how exhilarating it's been for you to be in control here. You aren't used to that, Delia, but I've seen you take to it. You possess a natural business ability and wonderful people skills, much like Dee did." She smiled. "As I watch you work wholeheartedly and with enthusiasm, I think of her, you know. I'd hate to see your best gifts squelched where you're not appreciated."

"But I might be appreciated, and I might really make a name for myself."

"Is that what you want? A big name? National recognition?"

"My family would certainly be impressed," Delia said longingly.

Maureen shook her head. "Oh, Delia. When are you going to stop trying to impress your family? Trying to do what you think they might admire? You need to find out what it is you want, and then be happy you've learned what that is."

She nibbled a mozzarella stick. "Like Tanner did in coming back here?"

"Perhaps," answered Maureen, "and not because I wanted him back. I wanted him to be happy. I never put pressure on him to stay in the Burg, and neither did Tom. We missed him, of course, when he moved to Atlanta, but we wanted him to pursue his own dream, find his own way. Learn what he needed to make him happy."

Delia leaned her chin on her hand. "He told me there was a day when he simply knew. Just like that. Knew he needed to come back here. That he belonged here and not in Atlanta anymore. Do you think I'll have a day like that? A knowing or an epiphany about what I should do?"

"Who can say? I certainly didn't." Maureen looked thoughtful. "You may not know it, but there were two men in my life before Tom. Maybe I should say boys. One in high school—he went off to college and met someone else. I thought my heart was broken forever for a few months. The other beau joined the military. I was in college by then. It seemed our relationship simply fizzled out over time. That's when I met Tom. He worked for an accounting firm I did part-time jobs for. His dream was to come to Gatlinburg and open an accounting firm of his own here."

"What was your dream?"

She finished off a bite of her sandwich before answering. "Well, mine was a little fuzzy, so I took a look at his." Her eyes warmed. "I kept coming up here on weekends with him to the mountains, and his dream gradually took a hold on me, too. I've never been sorry."

"You've loved it here in the Burg? And never wished for something more?"

Maureen pushed her glasses up on the bridge of her nose to look directly at Delia. "Honey, I came to the point where if Tom Cross had wanted to set up an accounting firm in Iceland I'd have gone with him. I mostly just wanted Tom." She had the grace to blush. "I loved Tom Cross with all my heart. There might have been a few men before him, but I knew a good thing when I found Tom."

"Did you know right away that Tom was the one?" Delia asked wistfully.

"Delia, there are as many different kinds of love stories as there are people. You won't find a pattern you can go by for love. What may have been my story won't be yours. I knew Tom for some time before something changed between us. Before my heart recognized him."

Delia sighed. "What a beautiful thing to say."

Maureen laughed. "Well, as you've seen, I'm a sensible, practical sort of woman. My head generally rules in most aspects of my life, and my heart has to work really hard to be heard sometimes. I eventually listened."

Delia stopped with her sandwich held in mid-air. "Well, I think you have a more tender heart than you think."

"Now, that's good to hear." Maureen smiled at her. "But I want you to tell me about Hallie, how she's getting along, and about your surprise visit from June Madison. I only just heard about that, you know."

Delia laughed. "Hallie is fine," she assured Maureen. "But it really was a scare that day when Mrs. Madison stopped by. Hallie peeked out the side window when her car drove up and almost freaked out. I had to stroll over to the door slowly and give Hallie a chance to pick up all evidence of her presence from the living room and then run upstairs to hide."

Maureen chuckled. "I'd like to have seen that. What brought June to your place, anyway? The fact that you've visited at the church?"

"Yes. I panicked at first—thinking it might be something else, but it was really only a standard church visit. She brought me a pound cake and some visitor information from Highland Church."

"So what did you think of June Madison?" Maureen finished off her sandwich as she asked.

"Well, I find Rev. Madison the more comfortable of the two to spend time with," Delia said honestly. "He's easy to be around. A very kind man."

"And?" Maureen pressed.

Delia frowned. "June spent a great deal of time telling me how special she was and how short of being special other people were. It got a little wearying, Maureen. Do you think I'm being overly critical of her, or do you think Hallie prejudiced me?"

"What do you think?" Maureen opened the container holding her cheesecake.

"Well, I've been around June several times since then, and I haven't revised my opinion." She stirred at her cola with her straw.

"June has some issues, that's for sure," Maureen agreed. "If she was anybody but the minister's wife, people would probably have told her off or socially snubbed her years ago. That actually might have been good for her. As it is, I don't think June is really aware of how annoying she can be. Also, the fact that she uses religion to justify her actions is particularly galling."

"You mean like gossiping in a mean way about someone, and claiming she's only telling you about it so you'll know how to pray for the person?" Delia reached for her dessert, too.

"That's it."

Delia crossed her arms. "I got really angry with her when she started talking like that about Hallie."

"What brought that on?" Maureen raised an eyebrow.

"She was upset that Aunt Dee left money to Hallie. Acted as though I should be upset with her that Hallie got what should have been mine."

Maureen snorted.

"Of course, that's how she started in, but then she confided that Hallie had tried to become overly involved with her son for years. Told me she and her husband sent John Dale out of state to college primarily to get him away from Hallie. She said she didn't want the good Madison-Ogle blood mixed up with Rayfield blood. I thought she became very unpleasant, raving on and on about her bloodlines and talking in a very derogatory way about the Rayfield family."

"The Rayfields are wonderful people. Don't you believe a word of that."

"I didn't. Actually, I made June somewhat mad at that point. I reminded her that Aunt Dee dearly loved Etta Mae Rayfield, Hallie's grandmother, and always told me the Rayfields were some of the best people she knew. I also told her Hallie Walker was my blood kin and cousin, and that I felt uncomfortable talking about her in a negative way." Delia tapped her fingers on the table. "I thought June would take a hint from that."

"Did she?" Maureen polished off the last bite of cheese cake.

"No." Delia shook her head. "It's almost as though she doesn't hear you, Maureen. She simply shifted her focus and started talking about Hallie's mother. Said it wasn't totally Hallie's fault she turned out the way she did, and that I shouldn't worry about it. As though that's what I meant! She claimed Hallie's mother was the real problem. She raved on and on about Hallie's mother and about how important the influence of a good mother is. Then she added what the Bible said a good mother was. Quoted scriptures for illustration. It was unbelievable. Next, before I could get in a word edgewise, she started into this big discussion on how she'd raised John Dale and his sister in the right way and how fine they'd turned out."

"That sounds like June, all right." Maureen nodded. "Not much on listening."

"I felt so glad when she left, but frustrated, too. I thought I'd be able to subtly put in a good word or two for Hallie, maybe help to heal a difficult situation. I hoped I might help change June's attitude towards Hallie."

Maureen patted her hand. "Instead, you felt like you were talking to a brick wall."

"I did." Delia sighed. "I wasn't able to help things at all, but I did realize Hallie didn't exaggerate about June's feelings toward her, no matter how twisted they are."

Maureen handed Delia a napkin. "Did Hallie listen in to your conversation with June?"

"Of course." Delia rolled her eyes. "I wish she hadn't. It only upset her more."

"I wonder how June will take it when she learns John Dale is married to Hallie and that she's going to be a grandmother?"

"I can't imagine, but she did talk at length in glowing terms about her daughter's little girl and about the new baby due any time." Delia took a bite of her dessert. "I gather she's going down to spend a month or two helping out. Rev. Madison is taking leave time to go down later, too."

"That will relieve some of the tension with John Dale having to sneak over through the woods to see Hallie and making excuses to his mother about where he is."

"He's putting in a lot of time working at the hotel, too," Delia added. "Hallie complains she doesn't see as much of him as she'd like."

"Well, Tanner says John Dale's over at your place nearly every time he drops by."

Delia rolled her eyes at that. "That's been sort of a problem in itself."

"How so?" asked Maureen.

"Well, you see." Delia struggled for the right words. "They're pretty intimate, and I've sort of wondered how to handle that. Like when they go up to Hallie's room for hours ..."

Maureen smiled. "Delia, I'd say that considering Hallie's condition, there's no question of how intimate they've already been. I can't see any point in the two of them pretending they're only courting all of a sudden. After all, as Hallie said, they actually got married last summer. Legal or not, they are an adult married couple, not two teens acting inappropriately in your house."

"I suppose," Delia replied, frowning.

"Why does that bother you?"

Delia toyed with her cheesecake for a minute. "They're not very discreet about their feelings. They touch a lot, get overly close and intimate, kiss right in front of me, and make highly personal remarks. They even act that way when Tanner is there. It's kind of embarrassing."

"Ah, that's young love. Totally uninhibited." Maureen smiled at Delia.

Delia felt annoyed. "You're saying I should be comfortable with that?"

"I'm saying you should be understanding. This is actually a young married couple who wish they had their own home and their own life. Instead, they're forced to sneak a life together on the sly. Be apart much of the year. Keep their love a secret. That isn't very easy. With you, they feel safe. They feel like they can act freely. It's really a compliment to you, Delia."

"I certainly didn't think of it that way," said Delia, feeling guilty.

"You get Tanner to take you out sometime when John Dale has the night off from work. Give Hallie and John Dale the house and an evening to be together on their own. That would be nice for them. If you don't decide to take in a movie or go to one of the theatre shows in the Burg, just come over to my house or go to Tanner's and hang out. Give that young couple some private time together."

Delia hung her head. "And all I could think about was how I felt."

"It's easy for you not to understand." Maureen pushed her plate back. "You haven't been married yet. Hallie and John Dale are still in what books call the 'honeymoon period.' It's normal, Delia."

161

Delia's Place

The door to the balcony opened and Tanner stuck his head out.

"What are you two girls talking about?" he asked, coming out to join them.

"Young love," answered his mother.

"Dang. And I missed that?" He grinned.

"You did," his mother answered. "How did your lunch meeting with the Rotary Club go?"

"Good." He plopped into an empty chair. "We had an administrator from the park service tell us all about the new Twin Creeks Science and Education Center being built off Cherokee Orchard Road. It's the building they've been working on the last year or so not far from Mynatt Park and the park boundary line."

"I saw an article about that in the paper." Delia brightened. "But I haven't been to see the new building yet, have you?"

"Not lately," Tanner answered. "But I'd like to see how it's coming along."

"Well, it's only about a mile and a half or so from Balsam Lane if you cut through the woods and catch Twin Creeks Trail over to the center," put in Maureen. "Why don't the two of you take a short hike over there and check it out? Tanner, you could take off from work early and get Delia out of doors. I worry that she's worked too hard here at the offices with the decorating. She needs a day outside. And the weather is beautiful right now."

"Good idea, Mom. Actually we could go now, Delia. I don't have any afternoon appointments, and the paperwork I need to do can wait. Also, Melinda Harvey said to tell you she's leaving for the day. Something about the paint needing to dry and set before she finishes the rest of the mural. So that probably frees you up."

Delia hesitated. She'd spent most of her time these last weeks with Tanner in groups, with Hallie and John Dale, here at the office with the other staff, or in social events with the gang. They'd settled into an easy friendship, and she wanted to keep it that way. She didn't want any more scenes.

As if sensing her thoughts, Tanner gave her a telling look. "It's a short hike, Delia, that's all. As Mother said, it's a nice day to get out. What do you say?"

"Well, all right," she agreed hesitantly. "But I need to talk to Melinda before she leaves and make a quick call. After that I need to run by the house, check on Hallie, and change clothes." She glanced down at her skirt.

"Fine with me." He stood up and glanced at his watch. "I'll check my messages before I leave and see if I need to make any call backs myself and then come by the house at Balsam to get you to hike at about two. How's that?'

Delia looked at her own watch. "That will be fine."

He leaned over Delia to kiss his mother on the cheek, and the musky smell of his cologne sifted across Delia's senses, causing her breath to catch. She could smell a hint of starch in his dress shirt and the faint aroma of mint on his breath from an after lunch peppermint he'd had at the restaurant. She closed her eyes to savor the scents while he stood so close.

When she looked up, he still leaned his arms on the table, listening to something his mother said—but watching her carefully. When he saw her eyes widen, he leaned closer to her, as if he planned to kiss her right there in front of his mother. Instead, he reached down and snatched the last bite of her cheesecake from her plate.

"Hope you didn't want that," he teased, standing up now and popping it into his mouth while giving her a slow grin.

Infuriating man. Everything with him was unpredictable. One day he acted all businesslike and professional, another day friendly, cute, and boyish. Then, another so subtly sexual it drove Delia nearly wild. It wasn't that he ever did anything she could justifiably complain about, like grabbing her, kissing her, or saying anything he shouldn't. There were simply those hints in the air.

She remembered the day that he passed her on the narrow stairs coming up from Crosswalk, and they both stopped on the stairway, staring at each other. Neither one moved for several minutes, as if some kind of electric awareness flickered in the air. Delia felt almost dizzy with it swirling around them, and when he leaned in towards her, she leaned back towards him in return, expecting him to kiss her. Wanting him to kiss her. It seemed what was natural and needed at the moment.

Instead, Tanner whispered just as their faces came close, "We're having it your way now, Delia. Let me know when you want it to change." He only touched her mouth with his finger and walked on down the stairs, leaving her there shaken and upset. The whole day afterwards felt horrible, and Delia tossed and turned in her sleep that night. She didn't know what she wanted from Tanner Cross, and she didn't understand what he wanted from her either. It was so irritating and confusing.

She looked up to see Maureen cleaning up their lunch remains. "Let me help you," she offered, trying to get her thoughts collected.

"I've got it," Maureen assured her. "You go in and finish up what you need to do, so you can get outdoors and get some sunshine."

"I do need to catch Melinda before she leaves." Delia hesitated, looking toward the door.

Maureen sent Delia a small smile. "Delia, thanks for helping me to get Tanner out of the office. I worry about him working too much. He's put in too many hours lately."

"He has?" Delia still felt somewhat disoriented.

"Yes." She stuffed the last of the plates and soda cans into a sack. "It will be good for both of you to take a break today."

"Well, you work too hard, too," Delia added, deciding to suggest that Maureen go along with them.

"I agree." Maureen dusted off her hands. "I'm taking off early today to go to dinner and a show with Mamie tonight, and I plan to work outside in the yard for most of the day tomorrow."

"Well, good," said Delia, the wind taken out of her sails with that reply. "You have fun tonight with Mamie."

"I intend to. You and Tanner have fun on your hike, too." Maureen turned toward the door—giving Delia a pat on the cheek.

"Everything will be fine, dear," she said before she left. "I believe in time you'll find the answers you're looking for. So don't worry."

Chapter 14

Tanner whistled happily while he changed into a pair of shorts, a t-shirt, and hiking boots. He was ready for some time with Delia by himself. He'd carefully given her space over the last month or so. She'd needed time to heal from all that business with Prentice and to recover from the disappointment of how her family handled her broken engagement.

He paused while tying his boot. "Delia doesn't know her father actually called me at work last month—asked me to talk some sense into her, so she'd come home where she belonged. I heard her mother sputtering comments in the background, egging him on. Boy, that was a moment."

Despite the awkwardness of the call, Tanner hadn't acted rude. He behaved professionally—assured Delia's father they shouldn't worry, that this time away was helping Delia strengthen and heal. Told them his mother was looking after her.

He talked about it later with his mother at the store. "Obviously they're concerned about her, but they talk about her like she's a child and not a grown woman."

Maureen listened thoughtfully. "In some ways, Delia does act young for her years, Tanner. She's led a sheltered life, but I've watched the work she's accomplished on this decorating project draw out her strengths."

Tanner agreed. He, too, had enjoyed watching Delia find her way around Gatlinburg, make contacts, find suppliers and workers for her design project, locate furniture and accessories—and come into her own this last month.

"The work she's doing for our office spaces is amazing, Mother. I had no conception of how good Delia was at her job, or how great the offices could look from her initial drawings and descriptions." Tanner shook his head. "Delia has a rare gift, that's for sure."

Maureen smiled. "Delia's making new friends, too. Bogan's wife, Rona, often takes her shopping or to lunch. She's friendly with Bess in the store. They already have their heads together about rearranging and redecorating in Crosswalk." Maureen pointed toward some changes they'd already made.

Delia's Place

"Delia's getting to know merchants and contractors around the town. Like her Aunt Dee, she's well-liked everywhere she goes for her genuine interest in others and her thoughtfulness."

Leaning against the front counter, Maureen looked thoughtful. "Delia has a special way about her. She notices everyday details, always seems to remember the little things about people most others overlook—a favorite color, food, or interest of theirs—or happenings or details about their lives."

"I've seen that." Tanner snagged a peppermint from the jar by the register. "I think that notice of detail is what makes her such a good designer."

Tanner knew, too—with certainty—that he was falling in love with Delia Walker. Probably most everyone else knew it, as well, except Delia. She still skated around him hesitantly, reluctant to trust him, even after nearly two months. She seemed unwilling to acknowledge, to herself or to him, how she felt about him. Tanner knew she had feelings for him, but failed to understand why she fought them so and felt afraid to relax with him.

He knew he teased her in this area, even enjoyed it sometimes. Got a kick out of seeing her respond to him despite her efforts not to. Other times, it drove him absolutely wild. These last weeks, he'd worked hard to keep himself busy. Put in overtime. Fished with Vesser and Perry. Tried to keep his hands off Delia, giving her time to heal, time to let her fears of getting hurt again die down—time to want more intimacy with him like he wanted with her. But the strain was telling on him.

Picking up his waist pack, Tanner headed for the door. He didn't need to carry much on this short walk with Delia, only a few essentials—a bottle of water and some trail mix for a snack up the trail. It was only a mile and a half to the new science center, and if Delia wanted to, they could walk further to the Ogle cabin before turning back. The shady porch on the back of the old cabin would be a nice place to rest before they headed home.

As he came around the side of Delia's house, he could hear voices on the screened porch. One was John Dale's. Obviously, he must be off work this afternoon.

"Hey, Tanner," Hallie called. "Come on in. John Dale and I have been making sangria. Come try some. It's great on a hot day."

"Sangria has liquor in it, doesn't it, J. D. ?" Tanner asked, using his old nickname for John Dale.

"Just a little wine mixed with all the orange juice and fruit." John Dale got up to pour a glass of the punch-looking beverage for Tanner.

"Well, I don't think Hallie should be having much of that." Delia pursed her lips in disapproval as she came out on the porch. She wore khaki shorts with a yellow t-shirt and had pulled her thick hair up into a ponytail to keep it off her neck for their hike.

"I'm only having a small glass, Delia." Hallie held her glass up for Delia to see. "We don't want little John-John getting tipsy or anything." She giggled. John-John was the name Hallie and John Dale used for the baby lately.

"Pregnant women are not supposed to drink." Delia crossed her arms primly.

"Don't worry, Delia," John Dale soothed. "I'm limiting Hallie to that one glass. And we only made a small batch to experiment with the recipe." He offered her a crooked smile and winked at her.

Like Hallie, John Dale was tall and leggy. Tanner guessed him over six feet tall with broad shoulders, narrow hips, and long legs. He had a strong square face, dark hair, chocolate-brown eyes, and thick brows—a good-looking kid who'd become a rather fine-looking man. Like many college-aged boys, he wore his hair long, curling around his ears and down his neck. Hallie reached a hand up to tuck a strand of it behind his ears, and the two of them looked at each other with a smoldering glance. Grinning, John Dale slid a hand over the top of Hallie's thigh, letting his fingers drift slightly between her legs.

Tanner heard Hallie's breath hitch and decided it was time to make a quick exit. Obviously the wine in the sangria had begun a trickle effect. Tanner sighed. Sometimes it was tough to be around these two lovebirds. He glanced at Delia and rolled his eyes, noting a slow flush spread up her neck. Tanner knew John Dale and Hallie's open intimacies embarrassed her.

"Let's get out of here." He took a last drink of the sangria and put the glass on the table. "The afternoon is getting away."

After a few quick goodbyes, they headed out the porch door. At the end of the yard, Tanner walked around a big snowball bush to find the trail that would wind into the woods, connect to Twin Creeks Trail, and then lead to the science center and Ogle cabin.

"Hallie really shouldn't drink when she's pregnant, you know." Delia grumbled behind him.

"I doubt they'll be drinking much after we're gone." Tanner laughed. "I'd say they'll be much too busy with other activities."

"Tanner!" admonished Delia.

Tanner shrugged and avoided a reply.

After a short walk, they came to a shallow creek crossing. Sweet Gum Creek twined through the woodland behind the houses at Mynatt Park.

"Here, let me give you a hand jumping the rocks here," Tanner offered. "Some aren't very stable and can be a little shaky." He took Delia's hand and helped her navigate across the stream. On the last rock she slipped, stumbling against him as she hopped toward the bank. Tanner snatched the opportunity to pull her against him for a minute, taking her face in his hands to study her.

Delia's eyes widened as she drew in a quick intake of breath, but she didn't pull away immediately. Tanner leaned over, brushing his lips over hers

Delia's Place

softly and experimentally. "I've wanted to do that again for a long time," he told her quietly.

He felt Delia stiffen with the kiss. He pulled away, walking on ahead of her and making a casual observation about an animal print along the trailside. Why was she so afraid of him, he wondered? He'd never hurt her or grabbed her, never forced her into more intimacy than she wanted. He simply didn't understand it.

To cover the awkwardness, he began to talk as they walked along. "This is a nice, easy little trail," he volunteered, trying to rekindle their former camaraderie. "The trail winds through the woods almost parallel with Cherokee Orchard Road. Here and there you may be able to see the road through the trees to your left." He gestured. "I've walked this trail hundreds of times because it's so close to the house, yet I always see something new each time. I brought my Scouts on this hike only last month. We hiked to the Ogle cabin and back, then cooked hotdogs at the park toward the end of the day."

"That sounds like fun." Delia helped him smooth over their awkward moment. "How many boys are in your scout troop?"

"Well, I started with five kids that needed a leader, but now the troop's grown to twelve. I'm keeping it that size so I can manage the boys by myself when we want to have outings. I also occasionally help Keppler with a younger group of Cub Scouts his boy Randy is in. There are ten boys in that group, mostly ages seven and eight."

"I remember when you were a Boy Scout," Delia reminisced. "I went with Dee one time to see you get your badges in a ceremony. You marched in the color guard carrying the flag at the beginning of the ceremony."

"I'd forgotten that." Tanner held back a tree branch for her.

"Tell me about the boys in your scout troop," Delia said encouragingly. So Tanner told her stories about his boys while they walked up the trail.

They soon arrived at another creek crossing, this one spanned with a split log bridge. LeConte Creek was broader with more cascades than shallow Sweet Gum. Delia started collecting pine cones after they crossed the creek, and Tanner enjoyed helping her identify them—the long, loose cones from the white pine trees, the prickly egg-shaped cones from shortleaf pines, the smallest ones, Delia called baby cones, from the hemlock tree. She spotted a few late flowers along the trail as they walked and surprised Tanner by knowing their names.

"Do you know this one?" he asked, pointing out a pinkish weed-like flower growing by the trailside.

"I know the butterflies like it." She smiled. "Look. There's one fluttering on it now."

"The flower is Sweet Joe-Pye weed, and the butterflies do love it." He squatted down and scraped the stem below the flower stalks with his fingernails. "Take a sniff," he directed, holding his fingers up to her.

She leaned over to sniff. "Ummm. It smells like vanilla."

"Yeah, nature's interesting, isn't it?"

"Wonderful. That's why I always loved coming to Dee's in summer so much. She always took me for walks in the woods. You came, too, a lot of times."

"I remember." He stood up and started up the trail again, Delia following. "Didn't you do outdoor activities in Virginia?"

"Not much. We lived in the city, you know. Most of our outdoor fun was in the parks, along the Potomac, or at the beach in the summertime. At Emerald Isle, we explored and played outside all the time."

"I like the beach, too." Tanner stepped over a rock. "We often went to the coast for our summer vacations."

"Where did you go?" she asked with interest.

"Different places. Down to the Florida panhandle, over to the east coast to the Carolinas or Georgia. We'd try to see a bit of the area while visiting. Dad and I liked to try the fishing at different spots. That was always a good time for us."

They talked about vacations until they came to the cut road leading back to the new science and education center—a rustic wood structure with peaked roofs and gables. Nearly completed by the park now, the structure sat among pine trees on a rocky terrain.

"What did they tell you about this new center at your meeting?" Delia asked, as they walked up the winding driveway for a closer look.

"It's primarily a place for studies involved with identifying and understanding different species of wildlife in the park. Scientists, biologists, educators, and even volunteers will be involved in the effort of collecting. When the center opens later, a huge climate-controlled storage area for specimens is planned. I gather people will be able to see different species here, and the facility will be a place for conferences, meetings, and hands-on activities for kids. I hope to bring my scout troop for activities when it opens. Maybe we can help in the collecting effort, too."

"It looks like they've used a lot of natural materials in the building," Delia observed. "I see solar panels in the roof."

"Yeah. The Rotary speaker said the builders made a real effort to create energy and water-saving features and to use natural materials for the building." They walked around peeking into the windows, and then sat down on the porch for a rest.

"Didn't this whole area used to have another name?" Delia asked.

"More than one," Tanner answered. "Most recently, the Twin Creeks Research Center. Previously different kinds of scientific research were done down the road there." He pointed. "The park superintendent and various staff members lived on the grounds, too. I guess they still do."

He paused to take a swig of water from the bottle he'd brought along. "All this land was originally donated to the park by the Vorhees family. Vorhees and his wife were rich northerners who moved here, bought a hundred acres, then built a main house, guest cottages, orchards, and a farm. You can still find apple trees in the woods if you know where to look. They also built a millhouse and waterwheel on LeConte Creek. A lot of mills were built on the LeConte at one time."

"Maybe they should have named this center the Vorhees Center to honor the original donors," Delia suggested, as they clambered down from the porch to start back to the trail again. "Speaking of names, does anyone know where the name Gatlinburg came from? I've always wondered about that."

Tanner laughed. "The town got its name from Radford Gatlin, an early 1800s storekeeper and postmaster in the area. Stories say he was outspoken and highly argumentative by nature. When the Civil War broke out, the people here in the mountains, over 1,300 at the time, voted pro-Union—Gatlin the one pro-Confederate vote. Evidently, he spoke quite vocally about his opposing beliefs. Sentiments ran high at the time, and he got run out of town—although some accounts say he left prior to that over other disputes. Anyway, the Gatlinburg name, already in place by then, stuck and was never changed.

"So Gatlins are not one of the old families here now?"

"No. And to be frank, I'm not sure where Gatlin went when he left here."

"It's sort of funny for a city to be named for a citizen run out of town." Delia giggled. "It makes a good story."

"This area is filled with great stories." Tanner led the way back on to the trail again.

"Tell me another one," Delia pleaded, following him. "Please."

"All right. I'll tell you one about a cemetery nearby." Tanner was glad she felt happy with him again. "If you follow the Roaring Fork Motor Nature Trail around the loop, you'll see a sign for Baskins Creek Trail on the left side of the road. A short distance up that trail is the Bales Cemetery. There are graves there for different families that settled this area—Ogles, Bales, Reagans, and others. Somewhere in that cemetery is also the buried leg of Giles Reagan. He lost his leg in a sawmill accident, and it's told they held a formal Christian funeral ceremony there just to bury his leg."

Delia giggled again. "Is there a gravestone for his leg?"

"Not that I've seen." Tanner smiled at her. "But the story is documented and held to be genuinely true around the area."

"I love the mountain stories and all the rich family traditions carried down among the people here in the Smokies." Her enthusiasm rushed into her voice.

"Maybe you ought to stick around the area and marry me, and we can create some mountain legends of our own together," Tanner teased. Peeking behind him to see a scowl cross Delia's face, he wisely changed the subject. "We're coming close to LeConte Creek again on the left." He gestured. "You can hear the cascades rushing over the rocks if you listen."

At the creek, Tanner involved Delia in looking for trout in a deep pool in the stream. He entertained her with stories about fly-fishing. It took him a while to get her mind off that last comment of his, but eventually he did. You couldn't blame a guy for trying, he thought. Besides, he'd wanted to test the waters.

Twin Creeks Trail rose gently through a nice woodland for about two miles before ending near the back of the Ogle cabin. A path wound between shrubs and trees to the back porch of the old cabin. From the front, another path led directly to the road. With easy accessibility off the Roaring Fork Motor Trail, the Ogle cabin received many visitors, but today Tanner and Delia found the place deserted and quiet.

Delia looked around. "This is one of the places where Hallie rested on her long hike when she ran away and came to Aunt Dee's."

"She's a plucky girl." Tanner walked up on the porch and sat down in the shade, leaning his back against the cabin wall. He patted the floor beside him, and Delia came to join him.

Tanner pulled out his trail mix for them to munch on and shared his water bottle. The July day was hot and both were sweating from their walk up the trail. Delia took her boots off to cool her feet. "Pretty toenail polish," commented Tanner, grinning at her.

She sent him a smile in return. "It's Hallie's," she told him. "Passion pink." As soon as she spoke the words, she realized what she'd said and blushed. They sat quietly after that.

"Do you mind if I ask you something?" Tanner said at last.

"What?" Delia replied absently.

"Why are you so afraid of me?"

Delia didn't answer, chewing her lip in that provoking way of hers, studying her hands instead of looking directly at him.

"I've known you since you were barely five years old, Delia. We played together summer after summer as children. We held hands running; I lifted you time and again so you could reach the high branches in the trees we climbed. We lay on the ground together side by side under the lilac tree, invisible to the world, talked and shared our dreams and thoughts. Sometimes you used my stomach for a pillow. When we grew older, we kissed in fun playing spin the bottle. We kissed more seriously when I was eighteen, you only thirteen."

Tanner paused for a moment, gathering his thoughts into words. "Now, whenever I touch you, Delia, you flinch. If I kiss you, you stiffen like I'm planning to rape you. I don't understand it. If I thought you felt indifferent to me, I wouldn't even pursue you, but I don't think that's the case. We have energy going between us. There are feelings. I'm drawn to you, and when I watch your eyes and the signs of your body, I can tell you're drawn to me. But when I act on it, you pull away like I've offended you or acted inappropriately—like I'm going to hurt you."

He scuffed his shoe against the porch thoughtfully, waiting for Delia to speak. She didn't, and the stillness stretched. In the quiet, they could hear the sounds of a squirrel scuttling under a nearby tree and the hum of bees on a clump of pink coneflowers against the side of a nearby shed.

Tanner cleared his throat. "Delia, I'm a pretty tough guy, but you're tearing me apart with this. You give me mixed signals, and they confuse me. It really hurts me that you don't trust me, that you act like I'd do something aggressive to you that you didn't want. Surely you know me better than that?" He threaded his hands through his hair. "I might get a little annoyed when my testosterone pumps up and you push me away suddenly, but I'll always respect your right to say stop at any time. Can you ever remember a time when I haven't?"

"You got mad at me that night at the park," she whispered, and he looked over to see she was crying.

"Yes. I was mad then, Delia. You hurt my pride, pushing me off unexpectedly, acting like I was ..." He searched for the words. "Some sort of creep trying to put the feels on you. I'm sorry if I got angry and scared you that night, but I didn't know what to think about how you acted. First, you acted warm, soft, and receptive; then, you acted all cold and shocked. You accused me of playing games with you ... of not being serious. You made it clear you didn't want to be more than friends with me after you'd flirted with me for days, giving me little kisses and invitations. So, yes, I did get angry that night, Delia. I think I had a reason."

"Maybe," she mumbled. "I guess you had a reason."

"You guess?" Tanner bit down on his temper. "So what about now, Delia? You need to tell me how you feel, so I'll know how to act with you. I want you to be genuine and honest with me here."

"How I feel about what?" she murmured evasively, still looking down at her hands and avoiding his eyes.

Tanner studied her. "Well, here, let's do a little test so we can be specific," he suggested, with a sudden inspiration. He scooted closer to her against the cabin wall until his body pressed against the side of hers. Then he linked his arm around her back and looped his leg over hers.

"All right, let's start with this. How do you feel when we sit close together—much like we used to as kids?"

"I feel funny," she whispered.

"I hope you mean funny good." He exchanged a knowing glance with her and noticed she didn't pull away. Smiling at her gently, he put his hands in her hair and turned her face so he could look in her eyes. He touched her face softly, tracing his fingers down her cheeks and jaw line and then underneath her ears, watching her all the time. "What about now, Delia? How do you feel now?"

"Really nervous," she answered honestly, swallowing.

"Why nervous?" he asked softly, moving a little closer.

"I don't know," she told him. "I guess I'm wondering if you're going to ... well, maybe if ..." She stopped and looked at his lips, wetting her own unconsciously.

Tanner smiled and touched her lips, tracing his fingers across them.

"My heart gets really scared now, Tanner. Wondering if you will or wondering if you won't. Wondering if I want you to or not. Afraid you will and afraid that you won't." She tried to pull her eyes from his, embarrassed at her own words.

He put his hand above the top of her breast where he could feel her heart beating, and heard her gasp. "I'm only feeling your heart, Delia. That's all; so don't get all panicky on me. Here." He took her hand and put it on his chest over his own heart. "Tell me what you feel with your hand?"

"Your heart is beating really fast." She looked at him in wonder. "And you're breathing harder."

"So are you," he told her smiling. "Your heart is beating faster now, too."

"Your eyes are changing somehow." She leaned closer to see and ventured a smile. "And I can smell that nice cologne you wear."

They sat close together staring at each other for a minute, reveling in the emotional feelings that played between them. It took a lot of effort for Tanner to hold back, to let Delia play this little game of exploring new emotions and reactions with him.

"Here, let's hug," he suggested, reaching over to pull her against him. She started to stiffen again, but when she realized Tanner only meant to hug—just as he'd said—she began to relax. Her fingers began to play softly across his back and then probed their way to the nape of his neck. Mercy, her touch felt sweet. Tanner followed her lead, letting his own fingers explore their way softly across her back.

He wondered about the past men in Delia's life at that point. Had they always pushed too hard, pressured Delia for more than she felt ready to give? Had they paid no attention to what she felt or what she wanted? He wished he could ask her about it, but he was afraid to break the good moment between them.

She laid her head against his chest. "Your heart is beating even faster now, Tanner. I think mine is, too. This is nice."

He swallowed. "The next step is kissing a little if you won't get upset about trying that out, Delia. We can simply experiment. See how we feel. See how you feel about it."

"Okay," she whispered.

He kissed her teasingly at first. Kissed the sides of her mouth, then touched his lips softly to hers, retreating before moving in once again. He watched her close her eyes and lean in for more. "Tell me how you feel now, Delia, and what you want." He spoke softly near her mouth, knowing she could feel the warmth of his breath. "Do you want little soft kisses or something more?"

"Something more," she murmured, licking her lips and stirring him. He angled in for a deeper kiss, but then after starting, pulled back, teasing her once again. Making sure she wanted him to go on.

She made some soft, little noises that nearly drove him crazy, pressing herself closer against him. He kissed her more intimately at that point, felt her soften against him at last, but even then he pulled back just when it began to get interesting. "Tell me how you feel now, Delia?" He teased his tongue around her mouth. "Does this feel good? Do you think we should do this some more?"

"I don't know," she started to say, but as Tanner brushed his lips over her closed eyelids and whispered kisses down her cheeks, she sighed. "Maybe yes, Tanner. I think yes." She'd started to breathe heavier now.

Tanner touched his lips and tongue against her mouth again, tracing slowly around her lips. When she began to open her mouth to him instinctively, he let his tongue tease into the edge of her lips and slip into her mouth. He wondered from the way Delia acted if she'd ever been kissed with any real mutual passion before.

They'd both heated up from the hugging, touching, and teasing kisses now. Delia stirred restlessly against him, moving closer to get more of her body next to his. Tanner knew he was in the catbird seat now, and he definitely wanted to stay there and not blow it this time with Delia. He forced himself to pull away from her and not move on to a more intimate stage.

"Are you still afraid of me now, Delia?" he asked her softly. He lifted her chin so her eyes would meet his but kept one finger tracing itself gently over her lips.

"Yes," she whispered back candidly. "But I don't think it's in a bad way. I've had excited feelings over some boys before. Sort of ...." She looked down in embarrassment. "But I've never had feelings like this. They scare me. They're so intense, so strong. So different. The scariest thing is that you're the one making me feel them, Tanner. I've known you forever, like you said. It feels weird, Tanner. I keep thinking you'll make a joke or suddenly jump up and holler, 'Last one to the house is a rotten egg!'"

Tanner chuckled. "I doubt I'm going to do that right now, Delia." He traced a finger around the neckline of her t-shirt, making her shiver.

"But doesn't it feel odd to you, Tanner?" she pressed. "That you feel like this about me, little Delia Walker? Doesn't it? Be honest."

"Okay, sometimes it does. I keep thinking Dee might walk in and say, 'Tanner Cross, what do you think you're doing with my niece?' That she'll scold me, send me home, and call my mother."

Delia giggled. "What do you suppose Aunt Dee would think about us starting to care for one another?"

Tanner considered this. "She loved us both, Delia. I'd say she would be happy. She's probably smiling down about now, wondering why we stopped kissing and started talking so much."

Delia tilted her head to one side to look at Tanner. "Could we do another really big kiss—and then stop and talk about it like we've been doing?"

"I think I can do that," said Tanner, grateful for anything at this point. He nibbled his way toward her mouth, making her giggle, and then began feathering little kisses around her lips until he felt her sigh and open to him. He shifted the angle of his mouth and began to kiss her more deeply. She gave a soft moan and pressed against him, joining him this time eagerly in the kiss. Thrilling him.

They explored with lips and tongue, filling their hands with each other's hair and letting their fingers drift and explore. The heat of rising passion began to surge between them. Tanner reveled in it until he felt a small hand move between them, pressing on his chest to stop. He pulled back reluctantly.

They stared at each other, both panting, the pupils of their eyes huge.

"I stopped." He managed to get the words out. "Do you feel okay?"

"I feel good." She smiled a little. "I feel like I don't want to stop. I feel the way I see Hallie and John Dale look at each other sometimes."

Tanner groaned, pulling her close against him again. "I hope you can feel some of the other changes happening here between us."

"Yes, you've grown in some other areas since we were kids, too." Delia giggled, surprising Tanner with her candor.

"You wanna play doctor again, like we did when we were small?" He smoothed a hand down her arm. "We can examine each other."

"I don't think that would be wise," Delia replied saucily. "I might find myself in the same kind of predicament Hallie is in if I played doctor with you."

Tanner traced his fingers over Delia's lips again. "Do you feel more comfortable with me now, Delia Eleanor Walker? Please say you do."

Delia's Place

"I do," she confided. "Tanner, I really do have feelings for you. It's odd because we've known each other forever, but I'm afraid, too."

Tanner waited, watching her and giving her a questioning look.

"I've been hurt so much thinking I'm in love. Wanting to believe someone might be the one. I've been disappointed so many times. I'm just now starting to feel okay again after all I went through with Prentice, and I'm scared to think of going through something like that again. Of trusting and starting to believe again. Of maybe finding it's not real after all. Of experiencing pain once more and disappointment."

Tears welled in her eyes as she spoke with total candor now. Thankfully, he'd gotten past her reserves today.

Tanner considered his tactics and next words carefully. "How about if we just take our relationship really slow—in little baby steps—like we did checking out our feelings today. We can explore it together. Spend time together. Kiss and hug sometimes when we want to. Wait and see. Believe me, Delia, I don't want to fall in love and get hurt either. It's the pits."

"It is." She nodded her head. "And I'd feel awful if I hurt you, Tanner. It would pain you and hurt Maureen, too, if my feelings weren't sure. Probably other people would be upset, too." She frowned. "Plus all the Jack Gang would hate me."

He smiled. She wanted so much to please others and not hurt anyone—so different from the polished and arrogant Melanie he'd spent so much of his time with in Atlanta. It amazed him that he'd ever believed he could live out his life with someone as insensitive to others as she'd been. Someone who thought of others primarily in terms of what they could do for her, how they could help her ambitions.

"Can we really, truly, simply go slow, like you said?" She turned hopeful eyes to his. "Can we keep it secret that we're starting to like each other? So no one will be disappointed if one of us changes their feelings or changes their mind?"

Tanner knew she meant him, although she suggested it might be either of them. "We'll go slow now and slow later, too," Tanner said, grinning and thinking ahead to how good that would be. Delia Walker had banked passions simply waiting for someone to set them free. He fully intended for it to be him.

"Don't worry, Delia." He kissed her nose. "For now we'll just act like we're good friends around everyone we know, and we won't tell anyone we're starting to like each other in a new way." As if they won't figure it out, Tanner thought, but he didn't say that to Delia. He knew how scared she was of being disappointed in love again.

She sighed. "Okay, that sounds good."

At that point, Delia noticed that she and Tanner still had their legs and arms wrapped around each other intimately. A little flush ran up her neck to her face.

Watching her reaction, Tanner felt his blood start to rush again.

She turned her eyes to him, trustingly now, and reached a tentative finger to start tracing it over his lips like he'd done with her before. "Maybe we could experiment a bit more, Tanner?" she suggested in a soft whisper. "With the kissing." She dropped her eyes for a minute, embarrassed by her request, but then gave Tanner a shy smile. "I've never been kissed quite that way before exactly. It was nice."

"Is that right?" He savored her words, letting his fingers slide up her arms slowly, teasing the soft skin on the inside of her underarms, moving his fingertips to her lips, watching her close her eyes and sigh. He kissed her again, fighting the urge to let his fingers drift down into the neckline of her yellow t-shirt. Delia responded more yieldingly than before now, making it harder for Tanner to keep his restraint in tack.

Tanner wanted her intensely but knew he'd made a lot of progress breaking through to Delia Walker today. He didn't want to press his luck. He felt almost glad when they heard a group of noisy tourists coming down from the road to see the cabin.

Delia jerked up, straightening her hair and clothes, nervously gathering up her hiking pack, and hurrying to put on her socks and boots again. By the time a family with several children rounded the corner of the cabin, she had a bright smile ready for them. Tanner, as a native, soon began answering their questions about the area.

About twenty minutes later, Tanner and Delia started their hike back down the trail in a new, more comfortable way. Delia no longer flinched every time Tanner touched her. She smiled at him often. They talked more easily. Occasionally they exchanged knowing looks, obviously both remembering their earlier time at the Ogle cabin. Still thinking about it.

"Hey, Tanner," Delia asked at one point, shifting subjects. "Why do you think Hallie's mother left her when she was so small? I've thought and thought about that. It seems to me there must be some reason why she did that."

"I don't know." He pulled back a branch hanging over the path. "I've thought about that before, too. Sometimes Mother and I have talked about it and wondered. Especially after Hallie worked in the store last summer. Mother grew fond of her."

"Hallie says it's probably because she grieved for Lawson so much after he died and that maybe Hallie reminded her too much of him."

"I don't think that really makes sense." Tanner frowned. "When my father died, it brought my mother and me closer. We were all each other had then."

Delia's Place

"I think there has to be some other reason," Delia analyzed. "I subtly probed the Walker family when I visited their business to buy furniture and get the chairs upholstered, but I never found out anything except that Lawson and Hallie's mother Sissy were very much in love. It seemed a great tragedy he lost his life so young."

Tanner looked thoughtful. "You know, the only odd thing I can remember when talking to the Walkers was a funny comment Vesser made one day while we fished together."

"Vesser is Lawson's brother, right?"

Tanner nodded. "We stood out in the stream casting together and somehow got on that subject. I don't remember how, but Vesser said something about it being his fault Sissy left."

"Why's that?" Delia voice sounded surprised.

"I have no idea. When I caught his comment and asked him about it, he changed the subject. Said he had to get some more bait. The topic never came up again."

She regarded him with interest. "Well, one thing I've learned is that things are never as simple as they seem."

Tanner considered this. "You'd think Sissy would have told Hallie by now if there was some important reason for her leaving."

"Maybe. Unless it was something she didn't want Hallie to know."

Tanner turned to grin at her. "Looking for a mystery to solve, Nancy Drew?"

"I might be." She lifted her chin. "I've also been wondering why my mother disliked my Aunt Dee so much. I mean, I always sort of accepted it as a given earlier, but now I'm starting to wonder what's really behind that, too."

Shifting the subject, Tanner asked, "How is your mother handling you continuing to stay down here?"

"Oh, she isn't happy with it." Delia rolled her eyes. "Keeps asking who I've sent out resumes to and what progress I've made looking for a position."

"Did you tell her about the job you did for the offices here? About the probes you've received from others in the area to decorate for them?"

"Mother and Daddy aren't taking any of the work I'm doing here seriously, Tanner. Gatlinburg is too small to matter to them. I'd need a metropolis to impress them—or to get coverage in a major magazine or something." She sighed.

"You'd really like to impress them, wouldn't you?" Tanner asked quietly.

"Silly, isn't it?" Delia admitted. "But I guess everyone wants their parents to be proud of them."

"They may not express it well all the time, but I think they love you, Delia."

"Do you think so?" She caught his glance.

"I do." He focused on her. "Look how often they call. Your brothers and sister Frances call, too. It's obvious they all care about you."

"I just wish I felt more assured that they cared," Delia fretted. "It's easier for me to see your mother cares for me than to know my own mother does. Mother criticizes so much and makes so many digging comments about things. Always makes me feel that I fall short. My brothers and Frances do that, too."

"Maybe it's because you've always been the baby," Tanner suggested. "Maybe it's hard for them to start seeing you as an adult—to treat you as an adult."

"Maybe." She kicked a stone in the path.

He turned to her and stopped walking. "Maybe you just need to keep acting like an adult until they all get the message."

"I'm working on that." She leaned over to pick up another pinecone. "But another thing I'm beginning to understand, in all this, is that I'm sort of different from my family. Actually, I'm more like Aunt Dee. I like simple things, simple pleasures. I like a dinner on the porch cooked by Hallie as much as a dinner in a fancy restaurant. I like a picnic with the Gang more than a gala evening at the opera. I enjoy a hike, like we had today, as much as a weekend shopping in New York."

Tanner grinned at her wolfishly. "Yeah, I really liked our hike today, too."

"Oh, you." She swatted at him. "I'm trying to be serious here."

So am I, he thought. So am I.

It wasn't long until they hopped Sweet Gum Branch again, walked down the path into Aunt Dee's back yard, and let themselves into the screened porch. In the house, they found John Dale and Hallie curled up on the living room sofa, their legs draped over each other, watching a movie. Tanner noticed Delia didn't show as much embarrassment seeing them coiled up together this time. Even with John Dale's hand draped casually across Hallie's breast.

"Do you have to work tonight, John Dale?" Delia asked, leaning over to unlace her boots.

"No. This is my day off," he answered her.

"Oh, good." She flashed him a bright smile. "Maybe you'll keep Hallie company tonight while Tanner and I go back to the office to check on some decorating problems. Plus we really need to drive to Sevierville, so Tanner can see this clock I've been looking at for the entry. It's an important piece, and I don't want to make the decision about it without his input. I thought we'd catch a bite to eat on the way. You guys wouldn't mind if we left for most of the evening, would you?"

John Dale's eyes brightened. "Well, no. Of course not, Delia. I told my mom I got called in to work again, and Ronnie Grimes, my manager, promised to cover for me if Mom calls at the Hyatt to check on me. I can stay here and keep Hallie company all evening."

Tanner noted that Hallie smiled at John Dale playfully.

Delia went out to the kitchen to put up her hiking pack and empty out her water bottle. Tanner followed.

"What was that about?" he hissed, so Hallie and John Dale wouldn't hear him from the other room.

"It was your mother's idea," she whispered. "She said they needed more time alone. Your mother suggested I tell them one evening when John Dale was off work that I needed to go out. To make up an excuse. She said it would be all right if I just went over to her house and hung out with her."

"That won't be necessary," Tanner assured her. "I know a nice Italian restaurant down in Sevierville I'd like to try out tonight." He paused. "Is there really a clock there you want me to look at? Or was that made up."

Her mouth curved in a smile. "No. I've really been trying to decide about one. Would you give me your opinion? I think the store is open late."

"You're on." He gave her a thumbs up. "I'll go over to the house, shower and change, and pick you up in half an hour. How's that?"

"That would be nice," she answered.

"Can we call this a date even though you asked me?" he teased.

"We're calling this an opportunity for John Dale and Hallie to have an evening together." She kept her voice casual. "Your mother reminded me they have very little private time alone as a young married couple."

"Maybe we can work out a little private time for Tanner and Delia to be alone together this evening, too." He winked at her.

"Maybe, but it will hardly be the same for us," she replied, on an oddly wistful note that made Tanner hide a knowing grin.

Tanner gave her a kiss on the cheek and left the house whistling. This had turned out to be a very fine day indeed. And the future looked decidedly brighter.

Chapter 15

The next morning, Delia sat in the kitchen, wrestling with mixed emotions about Tanner and their time together the day before. "I shouldn't have let Tanner kiss me again." She sighed. "Oh, it felt nice—in fact more than nice—but I still don't know if it's wise to get involved with Tanner Cross. Or with anyone right now."

She frowned in thought as she stirred milk into her coffee. "My goal this summer was to get my focus, figure out who I am in my own right, and chart my own direction for my life without letting others do it for me. That's the main reason I came here instead of going straight to my family at the beach. Mother and Frances always take over my life, start making all my plans for me, and before I know it, I drift along with their plans—getting no voice—like I've done so many times before."

Delia shook her head remembering. "They made my college choice, even blocked a scholarship offer because they thought the school too far from home, and they refused to let me take several good summer jobs I wanted. They opposed that wonderful camp counseling job out west. Refused to let me take that cruise ship job." She sighed, remembering a list of lost opportunities through the years.

"They always had a rationale for everything, but I think they primarily wanted to keep me close to home. They never had confidence in my ability to manage on my own. They always told me—more often than I care to remember—how I might fail more than how I might succeed." She poured cereal into a bowl. "Tanner was right in saying they mean well—and obviously love me. I know that, but their love is smothering and limiting sometimes."

Delia propped her chin in her hand. "When I look back, I see that I often chose companions who treated me the same way—strong-willed young men who thought more of their plans and welfare than mine. Who relegated me to more of an ancillary role that revolved around them." She winced. "Who smothered and limited me, too."

Delia's Place

Delia thought about Hallie and her spunky strength in planning for her own future and pursuing it. She remembered the arguments she'd heard between Hallie and John Dale—Hallie standing up to John Dale pluckily, pushing to see her own plans or ideas prevail in their discussions. Delia admired that. She wanted to be more sure of her own way, to have the courage to pursue what she felt was right for herself without being manipulated so much by others. She sipped at her coffee, wishing Tanner could understand that.

"You're up early," Hallie offered, coming into the kitchen.

"And you're up late." Delia looked pointedly at the apple shaped clock on Aunt Dee's kitchen wall.

"I seem to be more tired lately." Hallie sighed. "I'm into my fourth month now, and the baby seems to be taking more of my strength."

"Well, I think you're a very healthy pregnant woman," Delia told her, smiling. "Hardly any morning sickness, health problems, swelling, or other concerns many women face in their pregnancies."

"My pants are getting too tight." Hallie pulled up her shirt to examine her waistline. "I can't snap my favorite jeans anymore, and I've started wearing slacks and shorts with elastic waists most of the time."

"We probably need to get you some maternity clothes soon," Delia observed.

"Ugh. I'm going to get a real poke-belly, aren't I?"

Delia laughed. "You're raising a new life inside. You should know enough from growing up on a farm most of what will happen."

Hallie moved a skillet onto a stove eye and started fixing herself some eggs for breakfast. "What's the word for the day?" she asked, seeing that Delia had her devotional book and Bible laid open on the kitchen table. "Read it to me while I cook."

Since early that summer, Delia had been reading Aunt Dee's devotional books and looking up the corresponding scriptures related to each reading. She and Hallie liked a devotional book entitled *A Year's Journey of Words*. Each day offered a quote by a well-known man or woman of God that contained the "Daily Word" followed by a linked scripture that used the word for the day and suggested Bible chapters. Next the author provided personal discussion on using the day's word—and scriptures—to journey into a deeper faith. This book had become the girls' favorite and they read it and talked about the readings together every day over breakfast.

"Today's word is Walk," Delia told her. "The quote is one by a preacher and evangelist named George Mueller. It reads: 'If you walk with Him and look to Him and expect help from Him, He will never fail you.'"

"I like that." Hallie popped a piece of wheat bread into the toaster. "It reminds me of the one a few days ago about seeking, that if you seek God you'll find Him. I thought about that a lot while making candles yesterday."

Delia's eyes scanned down the page. "The scripture that goes with Walk, is one from Isaiah 30:21: 'Thine ears shall hear a word behind thee saying, This is the way, Walk ye in it, when ye turn to the right hand, and when ye turn to the left.' The author writes that if you need help about your way or direction, you should go to God, get alone with Him and seek guidance directly from Him. It says God walks with us individually in different ways, guiding us and helping us, speaking to us according to who we are and where we are in our walk and journey with Him."

Hallie put her plate of eggs and toast down on the kitchen table and sat down to eat. She took the devotional book from Delia and read some more of it on her own.

"I like this idea about God finding His own individual way of walking with us and talking with us." She tapped the page with a finger. "My Grammie Rayfield used to tell me God walks and talks with folks in different ways. She said God talked to her in the garden a lot, giving her principles that related to how things grew while she weeded flowers or picked vegetables. Dee used to tell me she took listening walks with God—that He talked best to her while she hiked or walked in the woods."

"Do you have a place where God talks more to you?" Delia asked her.

Hallie thought about that for a minute. "I always go to my prayer rock high on the hillside behind Grammie's farm when I need a big answer." She spread butter on her toast. "But I find God sort of talks to me while I work, too. You know, when I'm baking bread or making candles and stuff. Sometimes I get my best ideas then."

"I'm not sure I have a special place where God talks to me most," Delia confided, biting her lip and thinking. "But whenever I wanted to pray real hard about something or felt upset and confused, I usually walked down the street and slipped into the church sanctuary. Our church wasn't far from our house." Delia thought back, trying to remember. "On Sundays, I figured God was busy with all those other folks in church, but when I slipped in alone during the week, I always believed it only me and Him. Then I could sit there with all His holiness to myself. Silly, huh?"

"No. That's sweet. And what better place to talk to God than in a church." Hallie smiled. "With you being a decorator sort of person, you'd probably relate better talking to God in an actual place. You know, with the right ambience. All those beautiful stained glass windows at Highland would be enough to get anybody in a spiritual mood. I loved looking at those when I visited there."

Delia tilted her head, remembering. "Aunt Dee told me each one represented a parable in the Bible. She took me around and showed me all of them. Once I remember the minister doing a sermon on one of the windows when I went to church with Dee."

Delia's Place

Hallie paused between bites. "You know, I might have problems with June Madison, but John Dale's father is a good minister," she admitted. "In fact, he's a nice, gentle man—kind, thoughtful and wise. To be perfectly frank, I like June, too, when she's not trying to show off. She used to be an English teacher; maybe that's why she's kind of prissy and precise. But she really loves books and knows all about good books to read. She used to work in the library in Gatlinburg part-time, and when I was little, she'd help me find books to check out. When she talked about them, I'd get real excited and want to read them. She did the children's story hours at the library, too, and she was great. She used to have this box of hats. We'd all put on a magic listening hat along with her. It signaled time to be quiet and listen, so we could hear the story."

"I'm glad to hear something good about June," Delia said.

"There's a lot that's good about June Madison," Hallie admitted. "Look how nice John Dale turned out. June's simply too hung up about lineage and genealogy lately. John Dale says she got that way after he and Mary Alice grew up. He thinks she doesn't have enough to keep herself busy. If I had a better relationship with her, I'd encourage her to go back and work at the library again."

"I like the way you always look for the good in people." Delia smiled at her.

Hallie shrugged. "I told you, it was what Grammie always made me do. Think of the good things."

Typical of Hallie she changed the subject. "I wish I could come to your open house tomorrow, Delia. I feel awful I can't be there. I'm glad you sneaked me over one night to see how everything turned out, but I'd love to see everybody's reaction to the design job you did. It's awesome, you know. I'm really staggered at your talent."

"Why thanks, Hallie, but it was only a small job, really."

"You stop that self-deprecation right now." Hallie shook her finger at Delia accusingly. "That's a bad habit of yours. You did fine work over there, and you should accept praise for it gracefully. And you'd better do that tomorrow. You think of me whenever anyone compliments you, and you say, 'Why, thank you very much' ... and 'That's kind of you to say that' ... or 'I'm so glad you like it.' Don't you dare put yourself down or diminish the work you did by one little bit, you hear me?"

Shocked at Hallie's vehemence on the subject, she answered, "I'll try, Hallie."

"You do more than try," she challenged back, scowling. "You recognize and celebrate your gifts. God gave them to you, and He deserves better than you putting them down whenever someone notices them. You don't have to be prideful about it, but you should be respectful of your gifts and of yourself."

Delia winced, knowing she was receiving good advice from Hallie once again.

"John Dale's coming to your open house," Hallie continued. "And I told him to stay around close to you and to fuss at you if you started to put yourself down." She got up to get another glass of juice. "Maureen told me there's a magazine writer coming to take pictures and stuff at the open house, too. So you dress sharp and talk nice about yourself. Don't you be saying negative stuff he can quote later."

"What magazine?" Delia asked, shocked.

"Nothing for you to panic about," Hallie poured out her juice. "Just some local publication that covers new events and new businesses, but still, it's recognition."

"Do you think my black dress will be okay to wear?"

"Absolutely. It reeks of money and success." Hallie laughed. "I won't even ask how much you paid for that thing. But I can tell from how it looks on you that it's expensive. So it's just the thing for this event. Wear your signature pearls, too. I like those on you."

"I'm nervous," Delia admitted.

"Everybody is nervous before a big event. Especially one where they're in the spotlight." Hallie grinned. "Just don't let anyone know you're nervous. Simply walk around with grace and act like you do this kind of thing every day. No one needs to know you're nervous and flustered unless you tell them."

"I suppose," Delia worried, biting her lip a little in anxiety.

Hallie darted off onto another subject. "And by the way, thanks for giving me and John Dale an evening to ourselves. It was nice for us. I know you made up that business about needing to go out, so the two of us could have time together."

Delia lifted her chin. "I'll have you know Tanner and I did go over to look at that brass clock together, and we did eat out in Sevierville."

"I don't doubt that. But I saw the surprise on Tanner Cross's face when you started talking about your plans for the evening." Hallie laughed. "I thought he was going to poop his pants!"

"Hallie!"

"Well, anyway, both John Dale and I figured out what you two were doing for us, and we're grateful. Having a whole evening together gave us some good time to discuss things we needed to talk over."

"Have you convinced John Dale to finish out his senior year of college in Charleston?"

Delia's Place

Hallie shrugged. "More or less. Let's just say I've threatened him into it for now. But he still isn't happy about it. The only big thing in my favor is that you offered to stay here with me through the birth of the baby and after. John Dale thinks a lot of you, Delia. I want you to know we're never, ever going to forget what you've done for us, letting me stay here like this and taking care of me. Being willing to put your own life on hold to be here for me in a bad time."

Delia smiled at her. "I'm getting sort of fond of you, you silly nut. I'm actually getting sort of excited about the baby, too."

"Well, I'm glad you know a lot about babies and all that stuff. You'll have to teach me, Delia." She chewed on her fingernail. "I mean, I've babysat now and then, but I haven't been around little tiny babies a whole lot. I hope I'll do okay."

"It will all come to you as you go along, and if you keep reading all those books I bought you, those will help you, too. My mother used to say God gives women nine months of time to learn about babies and get ready for them, but most women are just too stupid to use that time wisely."

Hallie laughed. "I know your mother is a little direct and overbearing, but sometimes I like her outright honesty. At least she says what she thinks."

"She certainly does that, all right," Delia agreed, thinking of some of the conversations with her mother lately. Her mother was irritated Delia was still, as she put it, dawdling around Gatlinburg instead of actively networking to find a professional job and get on with her life. Delia could hardly tell her about Hallie and why she planned staying on here to help her.

Sensing the direction of Delia's thoughts, Hallie added, "You know, your mother did all right by you. She may not have done everything the way you'd have liked it, and she may not have done everything right, but she didn't run out on you. In her own way, she tried."

"Maybe your mother tried, too, in her own way." Delia met Hallie's eyes. "I think there must be a good reason for why she left when she did. Some reason that seemed right to your mother at the time."

Hallie shot Delia an irritated glance. "This isn't some big mystery you're going to find an answer to, Delia. My mother just put her own needs first and took off."

"Well, I still think there's more to it than that," Delia insisted stubbornly.

"Look. I've got to get started making some more candles," Hallie announced, getting up to put her dishes in the dishwasher and artfully shifting the conversation at the same time. "Maureen says my candles are really selling well at Crosswalk. I'm beginning to get a big nest egg saved up, too."

She turned to look at Delia. "Do you think you could look for a crib and maybe a chest of drawers and a changer for the baby's room we've been talking about? You could get some used pieces, and you and I could paint them up real cute. I can't afford new stuff, and the baby won't care anyway. They're not status conscious."

Delia smiled at her. "I've already been looking for things, and I've located several used furniture stores that carry baby furniture. Some thrift stores, too. I've actually already measured the room upstairs and started thinking about ideas."

Delia went into the other room for a minute and came back with a large children's picture book. "Look at this, Hallie. I found it in Aunt Dee's things. It has big Beatrix Potter color illustrations in it." She opened the book. "See? Peter Rabbit here." She flipped the pages. "Tom Kitten and Jemima Puddle-Duck over here. There's Miss Moppet and others, too."

She handed the old book to Hallie. "I thought we might frame the prints for the walls in the baby's room," she explained. "And then do the room in soft colors to match. There is even a Beatrix Potter fabric we could buy to make a quilt and curtains."

"Oh, what a wonderful idea! I loved these stories when I was little," enthused Hallie. "I can sew, too, you know. Grammie taught me. I can also knit."

Delia smiled. There were few domestic skills Hallie Walker lacked.

Her mind moving ahead now, thinking about the baby's room, Delia asked, "Do you think you might want the baby's furniture to be white, warm oak, or dark cherry? I could look for whatever you'd like, and maybe we wouldn't have to paint or refinish."

"I'd like a warm or dark brown color," Hallie said. "White is more for girls, and John Dale and I think the baby is going to be a boy. I'd like to bring out the blues, too, for a main color." She tapped a picture in front of her. "Maybe paint the walls a robin's egg blue."

"And if it's a girl?" Delia teased.

"Well, blue is one of my favorite colors," Hallie insisted, shrugging. "Robin's egg blue is good for girls or boys."

"Okay. Now I'll know what to look for," Delia said, getting up.

"Are you going in to the office now?" Hallie asked.

"Yes. I want to make sure everything is perfect for the opening tomorrow. Maureen, Tanner, and Lavonne are catering the refreshments, but I want to see that everything is arranged properly. Check it all one last time."

"Well, go make it nice," Hallie said, grinning. "And get the groceries I wrote on the list on the refrigerator on your way home. John Dale and Tanner are both coming for dinner tonight and they voted for spaghetti. So that's what we're having."

Later that day, Delia was coming out of the Garden Café after having a quick sandwich for lunch. She looked across the street at the Highland Cumberland Presbyterian Church and remembered the devotional message she'd

Delia's Place

read that morning. She also recalled Hallie's comments about how God often talks to people in different ways in their own special places. What had the devotional said ... that if you tried to walk with God, if you looked to Him, and expected help and guidance from Him, that He would give it to you? She decided she'd go over and sit in the church for a little while—to see if she could get some answers.

After a half hour of praying quietly, with no ready answers coming, Perry looked in to see her sitting in the church. "Everything all right, Delia?" he asked.

"Yes." She felt her face flush with embarrassment. "I was just spending time talking to God and hoping for some answers." Delia dropped her eyes.

"Well, don't get discouraged." He leaned an arm on the end of the pew where she sat. "The answers to prayers don't always come right at the moment we pray them, but sometimes come later at unexpected moments. The important thing to know is that whenever you pray, God hears. And He sends the answer in His own way at exactly the right time."

Hours later Delia was still thinking about Perry's words while poking through the shops in Laurel Village Mall looking for a gift for Frances' birthday. On an impulse, she stopped in an interesting gift shop called Nature's Little Corner to look around. She'd met the owner, Zola Devon, on several occasions and waved to her today as she entered the store.

When Delia came to the register a short time later to purchase a crystal music box for Frances, Zola glanced up and then stared at Delia in an odd way. "The answer you're seeking is in the midst of old things you haven't looked at for quite a while," she said.

"What?" Delia asked, confused.

"It's a message I received for you," answered Zola simply, starting to ring up the music box. "You're seeking an answer to a prayer, aren't you?"

Delia blushed, not knowing what to say.

Zola waved a hand nonchalantly. "Sometimes I see things or get answers to prayers," she explained. "It's odd, I know, but it was God's choice to give me that gift."

"So what does it mean, the answer is in old things?"

"I don't know that," Zola said honestly, beginning to gift-wrap the music box for Delia while she talked. "I just get the particular part I get. God will show you the rest at the right time." She pulled a mailing box from under the counter and began to pack the neatly wrapped gift into it, stuffing bubble wrap around it.

"Why didn't God give me His answer Himself?" Delia asked, somewhat piqued.

"Oh, God has His own ways of doing things," Zola replied matter-of-factly. "Maybe your receiving set isn't very well developed yet. Or maybe

God wants to get other people involved in helping you. He likes to do that, you know. Anyone who shares what God gives them with another person gets a blessing for the doing of it. That's nice for the one who shares, too. Spreads the blessings around." She paused thoughtfully. "I see that someone else shared with you today, too."

Delia remembered Hallie's words earlier and Perry's at the church. She studied Zola while she finished wrapping Frances' music box to mail, wondering about her.

"I'm only a regular person like you," Zola said, not looking up. "Weren't you just praying for God to speak to you? Why shouldn't He talk to me about you and use me to give you a small message from Him?"

"I don't know," acknowledged Delia. "But I'm not used to religion this way."

"I think it's deeper faith you're after now, not more religion." Zola smiled, running Delia's credit card for the purchase and handing it back to her. "Isn't that right? They're not always the same thing, you know. Faith positions you into more of a one-on-one relationship with God; religion puts you into a community of believers. The two serve different purposes."

Delia tried to wrap her mind around this concept.

"Here." Zola finished wrapping Delia's gift for Frances. "All you need to do is put the address on this and mail it now. I wrapped and packed it to keep it safe until it arrives."

"Thanks," Delia answered, suddenly remembering she'd never told Zola she'd bought the music box for a gift or that she wanted it wrapped for mailing.

"Uh, Zola ..." Delia started, intending to ask about this. However, the bells on the door rang, signaling the entry of more customers.

Zola put Delia's purchase into a Nature's Corner bag and handed it across the counter to her. "Don't worry," she said, smiling. "You'll find the answer you need at just the right moment. The important thing is that God has the answer already worked out, and He'll be sending it right along to you. You remember the word you were given today later when the time is right. It will confirm what you'll know in your own heart."

Delia left the store thinking over her odd encounter with the shop owner. She remembered that one of the words for the day a few weeks ago had been Mysterious. 'God works in mysterious ways,' the scripture had said.

"Mysterious isn't the half of it." She glanced down at the bag in her hand and shook her head. "God's ways seem downright peculiar at times."

Chapter 16

Tanner looked at the calendar on his desk. It was nearly the twentieth of August. Another month had slipped by since he and Delia took that hike to the Ogle cabin. Things had changed between them then, but not enough.

Twiddling with the paperweight on his desk, Tanner wondered about the relationship. "She acts warm and easy with me one day, then cool and withdrawn the next. Exasperating woman. Every time we make a breakthrough, she pulls back afterwards, purposely holding herself at length."

He looked at a picture of Delia from the Open House at Crosswalk tucked in his desk blotter. It proved a fantastic success for Delia, just as Tanner hoped it would. "The office was packed that day with guests and friends, Delia stunning in that sleek, little black dress and pearls."

Tanner fingered another photo of Delia with the Kirkpatricks. "Bogan and Rona showed up early, brought another pile of business cards for Delia, handed them out personally while they schmoozed with everyone." Tanner smiled. "Persuaded Delia to redo their offices at Mountain Productions, too. Even got her helping with plans for the new house they're building."

His hand moved to a copy of *Mountain Living* magazine. "Bogan's a mover, I'll give him that. He jockeyed to get one of their writers to cover the open house and write an article on it, spotlighting Delia's new business." The publication put the event coverage right in the middle of their August issue, and Delia's phone had rung off the hook ever since.

"She's blossomed in so many ways this summer and loved the 23rd birthday party the gang threw for her the week after the open house." He frowned remembering how terrified she looked when she opened his gift bag to find a ring box. "She twiddled that box around in her hands like it held a snake before opening it—her relief obvious to everyone when she found a pearl friendship ring inside and not a diamond."

He snapped a pencil in half remembering it. It irked him she'd been so relieved that she hadn't received an engagement ring from him. Not that he'd ever give one to her publicly that way. But it exemplified how Delia kept herself from taking their relationship to the next level.

"Ready for lunch?" a voice called. Tanner pulled himself back to the present and checked his watch. He'd promised to have lunch with his mother today, and, obviously, she was here and ready to go.

A short time later, they settled into a window table at the Garden Café and began looking over the menu. Tanner ordered a burger, his mother the blue-plate lunch special.

"How'd your fishing trip with Vesser go yesterday, Tanner?" his mother asked as they waited for their food to arrive.

He stirred sugar into his tea. "We both caught a few nice trout. Put 'em back, but had a lot of fun catching them."

She shifted the subject. "Is Vesser still worried about Hallie?"

"Yeah, it's weighing on his mind heavily. I got him to talk about it and learned something about that situation."

"What?" his mother asked with interest.

"Vesser feels more responsibility for Hallie than might be normal for an uncle. He claims it's his fault Sissy ran off after Lawson died and left Hallie behind."

Maureen looked up in surprise. "However could that possibly be his fault?"

He scratched his chin. "Well, I doubt Vesser would've told me if he hadn't been so upset about Hallie running away and Sissy being linked up with Jonas Cole. And there's been trouble over in Cocke County about Jonas—an accusation that he raped this fifteen-year-old girl. Her father's gone to the police, and a stink's flared up about it. No arrest yet though. A lack of solid proof, the authorities say. Seems it happened a while back but all of it's been weighing on Vesser's mind."

"Hallie was a smart girl to get away from that man." Maureen's eyes narrowed. "I only wish Sissy wasn't such a fool and could see what he's really like."

"Vesser's been thinking about that, too. He's come to the conclusion, like Hobart, that Hallie ran away for just cause. He blames himself for it—that he and the family didn't fight to keep Hallie from going to live with Jonas when he married Sissy."

"Well, the family didn't really know Jonas' reputation then."

"Nor did Sissy. And that's another reason Vesser's all torn up about this. He's afraid Sissy will wake up one day and see what Jonas really is. That he'll hurt her. The police investigation has uncovered a background of instability and past charges on Jonas in the state where he lived before. It doesn't look good."

Delia's Place

"That's disturbing. And I know that must worry Vesser since Sissy was once married to his brother."

"Well, it's a little more than that," Tanner told her candidly.

Maureen looked at him questioningly.

"Seems that Vesser fell in love with his brother's wife." Tanner lifted a brow. "He says he never meant it to happen, but that it did. Evidently, Sissy felt it, too. It was confusing for them. Vesser said he and Sissy made the mistake of acting on their feelings about the time Hallie turned two. He told Sissy a silly thing – that if anything ever happened to Lawson he'd take care of her and Hallie. Right after that Lawson got killed. Vesser says Sissy got it in her mind that the two of them wished Lawson dead, that it was their fault he died. Unreasonable thinking, of course, but Vesser said Sissy couldn't get past it. She fell into a hard depression, and then went into a wild stage with her life. Drinking and running around like she'd never done before."

"The mind in grief can get twisted," Maureen commented, shaking her head.

Tanner propped an elbow on the table. "Vesser kept hoping Sissy might get past it, but the next thing he knew she'd run off with Lou Clower to Alaska where Clower owned a hotel. Vesser believes Sissy felt she'd go crazy with all the guilt if she didn't get away. He waited ten years before he married himself, hoping Sissy might come back. Says he mainly married then because Mary Lou Horner got pregnant with his child—Isabel. Then Mary Lou died giving birth to their second child, Lawson. Now Vesser's raising a five-year-old and a three-year-old on his own. Said if he was the superstitious type he might feel downright cursed."

Tanner's mother stirred her tea absently. "You certainly did get a lot of confessions there on the stream."

Their food arrived, and they ate for a few minutes before talking more. Tanner's mother had always been an extremely discreet person, and Tanner never worried about sharing anything with her. No matter how personal.

"You know, I think it did Vesser good to finally tell somebody about this," he said at last. "I suppose if Delia hadn't kept pushing the idea on me that there must be some reason why Sissy left Hallie at only two years old, I might not have pushed on Vesser and gotten the answer at all."

She glanced up briefly. "Will you tell Delia and Hallie about this?"

Tanner scratched his chin in thought. "I might tell Delia. Otherwise, she'll likely keep pushing to find the answer herself. But I think Vesser or Sissy should tell Hallie. Don't you?"

"I do," his mother agreed. "I don't know why they haven't told her before."

"Would you want to tell me you'd cheated on Dad right before he died?"

Maureen winced. "Well, I can see their reluctance to share. It tends to shame Lawson's memory. And they'd risk Hallie's disdain, too."

"Yeah, it's tricky," he agreed, attacking the last of his hamburger.

"Speaking of Hallie, she's starting to look a little pregnant now," Maureen noted. "She'll be five months at the first of next month. Time flies, doesn't it?"

"Yeah, and John Dale is supposed to go back to school at the end of this month. That's not going to be easy for them."

"Things will work out somehow," Maureen said between bites. "Love has a way of working itself out."

Tanner made a face and snorted.

"You're thinking of Delia," his mother said candidly.

Tanner looked up at her in surprise.

"Everyone can see you're in love with Delia. Did you think I'd be the only one not to notice?"

Tanner swore under his breath. "Do you really think everyone else knows?"

"Just those who know you well, Son. Stop scowling so. It's not just your feelings that are evident to others. It's Delia's, too."

"Well, then, someone should tell Delia about her feelings." Tanner's jaw clenched. "Seems she hasn't gotten the memo."

His mother clucked at that. "Give her time, Tanner. She's still healing and afraid to get hurt. Trying very hard to find her own way and be her own person."

"And how long does that take?" he asked in annoyance. "It's been months now."

"It hasn't even been three months since her engagement ended, Tanner. Hearts don't heal overnight. You hardly dated the first year you came back from Atlanta, remember?"

"I was busy working," Tanner replied defensively. "I had a lot to do getting the business back in shape. Modernizing things. Branching out and growing our account base. And I was building my new house, too."

"All that's true. And you've done a fine job growing your father's business. He would have been proud. I'm proud." She smiled. "But that's not why you didn't date during that time. You feared getting involved and getting hurt again, too."

"I broke up with Melanie, if you remember. Not the other way around."

"Yes. And I remember you telling me what she said to you when you did. Melanie had a selfish, cruel streak, and you can't convince me the things she threw out when you broke up with her, and on many occasions before that, didn't hurt you. They did, Tanner. You had to have your season of recovery. You had to be ready to trust and risk loving again."

He threaded his hands through his hair. "Mother, you know I'd never hurt Delia. Never stand her up like Prentice did. Never treat her badly."

She reached across to pat his hand. "I know that, Tanner. And deep down Delia knows that, too. Otherwise, you'd never have gotten as close to her as you have so soon after her breakup with Prentice. Surely you can see that?"

Tanner picked at his french fries, pushing them around on his plate. These were not the words he wanted to hear.

"Delia has some other issues she's wrestling with, too." Maureen waved at the waitress to get some more tea. "She cares very much for her family's approval. She's finding it difficult to choose a lifestyle her parents might disapprove of."

Tanner's temper flared. "You think her parents would disapprove of me?"

His mother gave him a gentle look. "Not for who you are, darling, but you need to remember Delia is from very wealthy people. They want her to marry well, into their social strata. They have the connections and contacts to link Delia to a monied marital alliance and to help her get employed in a prestigious design firm. They don't want her to walk off on an alternate course like Dee did."

"Roland Ward was a wonderful man," Tanner bristled defensively. "And Dee loved him. She loved the business here, too. You know she did. She was happy here."

"I know that, Tanner." She laid a hand on his arm again. "But I also know she always had a secret sorrow that her family disapproved of her choices. That was hard for her, and Delia observed this. She saw her Aunt Dee practically disowned for her life choices. I think she fears they might do the same to her."

"Would they?" Tanner asked, finding it hard to understand that type of family thinking.

"I don't know," his mother said thoughtfully. "There were other reasons behind the family's disapproval of Dee's decisions that factored in."

"Delia always said there must be something. She believes a secret exists that explains why her mother disliked Dee so much. You'd think they'd be close since Charlotte married Dee's only brother. Charlotte had no sisters, either, from what Delia told me."

"That's true." Maureen nodded. "But she had one brother. That's where some of the bitterness is, Tanner."

"Tell me." Tanner pushed back his plate. "I want to understand."

Maureen sighed. "It was a long time ago, really, but Dee told me about it after we became good friends."

She stopped to think, picking at the last of her lunch. "Dee was in high school when her older brother Howard married Charlotte Chapman. Dee called it a gala and advantageous marriage. The Chapman's were a well-to-do family, and Howard wanted to make a match that would help him continue to expand the Walker business. Charlotte had money and a polish that Howard admired, and her family had contacts Howard wanted to cultivate."

"You make all of Delia's family sound very mercenary,' Tanner remarked, scowling.

"Arranged matches have occurred for thousands of years, Tanner." Maureen sipped at her tea. "But Dee said Howard also loved Charlotte. He liked her drive and strength. And she was very beautiful. Tall, statuesque, and blond."

"So why was that a problem for Dee?" Tanner frowned.

"I'm getting to that," his mother said patiently. "You see when Dee came out into Washington society, Charlotte asked her brother Richard to escort Dee to the various balls and events that form part of a debutante's debut. Richard became smitten with Dee, and Dee said before she hardly knew what happened, they became a pair and formally engaged. Richard, a West Point grad and young officer in the Army, went overseas on military duty shortly after their engagement. After he left, Dee came down to Arrowmont on a summer scholarship to learn about Appalachian arts."

"And met Roland," Tanner put in.

Maureen nodded. "Dee told me Charlotte and Howard disapproved of her even coming to Gatlinburg that summer. They knew she was interested in her roots here, but didn't want to encourage her building family ties with her poorer relations. Dee knew she looked like the Walkers and felt fascinated by the Walker family history. She called it her first defiant act, coming to Arrowmont when Howard and Charlotte had other plans for how she should spend the summer after her first year of college."

Tanner leaned forward with interest. "So you're saying when Dee met and married Roland it offended Charlotte."

"Worse than that." Maureen hesitated. "Dee and Roland eloped. Shortly after Richard Chapman received the notice of their marriage, he was killed in a bombing accident. Charlotte blamed it on Dee. She felt that Richard had been distraught and overly careless. She evidently talked to him before the accident and said he felt angry and upset."

Tanner frowned. "How could she blame an incident of war on Dee?"

"Well, obviously, very easily. If Richard had come home, met someone else, and lived happily ever after, Charlotte would probably have gotten over her anger with Dee in time. As it was, she never did. If you remember, she didn't even come to Dee's funeral and Howard only came briefly for the day."

"But they let Delia come to see Dee every summer," Tanner put in.

"Dee told me that Delia was an unplanned child. Charlotte planned every aspect of her life carefully, and Delia's birth proved more of an annoyance than a delight, showing up out of plan and so late in Charlotte's life. Dee

Delia's Place

said that was why she let Howard name her after his only sister and let Delia visit her in the summers. The other reason was because Howard insisted. He believed Dee had been punished long enough, and, of course, Roland died about the time Delia turned four. Howard thought letting Delia come to see Dee in summers was a kindness to his sister."

"There's something else you're leaving out." Tanner studied his mother's face.

She grinned. "As fate would have it, Delia was absolutely the spitting image of her Aunt Dee and the Walkers from the beginning. This seemed like a slap in the face to Charlotte, I'm sure. It's another reason why Delia isn't as close to her mother as her sister Frances is. If you've seen pictures of Frances, you've probably noticed she looks exactly like a younger version of Charlotte Chapman Walker—tall, sleek, and blond. In fact, all the children look more like the Chapman side of the family except Delia. Tanner, you have to understand this is one reason why Delia has struggled so hard to try to gain her family's approval. Why she's always felt less sure of herself."

"Well, it's a disgusting story," Tanner sputtered. "And my view is that Delia is well rid of a family like that."

"Now, Tanner. No one is ever well rid of their family, no matter how much pain comes to them through family affairs. There's always a hunger to be approved of by family. Plus it wasn't as though Delia wasn't loved or well provided for growing up. I think she continues striving, probably subconsciously, to get her family to fully accept her at last. She probably doesn't even understand all the underlying factors that colored her upbringing or the fire that hungered in her."

"I think Delia needs to know all this." Tanner crossed his arms. "She has a right to know these things."

"Will you tell her?" Maureen asked.

He looked at his mother. "I will if you won't," he replied honestly. "But I actually think this would be easier for her to deal with coming from you. She's come to love and trust you so much."

"That's why I've hesitated." Maureen sighed. "She so needed unconditional love and someone to trust in. I hate to put myself between her and her family."

"Then tell Hallie." Tanner grinned at the thought. "She won't have any trouble at all telling Delia. Just casually mention this story to Hallie, as though you thought she already knew about it. Hallie will go straight to Delia afterwards with the whole scenario. It will make Hallie mad as a wet hen on Delia's behalf. You know how fierce Hallie is about loyalties and how defensive she's become of Delia."

"That's devious, Tanner." Maureen cocked a disapproving eyebrow at him.

"Maybe," agreed Tanner. "But I don't think either of us could handle it as well as Hallie could. Or get away with it as easily as Hallie."

"You know," said Maureen thoughtfully, "I think Dee wrote all this down in journals she kept. Artistic people often keep journals, and Dee wrote in hers through those early, married years. She stopped writing them after Roland died, but I imagine she kept her journals somewhere."

"So you think this is all written out in old journals?" he asked.

"Well, Dee told me she wrote down every detail of how she met and married Roland. She laughed about it, too. Called herself sentimental."

"Where do you think Dee might have kept these journals?"

Maureen scratched her head, thinking. "If she kept them, I imagine they're in the attic or in one of the trunks in Hallie's bedroom upstairs."

Tanner considered this fact. "Perhaps you can toss that idea into your discussion with Hallie. After all, she's there all day with Delia out working. With the right bait, I'll bet Hallie will find those journals and dig through them to see if there's more confirmation of the story you mention to her."

"Do you really think we should do this, Tanner?" Maureen drummed her fingers on the table.

"Don't you, Mother?" Tanner dug deep for an honest answer. "I think it's long overdue for Delia to know about all these stories and subterfuges in her family. How can she ever get free of what she doesn't even understand?"

"You have a good point." She nodded her head in agreement.

Tanner finished off his iced tea and picked up the lunch ticket.

"I'll make an agreement with you," his mother said as they got ready to leave. "I'll spill the beans to Hallie about what happened with Dee and Delia's mother. I'm going over there tomorrow to get candles and that will give me the perfect opportunity. But I want you to persuade Vesser to talk to Hallie about what happened with Sissy. Hallie is getting ready to be a mother herself. She has a right to know about what happened in her own family, too."

"It's a deal," Tanner complied with a grin. "Wanna shake on it?"

"No. I think our agreement is quite enough," she pronounced with a prim look. "This isn't a joke meddling with people's lives, Tanner. I hope we're doing the right thing."

"I think we are, Mother. Wouldn't you want to know if you stood in Delia's or Hallie's shoes, always wondering and never knowing?"

She nodded. "Yes. And I'd be angry I hadn't been told before, too."

They walked back to the office, still mulling these issues over. When they walked into the T. Cross offices together, Lavonne met them in an agitated state.

"Oh, gracious heaven, Bill's just called to tell me about a problem over in Cocke County! It's got me real upset!"

Delia's Place

Bill was Lavonne's husband and an administrator with the Gatlinburg police. Few events went on around the Burg that Bill or Lavonne didn't quickly find out about.

"What's happened?" Maureen dropped her purse on a chair.

"Well, you know that mess we've been hearing about Jonas Cole in Cocke County? And maybe you remember those accusations by Ronald Crowley that Jonas raped and beat up his fifteen-year-old girl, Carleen, last spring? Well, evidently, Jonas' wife Sissy got into a bout with him about it. He hauled off and beat her up and put her in the hospital. Neighbors heard the commotion and called the police. But by the time they got there, Jonas had took off. Sounds like he kind of flipped out. A police report says he's on the run, armed and dangerous."

She paused to take a breath before going on. "Bill's on his way over to tell Hobart Rayfield, and Cas and Tabby at the old Rayfield home place, about what's happened. They're Sissy's family, you know, and they'll notify the rest of the Rayfields. One of Bill's officers went up to tell the Walkers. Bill thought you'd want to know, Tanner, since you and Vesser are close and all."

"Where do they think Jonas has gone?" Tanner asked, alarmed.

"Hiding out somewhere," Lavonne said. "Of course, they're looking for him. Sissy told the police over at Cosby that Jonas had been a little liquored up. They're hoping he'll turn himself in when he sobers. He's probably off in the hills somewhere, it being warm out. With Jonas in real estate, he knows the area real good. Probably knows where to hide for a spell."

Lavonne turned to Maureen. "That little Hallie, the girl who worked downstairs for you last summer, she was Sissy's daughter, wasn't she? Bill said he wished he knew how to get in touch with her. The police in Cosby said she'd run off to New York this spring. I'd say it's a good thing. Sissy cried and said Jonas threatened Hallie earlier, but that she wouldn't believe the girl then."

Maureen gave Tanner a pointed gaze.

They gathered more facts from Lavonne, and then Tanner said casually that he'd walk Maureen back over to her office across the hall. Claimed he needed to check on an item in the books there.

Once outside of Lavonne's earshot, Tanner and Maureen conferred. "I'll go tell Delia and Hallie about this," Tanner said. "They need to know about Jonas and to be extra careful."

"Well, Jonas won't be hunting for Hallie around here," Maureen lowered her voice. "That's a good thing, at least. He'll still think she's in New York."

"Yes. That's true." Tanner frowned. "But I still don't like the idea of him being on the loose in the area and making threats."

She bit on a nail. "Let's just hope he gets caught right away."

"The police may not be able to keep him long on just assault and battery, Mother. Especially if neighbors heard them having a vocal fight."

"Why don't you go up and see Vesser?" Maureen suggested. "He'll probably be needing a friend about now. And it might be a good time for him to go make peace with Sissy while she's laid up in the hospital. The two of them need to do some talking. I'll go over to see the girls and warn them to be especially careful."

"Okay." Tanner reached in his pocket for his keys. "I'll go now. I'd like to find out how Sissy's doing and how extensive her injuries are. The Walkers will have a report on her condition and Hallie will want that news. Despite their disagreements, Sissy is Hallie's mother."

Maureen put a hand on Tanner's arm. "You know, maybe now that Sissy knows the danger of Jonas, she and Hallie will be able to reconcile later on. I'm sure Sissy regrets not believing Hallie about Jonas. That could be good for Hallie."

"Maybe," agreed Tanner. "However, for now, I'm worried that a situation, already troublesome and dangerous, has just gotten worse."

Chapter 17

Delia hung up the phone after checking on Hallie again. It was the third time she'd called her today, using some excuse or the other, and Hallie snapped at her about calling the last time.

"I am fine, Delia. Quit calling me." She bit out the words. "Between you, John Dale, Maureen, and Tanner checking on me all the time, I can't get a thing done around here. Give it a rest! Jonas Cole thinks I'm in New York City. Whatever trouble he's in, it doesn't have anything to do with me!"

Hallie was right, of course. Delia knew she'd acted overly anxious about Hallie ever since Jonas Cole put Hallie's mother in the hospital a few days ago. But the situation troubled Delia nonetheless.

She tried to pull her attention back to the cost estimate sheet she'd penciled in for Bogan and Rona Kirkpatrick. She'd almost finished her plans for the design work on their offices. Delia smiled, looking at a recent photo of the couple she snapped at Mountain Productions. "They've been fun to work with this last month, both so enthusiastic about all my ideas."

Delia's eyes strayed fondly around her office—redecorated in rich reds and gold, with links to the Italian theme she'd used throughout the T. Cross and Crosswalk offices. She'd kept a few sentimental photos and items belonging to Aunt Dee, but the space now predominantly reflected her own tastes. She reached out to touch the engraved nameplate on her desk that Tanner bought her—a nice gesture, of course—but she'd been annoyed with him for doing it.

"I'm often annoyed with Tanner these days." Delia sighed. "And usually for little reason."

In fact, they argued yesterday before he went out of town to a CPA convention in Atlanta. She glanced at the *Mountain Living* magazine on her desk that started the argument. An article in the middle section of the magazine highlighted the Open House held here last month and recognized her as a new designer in the area. It was well-written with many splashy photos and had brought her many new business opportunities. She'd felt secretly pleased with the coverage. Until her mother called.

Evidently, Tanner sent copies of the magazine to her parents. "I thought they'd be pleased to see your work and the pictures of you," he said when she confronted him about it.

"You had no right to do that, Tanner," she stormed at him. "Mother used it as a launching pad to lecture me once more on how I'm wasting my fine talents here in this backwoods town. It whipped up my father, too, and he called telling me about a contact of his in D. C. looking for a young apprentice designer. He passed my name along to him, of course, and now the firm is putting pressure on me to consider a position with them. You know that I need to stay here for Hallie, and your interfering has now made that more difficult."

It hurt Tanner for her to lash out at him. Delia could tell. He meant well in sending the magazines, even though he hadn't asked her before he did it. Now, she felt guilty, of course.

Delia sighed. "How different my two worlds are. Here everyone thinks I'm wonderful. At home everyone always finds me lacking in some way. Frances says it's because I'm a big fish in a little pond here. But it's nice being well thought of, little pond or not."

The word for the morning in her devotional book had been Due—something about not withholding good from anyone to whom it's due when it's in your power to give them good. The scripture, from Proverbs, was followed by several other passages admonishing that you shouldn't do harm to a neighbor who's given only good to you and trusts you. Delia winced thinking about it. "Tanner's been good to me and I've repaid him many times over with unpleasantness and ingratitude. It would serve me right if he got fed up with me entirely."

Delia thought about this on her drive home. Perhaps when Tanner got back from Atlanta tomorrow, she'd apologize to him. She felt wretched thinking of the last words they said to each other before he left, remembering his angry eyes as he stormed out.

When Delia came into the house she found Hallie alone, piled up on the couch with a stack of books. Graham cat, draped across her lap, kept her company.

"Reading some new books on cooking?" Delia asked, coming in from the kitchen with a cola to sit down and talk.

"No." Her green eyes flashed. "I'm reading about your life and learning why your mother has always been such an ass to Dee Walker—and to you."

Delia's mouth dropped open. "Whatever are you talking about, Hallie?"

"It's all right here." She tapped the small books piled around her with her finger. "These are your Aunt Dee's journals from her young married years. I found them in a trunk in the upstairs attic."

"What possessed you to go hunting around in the attic?"

Delia's Place

She stretched out her legs. "Something Maureen said to me the other day when she came to pick up my new candles. She stayed for lunch, and we got to reminiscing. She said some things about Dee and your mother I didn't know. She wasn't gossiping; she thought I knew about it already. Chatted on about how Dee wrote so many things about her young years in journals. Wondered if you'd found them and read any of them. It got me to thinking."

"So you went snooping in my Aunt Dee's things?" Delia accused.

"She's my relative, too," Hallie snapped back. "Besides, I didn't want to throw out any of the ideas Maureen suggested to me until I knew if they were really true or not. I wasn't even sure if I should tell you."

"Tell me what?" Delia leaned forward. "Hallie, you need to explain to me what you're talking about."

"All right. All right." She waved a hand. "But you're not going to like it. I certainly don't."

Delia gave her an exasperated glance.

"Well, let's just say your mother is a bigger poop than we thought. She punished Dee for years for something that wasn't even Dee Ward's fault. Poor Dee. It makes me furious just to think about it."

"Hallie Walker." Delia's temper flared. "I know you have a tendency to make even the shortest story long and drawn out, but this is one time I really want you to get to the point."

"Fine," hissed Hallie. "Here it is in a nutshell. Your aunt Dee was once engaged to your mother's brother. Did you know that?"

"Richard?" Delia barely disguised her shock. "Mother's only brother who died in the military as a young man?"

"Yeah, that's the one." She nodded. "Evidently your daddy and Charlotte had him squiring Dee around to all those coming out debutante things rich girls go to in money-land. He took a shine to Dee and they got engaged. Dee wrote that it sort of happened before she could think. And that Charlotte and your father seemed pleased."

"What happened?"

Hallie glanced down at the book in her hand. "He was a hottie West Point officer and got sent overseas after he and Dee got engaged. Dee came here that same summer on her Arrowmont scholarship to learn Appalachian crafts."

"And she met Roland," Delia interrupted, sitting down beside Hallie.

"Yes, and fell in love with Roland. She wrote about it in this journal." Hallie tapped the small book. "She said she realized as soon as she fell in love with Roland that what she'd felt for Richard was only girlish infatuation."

Hallie scrolled her finger down the book's open page. "Dee says here that she knew Howard and Charlotte wouldn't be pleased she'd fallen in love with Roland. She feared, too, they'd find a way to keep her from marrying him, so they eloped. She wrote them after the fact and told them, and she wrote Richard at the same time."

"Oh. He must have been terribly upset," Delia said, remembering her own note from Prentice saying he'd married while they were engaged.

"You're thinking of Prentice," Hallie observed knowingly. "It's not the same, Delia. Dee had only been engaged about a month, with no marriage plans set."

"Still, it must have hurt him. And hurt Mother, too, for his sake."

Hallie nodded. "You're right on both counts there. Sorrowfully, Richard got killed right after that. Blown up by some bomb. Maureen said your mother always felt Richard's death was Dee's fault. That Richard felt upset, probably got careless, didn't think as sharply."

"But a whole regiment got killed when Richard died that day," Delia prompted. "I remember Daddy telling my brothers about it once. It was just one of those awful things that can happen in war."

"Well, your mother felt differently." Hallie put a marker in the journal and closed it on her lap. "She never forgave Dee for it. That's why she never came here to visit. Why Dee never came to your house—even with Dee your daddy's only sister. Even your grandparents felt bitter toward Dee for dumping Richard. And for eloping and getting married without telling any of them."

"What a mess." Delia swallowed the lump in her throat. "I guess I understand for the first time the quarrel between my family and Aunt Dee. I wish someone had told me."

"Honey, there was a lot they didn't tell you," Hallie pronounced.

"Now what are you talking about?" Delia asked, with a sense of dread.

"Have you ever looked in the mirror carefully? Who do you look like?"

She lifted a hand to her hair. "I look like my Aunt Dee."

Hallie nodded. "You took back after the Walkers in looks. Turned out to be the spitting image of your Aunt Dee, whom your mama hated. Get the picture, kid? Classic psychological transference."

Delia's head snapped up to meet Hallie's gaze. "Did Aunt Dee write that? That Mother loved me less because I looked like her."

"In a way. She wrote in one place that your father admitted it always bothered Charlotte that you looked like Dee. Evidently all the other kids looked more like Charlotte's side of the family."

Delia felt tears well up in her eyes. "That's true. They do. Especially Frances. She looks exactly like Mother. But I couldn't help how I looked, Hallie."

Hallie scowled. "Don't tell me that. Your mother's the one with the weird personal problem about that, not me. I'm simply the one who would like to punch her lights out right now. It really ticks me off she's made you pay

Delia's Place

all these years for a bunch of old, bitter feelings she harboured about Dee Walker Ward. I mean, how cruel is that?"

Delia started to cry.

"You go right ahead and cry, Delia." Hallie patted her arm. "You've got a right to. It's no wonder you've got issues with your family. They took old stuff out on you as a little kid, and you didn't even understand it. It makes me sick."

She looked up at Hallie, confused. "But they named me after Aunt Delia."

Hallie looked at her pityingly. "Dee wrote that your daddy named you. Your mother wasn't very excited to even have you, coming so late in her life. When you were born, you looked like Dee from the start. Your daddy saw the resemblance right off and wanted to name you after her."

Delia got up to get a tissue to blow her nose. When she sat back down, Hallie continued. "Your mother went right back to work and left you with Beeker. I guess we've got a better understanding about that now, too. Dee wrote here that the bond between you and your mother never developed the same as it did with her other children. Your daddy saw it, Dee wrote, and it worried him some." Hallie looked up at Delia. "Obviously it didn't worry him enough, the creep."

She crossed a leg with irritation. "However, when Roland died Dee wrote that your daddy softened. He wanted to make peace with Dee then, but your mother didn't want any part of it. That's when your father started coming for visits and bringing you along—you being Dee Ward's namesake. He felt sorry for Dee being widowed."

Delia put a hand to her mouth. "You're right. I was nearly five the first time we came here to visit—only a few months after Roland died. I didn't understand any of that. The next summer Daddy brought me again. He left me several weeks that time and Dee and I bonded. That's what she always told me. After that my parents let me come every summer."

Hallie snorted. "I guess they figured it a great way to get you out of the house."

"Oh, Hallie, that's an ugly thing to say." She slumped back against the sofa.

Hallie shrugged, unrepentant. "If the shoe fits."

"We shouldn't exaggerate, Hallie. All of these feelings may have been under the surface of things, but I do know my parents loved me. Even you've said so."

Hallie twisted impatiently in her seat. "I'm sure you're right, Delia. But you didn't deserve second best. You're a great person, and you didn't deserve to be treated differently for reasons that had nothing to do with you. To be hurt. It makes me so mad I could spit."

She jumped up impulsively and hugged Delia. "Please stay here with me forever, Delia. I'll always love you for who you are. That's what you deserve. Not any more of this twisted kind of love." Tears puddled in Hallie's eyes. "That's why Dee left you everything, Delia. She knew you needed it. She knew you'd been punished because of her. She knew."

Delia's eyes widened. "Oh, Hallie, you're right. That's why she did it. I've always wondered about it."

"She wanted to make it up to you," Hallie said. "But she loved you, too, Delia. It wasn't just guilt. She talked about you all the time to my Grammie and me. Showed us your pictures. Was so proud of everything you ever did. Put up all your drawings on the refrigerator, kept the cards and letters you sent her. I found them, too, in the attic. You were precious to her."

Delia cried now, along with Hallie.

"We're alike, you and I." Hallie reached for a tissue and handed Delia one, too. "It's another bonding between us. We've both known rejection since we were little kids and never understood it."

Delia blew her nose and shook her head sadly.

Hallie pulled back to look at her. "You're not mad at me for telling you, are you Delia?" she asked in a worried tone. "I know it's hurt you."

"No. I needed to know, Hallie. And I'm glad it was you that told me. It doesn't hurt so bad that way. You understand more. I don't mind you knowing." She sniffed. "I would have hated finding out all by myself."

Hallie patted Delia's hand.

"You need to look through all these journals sometime, Delia." Hallie gestured toward them. "It's sweet to read how much Dee loved Roland, to read about their times together. To share in those memories. And she wrote a lot about you and how much she loved you. You'll like that. It's nice. She even wrote about me. She talked about when I was born and when Grammie Rayfield first brought me to see her. Most of what's in Dee's journals will make you happy, Delia."

Delia bit her lip. "And what am I going to do about the other part?"

Hallie gave Delia a hard look. "You're older and wiser now, Delia. If it were me I'd have myself a nice little talk with my parents sometime in the near future. Give them a piece of my mind about how their little problems and prejudices have affected my life. Tell them I'd like there to be an end to it all right now, that I don't want any more scars and want to be valued on my own merit. Loved for who I am and not for who or what I represent."

Delia thought about her words.

"Don't let them hurt you, or dictate to you, or try to control or manipulate you for even one more minute in your life, Delia Walker," Hallie challenged, eyes flashing. "You hear me? They've had about all the misguided, twisted shots at you that you should give them. It's no wonder you've had so many problems with them. You've knocked yourself out trying to win in a no-win situation. Never quite figuring out the score. They ought to be ashamed of themselves. But now you're on to them, and you need to tell them they'd better straighten up and fly right." She punched a fist in the air.

Delia smiled through her tears. "Mercy. I wish I'd taped that so I'd remember it."

Hallie laughed. "I'll get on the phone if you want me to. I'd say I could hold my own with your mother."

"I'd say you could, Hallie." Delia laughed.

"You gonna be all right?" Hallie handed her another tissue.

"Yeah," Delia replied with a sigh. "In an odd sort of way, I actually feel better."

"Like a horse that's had its blinders took off?"

She smiled. "I'd probably have said I feel suddenly enlightened."

"City mouse. Country mouse." Hallie shrugged.

"Hey," Hallie said abruptly, changing the subject. "You want something to eat? I got so into reading this afternoon that I didn't cook. But we've got all sorts of leftovers."

"That sounds great. Let's go check out the refrigerator."

While they got out food in the kitchen and microwaved the leftovers, John Dale phoned. He was working up at the hotel, but he'd stopped on his break to call.

"Is John Dale okay?" Delia asked when Hallie hung up.

"Yeah, he's fine. But still spooked about Jonas Cole being on the loose and the police after him. He's driving me crazy about it. Made me create this code phrase to say in case there should ever be danger here."

"What's your code phrase?" Delia grinned.

Hallie rolled her eyes. "If there's ever danger, and I'm really scared and need to tell him there's a problem I'm to say, 'Don't forget to pick up the zucchini.'"

"What?" Delia giggled.

"Oh, it's a typical John Dale thing. He got it off television. You know, like in those shows where the victim answers the phone but can't say anything because the murderer is standing nearby in the house." She rolled her eyes dramatically. "So he says there should be some goofy code phrase you can use that wouldn't be a threat."

She snickered again. "And he thought of 'Don't forget to pick up the zucchini'?"

"He's a chef." Hallie shook her head and laughed. "He maintains that mentioning what to pick up at the store is the sort of normal thing you might say to someone familiar on the phone. That it wouldn't arouse suspicion."

"You mean like, 'Pick up a loaf of bread on your way home'?"

"Yeah, but he said it has to be something weird to be a good alert."

"Well, the zucchini thing would certainly fit in the weird category, that's for sure." Delia burst out laughing and Hallie joined her.

"He told this to Tanner, too. Can you believe it? The two of them were sitting there figuring out all this macho man stuff about how to protect us weakling women the other night. I could have punched them both."

Growing serious now, Delia paused in fixing two sandwiches. "It is scary to think of Jonas Cole out there and not caught yet. He really hurt your mother."

"Yeah, Tanner told me. He beat Mama up pretty bad. Broke a couple of ribs, blacked her eye, and broke her arm. The arm and some internal injuries were keeping her in the hospital for a while, but I hear she's coming home soon."

"She won't go back to their house, will she?" Delia asked, alarmed.

"No. She's going over to Uncle Cas and Aunt Tabby's at my Grammie Rayfield's old place. Cas and Tabby moved there after Grammie died, and they have a lot of room. Plus Mama is comfortable there. It's where she grew up. Uncle Hobart is right across the street, and Hobart's son and his family are down the road. There's a lot of family close around. The police chief for Pittman Center lives only two streets away, too. A lot of folks will be watching out for Sissy."

"Do you wish you could go see her?"

"In a way," Hallie answered, chopping up a banana into a fruit salad. "Tanner said she cried about me. Said she regrets she was so hard on me and pushed too hard trying to get back close to me. She's real sorry now about Jonas, too. Worried about whether he raped me and hurt me. Now that she knows about Carleen and what he did to her, she's more worried about me than before—when she only thought I ran away."

Delia put their sandwiches on a plate. "But you tried to tell her."

"Yeah, and she's remembering that now. Tanner says he went with Uncle Vesser to the hospital to see her. Vesser and Mama haven't been close ever since Daddy was killed. Tanner says they talked over a bunch of stuff at the hospital, and that it was good for both of them."

"I see," said Delia. She'd have to ask Tanner about that when he got back. Maybe if she hadn't snapped his head off about the magazines he had sent her parents, he'd have told her before he left. She sighed at the thought.

"Did you and Tanner have another fight before he left on that trip?" Hallie asked intuitively as they sat down at the table.

Delia hardly felt like hedging or lying tonight. In fact, she felt really tired of game playing, lying, and pretenses altogether. She wanted to be a more real and honest person from now on, no matter what.

"It was all my fault," she admitted honestly. She told Hallie then about the spat over the magazine article.

"Well, I'm glad Tanner sent your parents those magazines." Hallie stuck her chin up. "I'd like to see your success here rubbed real hard in their faces."

Delia shook her head thoughtfully, considering that.

Hallie leaned across the table and took Delia's hands. "You are a success, Delia. You don't need to have your parents' approval to be a success. Or their help. You can do it on your own. You don't have to keep trying to please them to make up for looking like Dee or for reminding them of old stuff that happened a long time ago."

"I know," Delia said.

And, for the first time, she thought she really did.

Chapter 18

Tanner was almost home. He glanced over at the clock on the dashboard noting it past 9:00 am. He'd been in Atlanta since early Wednesday.

He woke before five this morning and couldn't get back to sleep, so he decided to skip the final breakfast meeting of the convention and head for home. With so much on his mind, he hadn't enjoyed the meetings this year.

Before he left, he called Lavonne to let her know he'd be back early. It worried Tanner to leave town with Jonas stirring up trouble this week. But his fees and accommodations for the CPA convention were pre-paid, and he had commitments to speak in two Continuing Professional Development training workshops. He'd have let down a lot of people if he hadn't gone.

After quarreling with Delia the night before he left, he actually looked forward to getting away for a while. He got over that the first day away from her. He missed her. No matter how exasperating Delia could be, she swam in his blood now. It worried him, but there was little he could do about it.

"No fool like a fool in love," Bogan teased him last week. He'd caught Tanner eyeing Delia with longing at a potluck held in Keppler and Sherilynn's back yard. Tanner glowered at Bogan in irritation but made no comment in reply. He saw no point trying to deny his interest in Delia anymore to his friends. The two had been an item nearly all summer, although Delia still deluded herself that everyone thought they were only good friends.

He tapped the steering wheel as he barreled down the highway. "I got so mad at Delia before I left Gatlinburg that I forgot to tell her what I learned about Vesser and Sissy. She'll want to know about that—and she'll be glad I went to see Vesser and persuaded him to go visit Sissy in the hospital. Even went with him for moral support."

Tanner slipped around a slower vehicle. "I need to tell Delia and Hallie the bad news about Jonas Cole, too, if they haven't already heard—that Jonas is still at large, and that two more incidents occurred." He frowned. "Someone burned down the barn at that fifteen-year-old girl's farm. Lavonne says the police think it was probably Jonas, taking revenge on charges her family

Delia's Place

pressed against him. Then Sissy's house in Cosby was torched. Bill said she lost about everything she owned in the fire. The next morning, he was called in to see a bloody and mangled animal carcass found on the porch of the old Rayfield home where Sissy is staying."

Tanner clinched his fists on the steering wheel as he thought about his conversation with Lavonne that morning. "Bill thinks they're dealing with a real psycho now, set on revenge. He said he'd be glad when they catch Jonas Cole and lock him up right and tight. So far it's just been fires and animals, but who knows what's next."

The 'what next' worried Tanner. Even his mother was considering taking Hallie down to her sister's in Mississippi until Jonas could be found. She and Tanner knew if Jonas ever saw Hallie by chance that she might be in real danger. Tanner had seen what Jonas did to Sissy, and the remembrance scared him.

Tanner pulled into his parking space behind the T. Cross offices and sprinted up the stairs. It felt good to get out of the car after the long drive back from Atlanta. He'd grabbed coffee and a donut on the road, but the rumble in his stomach reminded him that he needed to rustle up some real breakfast soon. He hoped he might find Delia in her office, see if she'd go to breakfast with him. Have a talk. He was eager to see her.

As he walked into T. Cross's entry area, Lavonne greeted him warmly. "You've got someone in your office already." She pointed in that direction, raising her eyebrows.

"I just got in," hissed Tanner. "I don't really want to see anyone right now. Can't you get rid of them?"

"I don't think it's a client," she whispered back. "It's the minister's boy. Called me this morning early wanting to know when you'd get back. He's sat in there waiting for you about a half hour now."

Resigned, Tanner walked back to his office to find John Dale sitting on one of the chairs in his office with his feet propped on an ottoman. A pile of outdoor magazines lay scattered on the floor with another across John Dale's lap, flipped open.

"Hey, J. D.," Tanner said in greeting, walking over to shake his hand. "Surprised to see you out this early. Anything wrong?"

"Yes and no," John Dale replied with a frown. "I need someone to talk to, Tanner. I thought maybe you'd give me a few minutes this morning. I know you're just getting back and all that, but I'm off today, and I need to try to get some things resolved. I'm due back to Charleston soon." He frowned again.

Tanner could see the coiled tension in his eyes and strained movements. "Tell me in one sentence what the main problem is we're going to talk about," he instructed.

John Dale looked up with an anguished look. "I can't leave her, Tanner, and I don't know what to do."

"Had any breakfast?" Tanner asked him.

"Nothing much. Juice and a cereal bar. I left before the folks got up."

"Good. Let's go have breakfast at the Pancake House and talk. My treat." Tanner gestured toward the door. "I've been on the road since five, and I'm starved. I'll be glad for the company, and we can order one of those big breakfasts with everything."

John Dale grinned. "That sounds good."

A little later they sat tucked into a back booth at the Pancake House, drinking coffee and waiting for their breakfast order.

"All right. Let's have some more details now." Tanner sat back to listen.

"Hallie wants me to go back. She threatened to take off if I don't, to run away somewhere. She's real set on me going back to Charleston and finishing out this last year of college. But it's tearing me apart to think about leaving her. Especially with the baby coming. Tanner, that's my baby, too. I don't want to be down in South Carolina and not be here with her. She says she'll be fine, but what about me?" He stared miserably at Tanner. "I won't be fine. And, now with Jonas Cole on the loose, I can't see how I can even consider going off and leaving her. What if she gets careless—goes out and he sees her or something? I need to be here, Tanner. I can't go prancing off to college classes and frat parties at a time like this, and she doesn't understand. I can't talk reason to her."

Tanner poured out more coffee, waiting for John Dale to continue.

"She wants me to go back. Period. No discussion. Then wander home at Christmas and marry her again, all legal with Perry at his wedding chapel. But quietly so my folks won't know." John Dale gave a disgusted snort. "Then she wants me to go right back to school again in January. Not even be here with her when our baby is born. Wait all the way till June after I graduate to be with her and the baby. Let her stay on with Delia until then. Hallie and Delia have even fixed up a baby's room already."

He shot Tanner a hard glance. "It seems like they're making all these plans for my life and just expecting me to go along with them and like them. My voice hasn't seemed to matter a crap. Hallie's got it all planned out what is best for me and for her without much of a say so from me one way or the other."

Tanner shook his head in sympathy. "Women are tough to deal with sometimes, aren't they?"

John Dale nodded in agreement. "Yeah, and I gotta find a way to talk some sense into her right away," he insisted. "My folks expect to take me back to Charleston in two weeks. They want to go down early so we can visit with my sister Mary Alice and her family. And then visit my mother's brother

Delia's Place

Carlton and his family. I can move in the frat house any time before school starts, and they know that. But they have no idea what it's been like for me every year to leave Hallie and go off to school again."

A cloud of anger passed over his face. "It's hard not to hate them for that, Tanner, for being so callous about my feelings for Hallie. They always act like it's just some childish crush with her I'll get over. They treat me like I'm still a kid who doesn't know his own mind or heart. Think I'll outgrow Hallie like I did tinker toys or something."

"Dang, I still like tinker toys," Tanner put in with a grin.

John Dale sent Tanner a resentful glance. "I'm being serious here, Tanner. Give me some respect!"

"I know you are, J. D." He reached over to punch the boy's arm. "I was only trying to lighten things up."

The boy scowled. "Well, sorry, but I'm not in the mood for jokes right now."

Their food arrived, and the two stopped to eat, buttering up biscuits and pancakes, and digging in hungrily to eggs, sausage, and grits.

"What do you want to do?" Tanner asked eventually. "You haven't torn yourself apart over all this without coming up with some kind of answer."

He leaned forward. "I want to drop out of school, work, and stay here with Hallie. With the tourist season slowing down, I think I could find us an apartment we can afford. I can keep working at the Park Vista; they already told me they'd take me full-time. And if I look around, I might find a hotel where I can manage and live, get an apartment in the hotel Hallie and I can use. Some places give you lodging on site. I can finish school part-time at U. T. in Knoxville, a class or so at a time on student loans. My grades are good. I could transfer easily."

"What does Hallie think about this plan?"

He clenched a fist. "She hates it. She turns it into some Machiavellian melodrama where we'll struggle and starve in a garret, bitter with regrets."

Tanner ate for a minute, thinking. He wolfed down some pancakes he'd drenched in syrup while he studied on the situation.

"You know, I sat in on this leadership conference while down in Atlanta," he told John Dale thoughtfully. "The speaker talked about how one of the marks of leadership is how a good leader strategizes. Uses logic and ingenuity to find a better plan than his opponent so that he wins. A point he made was that this sometimes means changing course, gaining an edge by coming up with an unexpected alternative, even taking a calculated risk."

"So how does that relate to my situation," John Dale grumbled.

"Well, that's just it. Your plan isn't as appealing to Hallie as her own plan."

"You needed a convention workshop to tell you that?" John Dale said sarcastically. "We already know that. The woman's stubborn and set on her own way."

"Come on, J. D. ," Tanner encouraged. "Don't you think deep down Hallie really wants to be with you?"

"Well, sure, but she also wants me to finish school in Charleston." He wolfed down a glass of orange juice. "She doesn't want anything to get in the way of the plan we made for working with my grandmother in a bed and breakfast after I finish college. It's all she talks about. She thinks her getting pregnant threatens that. That my mom and dad won't pay for the rest of my school if they find out she's pregnant, that Grandmother Mary will renege on her plan to let us make her place into a bed and breakfast if I don't finish school. Etcetera. Etcetera."

"Okay. The girls are winning with emotion and getting us to think in the same way. Let's use logic and break this down in a different way."

"Like how?" John Dale forked another pancake to his plate.

"All right. First, what do you logically think your parents would do if you went to them right now and told them about you and Hallie?"

His eyes grew wide. "You mean, told them everything?"

Tanner nodded.

John Dale drank some juice and thought. "My father would be real disappointed, and he'd be embarrassed, him being a minister and all. My mother would be much worse. She'd freak out, threaten and blame Hallie. It would be hard to get her to see reason. You should hear how she's carried on about what's happened with Hallie's mother."

"Do you think they'd come around in time?"

"I don't know. Maybe if someone pressured them." He laughed. "It would take more than me to convince them to change their minds and attitudes."

"Who do they fear?" Tanner asked. "Who stands up to them and makes them back down?"

"What?" John Dale looked surprised. "Geez, I don't know. The mayor. The guy that heads the Cumberland Presbyterian churches; I can't remember his name right now. Grandmother Mary. Maybe Mary Alice's husband, Mark, because he's a hotshot dentist and from a wealthy family down in Charleston, or my Uncle Carlton for about the same reasons. He's a heart surgeon, teaches at the medical college, and lives in one of those old historic homes downtown in Charleston. Real prestigious stuff."

"Hmmmm," said Tanner thoughtfully. "In the middle of all that dialog, you mentioned your grandmother Mary."

"So?" He shrugged.

"Well, how do you think she'd handle this news about Hallie and you?" Tanner asked. "You said before she wants you to have her place, wants you to make it into a bed and breakfast. You told me she likes Hallie and has never opposed you marrying her. That's different than your folks' view."

"Yeah, Grandmother Mary likes Hallie," John Dale acknowledged. "Hallie's home place, Grammie Rayfield's farm, is right next door to Grandmother Mary's. The farms adjoin, you know. Hallie played all over both farms as a child. Grandmother Mary always loved her." He got a wistful look. "Hallie started coming to visit at my grandmother's when she first came to live at her Grammie's. She always brought Grandmother Mary things she cooked or wildflowers or something pretty she made. She did things for my grandmother. Took care of her once when she got bad sick with pneumonia. My mom was afraid to go over to help, thought she'd catch it, but Hallie wasn't. Stayed with Grandmother Mary until she got well."

John Dale warmed to his subject. "When my family moved here to Gatlinburg, and I started going to my grandmother's, she introduced Hallie to me. I wasn't sure I wanted to be friends with a girl back then at only ten. Especially one younger than me, with red pigtails and a smart mouth. But Hallie was always around when I went over and we became friends eventually." He smiled in remembrance.

Tanner interrupted his remembrances. "Your grandmother might be our trump," he suggested. "Let's think about it. Suppose you go talk to her and tell her all that's happened. Explain how you and Hallie tried to be honorable and respectful of the family even when it was hard. Remind her how you went off to college away from home when you didn't want to. How Hallie finished high school, and you only saw each other on holidays. Emphasize the fact that when the pressure grew too heavy last summer, you married Hallie underage, trying to be honorable. And assure your grandmother that you planned to finish college and please the family—but then had this unexpected situation."

"That's how we saw it," John Dale put in eagerly. "We really tried to go along with what everyone wanted us to do. Even when we didn't want to. We really did, Tanner. You can't know how many times I wanted to drop out of college, just come home to Hallie, but she always talked me out of it. Threatened me out of it." He frowned at that, obviously remembering numerous arguments.

Tanner laughed. "You'll never be bored with Hallie Walker in your life."

John Dale grinned at that, but then frowned at a new thought. "What can Grandmother Mary do to help with this even if she doesn't get mad?"

"I'm not sure, right off," Tanner answered honestly. "But I think she's our best chance for an advocate and a trump. If she gets on your side and, say, supports you staying here, maybe even lets you and Hallie live with her, that could be good. Or if she pushes your parents to let you take Hallie back to South Carolina with you, so you can finish college there, that could be good, too. Her pressure on them might be a persuader. You said your parents were afraid of her."

"That's because she's kind of like Hallie." John Dale finished the last of his eggs. "Strong, direct, and out-spoken. Grandmother Mary is also rich. I've heard my parents say that. She's helped all the family out a lot, too, including Mother and Dad when they were young and Mother's brother Carlton earlier in his life when he really needed it. They all know they owe her, and they respect her. Plus I think they all hope there will be some kind of inheritance from her one day, even if I get her old home place. Uncle Carlton doesn't want that place, even though he's oldest and the only son. He owns a big home in Charleston and a beach house, too. He wants to stay in South Carolina. His grown kids live around there. His work is there. It's meaningful to him."

John Dale flagged the waitress for another glass of juice before he went on. "My folks don't want Grandmother Mary's home place, either," he added. "They want to go back to Charleston when Dad retires or gets a church transfer there sooner. Dad's put in for one a time or two. No one knows that, so don't tell anyone, Tanner. But they want to live there. Mom wants to be near Mary Alice's grandkids, and she still has old friends from when she went to college there herself."

"I'm hearing you." Tanner flashed John Dale a smile. "Your grandmother sees you and Hallie Walker as her future. You plan to live with her, stay in the area. It will be the two of you who'll take care of her when she's older. She's already watched how faithfully Hallie took care of her Grammie Rayfield, knows she can count on Hallie. She probably also knows her daughter, your mother, wants to leave here. Without you and Hallie taking her home place and making a bed and breakfast of it, she might have to sell and go live with your mother and dad one day."

John Dale made a face. "Not in this lifetime. Grandmother Mary and my mother don't get along that well. They fight and disagree too much. She'd go live with Carlton and his wife before she'd live with Mom. She really likes Carlton's wife."

Tanner perked up at that. "Even better. She won't hesitate to stand up to your parents then, will she?"

"You might be right," John Dale said thoughtfully. "But you might be wrong. She might get angry and change her mind about everything. About all the plans. That's what Hallie is afraid of."

"Look," argued Tanner. "With a baby on the way, Grandmother Mary is going to figure all this out eventually anyway. Whether she's presented with the idea of being a great-grandmother ahead of time or after the fact, the two of you can hardly hide this story from her. What if she gets mad you didn't come to her about it earlier? Decides you left her out, didn't trust her? Women can get upset about that kind of stuff."

Delia's Place

"You're right," agreed John Dale, scratching his chin thoughtfully. "I never thought of that. Grandmother Mary told me once I'd never lied to her and that she always appreciated that.

"Shoot." His eyes grew round. "We could end up getting screwed either way with this. Grandmother Mary might be just as mad we didn't come to her earlier for help as she will if we wait to go to her later. She might see it like we didn't trust her or something if we show up next spring with a baby and already married."

Tanner nodded. "Like I said, women can be funny about stuff like that."

They sat and finished their breakfast, Tanner letting John Dale talk out his options of what he ought to do.

"I think I'm ready to go for the risk option." John Dale squared his shoulders. "I'd like to go and talk with Grandmother Mary. Maybe tell her my ideas but ask her advice, too."

He paused. "Besides, if Hallie and I are going to live with her for the rest of our lives, we need to know if she's going to be on our side if something goes wrong—if we ever mess up in the future. You need people who'll stand by you when things don't go well more than you need people to stand by you when everything's peachy."

"That's a good point," agreed Tanner. "And a piece of good logic, too."

John Dale leaned forward, catching Tanner's eyes. "Will you go with me?"

Tanner choked on his coffee. "To your grandmother Mary's?"

"Yeah, I'd really appreciate your support. You could help me tell Grandmother about Hallie being at Delia's and how you and Maureen have known about it."

"When do you think you want to do this visitation?"

John Dale looked at his watch. "Right now," he said emphatically. "Before I talk myself out of it."

Tanner sighed. "You don't want to sleep on it?"

"Nah, I'm scared to. Hallie can read me like a book. She might get suspicious, get me to slip up and say something. Talk me out of it or something. I've got to just do it. Like you said, take the risk and do it. Besides, it's starting to feel right. We need some power on our side that's family."

Tanner smiled, resigned to the inevitable. "Well, let's go then."

Twenty minutes later, Tanner and John Dale drove up the winding drive to Mary Ogle's Victorian farmhouse and parked. Mary was out in the front yard cutting late roses off the shrubs below the front porch. The big ornate, white Victorian house rose up behind her, with its wide, gracious porches, castle-like turret, peaked gables, and gingerbread trim. Around it spread a wide lawn, richly green in late August, with old oaks framing the picture. Barns and outbuildings scattered around the adjacent property, and a series of forested hills rolled up behind the entire scene.

Mary Ogle came forward and held out a hand cordially to Tanner. The quiet strength and wisdom Tanner always remembered about her still shone out of her eyes. Even in her late sixties, she was still a fine looking woman—her short hair still brown and only feathered with grey, her figure fit, her face warm with welcome.

"Well, do I not get a hug from my favorite grandson?" she asked with a smile, turning to John Dale.

John Dale hugged her with warmth, and Tanner noted the fondness with which she stroked his hair when he did so.

"You're just in time for some iced tea," she announced. "I was going to bring some out on the porch to drink since it seems too nice a morning for being inside. You two go sit down by the porch swing, and I'll be right out."

She came back in a few minutes, carrying a pitcher of sweet tea with fresh mint leaves floating on the top, their fragrance tinting the air.

They sat down on cushioned white wicker furniture in the shady corner of the Victorian's big front porch, and Mary poured out glasses of tea for them.

"I'd forgotten how beautiful this place was," Tanner remarked.

"Seems the last time you came out here was to fish the pond with John Dale one Saturday. Brought me two nice catfish for dinner, if I remember right."

They chatted cordially for a short time.

"Well, this visit has been real nice," Mary commented at a pause in the conversation. "But I think you'd better get on with telling me why you two came here to visit me today. There's something brewing under the surface here. I can see it hovering in my grandson's eyes."

John Dale nodded. Then he lifted his eyes to hers with a strong resolve and began to tell his story.

Tanner listened, only adding a comment or two of clarity where needed. He lent support to John Dale, too, when Mary asked him questions too difficult for him to answer. For example, Tanner clarified questions about Delia's background John Dale didn't know, and was able to tell Mary how much money Hallie earned over the summer continuing Dee's candle business. Gradually, the entire story came out and was put on the table.

Tanner felt pleased to see how calmly Mary heard them out. She was obviously relieved, too, that Hallie was safe and well at Delia's Ward's old place and not in New York City somewhere.

"You know," she confided to Tanner. "John Dale told me he knew where Hallie was and that she was all right." She paused and looked at John Dale sharply. "Now that I think on it, you never actually said Hallie was in New York, did you, Boy? You just kept saying you knew she was all right. For me not to worry."

Delia's Place

"Yes, ma'am."

"Hmmmm," she said. "And you think the best answer is for you to quit school and stay here with Hallie now?"

John Dale nodded and then told her again his ideas of how he could do that, that he'd been offered work at the Park Vista, that he could take student loans to finish up at UT, a course or so at a time.

Mary Ogle sat quietly through all this last discussion. When she made no response, John Dale became agitated.

"I'm real open for your advice and ideas, Grandmother," he offered, seeming to sense suddenly she wasn't on track with him.

"Well, I'm glad you said that," she replied smoothly, giving John Dale a little smile. "And I have to say I agree with Hallie that you should go back to Charleston and finish your senior year at the College of Charleston where you started. You've done well there, and you might lose credits trying to make a transfer at this late stage. Also, they hold a real pretty graduation ceremony at that old college, and I'd looked forward to coming down for it next May."

Tanner watched John Dale's face fall.

Mary reached out to put a hand on his knee. "I don't see any reason why Hallie can't go down there with you," she stated. "She'll be safer there than here with Jonas Cole still loose."

John Dale shook his head. "I live in the fraternity house, Grandmother. And housing around the college is really expensive. I couldn't afford an apartment in Charleston even if I could get loans to stay in school this year. Plus, you know Daddy and Mother told me they wouldn't pay for my schooling if I married before I graduated. They meant Hallie, of course, even though they tried to make it sound generic."

She refilled their tea glasses. "We all thought it would be best if you finished your schooling before you married, John Dale. Even I agreed. Hallie was only fifteen when you went to college—hadn't even finished high school. I knew she'd be eighteen by the time you graduated. That's still young, Son. Only a year out of high school."

"It seems like that's kind of irrelevant now," Tanner interrupted.

Mary gave him a silencing glance. "So it is," she agreed.

"I want you to know, Grandmother, that I'm purposed to be with Hallie this year," John Dale stated with surprising boldness. "I respect your opinions and I wanted you to know about everything, but I'm not going back to Charleston in two weeks without Hallie."

"I don't think you should," Mary replied with that same calmness. "Maybe I'd better explain. You see, when Carlton and Louise bought that big, ole house in downtown Charleston some years ago, I helped them with the financing. It has a very nice townhouse apartment over the separate garage wing. A lot of those old gracious homes have those, you know. My understanding with Carlton was, that if I helped with the financing, the apartment would always be mine while I was living. Whenever I go down to Charleston now, I stay in it. I like that. It gives me my own privacy."

She paused. "I don't go down there much. And I don't see any reason why you and Hallie can't use the apartment this year while you finish college. It's a nice little place, only about five or six blocks from the school. You could bike over if you didn't want to drive every day. There's a nice private walled yard behind the garage, and the whole building sits back quite a distance from Carlton and Louise's place. I think it would be ideal for the two of you. Personally, I find Louise delightful, and I think Hallie would like her. And with Carlton being a doctor, we'd all feel very safe about Hallie being next door to him."

John Dale sat on the edge of his seat now. "Grandmother, do you think it might work? What about my tuition and school fees, though? They're due next week, and when Mother and Dad find out about all this, they might refuse to pay them. Try to block all of this. And I might not have time to work out a school loan this late."

"Don't you worry about those school fees," Mary replied, waving a hand dismissively. "Vernon and June will pay them. I'll see to it. After all, this is their grandchild that's coming. And you've honorably married the child's mother as you should have. We can take care of that little age technicality quietly later on with a small ceremony like you planned, and nobody needs to know we didn't all know last summer the two of you got married when Hallie was underage." She clasped her hands in her lap. "I find people generally believe whatever you tell them, John Dale. Besides, it's unlikely Sissy would resist signing to let Hallie marry now, considering everything that's happened."

She turned to Tanner. "You know, despite these plans, I really think we should keep Hallie's whereabouts totally secret until Jonas Cole is caught and prosecuted. Even on bail he could be dangerous to Hallie. And no one will think to look for her where Carlton lives in Charleston."

Mary glanced out toward her rose bushes with a remembering smile. "I knew Hallie would never run away from her home and family without good reason. That child told me once, when we were mulching the roses, that she felt as much rooted and planted in the ground here in the mountains as our roses. She had that stubborn little expression on her face when she said that to me, and I knew it to be true."

"She still feels that way." John Dale grinned at the story.

"Well, that's comforting to me, Boy. I'm counting on the two of you valuing this old place and keeping it in the family."

"You know we will, Grandmother." He reached over to take her hand.

"You tell Hallie I'm going to slip over to see her next week before she leaves for Charleston. I'm fond of that girl. And of you, Boy," she confided,

Delia's Place

reaching over to pat John Dale on the cheek fondly as she said it. "I'll be looking forward to having you both move out here with me next June."

She stopped to count on her fingers. "My great-grandchild will be about five months old by next June. It will be a fine thing to have a little one about the place again. I'll have that little guest house by the orchard fixed up real cute for the two of you by the time you come back home."

John Dale got up to hug his grandmother warmly. "I'm truly grateful for your help and support, Grandmother. Thank you."

"Everythings going to be just fine now, Boy. You'll see. Now aren't you glad you didn't keep trying to worry all this out on your own?" she asked.

"I only wish my parents felt better about Hallie and cared for her like you do," John Dale admitted, scowling. "Hallie's real worried they may never accept her."

Mary Ogle chuckled. "Well, actually I've got myself a nice little ace up the sleeve about that. I planned to play it later on, but I think I might play it now instead."

"What are you talking about Grandmother?" John Dale questioned.

"Well, what's the biggest thing June worries over so much about Hallie?" Mary asked.

"That her mother ran off and married several times?" John Dale offered.

Mary waved her hand in the negative. "Even more than that."

"About her Rayfield blood," Tanner put in. "She's always talking about Hallie's wild Rayfield blood. And how she hates to see it mixed with the fine Madison, Ogle, Boone, and Heyward bloodlines."

"Bingo." Mary pointed in Tanner's direction. "So I've been doing a little genealogy and have found out some very interesting things."

"Don't tell me you're going to convince June she's got thieves and murderers in her bloodlines?" Tanner grinned.

"Better than that." Mary smiled smugly. "I've researched the Rayfields extensively over the last several years. Their heritage is even more impressive than my family lines, the Boones, Heywards, or even the Madisons on your father's side." She raised an eyebrow for emphasis. "Actually, there is a fine Rayfield Plantation right down in South Carolina June might like to see sometime. She also might like to learn how the Rayfield family links directly into President Andrew Jackson's bloodlines through marriage, and that several Rayfields fought in the Revolutionary War, and that a Rayfield actually sailed on one of the early British ships to America. Hallie has the lineage to join the Daughters of the American Revolution and the Colonial Dames, the latter of which June doesn't even have the credentials to join. I can't wait to see June's face when she learns that."

"Guess we'll need a President Jackson bedroom in the bed and breakfast now," suggested John Dale with a smirk. "Hallie and Delia cooked up this decorating scheme where each of the guest bedrooms here will be named after presidents, since our family is direct descendents of President Madison. We thought guests would like that."

"A nice idea," agreed Mary.

"And we can use wildflower prints of Susan Rayfield's in some areas of the house, too," she added, grinning like the cat who swallowed the canary. "Susan Rayfield is a famous wildlife illustrator, illustrated Audubon field guides. She's directly related to the Rayfield family, too. In fact, I think I'll give June one of those Audubon wildflower field guides for her birthday this fall. I ordered several copies through an online book company, and I've been trying to decide who to give them to."

Tanner laughed. "I had no idea you were such a clever and devious woman, Mary Ogle."

Mary sighed. "Actually my daughter, June, is a very clever woman, too, Tanner. She's simply gotten misdirected these last years. I actually think she's somewhat unfulfilled in her life. I wish I knew how to help her with that."

John Dale leaned forward. "Grandmother, Hallie talks a lot about how wonderful Mother used to be working with the children in the library. She still remembers stories that Mother told the kids at story hour and these special listening hats Mother used."

Mary looked pleased at that. "How typical of Hallie to look for the good. I'll be sure to tell June that. It would be nice for her to use her gifts and talents in some constructive ways again. She studied to teach, you know, and taught English until her children came. She always loved books and enjoyed researching subjects. She read a lot to you and your sister and saw to it that you both became readers. Perhaps she should go back to teach again or work in the library. Maybe if she found some interest again she wouldn't need to try so hard to make herself seem important." She pursed her lips. "Someone really needs to tell her it's rather boring and pathetic when she does."

Somehow Tanner felt it would be Mary who would tell June exactly that. And, in his opinion, the conversation was long overdue.

Mary insisted then that Tanner and John Dale stay for lunch. And, afterwards, Mary persuaded John Dale to stay and talk with her longer. She wanted him to climb up into the attic to look for an old baby bed, and go out to the guest house to help her decide how to start fixing it up.

"I'll drive John Dale back home later on," she told Tanner. "I need to go to Gatlinburg anyway. Besides, I'll have precious little time with the boy after next week, and we have a lot to talk about."

It was nearly two by the time Tanner started the drive from Greenbrier back to Gatlinburg. Eager to talk to Delia, he punched in her number on his cell phone. He thought he'd invite her to go out to dinner. There were so many things he had to tell her. He knew he could lure her to say yes by

Delia's Place

alluding to some of the mysteries he'd solved that she'd been so eager to get the answers to. In addition, he wanted to tell her the good news about Hallie and John Dale.

He'd almost started to hang up when she finally answered. And her voice sounded strained. Tanner wondered if she was still mad at him about the magazines. He hoped not.

Chapter 19

On Friday, Delia came back to the office by lunchtime, hoping to see Tanner. Lavonne told her that morning he planned to come in early from Atlanta.

She dropped by Bogan and Rona's first to check on the ongoing decorating work in process at Mountain Productions, and afterwards, met with a new client about another future job. An optometrist Delia met at the open house planned to move his offices to a larger location and wanted Delia to decorate the new space, focusing the décor around a fine collection of signed and numbered bird prints he'd collected over the years. Her mind already hummed with ideas for the project.

"Hi, Lavonne. Any messages?" she called, coming into the T. Cross offices. Lavonne did double duty in taking phone calls for T. Cross Accounting and for Crosswalk corporate. Now, in addition, she graciously handled Delia's calls related to her decorating jobs and prospects.

"Hey, darling." Lavonne sent her a smile. "Rona called. One of the painters has a question about something or other, and she wants you to call her back." She looked down at her phone notes. "Also, one of Tanner's clients called, too – Hiram Sheffrum. He wants you to redecorate his office and waiting room."

She glanced at Delia conspiratorially over the top of her cute red reading glasses. "To be frank, honey, I'd talk to Tanner before getting involved with Hiram. He loves to spend money, that's for certain sure, but doesn't always pay his bills on time. You might never get paid. And the man drinks entirely too much. He might be trouble to work with."

Delia laughed. "Maybe I'll tell him I have too many commitments." She glanced toward Tanner's office.

"Come and gone," Lavonne informed her, following her gaze. "Went to get breakfast with that preacher's boy. You know, the Madison kid."

"John Dale?"

"Yeah, that's the boy's name." She nodded. "Tanner hasn't come back since and probably won't today. My guess is he went home to unpack, mow the yard, and unwind. Those big conventions always wear you out—meetings all day and into the night. I'm sure Tanner's ready to take a break."

Delia leaned on her desk. "Any more news about Jonas Cole?"

"Nothin' much." Lavonne shook her head. "At breakfast this morning, Bill said that the police at Cosby had a lead. Seems a couple in Newport reported seeing somebody in an empty house nearby that matched Jonas' description. Police investigated, found food cartons and evidence someone stayed there. A check found the house one Jonas had listed as a realty agent; they plan to check out all his other empty listings to be sure he's not moving around between houses hiding out. He has keys to them all, you know; it would be easy for him to get in."

Lavonne tapped her head. "That man might be a little crazy, Delia, but he's smart. Anyway, I'm glad to know he was sighted around Newport. We don't need the likes of him down here with the tourist season still in full swing."

Delia went over to her own office to call Rona. The painters only wanted to know if she wanted the hallways painted the same color as the entry. After clarifying the paint color, Delia started a new file related to her meeting with Dr. Bradley. She always liked to write her decorating ideas down while they were fresh. She flipped through a furniture catalog next, looking for furnishings for the doctor's entry area. However, her mind soon wandered to Tanner.

She drummed her fingers on the table. "Maybe I can pick up a couple of deli sandwiches and take them to Tanner's for lunch. If he's mowing the yard, he probably didn't stop to eat yet. It's only noon. And he ate a late breakfast with John Dale, too." The idea pleased her. "I need to do something nice for Tanner to try to make up for being so unpleasant before."

Delia smoothed back her hair. "I want to tell Tanner what I learned about Mother, her brother and Aunt Dee, too. It makes so many things clearer." She looked across the room to the picture of Aunt Dee and herself on the bookshelf. "It was wrong how Mother blamed Dee for Richard's death. But Aunt Dee handled the breakup of her engagement badly, too—afraid of confronting Mother's disfavor."

She straightened in annoyance. "Well, I refuse to be afraid anymore. I can't help it if I look like Aunt Dee. Why should I be blamed or punished for that? It's stupid."

Banishing negative thoughts, Delia cleared off her desk and found her purse. A beautiful, sunny August afternoon called, Tanner was home, and Delia planned to take the rest of the day off. Checking out with Lavonne, she set out to find sandwiches at the deli on the parkway and maybe some of that fudge Tanner liked, the kind with the peanut butter layer on the bottom.

At almost one o'clock, Delia pulled in the driveway of Aunt Dee's place. She felt disappointed not to find Tanner at his place or his mother's. Perhaps he went fishing with Vesser—it was a great day for it.

"Oh, well," she told herself. "Hallie and I can eat the sandwiches. Then maybe we can invite Tanner and John Dale over for dinner tonight."

There wouldn't be many more nights for them to all get together, she thought. John Dale would leave for school next week. Hallie kept trying to act brave about it, but Delia had caught her crying several times. And despite John Dale's arguments to the contrary, Hallie still stood adamant that it was best for him to finish college in Charleston. It seemed like the two fought about it nearly every day.

Delia let herself in the back door. She dropped her purse on the kitchen counter and started toward the living room to look for Hallie.

"Hallie!" she called. "I'm home. And I've brought some sandwiches for lunch."

"Well, isn't that nice," drawled a man's voice. "You just come on in here and sit down, and we'll take a look at those sandwiches, you hear?"

Delia's breath caught in her throat. A strange man sat on the couch with a rifle propped across his arm pointed right at her.

"It's a real gun, girlie. And I know well enough how to shoot it, so you'd better mind what I say, and walk over here real easy and sit down."

Delia started across the room slowly, fear making her legs shake.

"Well, I can see you're not Hallie Walker. But since you hollered for her, I figure you know her. So I guess you and me will just wait right here nice and patient until she comes on back home. I've got a little score to settle with her."

"You're Jonas Cole." Delia breathed the name on a harsh whisper.

"I can see Hallie's been talking about me. And knowing that little cat, I doubt she had any good things to say either. Always causing trouble and spreading lies, that one." He ran a hand through his hair angrily, gesturing again for Delia to sit down on the couch opposite him.

As Delia did, Jonas reached across and grabbed the deli bag from her, causing her to gasp and pull back.

"I'm jest after the grub right now, girl." His brows drew together. "Haven't had anything to eat since early morning. And even then, not much. Hard to get nice meals when you're on the run. And thanks to Hallie, and that tattle-tale Carleen prissy-pants, I'm not likely to get many more for a season."

While Jonas Cole rummaged in the bag from the deli, Delia studied him. He was a little rough shaven now, his clothes soiled and not neatly pressed, but handsome none the less. He was tall, had a good build, and when he smiled, a certain charisma swirled about him. Delia could see how a woman might find him charming in a better time, not knowing the underside of his nature.

"What you looking at, girl," he snapped, looking up and catching her glance.

"Nothing," she answered quickly.

He'd found a sandwich and ate greedily now. As he ate, he dug pickles, chips, and fudge from the bag, spread them neatly on a napkin on the coffee table, and then pulled a liquor bottle from off the floor to sit beside the food. Delia saw that he was well into the bottle—a large one of bourbon.

He held the bag out toward her that contained the other sandwich. "I figure the rest here is yours." A half smile played over his lips.

Delia shook her head, her appetite gone with her fear.

Jonas studied her now while he ate. He still had the rifle propped carefully across his lap, and he put his hand on it every once in a while, as if reminding her that he had it close by.

"What's your name, girl?"

As Delia hesitated, he held the rifle out toward her face with a scowl. "I'm trying to be nice here, girl. It would pay you to be polite and mind your manners." He fingered the trigger on the rifle. "Now, once again, what's your name?"

"Delia Walker," she answered in a small voice.

He laid the rifle back across his leg again. "Delia," he said thoughtfully, drawing the name out slowly. "You kin to the woman who used to live here in this house?"

Delia nodded. "She was my aunt."

He ate for a minute, swigging down some more of the bourbon, too. Glancing down at the coffee table between them, Delia noticed a newspaper folded open to a short news article.

Jonas saw her eyes move to it. "Little write up about me here in the daily newspaper." He punched at it with a finger. "You look surprised at it, so I guess maybe Miss High-and-Mighty Hallie must have been reading it. Article says they think I burned down Sissy's house after she got out of the hospital."

He smiled a secret smile. "She should have come back home where she belonged. Been ready to say she was sorry and ready to be a good wife to me again. But, no." His eyes narrowed. "She went off with her Rayfield relatives, back to her old family place where she told me she never wanted to live again."

He kicked at the newspaper with his foot suddenly, startling Delia. "All this mess I'm in is her and her brat Hallie's fault. I never should have hooked up with them. I can see that now. And I intend to give both of them a few little lessons about messing with Jonas Cole before I leave here for good. That prissy Crowley brat, too. She sparked up to me, flirted with me, and stirred me up. Then she tried to play coy and shocked when I gave her the attention she asked for. I hate it when women do that. Tease and then don't want to pay for it. Ain't right, you know. Hard on a man. And they just think it's some kind of little game. Get all mad later when you don't play it their way.

"Hallie was like that, you know." His eyes gleamed at her. "Sashaying all around in front of me in her little nightshirts with nothing underneath. Coming out of the bathroom with not a stitch on but a towel. Laying around on the back patio in a skimpy little bikini. Showing me what she had right there under her own mother's roof."

Delia stayed quiet, thinking while she listened. Hallie had been Jonas's stepdaughter while she'd done all those ordinary things young girls do in the privacy of their own homes. How could Jonas Cole think she'd deliberately tempted him by just being natural in her own house? His logic was fatally flawed. And his views about women unnatural in some way.

Jonas took another swig of the whiskey. "Started catting around, too. But still tried to play like she was all sweet and innocent. I knew back in the spring something was going on with her and that little college boy. Him a lot older than her by a mile. Figured I could play that game with her, too, but she had other ideas. Thought I wasn't good enough for her."

"You were her stepfather," Delia protested without meaning to.

"So?" His temper flared. "I wasn't her natural father, and well she knew it. So did her mama, acting all horrified later on, talking like it was incest for me to look at the girl. I know what incest is. And it's not incest to act on what's invited with someone you're not related to. But that bitch Sissy slapped me for saying those words, and I had to defend myself then. A man can't let a woman push him around, you know. My daddy taught me that. And my mama knew how to stay in her place. My sisters, too."

Delia gave an inward sigh. No wonder he'd turned out the way he did. Growing up in an abusive home and now repeating the pattern. How sad.

"What's that look?" Jonas barked. "Feeling sorry for me? I don't need some little ole slip of a career girl feeling sorry for me."

Delia's eyes widened.

"I'm not dumb, girl," he snarled. "I read about you and all your fancy decorating work while I was waiting for Hallie. Read about you right there in this magazine." He stabbed a finger at it. "About all your degrees and all your possibilities." He mocked the article's words in a singsong voice as he said them.

"It's all right here." He flipped open *Mountain Living* to the article about her. "I can see real easy, right here, why you're having such success. Wearing that short little black dress with your nice, fine breasts about popping out. I guess any man would want to have you come decorate his office and then enjoy some sweet overtime with you after you're done."

Delia gasped. "That's not true!" she cried, without thinking.

Delia's Place

He arched out of his seat, never losing his grip on the rifle, and slapped her with his free hand. Hard.

"Watch your manners," he hissed at her, easing back onto the sofa.

Delia pulled back into the couch, holding her hand to her face, frightened even more now.

"Now, that's much better," he announced, looking at her with satisfaction. "That's the way a woman ought to look at a man, nice and respectful like."

He studied his watch. "I figure Hallie ought to be slipping back in here after a while," he told her. "Maybe the three of us can all have a little fun together. I might go ahead and try me a little of your nice wares right now except I don't want her to sneak in while I'm busy and get away from me again. We got a score to settle, she and I."

Delia huddled tighter into the couch, clutching a cushion to her— truly terrified now. This man was crazy, and unless some miracle happened, he planned to hurt both Hallie and her before it was done. Delia knew from Lavonne that Jonas had beaten Hallie's mother Sissy until she fell unconscious and raped her, as well. His own wife.

"I figured when I burned Sissy's house that she'd come around then, wanting to hunt through what was left of it, see if she could find some of her stuff. I hung around, hiding out, watching the house. Figured she and I could talk when she came. Maybe work things out." His finger strayed to the rifle trigger again. "Thought I could get her to leave with me. After all, she is my wife. Her place is with me. I figured to help her see that. She was always sweet on me, Sissy. I knew she'd come around after she got over being mad."

He stopped to eat the last of the sandwich and emptied out more of the bottle. "You can't imagine how surprised I was to see Miss Hallie Walker picking around in the ruins of that old house this morning early." He laughed. "Oh, she was wearing some kind of wig, but I knew it was her. Pulling out some old trinket here or there and crying over it. Silly girl."

Jonas scratched his head. "At first I thought she'd come back home from New York to see about her mother. But then, the more I thought on it, and about how sly and clever she'd always been, I figured she never left. Neighbors lived too close around for me to confront her there, so I thought I'd just follow her. See where she went. It looked to me like she had a little mound in front, too. Like she'd hooked herself up with a man and gotten herself knocked up. Thought I'd like to know a little more about that."

He took another long drink from the bottle. "She drove off after a while in an old beat up jeep. That your other car, girl?"

Delia shook her head no.

"Whose is it" he insisted, leaning toward her menacingly. Delia could smell the liquor on him now. He was surely drunk.

"I think our neighbor's," she answered him, afraid not to.

Tanner owned an old jeep, once his father's, that he drove when he went fishing or into the back roads of the mountains. Hallie must have used the key Delia had to Tanner's house, gone to Tanner's, and borrowed his set of keys. Mercy, whatever possessed her to be so foolish? To leave the house at a time like this? To take such a risk and drive over to Cosby? Delia could wring her neck for being so stupid.

"That her fancy man, the one with the jeep?" Jonas asked, his voice slurring a bit.

Delia shook her head.

"So who is he?" Jonas threatened, pointing the rifle at her again.

"The college boy," she answered, seeing no point in lying at this point. Besides, the man had an uncanny way of knowing when she tried.

He nodded, satisfied. "I knew it," he pronounced smugly.

"I thought you said you followed Hallie." Delia swallowed. "Why isn't she already here if you followed her?"

"Smart question," he acknowledged, biting into a pickle. "She got away from me. I thought I was keeping a nice distance from her, but she must have seen me as she started into Gatlinburg. Panicked then. Started cutting through traffic, turning off on side roads. I tried to keep up, but I lost her. But then it dawned on me where she might be staying." He tapped his head. "Dee Walker was a favorite of Hallie's, you know. Hallie buttered up to her, even got her to leave her a little money when she died. I got to thinking maybe she'd been hanging out here. So I came over to find out. I knew where it was from Sissy telling me. She picked Hallie up here sometimes when she worked with the old lady making candles."

He looked around. "You ought not to leave your house so easy to get into," he advised, laughing at his own joke. "Left my car hid out down a little side street, got in through the back. Didn't take me long to find things to let me know Hallie was staying here after I poked around. That's when I decided to just sit and wait a spell. The girl's bound to come back here sooner or later if her stuff's here. And she don't have no idea I'm here. So it'll be a nice little surprise for her when she comes."

Jonas offered Delia a slow, sly smile then. It reminded Delia of the excited face of a predator as it waited patiently to make its kill. She shuddered.

Delia tried frantically to think if there was anything she could do to protect Hallie from walking in on this monster. But nothing came to mind. She felt sure that even if she antagonized him and he killed her, he'd still stay and wait for Hallie, too. Then she wouldn't even be here to help at all. Or to comfort Hallie if they lived.

Her mind whirled, trying to think of ideas. Jonas, relaxed and easy, reached for the deli bag and proceeded to dig out the other sandwich and eat it.

Delia's Place

"No sense of a good sandwich going to waste," he said with a grin.

Delia tried to study the situation to evaluate any potential options. Jonas sat in the big easy chair clearly facing the front door. No one could come in without him seeing them immediately. Delia, alternately, sat on the couch across from him. She'd see anyone coming in the back door and through the kitchen first. But Jonas would hear them. He'd hear the car pull up, and he'd hear the back door open. Hallie was always noisy, too, calling out when she came in, banging around the kitchen as she entered it. Delia sighed with frustration. She doubted she could give any warning to Hallie before too late. Jonas was clever. He'd hear Hallie drive up in the car, be ready and waiting for her when she walked in. Even if Hallie drove the jeep to Tanner's first, Jonas would hear that noisy old vehicle on the street.

The phone rang then and nearly startled Delia out of her mind.

It startled Jonas, too, and he dropped a pickle on the floor, clutching his rifle up at the ready. They both stared at the phone with wide eyes as it rang.

Delia thought fast. "It will seem odd if I don't answer it," she said calmly. "Most everyone knows I'm at home. And my car is out front. If it's a neighbor or someone I work with, and I don't answer, they'll probably come over. Be worried." She let that thought hang there temptingly.

"So you answer it," he directed. "But you be short and sweet and sound normal. I'll be listening. If you give any kind of hint away to anybody that I'm here, you'll just be signing their death warrant when they come over here. And your own." He pointed the rifle at her as a warning, holding it on her as she picked up the phone.

"Hello?" she answered tentatively.

It was Tanner.

"Hi, Delia, I'm glad I caught you at home," he said cheerfully, as if nothing in the world was the matter. "I'm on my way down into the Burg right now. I got into Gatlinburg a little earlier today, and I've been out in Greenbrier for a while. How about if you and I go out and get something to eat later tonight? Does that sound good?'

"That sounds nice," she said in a shaking voice, keeping an eye on the rifle.

"You still mad at me, Delia?' Tanner asked softly.

"No," she answered softly back. "I'm fine."

"You sound odd, Delia. Is everything okay there?"

Delia knew Jonas could hear Tanner's words coming over the phone. He frowned at her in warning, touching his finger to the rifle trigger.

An odd thought came to Delia then. "Everything's fine here," she told Tanner breezily. "And don't you forget to pick up the zucchini at the store like you promised."

And she hung up.

"What was that all about?" Jonas groused.

"He'd promised to pick up something for me at the store, and I tried to say something that would seem real normal, so he wouldn't be worried."

"Zucchini?" he asked suspiciously.

"For Hallie," she answered simply. "She wants to make zucchini bread. You know she's always making those sweetbreads."

"Yeah," he said, accepting that. "She was a good cook. I missed that after she took off. Sissy worked a lot and wasn't as good in the kitchen." He scowled. "She should have stayed there to take care of me. And she shouldn't have run off like she did and worried Sissy."

He drank some more from the bottle, brooding.

Delia thought she counted every click of the old mantle clock after that, wondering if Tanner discerned her warning. Wondering if he'd send help, and if help would arrive before Hallie did.

Growing drunker by the moment, Jonas rambled on about his life and its injustices, alternating by bragging about his accomplishments.

"I served in the war when just a young kid," he told her. "Killed a lot of them Viet Cong. Helped keep our country safe. And I got crap appreciation for it from people here in the states. Made us mad over there, seeing those news flashes of war protests."

He looked up at Delia with a saucy smile. "Bet you didn't know I was that old, did you? Fifty-eight, but I'm still good where it counts, girl, so don't you worry." He chuckled. "No, siree. Don't need any of that Viagra stuff. Got real good genetics there."

Delia closed her eyes for a minute in dread. When she looked up, she saw Tanner at the edge of the kitchen doorway with his finger laid warningly over his lips. He held some sort of weapon and his eyes looked deadly serious.

She dropped her eyes to her lap, not wanting to give away any reaction to Jonas Cole that might endanger Tanner. In her mind, she said a short prayer. Before she could finish it, she heard a thud and looked up to see Jonas slump over, falling awkwardly off the sofa. Tanner moved quickly then, disarming Jonas, and squatting down to begin tying his hands behind him with twine from the kitchen.

Delia closed her eyes, wondering if she was going to be sick with relief. When she opened them, Tanner knelt there beside her, touching her, talking to her, asking her if she was all right. Asking her if Jonas had hurt her— probing the place on her face where Jonas slapped her earlier.

Before she could answer him, the front door flew open and two armed policemen rushed in. Another came in from the back. They quickly checked and properly handcuffed Jonas, and suddenly, the room that had seemed deadly quiet became a riot of noise.

Chapter 20

Delia Ward's little cottage on Balsam Lane had never known such pandemonium, and Tanner Cross had never felt such alternating fear and then relief in his life. Jonas Cole was no longer a threat, and Delia was finally safe. Tanner found the latter words rolling over and over in his mind like a mantra: Delia's safe, Delia's safe. She'd begun shaking and crying, and she had a foul bruise on her cheek, but she was safe.

Tanner sat on the couch with Delia wrapped in his arms now. The police officers had finished carrying the still unconscious Jonas Cole out of the room, and they talked back and forth in quick phrases to headquarters on their radios. Lavonne's husband, Bill Magee, had arrived on the scene. He was the one Tanner called as soon as he realized Jonas Cole must be at Delia's.

"Dadgummit, Tanner," Bill complained, slumping into the chair where Jonas Cole sat not so long ago. "You were supposed to wait until we got on the scene. What if you'd barged in here and got you or Delia shot?"

"Well, I didn't," Tanner bristled with an edge to his voice. "I did what I felt I had to do, Bill. Jonas was drinking heavily, his threats growing more aggressive. I was able to sneak into the house, and when I realized I had a chance to slip up on Jonas, I took it. I knew the house, where all the creaks in the floor were, and how to move in quietly. It's entirely possible that wouldn't have been the case with your officers. Jonas might have heard them as they started making their approach, trying to enter this little place. He might have panicked and shot Delia in the process. Bill, he was drunk and edgy. He had his rifle directly on Delia and his hand kept toying constantly around the trigger."

Bill shook his head with annoyance. "All the more reason to have waited, Tanner. The police are trained to handle these situations carefully. You know that."

Tanner glared at him. Delia had been in danger. He'd called the police, but he saw no reason to wait for them to arrive if he could do something to protect Delia sooner. His arm tightened around her protectively as he remembered those tense moments.

"I was so scared," Delia croaked, leaning into him. And this time nobody blamed her for the tears puddling in her eyes and spilling down her cheeks.

"Well, now, everything's turned out all right, little lady," comforted Bill, reaching over to pat her knee. "So you can calm yourself down. You can be real proud of yourself that you kept your head and thought to give Tanner that warning on the telephone. We're all real glad he caught the meaning of it, too, and got himself over here to check on what was going on."

"I was so afraid you wouldn't remember." Delia trembled against Tanner, her voice shaking. "Hallie said John Dale told you about their message, but I couldn't be sure you'd remember it."

Tanner would never forget the cold splinter of fear that hit him when he did. "I remembered," he assured Delia, stroking her face. "And, Bill's right. You were brave to tell me like you did and not to alert Cole."

Delia looked up at him. "I was so terrified, after I thought about it. I was afraid you'd just come barreling in, thinking it a joke, and that I'd cause you to get hurt. Or maybe shot." She shivered. "I took a risk to give you the signal, but I had to try something. Jonas kept talking about what he planned to do to Hallie when she came. He was so vengeful, and his thoughts so twisted, Tanner. Every minute, I was so afraid Hallie would come. So afraid of what would happen."

She sniffed and wiped at her eyes.

"Do you know where Hallie is?" Bill asked her.

Delia shook her head.

"Jonas said Hallie had been over in Cosby— that she went to where her mama's house used to be. I couldn't believe she'd do that, but he said he watched her there, decided to follow her. He said she saw him, and then she got away."

Delia relayed her story between hiccupping sobs.

Tanner gave Bill a scowling look. "Couldn't you let Delia calm down here before you ask her more questions? Let me get her something to drink, Bill. Help her get to the bathroom. Help her quit shaking and crying so much."

"It's just part of the job, Tanner," Bill replied with a serious cop's face. "And the sooner we get some officers out looking for Hallie, the better things will be for her. She's probably scared to death herself if what Delia says is true."

"I'll do anything I can to help Hallie," Delia insisted. "Please."

One of the officers put his head back in the door. "We're ready to transport."

Bill got up. "I'll go out and talk to officers Prichard and Dodson for a minute so they can head on back with Cole. Then Officer Breeden and I will come back and talk to Delia before we follow. Get an informal statement.

She'll need to come down for a full statement later on, but this will be enough for now. You help her into the bathroom and get her something to drink while I step out. Then we'll talk."

Tanner got Delia into the bathroom and back to the couch on wobbly legs. She threw up from the sustained stress, and he wasn't surprised. Afterwards, he helped her wash her face and get a drink; he even humored her by helping her put on a little makeup. As though it mattered at a time like this.

They came back into the living room as Bill and Officer Breeden walked back into the room. A wild-eyed John Dale followed behind them.

Bill gestured toward him and shook his head. "The boy was about to start a fight with the officers outside to get in, so I figured we'd better let him in here with us. He might know something to add to this situation that could help."

Tanner talked to John Dale to calm him down, assuring him Hallie hadn't been here, that she'd seen Cole and gotten away. It took a few minutes to get him settled down so he could update him. In the meantime, Bill and Officer Fred Breeden had pulled up a couple of extra chairs, so everyone could sit down in close proximity.

"I'm not talking about anything until all that stuff is out of here," Delia ordered tightly, pointing to the deli bags, food remains, and Cole's liquor bottle still left behind.

Seeing the stubborn set to her face and the red blotches on her cheeks, Bill nodded to Officer Breeden, and he collected everything up and bagged it in case anything might be needed later on. He sat the bag to one side, but after seeing Delia's eyes still looking at it pointedly, he got up and took it outside.

After that, Delia got the whole story out bit by bit. Calmer now, she told the details with a brave little clarity, keeping her tears at bay with effort, through most of the telling. His heart broke to hear what she'd been through.

"Tanner, let's have a description of this jeep Hallie's driving, since it's yours," Bill said at the end. "We'll put out an APB on it, get some officers looking for it—and for Hallie right away."

John Dale looked at Delia in anguish. "Why did she do this? Why did she take the risk and leave the house like that? I've told her and told her to be careful. She could have gotten herself killed. And you. What was she thinking, Delia?"

Delia shook her head. "I don't know, John Dale. A newspaper lay folded open here to an article about the arson at Sissy's house." She pointed to it.

"Dang press," Bill muttered. "Always printing up everything that happens and sensationalizing it. Stirring people up." He looked down at the article, hoping for answers.

Delia looked thoughtful. "I remember Jonas Cole saying Hallie was searching through the remains of the house, picking up what he called trinkets. He said he heard her crying and he called her silly for it."

Bill frowned. "She must have gone looking for something after she saw the article. People can get funny about sentimental things and forget reason."

"What can we do to help you find Hallie?" John Dale ran his hands through his hair in agitation. "She must really be scared wherever she is."

"What you can do is stay here in case she comes back. As Cole told Delia, Hallie didn't know Cole figured out where she was staying. If she comes back here, you call me right away."

John Dale nodded.

"And if any of you know any place where you think she might go, let us know that. We'll check out anything you can think of." He looked at Tanner pointedly. "And you let us do it this time, Tanner. Don't take off trying to do the police's job."

Bill and Officer Breeden stood on their feet. "The best thing all of you can do is stay here in case Hallie comes back or calls," Bill said. "We'll probably transport Cole on over to the Cocke County Jail in Newport when he comes to. But we'll keep looking for Hallie until we find her."

"I'll walk out with you," John Dale offered. "Tell you some places Hallie knows well that she might go to. Spots where we used to play together around the farms at Greenbrier. Places we used to walk and hike around here."

Tanner gathered Delia in a comforting hug as soon as they were alone.

"I'm so worried about Hallie." She fretted against his chest.

"They'll find her," he assured her.

The next several hours continued to be a hectic time. Tanner regretted it for Delia, but there was little he could do about it.

Maureen arrived, of course. Then others in the neighborhood, who'd seen the police cars, came by anxious, concerned, and curious. As typical in a small town, word spread fast about what happened. Also, as word of the search for Hallie leaked out, the phone began to ring off the hook with calls from Hallie's family. The secret was definitely out now that Hallie Walker was not in New York City.

Tanner and John Dale fielded the incoming calls, insisting that those who phoned call back on their cell phones to keep the line at Dee's place open. No one wanted to take the chance that Hallie might call and not be able to reach them.

A surprising visit occurred when Mary Ogle showed up at the door with Rev. Vernon Madison and June in tow.

"We've come to see what we can do," Mary explained, coming over to hug John Dale and Tanner, and then hugging Delia once she was introduced.

"I'm real proud of what a good friend you've been to our Hallie." Mary patted her cheek. "We don't deserve such kindness, considering the situation, but we're truly grateful to you." She looked pointedly toward June and Vernon.

"I've brought some food," June offered humbly. "I didn't think anyone would feel like cooking dinner." Her eyes dropped to the dishes she carried. "It's a casserole from the freezer and a fresh pound cake."

"How nice of you," Delia replied kindly, recognizing an olive branch when she saw one.

Maureen went to put the food in the kitchen while everyone pulled up chairs.

"Mary has told us everything," Rev. Madison said, looking at John Dale with significance. "You should have come to us, Son. I think you judged us harsher people than we are. We would have helped. We hoped you'd finish college before thinking of marriage, but surely, you know we'd understand this situation with Hallie."

He paused. "Actually, you and Hallie kept things so secret that when we heard Hallie went to New York, we thought you'd broken up or grown apart."

John Dale's eyes flashed. "Yeah, and I'll bet you both felt real delighted about that." He scowled. "If Hallie had been with me where she belonged, maybe none of this would have happened. Delia could have been killed here today, you know, and maybe Hallie, too, if she hadn't seen Jonas Cole following her and gotten away."

"Don't be overly harsh, J. D. ," Tanner cautioned. "We were all here, trying to watch over Hallie, and this still happened."

He nodded, but his expression remained sullen.

"Your parents have something to tell you that's important," Mary interrupted. "I think you ought to listen to them."

"Mary talked to your mother and me," Rev. Madison began. "And we all agree you should go on back to finish out your schooling at Charleston."

As John Dale's head jerked up, he added quickly, "We also agree Hallie should go with you. You two are married; you have a child coming. You should be together. And Mary has graciously offered to let you live in her townhouse apartment this year."

The room grew quiet.

"We will pay for your last year's schooling, of course."

John Dale tensed. "I'll work part-time. I'll make as much as I can to take care of Hallie and me."

"I know you will," his father replied kindly.

John Dale turned his eyes to his mother. "I don't want you being mean to Hallie," he told her. "She's a good person, and I love her. I won't have you acting catty to her all the time and trying to make her feel second class."

June flushed. "I think perhaps everyone misunderstood my feelings for Hallie." She looked down at her lap. "We just wanted the best for you, Son."

"Hallie is the best," John Dale shot back. "She's strong and kind and good. She's brave and talented, too. She worked out her own plan to escape when she knew she felt in danger from Jonas, and she's worked in Dee's shop and made candles all summer while she's stayed here. She cleaned and cooked all the meals for Delia in return for Delia letting her live here. A man couldn't ask for a better wife than Hallie."

John Dale's parents passed a look.

"I'm a man now," John Dale added, interpreting that look. "I turned twenty-one on my birthday. I'm not a kid anymore. I work hard every summer, and when I graduate I'm going to be a good husband and father."

Tears slipped down June's cheeks. "I'm sure you will be, Son," she assured him. "It's simply hard to realize sometimes that your children are all grown up. Especially your youngest. You'll understand that someday, I think."

He looked at her angrily. "I'll never make a big deal about ancestry to my kids, I can tell you that. And as it's turned out, Hallie's ancestry is as good as ours. Did Grandmother tell you that?'

June nodded and hung her head. She fought tears, trying to maintain her dignity in front of people not even her family.

Maureen seemed to sense the situation. "John Dale, obviously your family has a lot of things to talk about and come to terms with tonight. But Delia here has been through a terrible shock. I think she needs some peace and quiet now. And probably something to eat."

Maureen looked at Delia then. "Did you ever get lunch, child?"

Delia shook her head.

"I agree with Mother," put in Tanner. "It was good of you to come. But I think maybe Delia should rest now. You can talk all these things over later."

"You're right," Rev. Madison agreed, rising. "I hope we haven't been insensitive," he offered to Delia. "This has all been so traumatic. And I want to say again how much we admire you for what you've done for Hallie and John Dale." He paused. "For our family," he amended.

June and Mary stood up also, with goodbyes and concerns expressed again.

"Grandmother, do you need me to take you home?" John Dale asked Mary.

"No, Boy." She patted his arm. "You took the old truck, remember? And I drove my own car over afterwards. I can drive myself back just fine. It won't be dark for another hour or so. It won't be a problem. You stay here in case Hallie comes back or is found. And let us know when there's news of her."

"Us, too, Son," Rev. Madison added. "We'll be concerned, as well. I called people in the church to be praying for her safety, and we'll be praying, too."

It pleased Tanner to see Vernon Madison taking more of a stand-up role with his son about Hallie. June obviously still struggled with some

Delia's Place

emotional issues and acted defensive in several areas, but Vernon seemed very supportive.

As the Reverend left, he turned and offered his hand to John Dale. "Everything is going to be all right, Son," he said, clasping John Dale's hand when he only tentatively responded. "And I think you should stay here tonight if it's all right with Delia. When Hallie is found, she'll need your comfort and support. Also, I think it would be good for a man to stay here in the house tonight. It's been a hard day. I'd like to know someone is here tonight with Delia and Hallie."

Impressive, Tanner thought. John Dale's father thought of exactly the right thing to do and say.

John Dale straightened his shoulders and looked at his father with a nod. "Thanks, Dad." They shook hands and then John Dale reached out to hug his father.

Making an effort, he turned to his mother. "Thanks for bringing the food, Mother. That will mean a lot to Hallie." He gave her a stiff hug.

"I'll bring more tomorrow," she offered, eager to please. "Some of the women in the church will make things, too."

Finally, they left, and Tanner, Maureen, John Dale, and Delia sat, exhausted and not speaking for a while.

"What a day," Delia ventured at last, sighing. "You know, I think my life was really incredibly simple before I came here."

They all laughed, and the release felt good after all the stress.

John Dale shifted uncomfortably. "Listen, I'm sorry all of you got caught in the middle of that stuff with my folks." He dropped his eyes. "Especially you, Delia. You had enough to deal with today."

She waved a hand. "I wouldn't have missed that for the world. And I can't wait to see Hallie's face when she learns all this good news."

"You think she'll be okay about it?" John Dale asked anxiously.

"Yes, I think she'll be thrilled, like I'm thrilled for you." Delia reached over to pat his arm.

He squeezed her hand. "Dad's right, you know. We owe you a lot of thanks for all you've done for Hallie. And for me. I wish I could do something back for you."

She gave him an impish smile. "Well, you could go fix something for me to eat. You're a good cook, I hear. I haven't eaten since this morning, and Jonas Cole ate my lunch."

"Sure, right away. Right away." He jumped up, seeming glad to have something to do.

"I'll go help," Maureen offered. "This sitting and waiting to hear about Hallie is making me nervous."

Tanner leaned over to give Delia a kiss after both of them left.

"Ugh." Delia fussed, turning her head. "Don't kiss me now. I still taste awful. Remember I threw up a little while ago."

"I don't care." He tried to nuzzle closer again.

"Well, I do," she replied primly. "Besides, I want you to help me think, while they're not here, about where Hallie might be. I don't want her out there alone somewhere, after it gets dark later on."

Tanner glanced toward the window. "It won't grow dark until about seven with the days long."

"That's only two hours from now." Delia shivered.

"Well, that old jeep ought to be easy to find. There aren't many cars like that around. Bill and his officers will find it."

"I hope so," she said.

They talked quietly for a time about events of the day. Things Delia still needed to talk out. Get release from.

Then Maureen and John Dale brought food in to the dining room table and called them to eat. John Dale had heated up his mother's casserole, sautéed zucchini and mushrooms, and whipped up a nice salad.

"I thought the zucchini deserved recognition tonight," he said with a grin.

To all of them, it felt good to laugh.

Surprisingly, Delia ate. And the food helped to calm her.

John Dale, however, only picked at the food on his plate. "I keep trying to think where she would go," he grumbled. "I called Bill Magee again on his cell, told him a couple of more ideas where they might look. He said they had no leads on Hallie yet. None. Haven't found anyone who saw her and haven't found the jeep, either. Where do you suppose she is?"

He twisted the remains of his napkin nervously. "Knowing Hallie, she's probably hiding out where she knows no one would ever think to look for her."

Delia's face lit at his comment. "I think I know where she is," she exclaimed.

"Where?" John Dale asked eagerly.

"She's at the old Walker sisters' house behind Metcalf Bottoms."

John Dale frowned. "Why do you think she'd go to that old place?"

"Because of what she said when she took me there in May." Delia leaned across the table in her enthusiasm. "She said, 'I'd come here to hide out if Jonas Cole ever came after me. He'd never think to look for me here.'"

John Dale pushed his chair back. "I'll go call Bill and tell him."

"No." Delia reached out to catch his arm. "She'd freak if she heard cars driving in there. And you know the police would open the gate and drive straight to the house on that old settler's road. They wouldn't hike in." Delia looked at Tanner appealingly. "We need to hike in so she won't be afraid,

Delia's Place

Tanner. She'll be watching the road, and if she sees it's only us, she won't run. She'll know I remembered."

"I think Delia's right." Tanner flexed his fingers. "Besides, it's a long way over there. If Hallie's not there, we'd save some officers being pulled off the search nearer to the Burg by checking it out ourselves."

Delia got up. "I'm going to put on some jeans and get my hiking boots. I'm still wearing my work clothes." She looked at Tanner. "You go get your boots on and get your car. I'm too shaky to drive."

She turned to Maureen and John Dale. "Maureen, can you and John Dale stay here in case Hallie isn't at the Walker place and in case she comes back here?"

"I'll stay here," Maureen assured her. "Don't you worry."

Tanner caught Delia's arm. "Maybe I should go alone," he suggested. "You've been through a lot today, Delia. You should rest. If Hallie is there, I'll bring her back."

"No." Delia flinched. "She'll be scared. And if she sees me, she'll know it's all right to come out. Besides, I want to go."

Tanner sighed in defeat. Maybe it would help Delia to be busy and take her mind off the trauma of the day.

"I'm going, too." John Dale stood up. "It's driving me crazy sitting around here waiting. I need something to do, even if we don't find Hallie."

"She'll be there," Delia insisted. "I just know it somehow. And if you're going, John Dale, go find her boots upstairs and make her a sandwich real quick. She won't have eaten since this morning. She'll be hungry. Get some bottles of water for us to take, too. They're in the pantry closet."

"Will you be all right here alone?" Tanner asked his mother.

"I'll be fine," she answered. "I'll read a book and answer the phones. Fend off Bill Magee if he calls asking for one of you. I'll tell him you stepped out for a minute to pick up a few groceries or something."

"That's good." Tanner grinned, remembering how Bill felt about interference in police business. "I don't want anyone to know where we're going. I'll take my cell with us in case there's any news about Hallie here. You can call us. We may not be able to get reception once we get back up the trail, so don't get concerned if you can't reach us. But we can get calls while we're in the car coming and going."

In less than twenty minutes, they were out the door and on their way.

"It's nearly six now." Delia looked at her watch. "We should get there around six thirty. I think it will take us at least thirty minutes to hike in."

"We can get there faster than that," Tanner said. "I'll drive around and park at the old schoolhouse and we'll hike in from that point. That will cut distance off the walk."

"Good." Delia sighed. "Hallie will be scared when it gets dark there."

"Hallie's not scared of the dark," John Dale argued. "She's a country girl."

"Maybe." Delia's cheeks colored. "But I'll feel better if we get to her before dark. That old place is remote, and there's no electricity back there."

"I put a couple of flashlights in the trunk." Tanner grinned. "We may need them before we get back to the car."

They drove silently from Gatlinburg to Metcalf Bottoms, each lost in their own thoughts. Daylight lingered, and in the picnic area, the smells of hot dogs cooking on the outdoor grills trickled through the air. It being a Friday night, people could linger in the mountains later than usual, enjoying the evening and knowing they didn't have to get up to go into work the next day.

Tanner drove into the campground and across the creek, following Wear Cove Road and then turning to bump over an unpaved road to the Greenbrier Schoolhouse.

"I don't see the jeep." John Dale said with disappointment as they drove down into the schoolhouse parking lot.

"She'd hide it," Tanner countered, pulling up to park. "Let's look around and see if we can find it."

Glancing toward the metal gate blocking the road up the trail, Delia asked, "Could Hallie have opened the gate and driven in to the house?"

Tanner shook his head. "Not without having heavy metal pliers to cut the lock. And she didn't have that."

"Maybe she found a way to drive the jeep behind the gate," John Dale suggested.

"Then go look for tire tracks up there, J. D. ," he told him. "Delia and I will check around the school and in the woods behind it."

A short time later, Tanner found the jeep parked close behind the back of the schoolhouse. He and Delia didn't see it until they walked to the back of the grounds.

"She was smart," Tanner allowed. "She hid the jeep well."

"She's here." Delia breathed a sigh. "I just knew it, Tanner."

He leaned over to give her a kiss. "Remind me to marry you one day. I don't want a smart woman like you getting away from me."

"Let's go find her," Delia replied eagerly, disregarding his comment.

Twilight fell as the trio wound their way down the worn wagon road into the Walker sisters' farm place.

"Let me walk in ahead," Delia ordered, as the road opened into the farm area. "Hallie will be less scared if it's only me. I don't want her to panic and run."

John Dale grumbled over that, but conceded, at last. Delia had guessed right so far about everything else, and Tanner and John Dale had to respect that.

They stayed back, listening to Delia call out. "Hallie, it's Delia. Everything's all right and it's safe to come out now. Please don't run; it's okay, I promise."

A shadow emerged from behind the house, and then Hallie started running down the path to meet them—throwing her arms around them in relief. Soon, the four of them sat on the old Walker porch talking. Hallie wanted to hear everything that happened and be convinced Jonas Cole was locked up before she'd start back with them.

"Oh, Delia," she exclaimed, starting to weep at one point. "I had no idea he would come to Dee's place, that he'd figure out I was staying there. One reason I came here to hide was because I was afraid he might see me going back to the house. That he might follow me and hurt you. I tried to protect you by coming here."

Hallie blew her nose on her napkin. She'd eaten the sandwich John Dale brought her while they talked and now reached for his bottle of water.

"Let's go home," Tanner suggested after Hallie had calmed down sufficiently. "It's been a long day."

They walked back in falling darkness, Hallie and John Dale tagging along behind Tanner and Delia with their arms wrapped around each other.

"It's good to hear them giggling and talking about their future back there," Delia whispered to Tanner.

"It's good they still have a future," he replied solemnly. "If things had gone differently earlier, Hallie might have been hurt or even killed. You didn't see Sissy Walker Cole in the hospital like I did."

Delia shook her head. "I still can't believe Hallie risked going back to the house in Cosby to look for a ring and locket her grandmother gave her. She said they were the only things she really had from her grandmother, and she wanted to see if she could find them. She thought they might not have burned."

Tanner snorted. "It was impulsive. She admitted it—that she didn't stop to think. First her mother got hurt and then the fire happened. We didn't tell her about the fire earlier, you know, thinking it would only upset her more. But then she read it in the paper after you went in to work this morning."

"I'm sure she's sorry enough now she went out of the house for any reason. She knows she took a stupid risk." Delia stepped over a branch in the path.

"She's a plucky little thing though," Tanner admitted. "She said she actually found that ring and locket plus some other pieces of jewelry. They were in an old tin box she kept in the back of her closet. The closet area got completely blitzed, but the tin box—although charred—was basically in tact."

"Mercy, I'm glad this day's over." Delia reached for Tanner's hand in the gathering darkness. "I haven't really thanked you for coming to my rescue, Tanner."

"It's what anyone would have done," he replied, shaking off the compliment but glad of her hand in his.

"No, it's not." She leaned against him as they walked. "And I'll never forget it, Tanner. Never."

"The police were on the way, Delia. It would have worked out."

"Maybe," she admitted. "But you risked yourself to protect me. That was brave, Tanner. Things might not have worked out so well if a bunch of police officers came barging in."

"I don't think they'd have done that." He sent Delia a sheepish grin. "I only suggested that to Bill trying to justify what I did. The fact is I acted with my emotions more than logic. The woman I love was in danger. And I had to do something."

"I'm still saying thank you, Tanner." She reached up to give him a kiss on the cheek ... but before Tanner could pursue the kiss further, she giggled, breaking the moment. "You know you're going to be the hero of the day for weeks to come in the Burg. I can't wait to hear what the Jack Gang will have to say about this."

Tanner groaned. "You would have to bring that up right now."

Their conversation stayed light walking back to the car. John Dale drove Hallie home in the old jeep, while Tanner drove Delia and him in his car. At the schoolhouse parking lot, they finally got Maureen on Tanner's cell phone to let her know they'd found Hallie, and that she was safe. Tanner called Bill Magee, too, and told him they could call off the search for Hallie. He got another lecture from Bill about taking police matters into his own hands, but a less severe one than before. Bill felt too relieved, learning that Hallie was safe, to read Tanner the full riot act.

On the drive back to Gatlinburg, Delia fell asleep. Tanner pulled her head down onto his lap and enjoyed looking down at her as he drove home through the darkness. Smoothing her hair back from her face, he realized with an ache in his heart how much he loved her and how painful it would have been if he'd lost her. Tanner had told her again tonight that he loved her. Maybe if he kept telling her, she'd finally believe him. And maybe if he kept loving her, she wouldn't move away and leave him.

Chapter 21

Several weeks had passed, with September now settling over the mountains bringing shorter days and cooler nights. Delia noticed the sumac in the woods behind Aunt Dee's place beginning to turn red. Fall was on the way.

Delia's and Hallie's lives stayed busy with upheavals and dramas in the weeks following the arrest of Jonas Cole. To begin with, all of Hallie's Rayfield and Walker relatives descended in a storm on the little stone cottage at Balsam Lane. Neighbors and friends streamed in as well. The story of the day Jonas Cole chased Hallie and threatened Delia was told again and again.

"Tarnation, Delia, if I have to tell that Jonas Cole story one more time, I think I'm going to scream," Hallie declared one evening when the last of the day's company finally left, dropping off still another care box.

Delia glanced up at Hallie from the boxes they were sorting through, and laughed. "I think if I see one more box come in this house I'm going to scream."

Every day, family and friends brought over boxes, bags of clothes, toiletries, and other essentials for Hallie and Sissy—knowing they lost everything they owned in the house fire at Cosby. Also, once the news got out that Hallie was married and expecting a baby, the offerings began to include maternity outfits and baby clothes, plus every conceivable item imaginable for a new infant.

"What are we going to do with all these things you don't need or can't use?" Delia asked Hallie, as the bags and boxes piled up in the front guest bedroom and began to spill over into the living room and hall.

Hallie shrugged. "Everybody said to give whatever we don't want to Three Sisters Charity Shop. Some of the Rayfield sisters run the store, and that's where everybody takes their used stuff anyway. Mabel, Jeanne, and Estelle sell things in the store and give to charities or families in need, too. You know, families that get burned out or something, like we did."

"The sisters were some of the first ones to phone and ask us about sizes and all," Hallie reminded her. "Then they brought over some of the first bags and that little baby carrier. Isn't that the cutest thing you ever saw?"

Delia grinned. "It is."

"And look at these, would you?" Hallie cooed, holding up several tiny baby gowns in pastel colors. "Aren't they sweet? They've even got little mitts on the hands."

"Those fold over to cover the newborns' fingers so they won't scratch themselves," Delia explained. "Little babies have sharp nails when they're born."

"Oh, Delia," Hallie wailed then. "I'm going to miss you so much when I go. I won't know anyone in Charleston, and I'll be lonely everyday without you to talk to. And without my candle work to keep me busy."

"You'll be fine." Delia patted her fondly. "You'll have John Dale, and you'll soon make friends. You'll also live by Aunt Louise. Mary says she's very nice, and you know she's already called and chatted with you."

Hallie considered that. "She said she never had a daughter and looked forward to pampering me."

"Well, see?" Delia replied encouragingly.

Hallie frowned. "I'm not much for pampering. Or for fiddling about with rich society women. I'd rather be working and doing something useful."

Delia smiled, folding a small pair of baby overalls Hallie wanted to keep. "It's only for a year, Hallie. And the baby will keep you busier than you can imagine soon enough."

"I suppose," she groused. "But I look forward to getting back. Maureen said I can move all the candle making equipment over to the big shed at Grandmother Mary's when I come home and that she'll keep selling my candles in the store. She said you told her it was all right."

Delia nodded.

"Will you stay here until I get back?" Hallie asked anxiously.

"I'm not sure." Delia looked away.

Hallie scowled at her. "Tanner's in love with you, Delia Walker. Surely you know that. He wants you to stay. And, personally, I don't think your family are anything much to run home to. Even if your parents did haul ass down here when they heard about the stink with Jonas Cole, saying they were worried and all, I still don't like them."

That had proved another drama. Granddaddy Walker's brother Gordon called him in Virginia to tell him how proud they were of his granddaughter down here. He'd meant well, of course. But Granddaddy immediately called Delia's parents and they freaked out. They actually got on the first flight they could get to Tennessee and then rented a car to drive to Gatlinburg.

It hadn't been the best of family reunions. First, Hallie sat in on their initial tirades and criticisms, and she lost her temper and flew into them, sparing no words in telling them what she thought. She'd jumped to Delia's defense like an angry mother hen and volleyed Delia's parents with a stream of accusations and criticisms. It proved a highly volatile scene.

Delia's Place

Eventually, when things calmed down, and many issues got talked out, Hallie, in her usual chameleon style, graciously offered to fix supper for Howard and Charlotte Walker and told them she'd go clean the guest room for them. They declined and announced they'd already checked in at the big Park Vista hotel nearby.

This set Hallie off again. "Well, that's just what I'd have expected of you two. You come down here, supposedly worried about your daughter, and don't even make plans to stay over with her. Have to go to some fancy hotel instead."

They spluttered about Dee's place being so small and claiming they needed a good night's rest after such a long trip.

"Pooh," countered Hallie. "You just neither one wanted to spend the night at Dee Ward's house. Didn't want to stay with the memories, and didn't think it good enough for you. And that's the truth."

Delia tried to smooth things over, but her parents had been unwilling to prove Hallie wrong and stay at Dee's. And Delia knew her mother felt uncomfortable in the house while she visited.

"Probably worried that Dee's ghost would jump out and bite her," Hallie quipped later, laughing.

Delia's visit alone with her parents the next day hadn't gone much better. At their insistence, she met them at the hotel for lunch. They ranted on and on about Hallie's behavior—called Hallie common, which angered Delia. She defended Hallie and from then on seemed to spend the entire lunch visit offering defenses and justifications of some sort or the other.

She'd wanted to take her parents to see her office at Crosswalk, hoped to show them the design work she'd completed there. She even offered to take them to Mountain Productions to see the ongoing work in progress, but they expressed no interest. Made excuses to avoid seeing it. However, her father pressed his concern that Delia hadn't followed up with the design company in Washington. They evidently wanted Delia sight unseen and had tendered a good initial salary. Her parents stressed to her what a promising position this would be for her, how it could help establish her as a designer of merit. Delia knew the job a good opportunity, but it rankled her that it had been arranged without her even interviewing in person at the design firm.

She told Hallie, "They dismissed all the issues relating to Aunt Dee. Said I was overreacting. Claimed they'd never treated me any differently because I resembled Dee. Somehow they managed to make me feel small and petty for even suggesting any discriminatory behavior. They constructed a story of their own about everything that bore little relation to the story Dee Ward wrote in her journals."

"Hmmph." Hallie snorted. "It figures."

"They claimed Dee overreacted about things, tended to be emotional. Said she felt guilty after Richard died, that it strained their relationship. They claimed they often invited her to visit but that she always declined." Delia sighed.

"I'll believe that when pigs fly." Hallie tossed down the apron she was mending. "What other plots for your own good did they present, trying as usual to manipulate you?"

Delia winced. "They wanted me to pack and fly back home with them, sign the contracts for the job with Hazen House in Washington. They'd even talked to a realtor they knew and found me a townhouse in Georgetown."

"That's a swanky area, isn't it?" She picked the apron back up, stabbing her needle into it.

"Yes." Delia rubbed her neck. "And they didn't think it the least bit important that I had a commitment to finish my design project for Bogan and Rona at Mountain Productions, or that I'd signed a contract to do Dr. Bradley's offices."

Hallie raised an eyebrow. "And is it important?"

"Of course." Delia glared at her. But truthfully, she felt torn and confused after her parents finally left.

"Darling, do think carefully about your decisions at this point," her mother said. "It's your future that's at stake, after all. Your father and I are simply trying to help. We only want the best for you. Surely you realize that."

"What do you want, Delia?" Hallie asked, leaning toward her.

"I don't know," she admitted.

"Well, remember, you've got to make your own best decision, like my Grandmother used to tell me, and not the decision someone else thinks is best for you."

"I wish I knew what that was." Delia twisted her hands in her lap.

Hallie smiled. "You'll find a way to know, Delia." She studied the stitching on the apron. "Just be sure it's your way and not someone else's."

That nailed the problem, of course. There was the way her family wanted and the way Tanner, Hallie, and her friends here in Gatlinburg wanted. No matter which direction she selected someone would be displeased with her. And no matter which direction she picked, she'd wonder if she'd only chosen it to please someone else.

Delia found little time to decide at all in the hectic days before Hallie and John Dale left. Five days before Hallie left, Jonas Cole escaped while being transferred from the jail in Newport to the courthouse. The officers weren't quite sure how it happened, but it seemed a prisoner, released a few days before Jonas, got involved in the planning. The man arrived on the scene, created an altercation, and then managed to whisk Jonas into his car and away before the officers could properly respond.

Naturally, Hallie and Delia immediately panicked, wondering if Jonas would flee the state or try to retaliate again. It proved a tense time. John Dale moved into Dee's place and Tanner insisted on coming over to stay, as well. Bill Magee put a police watch on the house, and they all spent two anxious days waiting for news.

As it turned out, Jonas did try to retaliate, but this time he went after the Crowleys. It seemed he'd now convinced himself all his problems began when Ronald Crowley's girl Carleen claimed he raped her. He told jail mates everything that happened to him had been her fault. So Jonas went to the Crowley's this time for revenge, and in an armed scuffle, Ronald Crowley shot him. Jonas Cole died a few hours later in the hospital. Delia didn't know whether to feel sad or glad, her emotions so edgy and conflicting.

"In a way I'm glad for Mama," Hallie said when they got the news. "She won't have to get a divorce and won't have to worry about Jonas getting out of jail one day and coming after her again. It scared me, thinking about that. Jonas isn't the kind to forget a wrong, even an imagined one. He never saw his problems as his own, but always caused by someone else."

Thinking of Hallie's mother, Delia asked, "Will your mother buy a new house and go back to her job in Cosby? Or will she stay on with Tabby and Cas at the farm?"

"Actually, she's going to work at Vesser's furniture shop over on Glades Road and plans to stay in the apartment above the store." She smiled. "Vesser makes his handcrafted pieces in the shop but doesn't need the apartment since he owns a house nearby."

Hallie paused thoughtfully. "You know, Mama said that coming so close to being killed shook some sense into her. She told me she got to thinking about the past and how she hadn't handled things very well. We talked a lot about those years. I can't say I'll ever understand the guilt, fears, and superstitions she worked up in her mind or how she let them dominate her life choices. But living with crazy Jonas Cole helped Mama see some of her own craziness."

She shrugged. "Anyway, now that Mama's made peace with herself and with Vesser, maybe they'll have a chance for happiness. She didn't feel she deserved Vesser's love or to experience happiness with him after Daddy got killed. Even had herself convinced she didn't deserve me." Hallie shook her head. "She really did a number on herself."

Delia regarded her with interest. "Have you forgiven her now?"

"Well, yeah." Hallie laid the finished apron aside. "Nobody would want to see the woman suffer any more or be punished more than she's already punished herself. I don't see any point in staying mad, but we can't recapture the lost years. For me, she's more like an aunt or cousin now. I mean, I know she's my natural mother, but in my heart Grammie Rayfield will always be my real mother. She raised me and loved me when my natural mother was nowhere around."

Delia considered this. "Maybe you and your mother can build more of a relationship over time."

"Maybe." Hallie shrugged. "But it's my guess Mama will get her second chance more through Vesser. He never stopped loving her, you know, and being a widower, he has two kids to raise. Surprisingly, they've both taken to Sissy. A soft side comes out in her when she's with them that I haven't seen in a long time. A side I remember only from my own babyhood."

"You're looking at all this with a lot of maturity," Delia complimented her.

She folded the apron neatly to put away. "There's no sense in living in the past, Delia, or allowing it to overly affect your future. I see no purpose in letting the past keep you from living in the today with joy."

Delia relished the words. "Is that something your Grammie Rayfield taught you?"

"No, smarty pants," she returned sassily. "It's something I read in that devotional book of Aunt Dee's we've been studying. The word for yesterday was Forgetting and the scripture read: 'This one thing I do, forgetting those things which are behind and reaching forth unto those things which are before.' I memorized it because I wanted to remember it; it's from Philippians."

She paused to add pointedly, "Maybe you should memorize it, too."

Now, wandering around the lonely house, Delia wished she had Hallie here to spar with, talk to, and share with again. Mercy, she missed her. Hallie had been gone only two weeks, but it seemed like a huge aching hole still filled Delia's heart.

Delia wandered upstairs to the room where Hallie stayed, thinking about her. She walked past the baby's room, empty now of its furniture, its walls still a robin's egg blue. She sighed. "I need to bring the desk furniture back in here now that the baby furniture is gone." John Dale and his father had hauled all the baby furniture to Charleston in the church van, along with clothes, household items, and personal things the couple needed for their furnished apartment near campus.

"It makes me sad looking at this empty baby's room. I'll get started tonight changing it back to an office. It will give me something to do." She switched on the light in the upstairs attic and began to prowl inside it, looking for the furniture pieces she and Hallie stored away earlier.

Toward the back of the attic, Delia found the drapes she and Hallie took down from the office window. Lifting them up to examine them, she tried to decide whether they'd still coordinate with the now blue walls. She shook her head negatively and laid them back across the old trunk again.

Delia's Place

Noticing the trunk, Delia opened it to look inside. Maybe there'd be other drapes or fabrics she could use. Lifting off the top shelf of the trunk, she dug under an old sheet and then stopped in surprise. There lay Aunt Dee's blue dancing dress. Delia hadn't seen it in years. She pulled it out, smiling to discover it. Underneath it she found the old tiara, some mementos of Aunt Dee's, and a faded yellow scrapbook.

Distracted now, Delia sat down on the attic floor to look through the scrapbook. Inside, she found a youthful picture of herself and Aunt Dee on the first page with her own name scrawled across the bottom of the page in childish script. Delia put her hand to her heart in delight. This was her old childhood scrapbook! She'd completely forgotten about it. She caressed the pages lovingly. How she worked on this as a young girl. And how sweet of Aunt Dee to keep it.

Settling down with her back against the trunk, Delia began to turn the pages and reminisce. There were many pictures taken over her Gatlinburg summers, a little aged but still clear, even though pasted in place with household glue. She found pictures of the gang and of Tanner. Red crayon hearts were drawn around Tanner's pictures. She'd had a crush on him even then.

On other pages she found postcards and clippings from tourist brochures, the names she'd given to all the cottages and homes around Mynatt Park. Further on, she found house and room designs she'd drawn on notebook paper and then cut out and pasted into the scrapbook. Even then, she'd been drawing designs and planning decorating projects. Delia smiled in pleasure.

Beside the design drawings were homemade business cards created on colored construction paper and then cut out. Delia's Interiors. Delia's Designs. Delia's Decorating. She'd dreamed about a decorating career even at that young age. Underneath each card she'd carefully written the address of Aunt Dee's offices at Crosswalk. Delia shook her head. Obviously, she copied the address from one of Aunt Dee's business cards. She'd always been impressed with Dee's big office with its broad windows looking out onto the balcony.

In the back of the scrapbook Delia found more pictures, many of Tanner. Only twelve years old in one, tousle-haired and wearing braces. But still so cute. Grinning, tanned. And clowning around. Embarrassed about her taking so many pictures of him.

A stiff piece of yellowed paper fell out of the back of the scrapbook. Delia folded it open to find another sheet of old notebook paper. She felt her face flush as she looked at it. Across it she'd written in childish script: Mr. Tanner and Delia Cross. Mrs. Delia Walker Cross. Mrs. Delia Eleanor Walker Cross. And she'd drawn wedding bells around the words. What were these other names below, she wondered? John Tanner Cross. Anna Eleanor Cross. Thomas Dale Cross. Margaret Jane Cross.

Good heavens! She realized suddenly. Baby names. She'd listed potential baby names for her and Tanner. Planned her adult future with Tanner, naming babies, naming houses, planning out her childish career dreams. How cute and romantic.

She started to get up, realizing she'd never get the office set up mooning over old mementos here in the attic. But then a shiver touched her. Suddenly, she could hear again the words Zola Devon spoke to her that day in the shop: The answer you're seeking is in the midst of old things you haven't looked at for quite a while.

Delia sat very still for a moment. These were her old dreams here. She might have been young and she might have been romantic and silly, but these were her very own dreams. They weren't her mother's or her father's. They weren't Tanner's, Maureen's, or Hallie's. They weren't even Aunt Dee's. At this age, no one had ever made any specific suggestions to Delia about careers or her future life. No one had ever urged her in any one direction or another back then. In fact, at this age, Delia had been secretive with her imaginings. She never told anyone about her dreams to be a decorator, and she certainly never told anyone she had a crush on Tanner Cross.

She smiled into the dim light of the attic. She'd found her answer. Forgetting entirely about decorating the little office now, Delia got up and pulled the blue dancing dress out of the trunk.

"You knew everything back then," she whispered to herself, holding the dress up to look at it. "You knew for sure the first time Tanner really kissed you on your thirteenth birthday he was the one. You just forgot you knew. And you knew that you belonged right here with your own little business. You've been searching and searching, and the answer lay right here all along. It was always here." Delia hugged herself with the knowledge. "You belong right here."

She kicked off her shoes, stripped off her jeans and shirt, and slipped into the ice blue dancing dress. She hoped it might still fit; it had certainly been too large before. Reaching behind her, she pulled up the zipper. And, then, on a sudden whim, took the tiara out of the trunk and settled it on her head.

Out in Hallie's bedroom, she surveyed herself in the dresser mirror. The dress fit nicely now. She grinned at her image. She certainly filled out the top of the strapless dress more, too. In fact, the tops of her breasts bulged noticeably over the edge of the bodice. Delia giggled at herself, whirling around in the sparkling dress. The beads on the dress, and the rhinestones on the tiara, caught the light and shone as she moved.

Feeling sentimental now, Delia pulled out Aunt Dee's old record player and put on one of the thick, black records. The strains of an old waltz drifted out, and Delia began to dance around the room as with an imaginary partner. She closed her eyes for a moment as she danced, remembering another time.

Delia's Place

When she opened her eyes again, she saw Tanner lounging in the doorway, watching her with an appreciative gaze.

"I guess you forgot I was taking you out to dinner tonight," he commented.

Delia looked with alarm at the clock by the bed where Hallie had slept. Six o'clock! Where had the time gone?

Tanner saw her shocked glance towards the clock and laughed.

"There's plenty of time," he remarked softly. "Why don't I play prince to your princess once again so you don't have to dance with yourself?"

He stepped over and took Delia into his arms before she could think of a response. She didn't stop him either as he led her around the floor. It felt sweet to dance with him again like they had in this room so long ago.

"You're a more handsome prince than you were at eighteen." She spoke the words softly against his neck.

He pulled her away from him to sweep his eyes over her. "And you're definitely a more filled out princess than at thirteen. You know, I could practically see down that dress to your waist back then."

Delia gasped, but Tanner pulled her close again, continuing to circle her around the floor to the gentle music.

"You are a beautiful, beautiful woman, Delia Walker," he told her huskily after a few moments. "I think I knew I was a goner and in love with you from that first real kiss I stole right here when you were only thirteen."

"But you got engaged to someone else later." Her voice slipped out as only a whisper.

"So did you," he whispered back. "We just lost our way for a while."

"I know," she said on a sigh.

Tanner looked down at her, seeming to sense a new yearning in her, something different. Delia knew he saw clearly, too, that she wanted him to kiss her. She even wetted her lips in anticipation, her pupils growing dark.

"Just for the moment and the memory," she murmured, tempting him—stirring old memories of words he'd spoken to her long ago with another kiss in this room.

Tanner touched his mouth to hers. Delia sighed in pleasure and leaned into him with abandon. Taking the plunge, Tanner kissed her passionately with all his heart. She knew he reveled in the change he sensed in her.

"You know I love you, Delia Eleanor Walker," he told her boldly, as the waltz music on the record player drifted into a sweet and lilting stanza.

"I love you back, Tanner Harmon Cross," she told him with a smile.

Tanner, stunned for a minute, missed a step, almost waltzing on Delia's bare feet with his shoes.

A smile played over her lips.

"Do you really mean it?" She felt his heart beating fast against hers.

"I mean it," she assured him emphatically, smiling up at him. "It came to me this afternoon, looking through old things in the attic, that this is where I belong. I belong here with you, and this is where I want to establish my business. This is the place I want to live, where I want to be."

"Just like that, you suddenly knew?" he asked her, still stunned.

"You said it happened that way with you in Atlanta." She smiled at him.

"So it did," he remembered.

He pulled her close in pleasure. "You know, if you're going to stay here, Delia, you're going to have to marry me. I don't think I can keep being a restrained gentleman for very long after seeing you in that dress." He looked pointedly down at her breasts pushing out of the bodice and traced a finger across the top of them.

Delia closed her eyes and leaned forward against his hand.

"Oh no, you don't," he told her, grinning and pulling away. "I'm not letting you have your way with me until we're married. I'm afraid you'll use me and discard me otherwise. Take advantage of my innocence."

Delia giggled and smiled at him again. "Could we get married soon?" she asked. "I don't want a big wedding, just a small one with friends up at Perry's chapel. And I want Tracie to make the cake."

He gave a low whistle. "Is next week too soon?"

She considered that. "I really think I should try to plan a date when my family can come down. At least the ones who want to. I don't want to leave them out unless they truly don't care to attend."

"And if they object?" He touched her cheek.

"It won't matter," she told him, smiling happily. "I know my own heart and what I want."

"Well, I'm a lucky man if it's me you want."

"That you are," she told him saucily, pulling him down to kiss her again.

"You know that empty baby's room?" Tanner asked against her mouth a little later on. "I know something we can do with it. Maybe you shouldn't turn it back into an office again quite yet."

"Silly man," she told him, loosening his shirt and running her hands under it and over his bare chest. "If we have a baby, we'll have to put it downstairs close to us. That is, if we're still living here then. Will you want to live in your house instead?"

"No, it's smaller." He let a hand drift from her waist down to her hip. "We can rent out my place or use it as a guest house. And live in Dee's place here. Her house would be much easier to add on to. I've been thinking about how we could do that for a long time now."

"Oh, you have, have you?" she replied, chewing her lip and smiling up at him provocatively. "Were you that sure of yourself?"

"Delia, I was never sure of myself for a minute with you. But always foolishly hopeful." He kissed her again, in joy, smothering her laugh in the process.

"Who are we going to call and tell first?" Delia asked, her eyes shining. "Your mother? Hallie and John Dale? Maybe Bogan and Rona? You know what Bogan will say, don't you?"

"No, what?"

"He'll say, 'Whoo-eee, that sure is good news!'"

"And I'll be the first to agree with him." Smiling, Tanner whirled his princess around the room again.

Epilogue

A few weeks later in nearby Wear's Valley, Loreen McFee, bored with a quiet block of time in her temp job at Mountain View Realty, picked up the phone to call her sister. "Hey, Betty Jo, guess what I read in the paper. That accountant, Tanner Cross, you met at the barn dance is gettin' married." She scanned the newspaper announcement. "The paper says he's marrying some girl from up north near the DC area, Delia Walker."

"Too bad. He was real cute, and I'd been planning to go by his office to see if I could run into him again." Betty Jo smacked her gum in annoyance. "You know, Loreen, it continually irks me how these out-of-town women keep coming in and marrying up all our eligible men. It just ain't right."

Loreen twisted the old phone cord. "Speaking of eligible men, I hear that handsome single man I was telling you about, Kendrick Lanier, will be coming in this week. Lordy-dee, he's a tall, fine-looking man. I think I'll hang on to this temp job here a while—see if I can get to know him." She leaned toward the phone. "That naughty Jack Teague came in the other day, too. I'd bet one of these days someone's going to get themselves a catch in him."

"I don't know about that." Betty's Jo's voice sounded doubtful. "Everybody says he's a terrible ladies man."

Loreen laughed. "Well, maybe the two of us can go down to Gatlinburg and see if Zola Devon will tell us something about our future. Steer us in the right direction to snag a husband. We're not gettin' any younger, you know."

- ♦ -

To see if Loreen or Betty Jo snag the new bachelor moving to Wear's Valley, watch for the next book in the Smoky Mountain series, *Second Hand Rose*. And to learn whether Townsend realtor Jack Teague ever changes his womanizing ways, or if Gatlinburg shop owner Zola Devon has any more visions about future relationships, stay tuned for two more warm-hearted and enjoyable novels—*Down by the River* and *Makin' Miracles*.

About the Author

Dr. Lin Stepp is a native Tennessean, a businesswoman, and an educator. She is on faculty at Tusculum College where she teaches research writing classes and psychology courses. Her business background includes over 20 years in marketing, sales, production art, and regional publishing. She and her husband began their own sales and publications business, S & S Communications, in 1989. The company publishes a Tennessee regional fishing and hunting guide magazine and has a sports sales subsidiary handling sports products and media sales in East Tennessee. She has editorial and writing experience in regional magazines and in the academic field. *Delia's Place* is the fourth of twelve contemporary Southern romances in a series of linked novels set in the Smoky Mountains in East Tennessee.

For more about the author's life and interests and to keep up with signings, events, and future publication dates for future books in The Smoky Mountain series, visit the author's website at: www.linstepp.com

The photo above shows author Lin Stepp sitting on the porch of the Walker Sisters' cabin featured in this book. The homestead, not far from Metcalf Bottoms Picnic Area and Gatlinburg, is on the U. S. National Register of Historic Places.

CPSIA information can be obtained at www.ICGtesting.com
Printed in the USA
LVOW12s2157070414

380745LV00001B/209/P